ON PASSION'S WING

Clinging to Zeke tightly, Abby pleaded "Don't let go! Don't ever let go!"

"It's all right, Abbie girl," he told her quietly.

"No! If I let go you'll be gone! I know it! I'm just dreaming!"

"You're not dreaming, Abbie."

"Oh, Zeke, hold me just a little longer!"

He gladly kept his arms around her, and she kissed his neck, breathing in the wonderful, manly scent of him, running her hands across his broad, strong shoulders. He moved his lips back to her own in one long, lingering, hungry kiss, then he swung her up in his arms. She rested her head on his shoulder and asked no questions as he bent down and picked up her blanket while she still clung to him. It did not matter at the moment where he had been or why. All that mattered was that he was here now. . . .

ROSANNE BITTNER

SAVAGE DESTINY
Ride The Free Wind

ZEBRA BOOKS
KENSINGTON PUBLISHING CORP.

ZEBRA BOOKS

are published by

Kensington Publishing Corp.
850 Third Avenue
New York, NY 10022

Fourth Printing: July 1996

Printed in the United States of America

To my husband, Larry, and my sons, Brock and Brian, without whose support this series could not be written

My gratitude to Dee Brown, whose compelling book *Bury My Heart At Wounded Knee* inspired me to write a series about the Plains Indians. I am also grateful to other authors whose writings have both inspired and aided me to learn about the Indians: Will Henry, *The Last Warpath*; Donald Berthrong, *The Southern Cheyennes*; George Bird Grinnell, *The Fighting Cheyennes*; Stan Hoig, *The Sand Creek Massacre*.

Throughout this novel the reader will find references to Utah Territory, Nebraska Territory, New Mexico Territory, and Kansas Territory. Portions of these territories comprised what is now Colorado, Nebraska, Wyoming, and South Dakota. So that the reader understands specific locations, the major part of this novel is centered in present-day Colorado. The Arkansas River, around which lies the major territory of the Southern Cheyenne, is located in southeastern Colorado. Fort Laramie is located in southeastern Wyoming; the place of the "warm, bubbling waters" is in what is now Yellowstone Park; and the meeting place of the Cheyenne and Sioux for the Sun Dance Ritual is in the southwest corner of South Dakota.

. . . Don't make me leave you, for I want to go wherever you go, and to live wherever you live; your people shall be my people, and your God shall be my God; I want to die where you die, and be buried there. . . ."

Ruth 1:16–17

One

Thunder rumbled through the great peaks of the Rockies in one continuous, echoing boom, reverberating from peak to valley to peak and making the whole earth seem to shake. Black clouds rolled over one snow-capped spire, threatening everything below with a drenching spring storm. But Abbie was not afraid. In her brief sixteen years of life she had always hated storms, and in the mountains they were so much more frightening. But she was with Zeke, and when a woman was with Cheyenne Zeke, she was never afraid, not even of the elements.

The two of them guided their horses through a narrow, rocky ridge, both astride sturdy Appaloosas, the animals' brown coats spotted with white helping to hide their riders from whatever foe might lurk nearby. In the myriad of rocks and crevices around them, an enemy could easily hide, and in this year of 1846, a time when there were dangers of all varieties in this untamed land, one had to be very cautious and alert.

Abbie studied the broad shoulders of her husband as he rode ahead of her, the fringes of his buckskins swaying with the motion of his supple body. He was an experienced man of the mountains, bedecked with an array of weapons, all of which he could use skillfully to defend her if the need arose. A quiver of Cheyenne arrows was slung across his back with a bow, and he wore a handgun at his side. A Spencer carbine rested in its case

9

attached to the gear on his horse. But the weapon Cheyenne Zeke's enemies feared most of all was the knife he carried on his wide, leather weapons belt around his slim waist.

The knife's rawhide, beaded sheath was bright and colorful, with blue and red beads in the design of eagles. The handle of the knife that protruded above this sheath was made from the jawbone of a buffalo and wrapped with buffalo hide. But the razor-sharp blade, set into the jawbone handle with cast lead, was the source of Cheyenne Zeke's infamous reputation. The tip of the blade was slightly curved and could rip through animal—or man—in the blink of an eye, bringing instant death.

It was a big knife—fifteen inches from the buffalo tooth at the top end of the handle to the tip of the blade. And it belonged to a big man, who could throw it faster than a sharpshooter could draw a gun. Abbie had seen him use the knife, and that was something a person did not forget. Anyone who knew Zeke's reputation with the knife thought twice about doing battle with the tall, dark-skinned half-breed and usually decided against a confrontation. Those who chose a less wise decision did not live to tell about it.

His array of weapons was a stark contrast to the musical instrument he carried with his gear—a mandolin, which he played with as much skill as he used his weapons. The gentle music he made with the mandolin and his own smooth voice hardly fit the hardened, fighting man that was his primary personality. But he was only hard because life had made him that way; and he had taught himself to play the instrument back in Tennessee, where he'd often walked alone in the hills in which he'd found peace in his growing-up years. Sadly, as he grew older, the weapons were used much more often than the mandolin, but he still played and sang—for his Abbie.

Abbie smiled, a pleasant, warm sensation pulsing through her at the thought of being Zeke's woman. They had met in the summer of 1845, when he'd scouted for the wagon train with which Abbie and her family were traveling to Oregon. On that fateful journey, she'd lost her family, but she had come to know and love the half-breed, Zeke Monroe. If it weren't for him, she wouldn't have wanted to live at all in those first terrible days of being alone. Only the warm love and sweet passion she had felt for Cheyenne Zeke kept her going, and when their bodies finally came together in a night of terrible need and desperation, she'd understood why, of her family, she alone had survived. She was to be Cheyenne Zeke's woman, and there was no stopping that.

They were married late that summer at Fort Bridger. It had been an unlikely match, she being white and Zeke a half-breed. There would be many who would scorn such a relationship. But that didn't matter. Abbie knew in her bones it was a good match, a perfect match. Zeke had been her first man, and there would not be another in the life of Abigail Trent Monroe. He was her destiny.

"We'd best find a cave for shelter," Zeke spoke up without turning around. He didn't have to turn for her to know every feature of his finely chiseled face with the hard lines etched deeply from his life of torture and hardship—too deeply for a man only twenty-six years old. And there was the scar—a fine, white line that ran down the left side of his face—put there by an enemy Crow Indian, who'd died by Zeke's blade. But the scar and the lines of life did nothing to detract from his handsomeness. His eyes were fiery and dark, capable of showing the great passion that lay in his Indian soul, or of showing intense hatred when he was angry and vengeful.

"I agree," she shouted back. "We'll be drenched any minute!" She watched as, with agility, he guided his horse down an escarpment. He used an Indian saddle, a leather pad stuffed with buffalo hair. It provided a small, flat seat, not the large, horned, leather saddle most white men used and which made it easier to stay on a horse. Zeke sat the big Appaloosa as though he knew exactly how the animal was going to move, ready for every thrust of hoof and twitch of flank. Zeke knew horses, raised them and traded them. That was how he made

11

his living, along with doing some occasional scouting. But there would probably be no scouting for him now. He was married. He would not want to leave her.

He looked up to make sure Abbie was having no trouble getting down the same rocky pathway; for the descent was steep, and loose gravel skipped and bounced ahead of her as her horse's hooves slid slightly. She hung on tightly as Zeke headed back up toward her.

"I'm all right," she called out. He came closer and grasped the bridle of her horse, and their eyes held for a moment.

"I don't aim to lose another wife, especially when I've only had her with me for a couple of weeks," he answered. "Fact is, Abbie girl, there's more than one reason I'd like to find a cave to hole up in."

He flashed his handsome smile, a rare sight on Cheyenne Zeke, and Abbie felt the color rising to her cheeks. She wondered if this man would ever stop making her blush. Perhaps when she grew into more of a woman she would be able to control her emotions better. She smiled and dropped her eyes, and the man, who looked all Indian but spoke with the accent of a Tennessee-bred boy, carefully led her horse down the narrow pathway.

Abbie again felt a flutter in her young heart at the memory of his return for her that spring. He had left her at Fort Bridger the year before because of a severe arrow wound she had suffered when Crow Indians had attacked her wagon train. Zeke had removed the arrow himself and saved her life when she developed an infection from the wound. But the gravity of the wound, combined with the personal loss of her family and the hardships of the journey, had left Abbie too weak to go on to Oregon. Zeke had been forced to leave his new young wife at Fort Bridger while he guided the survivors of the wagon train to its destination. By then, winter hit the Rockies in full force, and Zeke had been obliged to wait until spring to return for her.

The mountain men who stayed at the fort and watched over Abbie had been good to her, showing nothing but respect for

Cheyenne Zeke's woman; for those same men had hunted and trapped with Zeke and respected the half-breed. But it was a long, cold, lonely winter for Abbie because she feared in one small corner of her heart that Zeke would not come back for her after all.

Then one warm spring day he was there! She saw him coming, his sleek frame set against the background of red rock and grand mountains, a part of the land and its wildness. He had come back; she belonged to him. And now she had nearly forgotten what it was like to be afraid. Cheyenne Zeke had promised her she would never have to be afraid again.

Abbie snuggled closer to her husband as the rain poured down outside the cave, its splashing and dancing enhanced by a waterfall near the entrance. The fall's flowing water music mixed with the steady beat of raindrops and made it difficult to tell if it was still raining without looking at the cave entrance to see. But Abbie did not care to look right now. A small fire flickered nearby to burn away the dampness of the cave, and she curled up, marveling at how soft and comfortable a buffalo robe could be, but knowing the best warmth came from two naked bodies lying close together.

Zeke sighed in his sleep and moved one leg over her. Only Abbie understood that beneath all the hardness and ferocity of this man lay an almost boyish need to be loved and wanted. He had known little of either in his young life. After being dragged by his white father from his Cheyenne mother and taken to Tennessee when he was only four years old, he had grown up in Tennessee, treated as something less than an animal. But his Indian blood had entrenched an inner pride in his heart that made him know he was much better than that—much better, even, than the people who looked down on him. He might even have been accepted eventually, if he had not made the grave mistake of falling in love with a white girl.

Some of her own people—men she knew—had raped,

13

mutilated, and murdered Zeke's first wife, and they had killed his tiny son. They had done it just because she "deserved" it for sleeping with a half-breed. But eventually those who had done that came to regret it, for each one met a violent death at the hands of Cheyenne Zeke, a man who knew how to prolong final death until his captive begged for it. For Zeke was half Indian, and the tribe whose blood he bore knew about those things.

That had been six years ago. Since then, when not wandering the western hills or trading horses or scouting, Zeke had dwelled with the Cheyenne, his mother's people. He dared not return to Tennessee, for he was a wanted man there. He had left behind his white father, his stepmother, and three white half brothers, all of whom he would likely never see again. The only thing of beauty he had salvaged from Tennessee was his music—the mandolin and his songs of the Smoky Mountains.

Now the Rockies were the only mountains he would know, and the only ones she would know. She shivered at the renewed realization of where she and Zeke were headed, to find his mother's camp and his Cheyenne half brothers. She wondered if she had been a little too confident when she'd told him she could live with the Cheyenne. She knew nothing about them. It was not that she was afraid of them, for Zeke had assured her his people would never bring her harm. But she feared they would not really accept her or that she would somehow make a fool of herself in front of them and they would laugh at her. Perhaps Zeke's mother would be displeased that he did not marry a Cheyenne girl.

Abbie shuddered slightly, pushed her face against Zeke's chest, and then felt his lips brush her hair. She knew her sudden trembling had awakened him.

"What's wrong, Abbie girl?" he asked quietly.

She ran her hands over the hard muscles of his arm and kissed the bare skin of his chest. "Nothing," she whispered.

He pulled back a little to study her eyes. "No lies,

14

remember? You know I can see right through those pretty brown eyes, Abbie."

She blinked back tears. "Oh, Zeke, what if they don't like me!"

"Who? My people?"

She nodded and he grinned, pulling her close again. "I have no doubt in my mind that they'll like you, Abbie girl. Oh, some will have to get used to the idea, and some will test you out. But mostly they'll tease you. The Cheyenne have a wonderful sense of humor, Abbie. They like to play jokes and have a good laugh. But they'll know you've lived differently—that you have to learn." He petted her hair and kissed it again. "And we don't have to go trekking all over creation with them, you know. We can build us a cabin on the Arkansas, maybe near Bent's Fort."

"I think I'd like to stay with them, at least try it for a while, Zeke. I've got no home, no people save you. And you have only the Cheyenne to call family. Wherever they go, we should go."

His lips moved down over her cheek, and she breathed in the sweet, earthy scent of him, the scent of man and power.

"For such a little girl, you're some woman, Mrs. Monroe," he told her. His lips covered hers while one big hand moved over her small body, so very gently in spite of its callused skin hardened from a rugged life of open air and leather and the hard work of mere survival. He cupped one breast, moving his thumb over the small pink nipple and arousing it, and she felt the surging tingle that always flooded through her at his intimacy. His lips moved down over her throat to that breast, lingering there to lightly taste the sweet fruit it offered while his hand continued down over her flat belly to find its way to the soft moistness between her thighs.

It seemed he had magical powers in those fingers—powers that made her weak and submissive. She soon forgot her fear of meeting his people, for she became lost in the man who hovered over her, wanting and needing that which is made more beautiful by love. She willingly allowed him to touch and

15

taste and explore; it was his husbandly privilege, but the pleasure she derived from it left no need for objections.

For some time he was lost in her. It was only during their lovemaking that Cheyenne Zeke was not in full control of his own being. A small, young white girl controlled him then, making him weak with desire. His love for Abbie was the only force that had power over him, and that power had compelled him to make her his woman even though all his good sense told him it was not a wise decision. For their marriage could bring her heartache. It could even bring her physical harm. How well he knew that! Yet he had to have her. And so he had made a pact with himself to protect her at all costs and to love her and be faithful to her. For she had made a great sacrifice in agreeing to marry a half-breed and turn her back on the much easier life she could have had if she had married one of her own kind. And so he would never leave her or betray her because this tiny girl who loved and trusted him so innocently, who had given over her virginity to him with such faith, was his whole world now. He had made his choice, and he was glad of it.

Her body seemed to be suddenly exploding, and she gasped. In her excitable youth this often happened. He could feel her sweet pulsing against his fingertips, and he knew she had reached her peak before he'd even gotten inside her. But that would not change her eagerness for intercourse. He smiled inwardly as he moved on top of her, pushing her legs apart with his knees and quickly entering her, filling her with his magnificent manliness and again marveling at the fact that he fit her at all.

She felt even smaller as his broad, dark shoulders and long, lean body cast a huge, misty presence above her. What a wonderful thing this was! Why some women thought it a chore was beyond her comprehension. It was so natural and right and pleasurable. Instinctively she arched up to him over and over, in spite of the pain that sometimes brought her, for Zeke was a big man. Yet he seemed to know the right time to release himself—when consuming her any further might really hurt her. She cried out his name and heard a soft groan from his own lips as his life poured into her. He lowered himself and enveloped her in his arms then, his body moist with sweat, his breathing heavy. He stayed inside her for a moment and then moved off her but kept her tight against him. They both lay quietly for a few minutes, their love for one another spoken without words. Then he kissed her damp hair, rubbing a hand over her back, thinking to himself that he could practically count every rib.

"You'll never suffer like she did," he told her with bitterness in his voice. "That's why it's best we stay with my people, Abbie girl. The whites just won't understand." He stroked her hair. "Oh, the few trappers and such that we'll run across in the back country would treat you all right—most of them, anyway. But if we lived in a white settlement or someplace like Saint Louis or Independence, they'd hurt you, Abbie. Ridicule you. I won't let that happen. You understand, don't you?"

"I understand." She kissed his chest. "But I'm not afraid of it."

"You didn't see what they did to Ellen."

"Don't think about it. You have me now. And we're out here in unorganized territory, away from Eastern civilization. People don't think the same way out here, Zeke. Just look at how Jim Bridger and his men treated me. They were so good to me."

"They're a different lot, free thinkers, men who aren't concerned about what's socially acceptable. They're close to the earth and the wild things, not so different from the Indian, who know the only thing that's right is being true to your own self. But the others, the Easterners who come out here and bring all their social customs and pious religion with them, their tailored suits and stiff corsets and their belief that whites are the superior race, they're the ones to stay away from, Abbie girl."

"Well, it doesn't matter. I love you and you love me, and

we're going to be with the Cheyenne. We'll be all right, Zeke. God wants us to be together. What people think will never bother me, as long as I have you. That's all that matters."

"You'll have to be awful strong and brave, Abbie."

She pulled back and looked into his eyes. "You're my strength and my courage. Look what I've already been through, Zeke, losing my whole family, taking that arrow wound. I've known pain and tragedy and death same as you. And I was raised to work hard. I was never pampered back there on that farm in Tennessee. I said we'd be all right, and I meant it. I don't want you worrying about it."

He smiled softly. "All right, my little *veheo*. I'll try not to worry." He kissed her lightly, and they curled up again under the buffalo robe as the rain continued to fall. *"Ne-mehotatse,"* he whispered. It was one Cheyenne word she had quickly learned, for it meant *I love you*.

Abbie relaxed again and closed her eyes, little realizing the kind of journey through life she had begun when she agreed to be Cheyenne Zeke's woman. That journey would take Zeke and Abbie and the entire Cheyenne Nation down a road over which they would never be able to return.

They had traveled from Fort Bridger through the Wind River Range of Utah Territory following the Sweetwater through the South Pass, then south, moving along the ridge of the Rockies but never getting too deeply into the mountains unless Zeke thought it was necessary for shelter or to hide themselves. Now it was May, the Moon of the Greening Grass, as the Cheyenne would call it. Never had Abigail seen such magnificent beauty as she beheld in this land that the Cheyenne loved. It was her first time in this part of the country. The Oregon Trail she had traveled the summer before on the wagon train did not touch this part of the Rockies, but followed Nebraska and Washington Territory. It was easy to understand why the Cheyenne loved this place, for if any land

18

was designed by the Great Spirit to be the most beautiful, it was this country of purple mountains and rushing waters.

The vastness of the great West was sometimes overwhelming to Abbie; it seemed at times that she and Zeke were the only living human souls within a thousand mile radius. But she could tell by Zeke's ever-watchful attitude that he knew otherwise, even though there was no life to be seen but a few antelope, some elk, and the small birds that sang and fluttered about. Occasionally an eagle would circle down, calling to a mate nestled somewhere in a high, hidden crevice, and Zeke would look up and watch, seeming to speak to the elusive master of the skies with his dark eyes. For his spirit power was from the eagle, and his Cheyenne name was Lone Eagle, derived from the vision he had experienced during the tortures of the Sun Dance ritual.

Abbie knew Zeke was mostly on the lookout for Ute Indians; a constant enemy of the Cheyenne, they often sneaked into Cheyenne country to raid and steal horses and women. The Cheyenne also had trouble with the Crow and Pawnee, but their ancient rivalry with the Crow was lessening somewhat, and a tentative peace pact had been made between the two tribes. Nonetheless Zeke doubted there would ever be peace between the Cheyenne and the hated Ute, and most certainly not between the Cheyenne and the Pawnee, who years earlier had stolen the Cheyenne's most sacred religious fetish, the Sacred Arrows.

Still, the Crow, the Ute, and the Pawnee were old, accustomed enemies. The white men worried Zeke more, for now they were filtering across the continent by the thousands, most of them only "passing through" Indian Territory for the present. But Zeke knew that one day more of them would stop just short of the Rockies to make their homes on Indian lands. He had enough white blood in him to understand what this would mean for the Indian.

Few Plains Indians had any knowledge of just how many whites lived in that mysterious land where the sun rises or of

19

how powerful the white man's advanced civilization was. Worst of all, they did not comprehend the white man's forked tongue; and this innocence, Zeke was certain, would be a real problem for his people when the white man came to take their lands. Zeke had seen land stolen from Indians before, and he knew the horror of what those white thieves could do to the red men who were moved off the land. Zeke had walked the Trail of Tears with the Cherokees when they were banished from Alabama. He had been hardly more than a boy then himself, hiding among the Cherokee refugees to run away from his white family in Tennessee. He had been discovered and returned to Tennessee, but he had never forgotten the hunger and deprivation, the filth and disease that had beset the once-proud Cherokee.

For her part, Abbie could not understand why there should be a problem. There couldn't possibly be bigger country than that which lay between the Mississippi and the Rocky Mountains. Surely there was enough land here for everyone! But whenever she expressed those thoughts to Zeke, he would smile sadly, telling her she sounded very much like his own Cheyenne friends and family who scoffed at his worries and did not concern themselves with the white-topped wagons that were invading their land.

Abbie was to cherish the peace and beauty of those first weeks of marriage to Cheyenne Zeke, for there was no one, either white or Indian, to bother them as they traveled alone through God's country, their horses plodding quietly. They would sometimes travel for hours without speaking at all, two small specks moving quietly beneath towering peaks of granite that looked down on them in absolute silence. Sometimes the wind that howled and groaned through the canyons seemed spooky and threatening. But Abbie would only have to look at her husband to know she should not be afraid.

Spring mountain wild flowers of buttercups and larkspur

and daisies greeted them everywhere. Their bursting life gladdened Abbie's heart, for just as the flowers bloomed again with each spring, so did life go on. She had lost all of her loved ones the year before, and was then an orphaned, inexperienced woman-child struggling in a strange land like a crippled fawn. But Zeke had stayed beside her and nursed her tortured heart. She prayed that some day soon his own life would sprout in her womb and she could give him the children he needed to take the place of his little dead son. He had helped heal her heart. Now she hoped to heal his own inner wounds with her love and with the children she would give him.

They traveled through sweet pine forest, staying mostly under the trees for shelter and less visibility. After dark, Abbie would listen to the wolves, howling and yelping, and she would snuggle closer to Zeke, telling herself she must get used to the sounds of the night and the wilderness. She would have to learn to listen with the Indian's ear so she would know when a rider approached or a herd of buffalo was nearby; to see with the Indian's eye in order to spot the enemy when that enemy was a mere shadow or a tiny movement miles away. She would have to become able to smell approaching horses, or nearby water and food. And she would have to learn to keep house the squaw's way, to live in a house of skins, sleep under buffalo robes, build a proper tipi fire, and dry and tan her own hides for clothing and shelter.

There would be no down-filled quilts. She would hear coyotes at night, rather than the ticking of a clock on a fireplace mantel. Her floors would be dirt instead of wood, and she would cook over an open fire. She would wear doeskin tunics rather than pretty dresses, and bathe in streams instead of hot tubs. But to do these things meant being with Zeke, and so she would bear it. What good were pretty things and the comforts of a fancy house, if a woman had to go to bed at night with a man she did not love? What good was there in polishing crystal, if she could not bear to have her man touch her in the night? And where could she ever find a man as fearless yet gentle; skilled and vicious in battle, yet kind in the night; wild in his Indian ways, yet civilized as a Tennessee-bred man? Where else but in Cheyenne Zeke would she find a man made up of so many men, all man, all courage, all loving.

"Just a few more days, Abbie girl," Zeke spoke up, almost startling her. She had been thinking deeply of what it would be like to meet Zeke's Cheyenne family, and Zeke seemed to be reading her thoughts. "Swift Arrow is the only one who might give us a problem at first," he continued. "But you just let me handle him. Most of my people still have a blind, innocent trust of the whites, but Swift Arrow doesn't have much use for them, especially after finding out what happened to me back in Tennessee. And he knows about the Trail of Tears." His voice trailed off, but Abbie caught the brittle ring to it. The horror of the experience still haunted him.

"Swift Arrow is the superstitious sort," he finally continued, "which means he'll probably think having you with us will bring us trouble. But he'll get used to you." He looked over at her and grinned, his eyes running over her body and down to the bare leg that showed beneath the slit tunic given her by a Shoshoni woman back at Fort Bridger. Her long, dark hair was braided and her skin was beginning to darken from long days of riding under the open sky. "By God, I have to say, you do look more Indian than white already, Abbie girl," he told her. "It won't be long before nobody will be able to tell the difference."

She laughed lightly. "Well, then, maybe we won't get so many remarks when we do go out among the whites."

His grin faded. "Just the same, we have to be careful. For one thing, if soldiers or government agents ever see you and know you're all white, they might come to try to take you away, figuring you're a captive of some sort."

"I am a captive," she retorted. "You captured my heart and I can't get away from you." She held her chin up proudly. "And just let them come and try to take me away. I'd fight them good as any Cheyenne woman would do!"

Zeke grinned and shook his head. "I reckon you would."

She puckered her lips thoughtfully. "Why is it, Zeke, that an Indian woman living with a white man is taken for granted, but a white woman with an Indian is different, supposedly wrong or sinful?"

He just shook his head. "Because the white man thinks he's better. Because it's ingrained in him to think that way. Because they don't understand the Indian at all, the beauty and spirit of the People and how in many ways the Indian is a whole lot better and a whole lot wiser, and a whole lot closer to heaven than most white men will ever be."

She looked over at him, studying the dark skin and long, black hair. "Why me, Zeke? Why not some Cheyenne girl?"

He stopped his horse and held her eyes with his own tender gaze. "We go where the spirit leads us, Abbie girl. *Maheo* led me to you. You could ask yourself the same question, you know. Why me and not some white man?"

She smiled seductively. "I have to say because God meant us to be together—like you believe. But also because the first time your hand touched mine, Mister Zeke Monroe, I thought little flames would shoot right out from my body. No white man I've ever met could hold a candle to you. When I saw you, I wanted you to be my man, and nobody else's."

Their eyes held and he suddenly wanted to find a place to bed down for the night. She would often blurt out such statements, words that sometimes embarrassed his humble nature but also made him want her. He grinned almost shyly and reached over to slap her horse's rump.

"Get moving, you little she-devil!" he teased. She laughed as her horse lurched forward, and he followed, watching her slim hips move rhythmically with her horse's gait.

They headed toward the Arkansas River, to meet destiny face to face.

Two

Senator Winston Garvey eased himself into a massive, leather chair, his heart pounding with excitement and his mind racing with the possibilities that lay ahead. He pulled a gold watch from his vest, peering down at it over a double chin. He wished Jonathan would get there soon, because the senator was hungry and was looking forward to a heavy lunch as soon as their meeting was over, with perhaps a little wine to celebrate the news.

War! President Polk had declared war on Mexico! The possibilities of riches that could be reaped from such a war were endless. He was anxious to get started.

Someone tapped at the door and the senator looked up. "Come in, Jonathan!" he spoke up in his booming voice.

A polished, well-dressed man entered, smoothly handsome but small in stature, and so neat that he appeared wooden. He nodded toward the senator as he came through the door.

"Good afternoon, sir," came his quiet greeting, as he approached and shook the senator's hand. "I've just heard the news. I know you've been waiting for this opportunity."

"We both have, and you know it," the senator replied, shaking the man's small hand vigorously. "Do you realize the wealth that lies in some of those Spanish rancheros? And God only knows how much gold might be out there in New Mexico Territory and in California. It's untapped land, Jonathan, and when we're through with Mexico, a lot more of it will belong to us. Do you have men ready?"

Jonathan Mack's dark eyes lit up with greed. "You know I'm the best business consultant you could have hired," he replied. "Of course they're ready. The first thing that's going to happen is there will be a run on the banks, especially in the border towns and in Santa Fe. The big traders out there—like the Bent brothers—have a good sum of money in those banks. They'll be afraid the Mexicans will take over and rob them." He stopped to light an expensive, thin cigar with his small, lily-white hands.

"So? Go on."

Mack puffed on the cigar. "With your financial backing, my men are already prepared to go to the bankers, promise as many of them as possible that we'll loan them whatever cash supplies they need to pay off their investors, at a very high rate of interest, of course."

The senator grinned. "Of course. And I want you to secretly buy up all the land you can. This is the chance of a lifetime! Anyone with any brains ought to be able to see that. When all that land comes into U.S. possession, people will flock out there like bees to honey, and I'll be the landlord."

Jonathan Mack puffed the little cigar again. If the senator got richer from his investments, he himself would also become richer, for the senator paid him well. "You sure people will go out there?" he asked the senator.

The rotund senator's eyes narrowed to reflect his scheming mind. "Dead sure," he replied flatly. "There's a westward movement going on that can't be stopped, Jonathan. Look how many are already heading west—thousands. It's just the beginning. They'll all head west looking for more land, more freedom, thinking the answers to their dreams lie out there. They'll go, all right, for a hundred reasons."

Mack fingered his cigar, watching the smoke curl upward. "There's one big stumbling block, you know, even if we defeat Mexico."

Garvey leaned back in the plush, leather chair, and it

squeaked under his weight. "What's that?"

Mack looked directly at him, his eyes suddenly menacing. Garvey wondered sometimes just how much evil the man was capable of committing. But it didn't matter. He was good at his job, which was to cheat and deceive people, and that was just the kind of man Garvey needed.

"Indians," Mack replied.

Senator Garvey burst into robust laughter, his big belly shaking from it. He waved Mack off with his hand. "Bull shit!" he scoffed.

Mack puffed the thin cigar again, not smiling. "Laugh if you want, Senator. But you're paying me to do this right, and I'm telling you the Indians will be a big problem. They're already causing trouble. They're angry over all the game the emigrants are killing, and all the trees they're chopping down along the trails west. They're mad about streams getting dirtied up, and most of all they're angry about the white men's diseases that have hit them hard. The Cheyenne alone lost almost half their people last year because of measles and whooping cough."

Garvey sobered and leaned forward. "To hell with the Indians. If they want to cause trouble, let them. They'll just be another thing to get rid of, like the damned coyotes and grizzlies. They'll find out soon enough just how powerful the 'Great White Father' in Washington can be, as well as the soldiers' guns."

Mack sighed. "Perhaps," he replied. "In time. But I've been doing some homework, Senator. I've not been out there, but I've been as far as Independence, and I've talked to men who know. They're fighters, Senator. A Plains Indian on horseback can outmaneuver and outfight the best soldier you could pick. Take my word for it. Those red devils will be a real problem."

"Then we'll just send out all the soldiers it takes to wipe them out."

Mack pursed his lips thoughtfully, rolling the thin cigar between his thumb and forefinger. "The best way to wipe them out is to kill off all the women," he suggested. "They have babies like rabbits. And kill the young ones, too. Little boys grow into big warriors, if you know what I mean."

The senator leaned back again. "I know what you mean. And if the soldiers wipe out a village of women and children here and there who the hell back here in the East will know the difference? It will simply be a military victory, our valiant men fighting the heathen savages of the Plains who raid and rape and scalp and commit atrocities against our innocent white settlers out there. The papers will help us in that department, Jonathan. They eat up stories like that, and so does the public."

Both men sat silently for a moment, while the senator rubbed his chin in thought and Mack puffed the thin cigar again. "What do you think, Jonathan?" the senator finally spoke up. "How else can I help?"

Mack leaned forward, resting his elbows on his knees, his black hair shining with the perfumed oil he used to slick it back immaculately. "You've already answered that for yourself, sir. Get started with the news. Start dropping hints about Indian trouble. Suggest that Congress begin right now doing something about it. Stay ahead of the game. Push for some kind of decision as to just where the American Indian stands in all this settling of the West. They aren't considered citizens, you know, so they have no rights. Begin suggesting right now that they ought to be put into special places—reservations of sorts—places where they can be watched and controlled. Point out that they should be made civilized, to live like the white man, to farm and such. That would keep them from wandering all over the place hunting buffalo. Educate them, but be careful not to educate them too much. Send missionaries out there to Christianize them. That would get rid of that murderous spirit they have. In short, do everything you can to wipe out their old ways, Senator. To wipe out their old ways is to wipe out the Indian."

The senator nodded. "You have a good point there. Wipe them out by taking away their means of survival—the hunt,

28

the buffalo, that sort of thing. Take away their religion and their land. Keep them begging. Maybe we can get rid of them without firing a shot. Maybe disease and starvation will do the job for us."

"Now you're beginning to understand," Mack replied in a slow, sure tone. "But go slowly and carefully, Senator. I doubt it will be done without gunfire, so we must at all costs make certain the public looks upon the Indians as the cruel and violent ones and the white settlers as the poor, innocent victims. We must never allow the story to turn the other way." He sighed and relit his cigar, which had gone out while he talked. "Time will take care of a lot of it," he went on. "The more the West is settled, the harder it will be for them. As you implied, they'll lose game and hunting privileges. They'll begin to starve. And their low tolerance for white man's diseases will take care of more of them in the future."

The senator smiled. "You're a good man, Jonathan. You've got a head on those shoulders."

Mack stood up. "That's what you pay me for, sir."

The senator rose also. "How about lunch? I'm ready for a good beef steak. You ready to eat?"

"Sounds good to me. By the way, sir, how's the wife?"

The senator's eyes darkened somewhat. "Susan is fine," he answered rather coldly.

"You got yourself a young one there, Senator."

The senator pulled out his watch and looked at it again. "Money can get a man a lot of things," he replied. He put on a grin. "By the way, she's going to have a baby in just a few months."

"Well, congratulations, sir," Mack told him, putting out his hand again. The senator shook it quickly and walked to the door, grabbing his hat.

"I'll tell you what's even better than a young wife, Jonathan, if you can keep a secret." He hesitated and gave Mack a sidelong look that told the man he expected his words to be confidential.

29

"And what might that be?" Mack asked with a knowing grin.

Garvey leaned closer. "Having another young lady on the side," he replied. "One who will do anything—and I mean anything—for money."

Mack raised his eyebrows. "And may I ask who this very greedy and willing lady is?"

"You may." The senator lowered his voice. "Her name is Anna Gale."

Mack pondered the name. "Anna Gale. Not the young singer over at Hillary's Saloon?"

"The same." The senator's lips curled in a wicked grin. "Quite a young lady, that one. We're thinking about getting her into the business of prostitution. She's an orphan—learned her trade in the streets for survival. She's quite beautiful, too. Young and very good, and I don't mean just at singing." He gave Mack a warning look. "I trust your lips are sealed."

Mack nodded. "Nothing goes beyond these walls."

The senator studied the man's eyes. No, Jonathan Mack would not betray him. He was too greedy to risk falling out of the senator's employ.

"We have a lot of things to talk about, Jonathan," Garvey stated. "Let's go discuss business over lunch."

Mack nodded, and they left the high-ceilinged room that smelled of oak and leather and wealth. As they walked, Mack pondered the other ways he could get rich when he went West to take care of the senator's business. War meant guns—and two factions that would need them. Working both sides of the issue just might make a man quite wealthy, if he was clever enough. And Jonathan Mack was a clever man.

"Your father and I go soon," Gentle Woman told her son. "Your father must teach Little Rock about the hunt. It is Little Rock's first time chasing real buffalo."

Red Eagle swallowed a piece of deer meat. "Yes. You should

30

go. My brothers and I will wait here with the rest of the clan until the runners tell us where the tribe will meet for the hunt."

As was the Cheyenne custom, Red Eagle's father, Deer Slayer, would teach Red Eagle's cousin, Little Rock, the ways of the warrior, just as Red Eagle and his brothers, Swift Arrow and Black Elk, had been taught by their father's brother, Dog Man. Dog Man was Little Rock's father, and a brother to Deer Slayer.

Gentle Woman stopped her quilling and looked at Red Eagle, eighteen summers old now, a fine son with handsome features and a skill with weapons. But she was a little worried about the way he liked the white man's whiskey. The boy felt her watching him and met her eyes.

"I did not drink the firewater today," he told her, reading her thoughts. She smiled softly and sighed.

"That is good," she answered. She reached over and stirred the coals of the fire. "Do you think he will come this spring?" she asked.

Red Eagle swallowed one more piece of meat. "I think he will. Zeke always shows up in the spring. He will come, Mother. We will wait here for him."

Her eyes teared. "There was a time when I thought I would never see my half-blood son again."

"That is in the past. He was taken from you as a little boy, and he returned a man. *Maheo* brought him back to you."

She returned to her quilling, working the painted quills across the front of a leather vest. "I know I should not worry. There is no finer warrior, even though white blood runs in his veins."

"He is not like a white man. He is not even like the *Voxpas* we have known. That kind—they smell white and are weak!" He made a spitting gesture. "Zeke is not like that."

"Your half brother lives in a tortured world, my son. Always he will be torn. I am happy that you and your brothers accept him as a Cheyenne."

31

"He is *Nis'is*."

"*Ai*. You are of the same blood."

Red Eagle chewed the meat from the bone until the bone was clean, then threw the bone to a dog that lay in the shadows.

"The chiefs will tell us to meet farther to the rising sun, I think," he told his mother. "Maybe at the Smoky Hill River. The whites have caused us much trouble in finding the buffalo. First they chase the buffalo to the Rockies. Now there are many more whites on this side of the mountains, and the buffalo run back the other way. They are caught between. Soon there will not be a place for the buffalo to go."

The woman nodded. "*Ai*. And soon there will not be a place for the Indian to go. I fear for the Cheyenne. Game is getting scarce, and the white man brings the terrible sickness."

Red Eagle grunted disgustedly. "Because of them my brother has lost his wife and child. Swift Arrow will not easily forget that it was the white man's disease that murdered my sister-in-law and my nephew. Nor will I soon forget!"

"You must be careful," Gentle Woman warned. "Young blood and hot tempers bring trouble to all of the People."

"There are some things a man must do," he shot back, suddenly rising. "It is not right that these pale faces can come into our land and claim it is theirs. It is not theirs!"

"It is no one's," his mother reminded him. "It belongs to the spirits."

Red Eagle smiled sarcastically. "And do you think the white man understands that?"

She dropped her eyes, and Red Eagle thought to himself how lovely his mother still was, with only a little gray in her still-lustrous hair. "No," she answered. "But we must think and be cautious in the ways we respond to the white man. You wait until Zeke comes. Talk to him. He understands the white man. He will come soon. You will see. He always comes before we leave for the hunt."

Red Eagle sighed. "You and father go tomorrow to Little Rock's clan. Others will go tomorrow also, and it is a long

32

journey to the north before you will reach them. Swift Arrow, Black Elk and I and some of the others will wait here. We will meet you soon."

She nodded. "*Ai.* But promise me you will be careful, my son. You will not bother the whites?"

He snickered. "We will not bother them." He kicked at a little stone. "I go now. I want to ride. I need to ride and feel the wind in my face. It is a good feeling."

She smiled softly. "Yes. A man needs to feel the wind in his face. You are restless tonight, my son."

"I am anxious to go on the hunt."

"Perhaps it is because there you will see the Arapaho girl?"

He glanced at her in surprise and was suddenly embarrassed. "You know?"

She laughed lightly. "How could I not know? Mothers always know these things."

He grinned and looked away.

"She is lovely," Gentle Woman told him.

"*Ai.*"

"You should find a white-tailed deer and kill it, my son. Keep the tail and it will bring you luck with women."

He shrugged. "I go now."

He ducked out of the tipi and Gentle Woman's heart swelled with pride. She had borne fine sons, good sons, three of them full-bloods and Zeke, the half-blood. Even though he had a Cheyenne name, Lone Eagle, it was not often used, for Zeke cherished the name he'd earned through his vision. He had fasted and suffered to get the vision. Now he used the name only when he participated in tribal ceremonies. But his brother, Swift Arrow, often referred to his half-blood brother by his Cheyenne name, as did many of the elders.

Gentle Woman reached over and put another stick of wood on the fire to keep the meat warm for her husband, Deer Slayer. She watched the little flames and remembered the terrible pain in her heart the day Zeke's white father had dragged him away from her, after selling her to the cruel Crow

33

buck. Never would she forget that day, nor the day when her Zeke found her again after searching for many months. He was twenty-one summers old by then, a grown man. And he had suffered much because of his mixed blood. The story he had told her about his young wife and son being murdered by white men had made her weep.

Now his place was with his mother's people, who understood and accepted him. He could not go back to that place called Tennessee, for he had killed the men who had tortured his wife and child. It was good that he had killed them—fitting—the proper thing to do in his revenge. But the white men did not understand. They would hang her son if he went back. That was why she worried now. Perhaps someone had taken him back to that place where his white father lived. Perhaps they had hung him after all. She always worried when he was gone for so long. She had not seen him for over a year. He had not come back for the hunt after taking his horses to the big city called Independence to trade. Deer Slayer had told her he was probably acting as scout again for a wagon train, as he had done before. But there were many dangers in this land. Many dangers.

She sighed and returned to her quilling again, her fingers bleeding from the sharp porcupine quills. Yet she knew her sore fingers would be worth it. The vest was for Zeke, if he came back. She wanted to give her half-breed son a gift, for it had been many, many months since she had seen him. And as always, she wanted to assure him that at least the Indian half of his family loved him.

Col. Stephen Watts Kearny walked up and down the lines of volunteers, men who had offered their services in the taking over of Mexican Territory. The news of President Polk's decision to declare war on Mexico had traveled quickly, and men were pouring into Fort Leavenworth to volunteer for the great "adventure."

34

The colonel's boots squished in the Kansas mud that had been created by the spring rains. He silently studied the motley group of would-be soldiers. There were no Unionized states in the western territories yet, except for Texas; therefore, there was no official draft in the Western lands. It was a place ideally suited for men who were running from the law in the East, for those who wished to avoid the regular army and its strict disciplines and for men who had no morals and wanted total freedom. That was why many of these men had come west in the first place, and these were the sorts of men Colonel Kearny would have to work with: whiskey traders, trappers and hunters, panhandlers, fortune seekers. And those who volunteered to join in a war were usually the worst of all; losers who had failed at everything else and were ready to try something different. Joining the army to kill Mexicans would be an easy way to be paid for adventure and to receive free meals to boot.

But at least for the most part these men were experienced at living in the Western lands. They were rugged, unkempt characters who found it easy to live with the elements and cared little about bathing or eating on fancy plates. There would be little bathing, and certainly no fancy plates on this mission. The Western Army needed men to whom the ground was their bed and the stars their roof. Men like these would do little complaining, but making them obey orders would be difficult; for they were an independent lot and accustomed to making their own rules.

"Gentlemen," Kearny spoke up. "First I wish to thank you for volunteering to help in the fight against Mexico."

"Them oily-skinned bastards will soon find out who's best!" one of them blurted out. Kearny shot the man a scowling look, and a blond-haired middle-aged man standing next to the man who spoke nudged the first man and told him to shut up. The blond-haired man appeared much cleaner than the others and seemed a little more intelligent, too.

"All of you just shut up and listen to the colonel," he

warned the others. "If you're gonna be in this army you've got to do like he says and not talk unless you're asked to."

The colonel smiled. "Thank you, sir." He stepped closer. "And what is your name?"

"Ward, sir. Casey Ward."

The colonel looked him over, happy to see that even though Ward wore the buckskins so common to this land, his were at least clean.

"Well, Ward, these men seem to listen to you. As of this moment, you are in charge of this particular group."

Ward grinned. "Thank you, sir."

Kearny smiled tolerantly, almost laughing to himself at how he was forced to pick his officers from men such as these. He wondered to himself if America could truly win this war, in spite of Gen. Zachary Taylor's impressive victories along the Rio Grande.

The war had already begun well before it was formally announced in Washington, and many of those volunteering were arriving because of the exciting news of Taylor's victories at Palo Alto and Resaca de la Palma, not because they knew the President had made the word *war* official. The fact remained that this was a ragtag bunch of men with no training, and they would be going into hostile lands that were rugged and unbearably hot and full of snakes.

"I shall continue, gentlemen," he went on. "I want you all to understand what you have volunteered for. And anyone who wishes to change his mind may do so without retaliation by this army and without ridicule." He continued to parade in front of the men. Colonel Kearny commanded attention just by his disciplined appearance; his neat, blue uniform decorated with many badges and stars, and his pleasing but stern visage, with its kind but determined brown eyes and prominent, straight nose. He was a man with twenty-seven years of experience in the service of his country, and was now in command of the Western forces. He was a stern officer, but a fair man.

36

"Volunteers who are now assembling at New Orleans will also be taking part in this great plan of ours," he continued. "In one month we will be leaving this fort and will take the Santa Fe Trail all the way to the city of Santa Fe, which we will secure before going on to California."

"California!" someone mumbled in surprise.

"Yes, California," Kearny answered him. "General Taylor will continue to secure the Rio Grande area, and we will march onward to claim other disputed territory. We have already proven our power to the Mexicans by taking over Texas. Next we'll go to New Mexico Territory and California."

The men grinned and nodded.

"Just remember that this will not be an easy journey, gentlemen. The Western lands are hot and cruel, with little water that is drinkable, thorny plants that tear at your clothes, and a sun that scorches the skin. We will be traveling in the hottest season. The snakes and the wolves will follow us. But I know that all of you are experienced in such things. You will do just fine."

"What about Indians, sir?" One of them spoke up. "Are we allowed to shoot them that gives us trouble?"

Kearny scowled again. "You will shoot no one without orders. I don't expect a lot of trouble from the Indians."

"Well, sir, excuse me, but . . . uh . . . we do. They've already been raidin' some of the supply trains between here and Santa Fe, takin' food, guns, whatever. Some of them Comanches is bein' paid by the Mexicans to make trouble."

"They won't bother an army the size of which I will be taking to California," Kearny replied. "My job is the Mexicans, not the Indians."

Casey Ward cleared his throat and spoke up. "Colonel Kearny."

"Yes, Mr. Ward?"

"Well, sir, part of the reason some of us joined up was to get some experience so maybe we could step in and maybe be officers in the army that will be set up to fight Indians. We were hoping after this campaign that you'd put in a good word for us."

Kearny frowned. "What are you talking about, Ward?"

The man fumbled with his hat nervously. "Well, sir, Agent Fitzpatrick, Broken Hand Fitzpatrick, he's been talkin' about how we need a better army out west here—one that can handle the Indians. He figures the men best at that would be men like us; we've been livin' among the redskins for quite some time now. We just figured we could get in on the ground floor and—"

"Fitzpatrick is not a regular soldier, Mr. Ward," Kearny interrupted irritably. "He is a scout turned agent. He knows nothing about soldiering. And Washington is not extremely interested in the Indians at the moment. One war at a time, Mr. Ward."

The man swallowed. "Yes, sir. We just thought—"

"Let Congress do the thinking, Mr. Ward. If an army is needed out here for Indians, one will be established. And it will be made up of regulars. I am aware of Fitzpatrick's feelings, but many of us feel his worries about the Indians are exaggerated. It is hardly conceivable that a few uncivilized red men can even consider going against the United States Army. In fact, for your information, there is much talk about making a treaty with the Indians, one grand treaty that would take in most all of the tribes and would set aside quite a large piece of land for them. That should keep them quiet. For the moment, my orders are to take New Mexico and California, and we shall do it." He nodded to Ward. "You, young man, will exercise these men regularly and get in some target practice." He scanned the entire group of straggly haired, mostly bearded men. "More guns and ammunition are on the way from the East, gentlemen. We should be well supplied. Be here at this same time next week and I'll let you know of any news I have learned between now and then." He started to turn. "Oh, and I would suggest you get your hair cut, at least to your neckline. A shave wouldn't hurt either, but I won't insist on it." He turned and walked to his quarters, shaking his head at the task before him. Some were too young, much too young. He didn't like to see young men die. And the others, the older ones, they would be difficult to command. This was not going to be an easy expedition.

Jonathan Mack made ready to depart, his dapper gray suit hanging neatly in the corner of Anna Gale's room. The seventeen-year-old orphan girl who sang in Hillary's Saloon was as good in bed as the senator had said she would be. He glanced over again at her willowy, young body as she lay stretched out naked on her bed, watching him dress.

"You are worth every cent I pay you, my dear," he told her. "Too bad I have to go to Santa Fe for the senator. I shall miss you."

She sat up and shrugged, shaking out her long, dark, tangled hair, then lighting one of his thin cigars and smoking it herself. "I'll miss you, too," she lied. "I should say, I'll miss your money."

Mack laughed. "I'll bet you will! But you'll find others glad to pay for a roll in bed with you. You are delicious, my pet."

He did not catch her look of disgust. An orphaned girl in the city soon learned there was only one way to earn her keep. She had always been told that to be an orphan, especially one abandoned as a baby, was a shameful thing, and that there was no future for orphaned children. That had proven true. The only jobs available were those requiring hard labor in factories that dealt in cheap child labor, eighteen-hour days and whippings for falling asleep on the job. She had discovered she could make a lot more money and live a lot more comfortably by singing in saloons and sleeping with men.

A man who was a foreman at one of the factories where she had formerly worked had taught her on one cruel night what little girls were made for; and other than her horror and disgust, she had learned one thing from that night. Men liked doing these things, so perhaps she could get money by doing them.

Until now the way she made her living meant nothing to her but a few moments of naughty pleasure and a lot of money. Of course, some nights were not as enjoyable as others. The nights Jonathan Mack came to see her provided no pleasure. He was a small man, in every way, and he disgusted her. But he paid well, so she pretended he excited her.

"You coming back?" she asked him.

"Oh, I suppose. I have a lot of business to take care of for the senator."

She took a long drag on the cigar and laid back again, bending one knee and flagrantly exposing herself. He stared at her as he finished dressing.

"Santa Fe," she said rather wistfully. "Maybe some day I'll go out there. Sounds exciting."

"It's a dangerous land, Anna. A cruel land for one who isn't prepared."

She just grinned. "I wouldn't be afraid. Maybe some wild Indian would grab me and rape me." She laughed aloud. "Imagine that! Anna Gale—raped!" She laughed again, reaching over and setting the cigar in an ashtray. "By golly, I just might go," she said matter-of-factly. "I'm going to think about that."

Mack pulled on his shoes. "I would wait until this thing with Mexico is over."

She glanced at him. "Why do you care?"

He snickered. "I don't—not about you, anyway. I just care that the senator likes you and he'd be upset if you left him just now."

She sneered. "Yeah. That young wife of his has an awful lot of headaches lately. I don't think the senator does much for her in bed." She laughed hard again. "Fact is, he doesn't do

40

much for me in bed either. It's like having a two-ton elephant sweating over you."

Jonathan Mack laughed with her and came to sit down on the bed beside her, grasping a full, firm breast in his hand and studying the pink nipple. "I'm not like a two-ton elephant, am I?" he asked. She looked down at his small, white hand.

"No," she replied, deciding she'd best not elaborate.

He moved his hand over her body, touching her in places that had become familiar to him, his face flushed again. "I think I just might truly miss you, Anna," he told her. "Not many girls are as good as you."

She smiled. "That's why I charge so much."

He bent down and kissed her breast, then moved up and kissed her lips bruisingly. She was glad when he stopped, for his mouth tasted of cigar smoke. He sighed and rose from the bed.

"Take care, Anna dear. And . . . be good."

They both laughed at the remark, and he pulled on his suitcoat. He walked out without another word.

"Good-bye, little creep!" she sneered under her breath as she watched him go down the back stairway. Another man coming up the stairs passed Mack. He was the owner of the saloon, come for his pay for room and board. He would get it, the usual way. Anna snickered to herself, wondering what the man would do if he knew his own fat wife had also been up the stairs to see Anna Gale.

At his own apartment, Mack hurriedly finished his packing. Santa Fe would mean wealth to him in more ways than one. The senator had told him about the guns that would be shipped to Santa Fe, to replenish Colonel Kearny's troops before they moved on to California. The guns would arrive at that city sometime in August.

Mack had been to see the man whose responsibility it was to

order and ship the rifles. A little extra money had convinced that man to list in his book a shipment of one thousand rifles. But two thousand would be shipped. Mack would pay for the second thousand himself, and they would go out by a separate shipment, in wagons marked PIANO PARTS. They were destined for a special meeting place south of Santa Fe, where they would be sold at a very high price in gold to the Mexicans. Who cared that some of the rifles might fall into the hands of Comanches or Apaches paid by the Mexicans to help in the war by raiding Santa Fe supply wagons? That was not Jonathan Mack's concern. He would be living comfortably in Santa Fe, conducting the senator's legal business. No one would suspect he had made the arrangement. The man he had paid to secretly manufacture and ship the other thousand guns could be trusted, for he was greedy. That was the best kind of man to deal with if one wanted secrecy.

It was all working out very well. Jonathan Mack would get rich off the senator and live royally in Santa Fe while making a second fortune in smuggled rifles. It was a good plan.

"Manifest Destiny," he mumbled to himself. He liked that phrase. New York Editor John O'Sullivan had first coined the phrase when he declared in his writings that the West must not be ignored, for in those untamed lands lay unimaginable beauty and untold wealth. And O'Sullivan had also declared it Divine Providence that was the destiny of America to claim and hold all lands between the Atlantic and the Pacific, and to open those lands to the multiplying millions of citizens who bulged at the seams of the East.

Yes, it was America's destiny, and many men would get rich from the fruits of that destiny. Jonathan Mack planned to be one of them. He closed his suitcase and lay down on his bed, falling asleep to the busy sounds of carriages and city life after dark. He would be leaving very early in the morning.

Out in Utah Territory, where the land was still mostly untouched by the impending surge of new settlement, Cheyenne Zeke and his new young wife slept. There were no sounds of carriages and people. There was only the dead silence of the mountains, and the occasional yip and howl of a coyote. And as Mack lay worrying about ways to become richer, Abigail Trent Monroe lay worrying about being accepted by her husband's people—the Cheyenne. There would be no riches for Abbie. But then she was already wealthy. She had Zeke.

Three

Abbie was not surprised when trouble came, for it had followed her all the way from Tennessee; and seldom did Cheyenne Zeke venture anywhere without finding it close at hand. They were only two days from where Zeke figured they would come upon his people's camp when he suddenly halted his Appaloosa and dismounted, studying the ground intently, bending down to look closer, and then looking out across the horizon.

"What is it, Zeke?" Abbie asked him.

"Crow," was his only reply. His face was both worried and puzzled. Abbie shuddered, memories still fresh in her mind of the awful pain of the Crow arrow she'd taken the summer before when the wagon train had been attacked. She remembered the Crow faces, painted a hideous black with white around the eyes, and she knew they sometimes stole women for slavery or trade. "Got to be careful," Zeke finally spoke up, scanning the horizon full circle. "I don't like surprises."

Abbie already knew Zeke's fighting skill, but one man could take on only so many others and still win the battle. If they did not stay alert, Abigail could become a Crow buck's woman at any time, perhaps later to be sold to a Blackfoot or a Ute or maybe to the Mexicans. She pulled her own Spencer from its resting place on her saddle. Abbie knew how to use a rifle. She had already killed two men with it.

Zeke remounted his horse in one quick movement. "We'd best stay in the trees," he told her. "These tracks tell me it hasn't been long since they were here. My guess is they're far enough ahead that they don't know we're here, but we can't take chances. From now on keep your voice low and do everything I tell you."

"I'm not afraid," she replied quietly. "I'm with you."

He shot her a glance that showed the worry in his eyes. "I'm only one man."

"That's all it took to rescue me a few months back, as I recall."

"I had the upper hand then. I surprised them."

"You always have the upper hand, and you know it. The only one who can outsmart Cheyenne Zeke is God himself."

He snickered. "You young girls fantasize too much," he replied. She smiled and felt the pleasant warmth in her groin again.

"I haven't had one fantasy about you yet that didn't turn out to be true," she told him. He just grinned and shook his head, riding forward beneath the green pine trees.

The fire they made that night was a very small one, built in a shrouded crevice where it would be difficult to spot the flames from any direction. It was just for a little warmth against the cold, mountain air. Zeke would not let Abbie cook, for fear the smell of food would wander on the wind and be caught in the nostrils of some alert Crow buck.

"I thought the Crow and the Cheyenne made up," Abbie told him as they sat close together near the flames chewing on jerky.

Zeke laughed lightly. "You make it sound like young lovers. But if you want to use the phrase, they did 'make up,' so to speak. But there're always some young bucks looking for a fight so they can show their stuff, Abbie. Young Indian men like to do battle. It's in their blood, the need to show their

46

strength and their courage to the women, to steal horses from an enemy tribe and ride into camp with the stolen horses, sitting proud and straight, and to be praised for their bravery and cleverness. It's the way they are, Abbie girl, proud and free and always ready to show their fighting skills. I expect this is a small party of young ones down here away from their own country, looking to show the Cheyenne that the Crow are better than they are. But you don't find better fighters than the Cheyenne. The only good thing about knowing there's some Crow sneaking around these parts is that it must mean my people aren't far away, else them Crow wouldn't be skulking around like they are. If that's the reason, then it means my people haven't broke spring camp yet to rendezvous for the buffalo hunt."

He stopped to take a swallow of water from his canteen.

"I expect the Council Chiefs have sent out runners by now to tell us where the tribe will meet for the hunt," he went on. "If Crow are close by, it could mean trouble for a small camp. I'm hoping that tomorrow we'll reach the Cheyenne in time to warn them. I have plans to circle in another direction tomorrow and reach my people before the Crow do."

Abbie sighed. "I don't understand why they have to fight at all."

Zeke pulled her closer. "It's inborn, Abbie. Indians have been fighting each other for hundreds of years. It's the law of survival, fighting over hunting grounds, places where the water is best, women, whatever. Indian ways are so different, I expect most whites will never really understand them—that gut need to show courage and manhood. It involves the Indian's very attitude toward life and death. I hope someday you'll understand how the Indian thinks, his religion and beliefs. It's a beautiful, spiritual thing when you get to know it, Abbie girl. The Indian has a closeness with nature and all living things that most white men have never experienced and never will. Doing battle is just kind of an ongoing part of life and death and religion and visions and all of it." He let go of her and moved out from under the blanket, walking over to his Appaloosa.

"It's so . . . barbaric!" Abbie replied, staring at the flames of the little fire.

"Perhaps." He stood near his horse, looking out at the darkness. "To someone like you it would be." She did not see his eyes peering into the surrounding shadows or his hand tightening on the Spencer carbine he'd carried with him when he'd walked to the horse. "But it's no more barbaric than the way the whites treated the Cherokees on the Trail of Tears. Not near as barbaric. The Indian most always fights for a reason, kills his enemy for a reason, even if it's just for the sake of vengeance or to steal something they need. But there was no reason to push the Cherokees out of Georgia and Tennessee. They were civilized, Abbie; had their own settlement, log homes, even had their own newspaper, printed in English and Cherokee. They were independent and educated, bothering nobody, doing their best to live like the white man and stay out of trouble. But the whites wanted the land where they lived, so they got rid of them—stole everything they'd worked for and sent them on a long walk of disease and starvation and death."

He walked slowly back to her, trying to act as though nothing was wrong.

"Some day all Indians will have to stop their fighting and work together for survival against the white man. I feel it in my bones, Abbie.

"The same thing that happened in Georgia and Tennessee and everyplace else back East will happen right here in Utah Territory, the Black Hills, all across this country, until there's no place left for the Indian to go."

"Oh, Zeke, I hope you're wrong."

"So do I. But I don't think so. For now, you shouldn't worry too much about the tribal wars when you're with the Cheyenne. They're peaceable enough, except for an occasional uproar with the Pawnee. That's one enemy they'll probably never make peace with. And they'll put up one hell of a fight if

48

somebody brings trouble to them. There's nothing more dangerous than a vengeful Cheyenne warrior."

She smiled with pride. "That's already obvious from the times I've seen you fight," she answered him.

"Well, Abbie girl, I expect you're about to see it again."

"What?" She quickly turned her head to look up at him.

"Turn back around and don't move a muscle," he told her calmly. "Whatever happens, sit like you don't know there's anything amiss. I just want whoever is out there watching us right now to think I'm going into the bushes just to relieve myself and you are calmly waiting for me by the fire."

Her heart pounded and her face drained of color. She continued to stare at him, starting to rise.

"Damn it, Abbie, do like I say!" he ordered, trying not to show his anger so that the conversation appeared normal. "Look back at the fire and pretend there's nothing wrong. Hold out your hands like you're warming them."

She blinked back tears and swallowed, afraid for herself and for Zeke. It was obvious now that someone or something was close by. She couldn't imagine how Zeke knew, but she did know he would die protecting her if he had to. She looked back at the fire.

"I'm gonna walk away from the light for a minute, Abbie. You trust me, don't you?"

"You know I do!" she squeaked.

"Then whatever happens, even if a Crow buck comes screaming out at you, you stay right there, understand? If you go for a weapon, he'll kill you. But he won't get a chance to touch you, Abbie. I promise you that."

Her mouth felt dry and her palms were wet. She only nodded. "Zeke?" she said after a moment. "I love you." She waited a moment, and all was silence. She turned to see him. "Zeke?"

He was gone. She turned back to the fire, her ears highly alert now, waiting for some sound. She jumped when she heard a thud and a grunt. Was it Zeke? Her heart pounded so hard she thought perhaps she would die. Several silent minutes passed, the outer shadows seeming blacker because of the flames of the fire. Abbie closed her eyes and prayed harder than she had ever prayed in her life. Then she heard a rustling in the underbrush nearby.

"Zeke?" she choked out in a frightened voice.

Her reply was a piercing yelp. A Crow buck jumped into the firelight, his black, painted face with the white around the eyes making him look like some kind of monster in the darkness. Abbie screamed and scooted back.

The grinning buck headed for her, his knife pulled and gleaming in the firelight. Abbie's breathing came in quick gasps, and her eyes darted around the dark perimeter of the fire's light. She was desperately afraid now that the thump and groan she had heard had been Zeke and not the other way around. She scooted back more as the Crow's eyes moved over her body, resting on her white legs. He licked his lips. This one would make a fine captive, a valuable slave! He reached down for her, but then a large, dark figure came roaring out of the shadows behind Abbie, ramming into the Crow man with terrific force and lunging the Crow backward so that his bare back fell into the hot coals of the fire.

The Crow's screams of pain were mingled with Abbie's own screams of fright and horror, and for a brief second Zeke's own huge and infamous blade flashed in the moonlight before it came down with terrific force into the Crow's chest. Abbie covered her eyes and looked away, knowing from things she had seen before that Zeke would rip the blade down through the Crow's midsection before he pulled it out of the man's body.

Zeke finished the job quickly, taking a moment to deftly carve off a piece of the Crow's scalp, his Indian instincts and fighting pride compelling him to take this trophy to show to his brothers. He glanced at Abbie, who was still turned around, shivering and keeping her eyes covered. He had to grin at the sight. He walked over to hide the scalp under his gear and then wiped the blood off his knife onto the grass before shoving it back into its sheath. The next thing Abbie knew, Zeke was grabbing her up in his strong arms and pulling her close. She clamped her arms around his middle, shivering and crying.

"It's all right," he said soothingly, kissing her hair. "There was only the two of them."

"I thought they'd killed you!" she whimpered, burying her face in his chest.

Zeke grinned. "What happened to all those fantasies about your courageous warrior?" he teased.

"Oh, Zeke, don't joke with me!" she answered, her body jerking in a sob.

He patted her shoulder. "Don't cry, Abbie. I hate it when you cry. Everything is all right." He gave her a reassuring squeeze and led her to a supply pack. He freed a rolled-up buffalo robe and let go of her long enough to spread it out for her. "Sit down and turn around while I get that Crow's body out of here."

She sank down obediently, shivering from fright and the aftershock of having a painted warrior lunge at her in the eerie firelight. She could not stop her tears as she turned away while he dragged the body off into the darkness.

"What about the rest of them!" she called out in a choked voice.

"I expect these two were sent back to see what was behind them," he replied from the shadows. There was a loud rustling and then the sound of falling rocks, and she knew the body had been thrown down the small embankment near the edge of the crevice where they were camped. "We must be closer than we think to these devils," he added. He made a grunting sound, and she knew he was moving the second body. Again there was the sound of falling rocks. "You'd best get some shuteye, Abbie, 'cause we'll be leaving here before the sun rises." He reentered the light of the fire and walked to the supply pack again, removing another rolled-up robe. "When them two don't show up in the morning, the rest will come to find out

51

why, and I aim to be far from here when they do," he continued. "We'll make some fast tracks come full light and get the hell on down to the Arkansas and find that Cheyenne camp." He walked over to her, bringing the robe, and she saw that his face was strained and damp.

"Zeke?" she asked in alarm. "Are you all right?"

He squatted close to her, throwing the robe over her, squinting with obvious pain. "Just that damned old bullet wound from last year," he told her. "Gives me a little pain once in a while when something hits it just right. That Crow got a knee into it."

He saw the fear and sorrow in her eyes and put on a grin for her, touching her hair.

"Nothing to worry about, Abbie girl. You did a right good job digging that bullet out like you did."

New tears welled in her eyes. "Maybe I did something wrong!" she lamented. "I never took out a bullet before, Zeke. What if I did it wrong!"

He put a hand on each side of her face and held her head firmly, his dark eyes holding her own, his handsome face glowing bronze in the firelight. "You did just fine, Abbie," he said calmly and quietly. "Just fine. If you hadn't been so brave as to do that, I'd have died for sure. Now I'm telling you not to worry. That's the way with old wounds, child. Sometimes they just pester a man to his dying day, but they never really do him any harm. I expect something just healed funny on the inside, maybe so's something goes pestering a nerve once in a while just to be ornery. It's nothing to worry about, Abbie. Scar tissue often gives a man pain when it's hit just right."

She put her hands to his wrists. "Are you sure?"

"Yes, ma'am, I'm sure." He bent forward and kissed her forehead. "Now lay down there and get some sleep."

"I don't know if I can."

"Well, give it a good try. You'll need it. Do it for me." He kissed her lightly on the lips and she lay down. He tucked the robe around her face, now gentle again in spite of just having killed two men. His ability to be violent one moment and soft the next always amazed her, but she knew instinctively that his violence would never be used against her own person. He walked back to their supplies and pulled out an Indian blanket. Throwing it around his shoulders and returning to her side, he sat down close by and positioned his rifle beside him. The big knife he used with infamous skill rested in its sheath at his side, and she knew he would sleep with one eye open that night, in spite of his pain.

She watched him as he crossed his legs Indian style and stared at the little flames of the fire, and she wondered just what passed through his tortured mind in the still of the night, when memories were always so much more vivid. It had not been a happy life for him. But she would make sure he was happy from now on.

"I do love you so, Zeke," she told him quietly.

He glanced at her with a sidelong grin, and she wondered with a sudden, fierce jealousy how many women had shared his bed. But there were some things a woman didn't ask a man like Zeke.

"Woman, if I wasn't worried about enemy Crow tonight, I'd be under that buffalo robe with you."

She smiled, and he knew she was blushing, even though it was dark. "You're always welcome under my robe," she teased provocatively.

His eyes held hers for a moment, then scanned the small, almost undetectable rise she made under the robe. Such a child she was, yet all woman when he was inside of her.

"Get to sleep before I give you a good spanking," he answered.

She laughed lightly. "You might scare those devil Crow and the grizzly bears, but you don't scare me, Zeke Monroe!" she chided.

He grinned more. "That's big talk from such a little girl." He reached over and tousled her hair. "Now go to sleep. I mean it."

"Yes, sir."

She closed her eyelids, and for a few moments he stroked her hair gently, making her sleepy. It was not many minutes before she drifted off, unaware of the heaviness that was upon his heart over the sudden worry about what living with him could mean for her.

"God, I love you, Abbie girl," he whispered. He took his hand away and hunched over more, pulling the blanket closer around his neck and tuning his mind and ears and senses away from his pain and in to the night sounds and the surrounding shadows. The Lone Eagle would keep a close watch this night, for he had his mate to protect.

The next day brought the signs of life Zeke had been hoping to find. They crested a ridge to see smoke wafting up from the tops of trees that stood in a valley ahead of them and the Arkansas River meandering quietly through a green valley. Zeke halted his horse and squinted, trying to see through the thick pines below.

"Is it the Cheyenne?" Abbie asked quietly.

"Most likely. But we can't take a chance that it isn't." He circled around to the right, guiding both horses amid the trees along the steep embankment, a treacherous but safer approach to the camp if they did not want to be seen right away. They worked their way sidewise and downward until they reached a rocky hill not far above the camp and stopped again. A circle of tipis lay below them. Zeke stared down at the settlement for a moment, then nodded.

"It's a Cheyenne camp, all right—my own clan, to be exact," he said with a grin. He pointed his finger. "That one down there, the lodge second from the river's edge, is the tipi of my brother, Swift Arrow. I can tell by the flying arrows painted on it." He turned to look at her. "The women always paint their tipis with whatever design they like, each one can be individually recognized as belonging to a certain family. Swift

54

Arrow's wife painted theirs in honor of her husband."

Abbie arched her eyebrows. "I'll have to build and paint a tipi, won't I!"

Zeke winked. "You'll learn. The women will teach you, and the ones who paint well will put designs on it for you." He looked back at the camp. "I'm glad we got here before the Crow did. That tipi over there is—" He never got to finish his sentence, for just then there was a terrible shriek behind him. They both turned to see at least fifteen Crow warriors riding toward them, screeching and grinning at the glory of battle.

"Ride, Abbie!" Zeke ordered, slapping her horse on the rump. "Get down to that camp!"

Abbie's horse took off at a gallop, and she had no control over its movements. Clumsily she removed her rifle and tried to fire it toward the Crow behind her, but she knew her shot would mean nothing, and it could hit Zeke. Her heart pounded with fear for Zeke, who was staying behind to keep the Crow from getting Abbie before she could reach camp. She could hear no gunshots and wondered if Zeke had been killed by a Crow arrow or hatchet. There were pounding hooves behind her—more Crow braves. She was surprised they would follow her right into a Cheyenne camp; but just as Zeke had explained, these Crow were looking for a good fight, and she knew if that camp below was full of Cheyenne bucks, a good fight was just what they would get.

Rocks rolled down the hill ahead of her and dust flew, and she could see men coming out of lodges now, some already mounted and riding up the hill.

"Crow! Crow!" Abbie screamed, not knowing what else to say. She bent low, dodging the hated arrows, remembering the horror of feeling an arrow in her body the year before. Some Cheyenne warriors stood outside with bows and arrows, others with hatchets and paggamoggons and quirts, but there were none with rifles.

Abbie's horse stumbled and fell on its side. Abbie rolled off the animal and kept sliding due to the momentum she had already gained in her fall. When she finally came to a stop, her·· legs were badly scraped, but she had managed to hang on to her rifle. She quickly got to her knees and cocked the Spencer carbine that had once belonged to her father, aiming it at a Crow warrior closing in behind her. She fired and the Indian screeched and fell from his horse. The animal galloped past Abbie and the Crow's body landed beside her.

"Zeke!" she screamed, worried now. She searched the hills above desperately, but could not see him. Several Cheyenne horses went thundering past her up the hill after the Crow, and someone strong was picking her up then, grabbing away her rifle.

Abbie turned to look up into a stern, dark face. The Cheyenne man set her on her feet and motioned for her to walk the rest of the way down the hill to the tipis.

At first she just stood and stared in awe at the man. So, this was a true Cheyenne, the kind of man whose blood ran in Zeke's veins. She had seen Crow and Shoshoni and Sioux Indians, but she had not seen a true Cheyenne. It suddenly hit her that she was really here, in a Cheyenne camp, that of Zeke's own clan! She was frightened and confused, worried that Zeke would be killed and she would be unable to explain her presence. For the first time she wondered if she had done the wrong thing to come here. The man who had picked her up grunted with irritation at her hesitancy to obey his order to move, and he gave her a nudge. She quickly walked the rest of the way down the hill, the Cheyenne man behind her, leading her horse and still carrying her gun. When they reached camp, the man motioned for her to enter a particular tipi, and from the look on his face, she knew she had better obey.

She entered the dwelling, surprised at its neatness. Its sweet, smoky odor was not unpleasant, and all around the inner lining were bright paintings of horses and warriors. The man who had brought her there studied her curiously for a moment; then he left.

Abbie hurried back to the entrance and peered out. Dogs

scampered about excitedly, barking and running, many of them bounding up the hill after the Cheyenne ponies. She could hear war whoops and see glimpses of men and horses amid the trees, but nothing was clearly distinguishable, and it was impossible to tell which man might be Zeke. She wondered why she heard no gunshots; that frightened her. Zeke had a rifle and a handgun. Surely if he were alive, he would be using them.

The man who had pushed her into the tipi now thundered up to the entrance on a painted pony, his bare legs glistening in the sun. He was handsome, but nearly naked, wearing only a breechcloth. Abbie thought he resembled Zeke, but she was too embarrassed to stare at him, and she looked down at the ground. His horse pranced around in a circle.

"Who are you, white woman?" he demanded to know.

She swallowed and looked up at him. "My name is . . . Abigail," she replied. She took a deep breath. "Abigail Trent Monroe," she added louder. "I am Zeke Monroe's wife."

The man's eyes grew large in surprise.

"Cheyenne Zeke," Abbie said in a braver voice. "Zeke said this was his brother's camp. We were coming here to meet them when the Crows started chasing us."

The man studied her sullenly, eying her carefully as though she stood before him naked, and she was suddenly terribly afraid. What on earth would she do if Zeke were dead? The man glanced up the hill, then back at her.

"How many Crow are there?"

"I don't know for sure . . . maybe fourteen or fifteen." Their eyes held a moment, as he glared at her, the muscles of his young face flexing in a mixture of excitement and shock and anger.

"It is true? You are Zeke's woman?"

"It's true. We've come from Fort Bridger where we were married a few weeks ago. We've been traveling about a month—coming here to meet Zeke's brothers."

He sneered at her as though he did not believe her. "You are

57

white! Zeke would not marry a white woman!"

She frowned, her anger rising at his obvious dislike of her. "How would you know who Zeke would marry?" she retorted.

"I am his brother! Swift Arrow!" the man growled.

Her heart pounded. Of course! She glanced at the tipi to see she had been taken to the one with the arrows painted on it. She looked back at him, losing some of her anger then, not wanting to offend him. So . . . this was the one Zeke had said would be difficult to win over. And now she understood why he spoke English. Zeke's mother spoke it, having learned it from her white husband. She folded her arms in front of her.

"Just the same, I am Zeke's wife," she told him in a gentler tone.

He snickered. "White woman bring bad luck to the Cheyenne! My brother has chosen foolishly!" He whirled his horse and rode up the hill before Abbie could reply.

She watched him disappear into the trees, the blood draining from her face. His words had cut deep, and her mind raced with confusion and hurt. Her body began to shake from the shock of her rude greeting, combined with her flight from the Crow and her fall. Her worry over whether Zeke was alive or dead only made matters worse. She choked down a frightened sob and retreated into the tipi, looking around again at the inside of the dwelling place that was so foreign to her. It was much bigger and more pleasant inside than she had expected, but at the moment these things didn't matter. She huddled down beside the doorway to pray.

"Dear God, what am I doing here?" She could not stop the tears from flowing, and when she looked down at her bleeding legs, she only cried harder, feeling like a tiny girl rather than the brave woman of Cheyenne Zeke. "God, don't let him be dead!" she squeaked. "Don't let him be dead!"

Four

Abbie heard the sound of thundering hooves coming toward the river, and she knew the Cheyenne bucks were returning. She quickly wiped her eyes, determined she would not cry in front of Swift Arrow. But if Zeke was not with them, she knew it would be impossible not to burst into tears of pure fright and confusion. She blew her nose on the hanky she kept in the little supply pouch that hung from the belt of her tunic, then peeked cautiously out of the tipi as the horses pounded into the small camp. Zeke was with them!

Her heart leaped with joy and relief and she hurried out of the tipi as he slid from his horse before the animal even came to a stop. All of the men were laughing and apparently joking, but they spoke in Cheyenne and Abbie could not understand them.

Zeke hurried to Abbie while the others bantered, shoving one another around, hooting and mimicking the Crow. It was apparent the Cheyenne had chased off the attacking Crow bucks, but not without a fight, for Zeke's skins were spattered with blood. Abbie lost her smile of relief when she saw it, and Zeke saw the fear in her eyes.

"It's Crow blood, Abbie girl, not mine," he told her with a grin on his face. "He's bad wounded, too. I doubt he'll survive the night. But at least he's gone now—picked up and carried off by his friends who turned tail and ran."

"Oh, Zeke!" she said in relief. She hugged him around the middle and he returned the embrace, but only for a brief second.

"Not here, Abbie," he said quietly. "Cheyenne men don't show their affection openly." He pulled back and winked at her. "They save it for inside the tipis."

She blushed at her awkward mistake and pulled back, wanting to cry again, and he saw that her eyes were red and swollen.

"Abbie, are you hurt?" he asked, beginning to look her over. She only shook her head, knowing that if she opened her mouth she would show her childishness. "You are!" he frowned. "Your legs are all skinned up!" He stooped down to get a look at them, then rose and met her eyes. "What happened?"

"I just— My horse fell," she replied in a quivering voice. "I slid down the hill and—oh, Zeke—I thought they'd killed you! I didn't hear any gunshots, and—"

He put his fingers to her lips. "Abigail Monroe! You know no Crow can lick a Cheyenne! And a real warrior doesn't use a gun, Abbie, not if he can help it." He took on a proud look not unlike the one his own brother, Swift Arrow, had assumed earlier. "A real warrior gets close to his enemy!" He grinned and yanked his knife from its sheath, suddenly seeming like a changed man as he turned and faced the still-celebrating Cheyenne men. "He kills his enemy with weapons that require close fighting!" he continued. "He counts coup, touches his enemy, kills them with his own strength and skill—not from far away, hiding behind a rock with a gun! Guns are for white men who are too afraid to get close to their enemy!" He let out a war whoop and held his knife in the air, and the other men began hooting and hollering again.

Zeke's Indian blood had surfaced, and Abbie could see he was just as caught up in the excitement of the small skirmish as the others were. He howled and laughed with the other men, concentrating on three in particular, whom he greeted hardily with a firm Indian handshake and a look of genuine affection in his eyes. There was the same affection in the eyes of the three men. Abbie recognized the half-naked Swift Arrow and knew the other two must also be Zeke's brothers.

She felt a strange tinge of jealousy at Zeke's ability to share the Cheyenne culture with these men and to understand them. It seemed to her this was a part of him that would never belong to her, a wildness she would never be able to completely control.

Something moved at her right, and Abbie turned to see four women standing and staring at her, several children hiding behind them and gawking at the newcomer. Abbie was amazed that she had not known until now that there were any other women around. She supposed they must have been hiding in tipis with their children until the battle was over, and that it was only now that they were aware of the presence of a stranger. Their faces were not unkind, and one smiled. Her face was broad and round, and her dark eyes sparkled with enthusiasm. Abbie liked her right away without knowing her. The woman carried a papoose on her back, and Abbie was curious to see an Indian baby, but by then the warriors were quieting and beginning to turn their attention to the strange white girl who had invaded their camp crying "Crow!"

Abbie stood a distance from them, turning her eyes from the Indian women and looking at the men again, realizing the attention was now being directed at her. Their interest had been drawn from the Crow skirmish to one small, white girl, and she felt awkward and embarrassed. The men's laughter and celebrating dwindled, and their eyes grew curious. Abbie stepped back a little further when they began to circle her, and Zeke was at once at her side, motioning to the three men he had so hardily greeted.

"Come here, my brothers, and meet my new wife!" he told them in English. Swift Arrow looked at Abbie haughtily while the two younger ones looked at each other, then back at Abbie, scanning her with their eyes and again making her feel undressed. The two younger ones grinned and nodded to her, their eyes friendly, but Swift Arrow remained sober. All three stepped closer.

"Abigail, the ornery one there is Swift Arrow," Zeke told her teasingly. "That one is Red Eagle," he went on, pointing to a younger man, the shortest of the three, but just as fine-looking as Swift Arrow. "He's eighteen summers. The youngest one here is Black Elk. He's seventeen summers—only one year older than you, Abbie."

Black Elk was more slender than the other two, the muscles of his arms round and hard but not as full and powerful. His nose was sharp and prominent, his skin darker than the others. He was not as handsome as Swift Arrow and Red Eagle, but was still fine-looking in his own right, on the threshold between boy and man. He put out his hand white-man style and Abbie took it hesitantly. He closed a warm hand around her own, shaking her hand vigorously.

"She is pretty!" he told Zeke sincerely.

Zeke grinned. "That she is," he replied proudly. "Her name is Abigail, but she is called Abbie. She's sixteen summers, Black Elk—and don't get any ideas. She's mine."

Black Elk laughed and looked around at the others. "Zeke's wife," he told them in the Cheyenne tongue, pointing to Abbie.

Their reactions were mixed, some scowling at her, others smiling, and some just staring at her with blank looks. Swift Arrow stood with his arms folded, looking down his handsome, prominent nose at Abbie. His thick, dark hair was neatly braided and decorated with beads, and there were three coup feathers at the base of his neck.

"You left something out, my brother," he spoke up to Zeke, shifting his eyes to the man. The others quieted, aware of Swift Arrow's bad temper. "She is white!" The words were sneered. "We need no white women in this camp! We need no white women in any Cheyenne camp! It is bad luck! White women are weak. Look at her eyes! Already your woman has been crying!"

Abbie looked down at the ground, ashamed of her own tears and feeling as unwanted as a plague. Zeke bristled, stepping

62

closer to his brother. "I'd say under the circumstances she's done pretty damned good up to now," he replied, trying to stay calm. "And you don't know anything about her yet, Swift Arrow. When you know about her, you'll know she's not weak. And you'll respect her the same as if she were a Cheyenne wife, because she's my woman, Swift Arrow, and a good woman!"

Swift Arrow's dark, angry eyes blazed. "You told us once that you will never again marry a white woman! We wait here for you faithfully, caring for your horses! And what do you do but return with a white woman at your side!"

Zeke moved back over to Abbie and put his hands on her shoulders. "Hold your head up, Abbie girl," he told her firmly. "Look at these men." Abbie dutifully raised her eyes, scanning the assortment of dark faces and breechcloths and vests and leggings and long, black hair. The tears in her eyes blurred her vision and made the Cheyenne look alike—dark enemies who wanted no part of her. Never had she felt such a foreigner. "These are my friends, Abbie, and three of them are my brothers—blood brothers." He accented the last two words. "This woman is my wife," he told all of them. "She has suffered greatly over the past year. I have brought her here with me to find the peace all of you know I cannot find in the white man's world. She has given up everything to be at my side—all the comforts of the white world, her very way of life—given it all up just for me! She is not weak! She is strong, and good, and obedient. She is my woman, and that is the way it is."

Swift Arrow turned his head in disgust.

"There is much she has been through," Zeke continued. "And when I bring her before the council and before my mother, I will request my brothers and all of you to attend, and then you will know her story. It is a sad one. She knows suffering and grief, just as our people have known these things . . . and as I myself have known them. And all of you should know that this tiny woman has killed two Crow bucks: one was among some outlaws who attacked and brutalized her and the other attacked the wagon train she was with. She has even taken a Crow arrow in her back. She almost died from the wound, but the Great Spirit saved her—for me!"

Those who understood English exclaimed over her courage, and most wore broad smiles of approval, as Zeke retold the story in the Cheyenne tongue for those who did not understand. The Cheyenne women grinned and whispered and continued to stare at her. All seemed impressed, and even Swift Arrow had turned to glance at her in surprise when Zeke mentioned she'd even suffered a wound from a Crow arrow.

"She has killed three Crow!" Black Elk spoke up with a boyish grin. He pointed to a dead Crow Indian halfway up the hill. "That one. I see her shoot him, after she fall from her horse. Maybe we make her a woman war chief, huh?" Some of them laughed with good humor, and Black Elk voiced his feelings to the others in his own tongue. They were warming to her now, and Abbie began to feel more at ease. Zeke grinned with pride, but Swift Arrow began to scowl again.

"No white woman can be counted among the brave Cheyenne women!" he grumbled. Zeke stepped closer to his brother again, reaching out and putting a hand on the man's shoulder.

"What is it, Swift Arrow?" he asked quietly. "Always you have been the suspicious one, but it is not like my brother to be rude and insulting. She is only a small girl, and she is frightened. It was my wish that my brothers would help her feel welcome among our people."

Swift Arrow met his half-blood brother's eyes. "She is white!" he repeated. "She will bring disease! If not for the white man's disease, my own wife and child would not have died of the ugly spotted fever!" He spit out the words bitterly and turned away, and Abbie watched the two of them, suddenly losing some of her hatred for Swift Arrow.

Everyone quieted, and the little circle of men began to break up. The women disappeared as quietly as they had appeared, and Zeke's two younger brothers remained, watching Zeke, who stood staring with pity at Swift Arrow.

Black Elk touched Zeke's arm, embarrassed at Swift Arrow's words. "It is good to have you back, my brother," he told Zeke. "Our mother was worried. She has gone on ahead to meet up with Dog Man's clan. Our father is to teach Little Rock about the hunt and prepare him. Soon we must all leave for the hunt."

Zeke nodded, but kept his eyes on Swift Arrow. "Abbie and I will be going along," he replied. Black Elk looked over at Abbie in surprise, then nodded to her. He turned to his brother, Red Eagle, and Red Eagle motioned that they should leave Zeke alone with Swift Arrow. They left quietly, and Zeke and Swift Arrow and Abbie were left alone.

"I'm sorry, Swift Arrow," Zeke spoke up quietly. "When I left, you had been married to Weeping Woman for only two or three months. I did not know there was a child. When did this happen?"

"Six moons ago," Swift Arrow replied, his voice sounding suddenly too weak for such a powerful man. He turned to face Zeke, his eyes full of hatred. "It was the white man's disease! In this past winter, my brother, while you have been gone, we have lost almost half of our people! Do you understand? Half of the whole Cheyenne nation was gone in only two moons because of the white man's dreaded spotted disease! Women. Little children. Even warriors. Men who could defeat any man in battle died like women from the dreaded disease. They could not fight that. And now you bring a white woman into our camp!"

Their eyes held in a challenge, and Abbie swallowed back her tears. Zeke's eyes began to soften. He had lost a wife and son of his own. He knew the hurt.

"I understand your feelings, my brother. But Abbie is just one little girl. She's had the spotted disease, so she can't get it again. They say you only get it once, and then it can't hurt you anymore. And it's only when you find the whites in great numbers that the disease can take hold. Abbie has been with

65

me now for six weeks. Before that she spent the winter at Fort Bridger, with strong, sturdy men where there was no disease. It's been a long time since she's been around whites fresh from the East. They are the ones who bring the disease, Swift Arrow—the ones fresh out here in big numbers. Don't blame what happened to Weeping Woman on Abbie. I'm asking you as a brother to accept her and make her feel welcome. And I'm truly sorry about your wife and baby. I've felt the loss, Swift Arrow. You know that."

Swift Arrow seemed to soften slightly. He sighed deeply. "All right," he told Zeke. "I will not interfere. But some of my anger is not at the white woman. It is at you, for I fear you will feel the hurt again. How many times did you say you would never again marry a white girl?"

"I know what I said. But that was before I met Abbie."

Swift Arrow glanced at her, then back at Zeke. "She must be an unusual white woman for you to make her your wife."

"She is. She's good, Swift Arrow, good and true."

The man's eyes remained belligerent, but it was obvious he had a great deal of respect for his half-blood brother.

"My tipi is the one with the arrows painted on it," he told Zeke. "Just behind your woman. Our mother always puts it up for me. Now I give it to you. It shall be your dwelling until your woman makes one of her own, if she can learn!"

Zeke recognized the friendly gesture, even though Swift Arrow had added the last sarcastic remark.

"Thank you, my brother."

"I do it only because our mother would wish it and because a man needs a place to be alone with his woman. You are my brother. I would not deny you shelter." He turned and walked away, calling out to Zeke as he departed. "Tonight we will make big fire—have council." He stopped and turned to look at both of them again. "You bring woman." He turned away again and Zeke looked at Abbie, whose mouth was set in a hard line of anger at Swift Arrow for his digging remarks.

"Believe it or not he's starting to like you," Zeke told her.

She sighed and looked down. "I find that hard to believe, Zeke."

He walked up to her and put a hand on her shoulder, leading her inside the tipi. "He's given us this dwelling place," he told her. "That's quite a gift. Sit down over there on that buffalo robe, Abbie, and let's have a look at those legs. I'll go out and get some bear grease from my supplies."

Abbie turned up her nose. Bear grease did not smell very good, but it did work wonders on abrasions. She decided that if the Indians used it, she might as well get used to using it also.

She sat down wearily on the buffalo robe, staring around at the lovely paintings on the inside of the tipi and feeling very sorry for the wife of Swift Arrow, whom she would now never meet. She had to feel sorry for Swift Arrow in that respect, and she could not fully blame him for fearing she would bring disease to their clan. She could only pray she would not.

Zeke returned a moment later with his parfleche and a canteen. He sat down beside her and put an arm around her for a brief moment. "Everything will be all right, Abbie," he told her. "You just let me do all the talking for a few days." He gave her a squeeze and moved around in front of her. He pushed up her tunic, and his hands looked large against her thin legs. "You still need to put on a few pounds, woman," he told her.

She smiled wistfully. "Mama used to call me her little bird," she replied. The thought of her dead mother brought an ache to her heart, reminding her she had no family now. There was only Zeke. All she had in the world sat in front of her now . . . this precious man who was her dearest friend and who had stayed by her side when all else was lost.

He poured some water from his canteen onto a piece of clean cotton cloth he'd taken from the parfleche. He dabbed the cloth on her legs and she jumped with pain. He hesitated, glancing up to see the tears in her eyes.

"Sorry, Abbie, but we ought to clean these up a bit before I put the bear grease on them." He continued washing them as best he could. "And try not to think about sad things right now," he added. "You have the present to think about, honey. Don't burden your mind with memories of the past."

She sat quietly and watched him, as he applied the bear grease with great care and gentleness. Again she was amazed at how he could be a fierce warrior one moment and a gentle husband the next. She quietly studied the finely chiseled features of his face. He loved her. Of that she was certain. He was here now, and she didn't have to be afraid.

Someone called Zeke's name from outside the tipi, and Zeke turned and replied in the Cheyenne tongue. He set the bear grease aside as Red Eagle, his middle brother, entered, followed by the friendly, round-faced woman Abbie had seen standing outside watching her. A small girl, perhaps two years old, followed the woman, clinging to her mother's tunic, and a little boy, slightly older, was behind the girl.

Zeke greeted them all, and the children stood staring at Abbie as though she were a strange spirit who had come to eat them. Abbie's first thought was how beautiful the children were, their skin smooth and brown, their eyes almost too big for their small faces. She had seen many other Indians in her few months in untamed territory, and she was sure the Cheyenne had to be the most handsome. Their appearance was clean, their stature proud, the colors of their clothing and dwelling places bright and lively. Their long, jet-black hair was soft and clean, neatly braided or twisted into plaits with brightly died cloth and beaded rawhide strips.

Red Eagle glanced at Abbie, amazed at how white her legs looked. Abbie felt embarrassed, and quickly pulled down her tunic. Red Eagle looked at Zeke. "This is Tall Grass Woman," he told Zeke. "Wife of Falling Rock. You remember her?"

Zeke nodded to the woman. "I remember."

Red Eagle reached over and took something from Tall Grass Woman's hands. "She bring gift for your woman—to welcome her." He shook out the cream-colored doeskin dress, beautifully painted and decorated with quills and beads.

Abbie gasped with delight, and Zeke smiled, reaching down

and helping Abbie to her feet so that she could take the tunic and hold it up to herself.

"She make tunic for her sister, who die of the spotted disease before Tall Grass Woman can give dress to her. Now she want your woman to have the dress. She say someone pretty like the white woman should wear it."

Abbie looked up at Zeke, her eyes tearing. "Oh, Zeke, I can't take it from her. It's too lovely!"

"You must take it. She'd be insulted if you didn't."

Abbie turned to Tall Grass Woman. She laid the tunic over one arm and touched Tall Grass Woman's shoulder with her other hand. "Thank you!" she told the woman. She looked up at Zeke. "How do I say it?"

"Ha ho," Zeke answered. "It means thank you."

Abbie repeated the words to Tall Grass Woman, and the woman smiled proudly, reaching out to touch Abbie's cheek.

"Wagh!" she said, nodding her head vigorously. *"Wagh!"*

"She says it is good," Zeke told Abbie. "She means it is good that you are here."

"The little boy is her son, Wolf's Paw," Red Eagle told Abbie. "He is four winters old. The little girl is Magpie, and she is two."

The children moved further behind their mother, peering at Abbie with big, brown eyes.

"Oh, Zeke, Indian children are so beautiful!" Abbie exclaimed. "I can't wait until we—"

She blushed and looked down, forgetting that Red Eagle could understand English. Red Eagle and Zeke eyed each other and suppressed their laughter. Abbie swallowed, still looking at the ground.

"Please tell Tall Grass Woman how . . . how grateful I am. I need the tunic badly," she told Zeke. Zeke felt sorry for her embarrassment, and he reached over and put a hand reassuringly on her shoulder, not caring if Red Eagle saw him show his affection. He spoke up to Tall Grass Woman, thanking her again, then left Abbie for a moment to reach into

69

his parfleche and retrieve a handful of blue trade beads from a pouchful he had purchased at Fort Bridger to bring to his mother. He knew how highly prized beads were to Cheyenne women, and he handed them to Tall Grass Woman. Her eyes widened and she exclaimed excitedly over them, nodding to Zeke, then to Abbie, then to Zeke again, smiling and jabbering in her own tongue. She nodded once more and then scurried out with her children.

Zeke put a hand to Abbie's waist and urged her to sit back down. She carefully laid the tunic out beside her on the buffalo robe, overwhelmed by the beautiful gift from the Cheyenne woman she had never even met until today.

"It is good you give her the beads. She is happy," Red Eagle told Zeke as the two men sat down also. Zeke picked up a stick and stirred the small fire Swift Arrow had built inside the tipi that morning to ward off the chill of the early hours.

Zeke looked at Abbie. "When an Indian gives a gift, it is the custom to give something in return to show your gratitude," he told her.

"Oh. Then I'm glad you gave her the beads," she replied.

Red Eagle glanced at her; then he looked at Zeke. "There are many customs she must learn if she is to live here among us." Their eyes held.

"I need her, Red Eagle," Zeke said openly. "I want to be with the Cheyenne, and she has agreed to stay with me. How are the others taking it—besides Swift Arrow, I mean?"

"They do not mind so much. It is only Swift Arrow who is so angry. The others, they know you are a great warrior, in spite of your white blood. They respect your decisions, as I do." He grinned a little. "And they know it is your white blood that keeps you looking at the white women, just as the Cheyenne like to look at their own women—and at the Arapaho women. They are all pleasant to watch."

They both laughed lightly, and Abbie had to smile. She looked down again, feeling as though perhaps she should not be sitting in on Zeke's conversation with his wild young brother.

But Zeke reached over to take her hand and he squeezed it consolingly as he continued talking.

"Did we really lose half our people to the measles, Red Eagle?"

The young man frowned. "Many. Hundreds. It was very bad, very bad. There was also the coughing sickness. I myself am bitter toward these whites who come through our land." He glanced at Abbie again, then back to his brother. "I do not blame your woman for these things. She is only one small girl. But you should know that our feelings toward the newcomers from the East are not good, my brother. They bring disease. They cut down the trees and make the water foul. They leave behind dead animals and filth. They shoot at us without reason and kill our game. When they kill an animal, they take only a little of the meat and leave the rest, wasting the blood and the bones and half of the meat. We fear for our future, Zeke."

Zeke nodded. "I understand."

"Yellow Wolf speaks like a woman now," Red Eagle went on, referring to one of their chiefs. "The disease frightened him. Now he speaks of asking for protection from the Great White Father in Washington. He says we must do as the white man does—plow the earth and raise cattle and plant seeds." He waved his arm and spit toward the fire. "He expects young men who are strong and eager for the hunt to give up the hunt and be like women! I will not live that way! Nor will our brothers. Digging in the earth is woman's work! And what does a man do once the seed is planted? Sit and watch the earth? Wait for the seed to sprout and grow?" He sneered and pulled out his knife, using it to trace nervously in the dirt floor. "He might as well put a shawl around his shoulders like an old woman and shrivel up and die!"

"I know how you feel, Red Eagle," Zeke answered. "But I also know the white man. And the more of them that come out here, the harder it will be for the Indian to find food, to roam wherever he wishes for the hunt, even to war against other tribes. Yellow Wolf sees this. He sees a change coming. I don't

71

like it any more than the rest of you. But I see a day coming when the Cheyenne will have to make peace with the Crow and the Ute and Pawnee; a day when all tribes will have to fight as one against the white man. Either that, or they will have to bend to the white man's will. Not to bend will mean death, Red Eagle. I feel it in the wind."

There was a moment of silence. "I hope you are wrong, my brother, for the Cheyenne will never bend!" He glanced at Abbie. "What will she do if the day comes that we must fight? Who will her weapons be used against?"

Abbie returned his look boldly. "I will be with my husband's people," she answered.

Red Eagle grinned a little. "Which people? He has two people."

"He has one people!" she answered defiantly. "The Cheyenne!"

He nodded and looked approvingly at Zeke. "Perhaps she will learn to be a good squaw sooner than I think."

"She'll learn," Zeke answered with a grin. "And she doesn't speak with a forked tongue as some whites do. She has given up much to be with me. That alone should win your respect. And when we have spoken to our mother, you will know and understand my wife better."

Red Eagle nodded. "You say you will go on the hunt with us?"

"We will go."

"We will leave in the morning to catch up with our mother, who goes north to Dog Man's clan. We will probably hunt at the Smoky Hill or Republican River. It is said that is where the buffalo have gone, but there might be trouble crossing the Santa Fe trade route."

"Why? We've always ridden through that area."

"There is talk—at Bent's Fort. They say the Mexicans to the south of us are making great trouble. They speak of a war between your white brothers and the Mexicans. Many soldiers will be coming."

Zeke frowned and looked at Abbie, then back at his brother. "I heard a few rumors at Fort Bridger."

"At Bent's Fort the traders speak as though there is already a war. And they say some of the Comanches are being paid by the Mexicans to make trouble for the Americans."

Zeke reached behind himself and felt in his parfleche for his corncob pipe. He pulled it out and lit it, while an eerie silence hung in the air.

"Zeke?" Abbie spoke up quietly. "Maybe there's a war going on we don't know about." She hesitated when Red Eagle looked at her as though she had no right to be talking. Zeke puffed on his pipe and eyed Red Eagle.

"I won't deny her everything, Red Eagle," he told his brother. "She's a smart girl with a mind of her own, and if she wants to speak she can speak."

"A Cheyenne woman holds her tongue when the men are talking."

"Outside she'll hold her tongue. But within the privacy of our dwelling place she can speak as she likes. And you know as well as I do there are plenty of single-minded Cheyenne wives who speak their pieces to their men in privacy."

"Only when they are alone," Red Eagle replied, tracing in the dirt floor again.

"You're my brother. She can speak in front of you." He looked at Abbie. "I'm thinking the same thing, Abbie girl," he told her. "If it's true, more soldiers will be coming to Indian Territory, followed by more settlers. And if the damned Comanche are raiding, you can bet some of it will get blamed on the Cheyenne by people who don't know one Indian from another."

"This is what we fear," Red Eagle put in.

"Back home in Tennessee"—Abbie spoke up again—"there was talk about Mexico way back before Pa and us even left. Folks said as how since we had Texas, maybe we ought to go for more and take in New Mexico and California."

Zeke puffed at his pipe and nodded. "And knowing how

73

greedy most whites are for more land, they'll go after it."

Abbie watched them both, feeling as though she were being drawn into a destiny over which she had no control. "But a war with Mexico, that doesn't have to bother us any, does it, Zeke?" she asked hesitantly. "I mean if they want to fight the Mexicans, so what? You and I and the Cheyenne, we can just go on about our business."

Red Eagle looked at her, his eyes scanning her quickly again, dropping last to her white ankles. She was pretty, of that there was no doubt. And she was soft spoken, even if she did speak when she shouldn't. And there was something about her . . . a certain quality that told a man she would be a fine woman some day.

"When you have been with us awhile," he told her, "you will understand that anything that happens with the Americans has much to do with the Indian. If there is to be war with Mexico, it is as Zeke said. More soldiers will come. And with the soldiers will come more settlers. And if they take more land, then even more will come, searching for the gold and for the power the white man finds in owning much land. But he does not own the land, nor does the Indian. It belongs to the spirits. *Hesek*, the mother earth, is sacred. It is here to be used by all those who pass through it. But no one has the right to own it and tell others they cannot use it. This is a strange custom of the white people I do not understand—always to be owning land and buildings and much gold. Our people do not understand such thinking."

Zeke nodded. "I agree this can only mean more trouble. There is vague talk at Fort Bridger about a big treaty with the Plains Indians. You heard anything like that?"

"*Ai*. Broken Hand is now an agent. We hear he has told the Great White Father there should be such a treaty. But both of us know the white man's word cannot always be trusted."

Blue smoke curled up from Zeke's pipe. "True. But if they offer a big chunk of land to the Indians, it might be wise to consider taking it."

"It is talked about whenever council is held," Red Eagle told him, shoving his knife back into its sheath. "But most of us do not want such a treaty. It is not right that the Indian should be put on one piece of land and told to stay there. We cannot live that way."

"There may be no choice in the end, Red Eagle."

"*E-have-se-va!*" Red Eagle spit out the word. "No good! No good!"

Zeke shook his head, knowing how difficult it was to make his Cheyenne brothers understand about the whites. "Well," he said, setting down his pipe, "it's something to be considered, Red Eagle." There was a moment of strained silence before Zeke spoke again. "How are the horses coming along?"

"Good. Some fine young ones were dropped this spring. You will be happy when you see them. We have taken good care of them."

Zeke grinned, and Abbie felt relieved at the change of subject. "There're no better horse breeders than the Cheyenne," Zeke replied to his brother. "I owe you and Swift Arrow and Black Elk," he added. "You're welcome to eat with us any time, and I want each of you to pick out one of the best mounts for your own." He looked at Abbie. "A good horse is worth just about as much to a Cheyenne man as his wife," he told her with a wink.

"Oh?" Her eyebrows went up in mock offense. "Then you'll have to take me out to see my competition."

Zeke laughed lightly and looked back at Red Eagle, who was grinning himself at the remark.

"I'll pay you cash money for your work as well," Zeke went on to his brother. "You can use the money to get supplies at Bent's Fort. As the hunt gets leaner, you'll need the white man's dollars to get some of the things you will need. I'm taking the horses to Independence after the hunt. I have money in a bank there. I can get good prices for the horses, too. That's where most folks congregate to come West. They'll pay good for sturdy horses, and my Appaloosas are some of the best. Long as we can't stop the damned whites from coming, we might as well take advantage of their needs, Red Eagle. God knows we'll have plenty of needs of our own as we lose more hunting ground."

Red Eagle grinned. "With the white man's money we can also buy the white man's firewater!" he told his brother. "For now, Red Eagle trades robes for the whiskey."

Zeke's face darkened with anger at his brother. "You've been trading robes and supplies for whiskey?"

Red Eagle straightened defensively. "The firewater makes us feel even braver! And it helps us have visions. It is good medicine! Good medicine!"

"It's bad, Red Eagle! Very bad! You leave the whiskey alone!" Zeke told him.

The man frowned and waved him off. "Whiskey good. Only one buffalo robe buys whole bottle!"

Zeke's eyes narrowed in disgust. "They water it down, Red Eagle! They sell you two cents worth of whiskey and in return they get five dollars for the robe back in Saint Louis!"

Red Eagle shrugged. "Perhaps. Money means something only to the whites. So, let them get their money for the robes. We will have our firewater! Even now I have some in my parfleche. I drink some every day. When I do, I feel more alive."

Zeke rubbed a hand over his eyes and sighed. "If anything destroys our people, Red Eagle, the firewater will do it more quickly than white man's diseases and soldiers' rifles combined!" He looked back at his brother. "I speak the truth, Red Eagle. You think the firewater gives you power, but it's bad for you. It keeps you from thinking wisely. It will get you in trouble with the soldiers. And even though it makes you feel stronger, you are actually weaker when you are full of the firewater!"

Red Eagle grinned. "Always you worry about us. We are fine, proud Cheyenne—best warriors on the Plains! A little whiskey will not harm us. I only drink a little each day."

"It's habit forming. Each day you'll want more and more, Red Eagle, until it destroys you. I speak the truth, my brother. Listen to me!"

Red Eagle suddenly rose, his eyes hot with anger. "Do not speak in such a way in front of your woman!"

Their eyes held in a challenge, and Zeke rose also. "I speak to you in such a way because I care about you, Red Eagle. Does our mother know you have the whiskey?"

"Our mother no longer has anything to do with what Red Eagle chooses to do or say or eat or drink!" the man shot back. "I am my own man!"

Zeke knew he had greatly offended his brother by scolding him in front of a woman, especially a strange white woman. He forced back his anger and nodded.

"Of course you are," he said calmly. "Forgive me, Red Eagle. I still think of you sometimes as a small boy."

"I am not a boy! I am a man! And I ask you to let me have some of the horses as payment for caring for them. I want to use them as a gift to Red Dog, an Arapaho, when we go on the hunt. I . . . I wish to marry Red Dog's daughter, Yellow Moon."

Zeke's face brightened. "You wish to marry?"

"*Ai.* I have been watching Yellow Moon since I was only fifteen summers. I have killed the buffalo and I have had a vision—and now I am a man. I have learned that Yellow Moon has had her first"—he hesitated and glanced at Abbie—"that she is a woman now," he finished. Abbie blushed deeply at the meaning of the words. "She is fourteen summers. It is . . . difficult . . . for us not to be together. I wish to marry her after the hunt."

Zeke nodded and put out his hand, and Red Eagle grasped his wrist. "You may have four horses, Red Eagle. Is that enough?"

"*Ai.*" The young man nodded. "It is as you say about your white woman. I need Yellow Moon as much as a man needs to breathe."

77

Zeke grinned. "I understand, my brother." Red Eagle started to release his hand, but Zeke kept a firm grip. "Be careful with the firewater, Red Eagle. Remember my words. I speak them not to dishonor you, only to warn you—because you are my brother. I have seen what whiskey can do to men."

"You drink it. I have seen you."

"*Ai.* But I know what it does, and I am careful. And the whiskey you buy from those traders—it's full of water and sugar. I've seen them mix it myself. They know the red man likes sugar and that he will drink so much of it that he will be destroyed. I have white blood in me, Red Eagle. It does not affect me the same as my full-blood brothers. Don't let them destroy you that way."

Red Eagle grinned. "Always you worry too much about such things," he told Zeke. He looked at Abbie, then back at Zeke, who finally released his grip on Red Eagle's wrist. "We hold council soon," Red Eagle told Zeke. "We talk more about the soldiers and Mexico. We tell you what has been happening while you have been gone." He walked to the tipi entrance, then hesitated. "Bring white woman. The others want to look at your new wife again. She should wear Tall Grass Woman's tunic. But be sure she sits behind you and does not speak too much. Tomorrow we go north."

He quickly left, and Zeke walked over and tied the leather straps of the animal-skin entrance flap so that it could not be opened. He turned to look at Abbie. "Think you can keep quiet at the council, woman?"

She smiled. "I'll try. But it isn't one of the things I do best," she answered.

Zeke chuckled and walked over to where she sat. "White women do seem to talk a lot," he told her. He sat down beside her. "How are your legs?"

She shrugged. "They don't hurt anymore."

He pushed her tunic back up to look at them and then pushed it up further, lightly stroking her thighs and sending the pleasant tingle through her body.

"Do you think I'll be accepted, Zeke? I want so much for them to like me."

He moved one hand up further, rubbing it along the side of her bare bottom. "They already like you, Abbie girl," he told her. "Let's both wash and change and we'll go out there and you can get to know them better."

"Will you wear that lovely white, beaded buckskin shirt that I like so much?" she asked. She had only seen it on him three times, that fine, beautifully decorated and bleached doeskin shirt he wore only for special occasions. He looked grand and handsome in it, its bleached whiteness only accenting the dark, provocative air about him.

"Whatever you want me to wear," he told her. He unlaced the front of her tunic. "I'll have to kill lots of deer and buffalo, Abbie girl, so you can sew the skins into some clothes for us. The women will like teaching you."

She nodded, feeling a shiver of excitement when he pulled her tunic down over her shoulders, exposing her small breasts. He toyed lightly with one nipple, arousing it and making her blush.

"Zeke," she whispered, looking down. "What if someone comes?"

"No one will come." He leaned forward and kissed the pinkish scar left from her arrow wound, where the arrow had exited just above her left breast after entering her back. The scar brought back the ache in his heart, the terror he had felt in thinking she might die from the wound, and he recalled the agony he'd experienced at watching her scream with pain when he had to cut her to relieve the infection.

But it was over now. She was alive! And she belonged to him! Her breathing quickened as he pushed the tunic down to her waist.

His lips covered her mouth with their sweet moistness, and he laid her back gently, pushing the tunic down more. She thought to herself that he had been right about how practically and comfortably Indian women dressed. Their tunics were

79

soft, and to be free of undergarments was to be free of stiff corsets and pinching supports and hot layers of petticoats and ruffles. In this land a woman had to dress so that she could move quickly and could work without being burdened by stiff, hot clothing. And then, of course, the tunic made it much easier for a man to bed his woman. The freedom of the clothing seemed to bring a physical freedom that was also a sexual one.

She lay still and let him look at her as he sat up and carefully removed her tunic so that it did not rub against her sore legs. Then he stood up and took off his own shirt and leggings. She drank in his lean, hard body, and felt the excitement and glory of being wanted by a man who knew no fear—a man who was as skilled in his bed as he was in battle. He removed his loincloth to reveal the part of him that was a powerful and masculine extension of his body, its power lying in its ability to make her lose all resistance to him, to make her cry out at the ecstasy of taking it inside herself and therefore claiming the man himself. There was an urgency about him now. Fire flickered in his eyes at the excitement of the recent hand-to-hand battle with his Crow enemies, combined with the joy of again being with his own people.

He quietly moved on top of her, being careful of the abrasions on her legs. "Welcome home, Abbie girl," he told her. She felt the near pain of his first entrance and cried out, and the inside of the tipi became a dusky swirl of paintings and smoke and Indian weapons and trappings that hung inside. He whispered something to her in the Cheyenne tongue, and Tennessee and the white world she had once known were rapidly becoming a blurred memory.

Five

It began when Mexico successfully separated itself from Spain in 1821. No longer could the King of Spain forbid Mexicans to trade with foreigners. No longer did foreigners have to worry about being arrested or having their goods confiscated for entering Spanish Territory. It had become Mexican Territory, and with an initial load of merchandise costing thirty-five thousand dollars, a United States merchant could realize up to two hundred thousand dollars on the sale of popular American goods to Mexicans. There were millions to be made, and of course, some men were willing to make the investment and to take the risks involved in shipping their wares to Sante Fe, the primary trading point.

Thus was born the Santa Fe Trail, an eight-hundred-mile journey between Independence, Missouri and Santa Fe, New Mexico. It soon became a two-way road, as Mexicans traveled north into the United States with their pack trains of Spanish goods for sale to American merchants. The trail was shortened just slightly by the discovery of the Cimarron Cutoff by William Becknell, a trader from Franklin, Missouri, who nearly died from lack of water, along with the thirty other men who accompanied him on his first journey via a different route. But they had discovered a stream of drinkable water; and so, the Cimarron Cutoff became a feasible shortcut, although not everyone chose to use it.

But this birth of trade and the opening of new westward

trails only brought more settlers into Indian Territory. And it also brought a hunger on the part of the Americans to possess the Mexican territories that lay so close to their newly acquired state of Texas. A major factor in prompting their desire to make New Mexico and other Mexican territories a part of the United States was the fact that Mexico had begun to tax merchandise that arrived at Santa Fe and at other points for trade. Governor Manuel Armijo, a pompous, eccentric and vicious Mexican ruler, began charging five hundred dollars for every wagonload of trade goods that arrived at Santa Fe from the United States.

When rumors spread throughout Mexican Territory that the Texans intended to claim the Rio Grande as their western border, Governor Armijo knew this would mean the loss of Santa Fe and Taos, and the Mexicans in general feared the wild, "godless" Texans, who, they were sure, would pillage, rape, and murder their people once ownership of Mexican territory was established. Thus began the buildup of a Mexican Army and the attempt on the part of the Mexicans to defend their territory in a war that had not truly begun and was still mostly more fear than reality. This situation turned into a real war when the men from a Texas expeditionary peace force were captured and sent on a two-thousand-mile forced march through waterless, snake-infested desert land to Mexico City. Governor Armijo's orders to the sadistic leader of the march: "If any pretends to be sick or claims he cannot march, shoot him and bring me his ears." When the march was completed, five sets of ears were presented to Governor Armijo in Santa Fe.

Danny Monroe was twenty when he arrived at Fort Leavenworth to join the forces that would march on Santa Fe. A tall, quiet Tennessee boy who proved to be very skillful with a rifle and good at taking orders, he was recognized at once by Colonel Kearny as one of the better recruits. Like most of the other young boys who had joined up, Danny had felt a restless need to leave the boredom of his father's backwoods Tennessee farm and seek his fortune in the West; and one very good way for a poor boy to learn about that untamed country and have a meal in his belly every night was to join the Army.

But for Danny, going West held even more meaning. Since he was fourteen years old, Danny had not seen his half-blood brother, Zeke. He was not certain he would even recognize Zeke now. But once he became familiar with the land, Danny intended to find his brother. Why he needed to find him, he was not sure. Perhaps he wanted to talk to Zeke face to face and to find out the truth about the murders in Tennessee— whether Zeke had truly killed all those men, and, if so, why he had done it.

In Tennessee, no one in Zeke's white family had sympathized more with what Zeke suffered for being a half-breed than Danny. Being the oldest of Zeke's three white half brothers, Danny was the one most familiar with Zeke's growing-up years: the torments, accusations and insults, the abuse and neglect from the boys' mother, Zeke's stepmother; and finally the murder of Zeke's young wife and son. Danny had never believed Zeke had killed his wife and little boy as the authorities had said. He was certain white men had killed Ellen Monroe and her son, and that was why Zeke had murdered all of them.

Whatever had happened, Danny wanted to know the truth because he had always held a special love in his heart for Zeke. Once Zeke had gently and lovingly nursed Danny's puppy back to health after it had been attacked by a bear. Danny remembered that. It was then that he had recognized the gentle side of his half-breed brother and had seen in his eyes a need to be loved and accepted. No one else had cared about the puppy; their father had wanted to shoot it. But Zeke had hidden it in the swamp and had stayed there with it for three days, until the animal had obviously improved enough so that no one would shoot it when he brought it back. After that he had continued to nurse it until the puppy had no sign of injury. It was an event that had remained vivid in Danny's mind, and one that made Danny certain that Zeke Monroe was not the vicious, bloodthirsty killer that their friends and the local authorities had made him out to be. The compelling urge to know the real truth and to find out what had happened to Zeke had grown inside Danny Monroe until he could no longer quell his curiosity. And so, he headed west, joining up with Col. Stephen Watts Kearny's volunteers. He would be among those who would march to Santa Fe.

Abbie forced her legs to walk, desperately trying to ignore the pain in her feet. Refusing to heed Zeke's pleas to ride, she walked behind the Cheyenne men, who rode horses, preferring to remain with the Cheyenne women and prove she was as strong as they.

"If the Cheyenne women usually walk, then so will I!" she told Zeke stubbornly every night as he rubbed her tired and callused feet with bear grease.

"Cheyenne women of wealth ride," he repeated. "You're a woman of wealth. I have many horses. To the Indian that is like a white man having his pockets full of gold. They wouldn't think anything of it if you rode, Abigail."

"That isn't the point," she answered. "I've seen how Swift Arrow watches me. He's waiting for me to prove my weakness. I'll not show him any such thing. He'll soon learn I'm just as strong and brave and industrious as any Cheyenne woman. He'll soon learn that his brother chose well!"

"He already knows I chose well. He just won't admit it."

"Then I'll make him admit it," she answered bitterly.

Zeke wanted to force her to ride, but he knew she was not trying to prove something only to Swift Arrow. She needed to prove something to herself as well; and if they were to live among the Cheyenne, he must let her find out whatever it was she had to know and help her learn the Cheyenne way. But after the fourth day of their journey northward, he knew he could not let this situation go on. She did not look well, and he sensed it was something more than just sore feet. Abbie was physically strong, in spite of her tiny frame. But she was growing paler and thinner, and when he saw her vomiting on the fifth morning when she went out to get a bucket of water, he decided he would exercise his husbandly duty of commanding that she obey him and ride.

She protested weakly and vomited again as he held her from behind. "You'll ride or I'll tie you to a goddamned travois!" he told her. "I've let you have your way, Abbie girl, but this is the end of it."

"Swift Arrow will laugh at me," she protested, beginning to cry.

Zeke took her to the edge of the stream and bathed her face with cool water, and she bent down to rinse her mouth.

"If he laughs I'll beat the hell out of him," Zeke told her. "He knows I can do it. You'll ride, and that's that." He pulled her hair back from her face and gently rubbed her back while she rinsed her mouth again. She sat up straighter and breathed deeply. "Look at me, Abbie," he told her gently.

Her body jerked in a sob, and she turned to face him. Taking her chin in his hand, he studied her eyes.

"How long have you been getting sick like this?" he asked her.

She shrugged. "Off and on for a couple of weeks. But the last three mornings it's been regular."

He sighed and closed his eyes for a moment. "I'm not ignorant about women, Abbie girl. You're pregnant, aren't you?"

Her eyes filled with tears. "I think . . . maybe. I . . . didn't want to worry you. I wanted to be like the other Cheyenne women."

He had to grin, and he pulled her into his arms. "Well, for your information, if a Cheyenne woman has trouble with a pregnancy, her husband doesn't make her walk all the time and do hard work." He kissed her hair. "Abbie, children are all-

85

important to the Cheyenne. The men don't want their women to be losing babies. Just because you're white doesn't mean problems with having a baby make you any weaker. Cheyenne women have the same problems sometimes, especially the very young ones." He pulled back and kissed her eyes. "Damn it, woman, you're going to have a baby—our baby. Ours! Do you know what that means to me?"

"I hope you're happy," she whimpered.

He grinned. "Happy?" He kissed her lips lightly. "Jesus, Abbie, how could you think I wouldn't be happy about that? It's wonderful, and I love you." He hugged her tightly. "No more walking, Abbie, understand? No more."

He helped her to her feet and back to the tipi, making her sit down inside while he made breakfast for them; then he began packing the robes and utensils on their travois. He tied the travois to Abbie's horse and began dismantling the tipi himself, a job which Abbie had learned quickly and had already become adept at doing.

Abbie sat outside on a log, watching Zeke with loving and grateful eyes, happier now about her pregnancy because he finally knew and she didn't have to try to hide it in order to prove she was as strong as the Cheyenne women. But she felt uncomfortable when she noticed Swift Arrow watching from his campfire. She could feel him laughing inside himself, and she wanted to cry. The others in their small party had taken to her quickly, and she had become good friends with Tall Grass Woman. The two of them had developed a method of communication, Abbie learning some Cheyenne words, Tall Grass learning some English, and the two of them getting by most of the time with awkward sign language.

Abbie liked Tall Grass Woman. It was good to have a woman friend. It had been a long time since she'd had one, for she'd had no mother now for over two years, and she had left all her girl friends back in Tennessee a year ago when her father had decided to come west. After that her only friend had been her sister, Lee Ann. Then Lee Ann was murdered, and there was no one. During the long winter at Fort Bridger, while Abbie waited for Zeke to come back from Oregon, there had been only burly, uncivilized men to talk to, and a few Shoshoni women who spoke no English. Now she had a woman friend again, and it was good. Perhaps she would have more friends after their party met up with Zeke's mother's clan and the other Cheyenne who would congregate for the hunt on the Smoky Hill River.

The only problem now was Swift Arrow. He remained aloof and still insisted Abbie was bad luck. Although he hadn't actually voiced his feelings to Zeke and Abbie, they were obvious by the look in his eyes and the way he watched her, ready to use any excuse to say "I told you so." Abbie felt he would gloat if she showed any weakness, and he was gloating now, so much so that he felt compelled to rise and walk toward them with a grin on his face.

He came to stand near them, his arms folded in front of him, his haughty eyes watching his brother dismantle the tipi.

"How is it that you do this woman's work?" he asked Zeke, unable to withhold the chance to discredit Abbie.

When Zeke stopped what he was doing and turned to face his brother with dark, angry eyes, Swift Arrow lost his smile and dropped his hands to his sides.

"Abbie is going to have a baby," he told Swift Arrow. "She's been sick. My first wife miscarried and almost bled to death once, Swift Arrow. And the son we did have was murdered. I don't aim to lose another wife or child. Plenty of Cheyenne women have this same problem, so I don't want to hear you direct one insult toward Abbie, or I'll make you beg for forgiveness, brother or not. Do you understand me?"

Their eyes held in a challenge for a brief moment, then Swift Arrow's softened slightly. "I understand you," he replied. He glanced at Abbie, then back at Zeke. "She is very young for this."

"Yes, she is. That's why I intend to be extra careful."

Swift Arrow stood and watched awkwardly as Zeke returned

to taking down the tipi. Then he walked up to Abbie.

"It is customary that an uncle be appointed to train a son in the Cheyenne ways," he told her. Abbie met his eyes, realizing that in his own way he was telling her he was glad she was having Zeke's child and was offering his services in the child's upbringing. She rose and faced him, and Zeke listened but did not turn around. If anything was to be settled between Abigail and Swift Arrow, it had to be done between the two of them, and no one else could bring them to an understanding. But he had faith in Abbie. Someday Swift Arrow would recognize the quality of the woman.

"I'll remember that," she replied to Swift Arrow. "And if I have a son, I hope he's as proud and strong and skilled as his Cheyenne uncles. He will be raised as a Cheyenne, Swift Arrow."

The man nodded, suppressing a grin. "I accept your praise and thank you." He started to walk away, then turned to look at her once more. "You shall ride from now on and not walk," he told her. "I will explain to the others." He glanced at Zeke, who had turned to face him, and their eyes met in brotherly understanding. Swift Arrow looked back at Abbie. "But your husband should not do woman's work," he added. "Tonight the other women shall help raise the tipi, so that Zeke can smoke with the men. They will not mind. They will be happy to know you are with child. They will help you."

He turned and left before Zeke and Abbie could reply. Zeke looked at Abbie and grinned. "Give him time," he told her. "You're some woman, Abbie." She smiled and sat back down while he finished dismantling the tipi. This life was not so bad after all.

The wheels of Jonathan Mack's coach bounced and jolted over rough Kentucky roads, but the plush interior and the leaf springs of the Carroll Coach in which he rode made Mack's ride a comfortable one. He sat back and lit another thin cigar, grinning at the thought of the wealth that lay waiting for him in Santa Fe. Senator Garvey had given him complete license to loan, invest, and purchase in any way that would bring the biggest profit. But the pay he would receive for such work would be only part of his profit. For at this very moment, two very large, well-packed wagons were on their way to St. Louis, where they and Jonathan Mack would ride a steamboat across the Missouri River to Independence. There, Jonathan would hire another coach, with guards for his own safety, to take him to Santa Fe. The wagons would go to a point farther south, where the smuggled rifles and dynamite they carried would be sold to the Mexicans for pure gold.

It was all arranged. Reliable men were being well paid to watch the wagons until they arrived at Independence. There, Mack would hire a good man who knew the back country to take the wagons to Santa Fe by an alternate route. Other men, paid by Mack, were already on their way to Mexico to make a deal for the exchange of gold and rifles and to set up the place where the wagons were to be intercepted before reaching Santa Fe.

The Mexicans were desperate for rifles, for they knew it would not be easy to defeat the Americans and neither their government nor their army was organized. If this deal was successful, Mack planned to arrange for more smuggled shipments. When the war with Mexico was over, perhaps the Indians would trade valuable skins and gold for the firearms.

The only hitch might be finding a good scout to take the guns from Independence to the rendezvous point. It had to be a man who was very familiar with the rugged southwest back country, as well as with Indians. There was not such a man among those he had hired, but he was certain he could find one in Independence, where such men congregated to lead the wagon trains West. And perhaps it would be best if the scout he hired did not know the wagons carried smuggled rifles. That way he and the second driver would not be tempted to do their own dealing on the side. Mack would make certain the drivers he hired would think the wagons carried only whiskey and piano parts for the fancy saloon he planned to open in Santa Fe. After all, the wagons would indeed carry those items. It was just the "extra" cargo the drivers would not know about—not until the Mexicans intercepted them at a place called Devil's Pits.

He looked out at the mountains of Kentucky. The mountains of the great West were supposedly much higher and more majestic than these. But Jonathan Mack cared little for the beauty of the land. To him it was of no importance. He did not like the idea of living in the rugged, hot, and dusty West, with few Eastern comforts; but he knew that anyone who got in on the ground floor there could become a millionaire because of the explosive settlement that was sure to occur.

And so he would bear the heat and filth and snakes and thorny plants; for all that mattered was to get rich. Perhaps he could open a dance hall and a whorehouse. Nothing brought more money in the West than good whiskey and loose women, for both were hard for a man to come by. The few women that were already out there were prim pioneer wives and their few chaste daughters. The thousands of men who had gone west to find their fortunes needed women, the kind that were fast and easy. Jonathan Mack would find them and supply them—for a percentage of the profits, of course.

He thought of Anna for a moment. Few women would be that good or that pretty, but he would find some. He wondered if perhaps he should have asked Anna to come along. But then the senator would not have liked that. Anna was his favorite.

It was the middle of May when Zeke and Abbie and their small party reached the sprawling Cheyenne and Arapaho village. They crested a rise, and Abbie's heart pounded with apprehension when she looked down on over four hundred lodges. She pulled her mount to a halt, and Zeke could feel her doubts and fears. He motioned for the others to go on ahead of them.

"I will tell our mother you are coming," Black Elk told Zeke. "She will be happy." He rode forward, yelping like a wild dog, and galloped into camp, causing a stir among the women who sat stitching and visiting and the men who were busily preparing their weapons for the hunt. Runners had been sent out, so most of the Southern Cheyenne were congregated for the buffalo hunt, as were many Arapaho.

Swift Arrow rode up and stopped beside Zeke. "I will prepare the village to receive your white woman," he told his brother. "The chiefs will want a council, I am sure."

Then Swift Arrow rode forward with the others, and Abbie watched them ride into the village, becoming lost among the fifteen hundred or so Cheyenne and Arapaho who immediately surrounded them, including children of all ages and the ever-present dogs. Abbie turned to Zeke, her face pale.

"Zeke, there are . . . so many! Is that . . . all of them?"

Zeke grinned. "No, Abbie girl. That's just part of them, a small part. There are a lot of Arapaho down there as well."

She swallowed and looked back at the village. "I . . . don't know if I can go down there, Zeke."

He reached over and took her hand. "Do you think they're going to behead you and boil you in a pot?"

Her eyes teared. "Don't joke about it, Zeke." She turned to face him. "Don't you realize how somebody like me feels in a situation like this? I . . . I didn't expect . . . so many!"

He squeezed her hand. "Abbie, I was once the only Indian among hundreds of whites, remember? And I was just a little boy, with no one who loved me the way I love you. No one was willing to protect me, not even my white father. I know exactly how you feel. But you have me, and you don't have to be afraid, Abbie."

"I'm not afraid, really. I'm just . . . oh, Zeke, I want so much for them to accept me. I know how important it is to you. What if Swift Arrow says something bad about me? What if—"

"He won't. He knows he doesn't have the right. He'll leave it up to their own judgment. It's the band chiefs who have to

91

approve, and the dog soldiers and priests."

She looked at him again. "And what if they don't want me there?"

"Then we'll just have to leave. That's all. They won't harm you, Abbie. They're just people, and they're a beautiful people, Abbie. Understanding. When they know about you, they'll let you stay. They may ask you to stay away from tribal ceremonies and religious gatherings. But they won't ban you, because you belong to me."

She looked back at the lodges, noticing they were set in neat groups of circles, the entire group making up one large circle.

"How do they know where to put up their tipis?" she asked. "Do they argue over the best spots? There are so many of them!"

Zeke let go of her hand and pulled a cheroot from a small pouch on his weapons belt. He lit it and slung one leg crosswise over his horse's back in a relaxed position. He took a puff on the cheroot and pointed.

"See the opening—where the circle is incomplete?"

"Yes."

"The lodges are always arranged in one large circle, and the camp opening always faces east, toward the rising sun, the greatest power. The village is always placed on the south bank of the river. The Tribal Council assigns the locations of each band within the bigger circle, and each band then builds its circle of tipis, also with the openings facing east. The larger circle is nearly a mile around. Each band is made up of one to four clans—family units—sometimes more. We will be with my mother's clan. Most Cheyenne women remain with their mother's clan when they marry, and the man leaves his family clan, unless for some reason that can't be done. Each band has a chief who is over all the clans within the band."

She shook her head. "I hope I'll remember all of this some day."

"You will."

"Do the dog soldiers live apart from the others?"

"Not usually. They're the primary warriors, the most respected and honored of all the fighting men. Swift Arrow is a dog soldier. My other two brothers want to be, but they haven't gone through the sacrifices yet. Red Eagle will suffer the Sun Dance ritual this summer. At any rate, the dog soldiers usually live among their own clans, but they don't answer to a band chief. They answer only to their own military chiefs. But there are soldier societies within the bands. They are fighters, too, but not dog soldiers. They answer to the band chiefs, and they are the ones who plan the hunt. All those who participate in the hunt must do exactly as the soldier society tells them. To disobey could mean a whipping, and to disobey more than once could get a man's tipi burned and his horses shot."

Her eyebrows went up. "Oh, my!"

Zeke grinned and watched her, knowing what a difficult thing it would be for her to ride into a village of dark-skinned, half-naked people who appeared savage and violent to her. Aside from Swift Arrow's cool attitude, the few they had been with up to now had been friendly and kind, but their number had been small. This was an entirely different matter.

"Were you ever a dog soldier?" she asked Zeke.

He puffed the cheroot. "I've suffered the Sun Dance ritual. And I've proven my skills. They all know better than to go against me with a knife, and they know I can fight as good as any of their best dog soldiers. But I'm half white, Abbie. I can't hold the title of dog soldier, especially since I'm also gone a lot of the time. Nevertheless, they show me the same respect as their better warriors receive. I feel very honored. It's only because I've had a vision and have a Cheyenne name, and because I successfully accomplished the Sun Dance sacrifice."

"You never told me what you had to do. I've only seen the scars it left."

He frowned. "I'll explain it sometime. I don't think you want to hear it right now. I'm not even sure you should ever see it, Abbie. To an Indian it's a great honor . . . an important and religious ceremony. To a white person . . . well . . . I

93

suppose it would seem . . . barbaric . . . as you once said about . .
the fighting among the tribes. You have to have a very deep
understanding of the Indian to understand the Sun Dance."

"I want to understand."

"I know you do. But let's take one thing at a time. This is
today, and for today we simply have to go on down there and
meet the Cheyenne—and my mother. And when I've told them
about you, you'll be accepted. I have no doubt." He threw
down the cheroot and picked up the reins of her horse, starting
to lead it down.

"Oh, Zeke, let's go back!" she spoke up.

He turned to look at her. "What is there to go back to,
Abbie?"

Their eyes held. "Nothing," she replied in a near whisper.

"Then let's ride forward, Abbie girl. You just sit proud and
tall on that horse. Cheyenne Zeke is coming home to his
people. My brothers just herded my prize horses down there
for me. Now I'm coming, with my wife who's carrying my
child. I'm proud to take you down there."

They rode forward, toward the sea of brown faces already
gathered at the edge of the village and staring up at Cheyenne
Zeke and the white woman he had brought home.

Abbie sat proudly on her mount as Zeke had instructed her
to do. When they reached the edge of the village, Zeke
dismounted and walked, leading both her horse and his own
into the huge Indian settlement. Little children ran merrily
around the animals and dogs yipped and leaped about the
horses' legs. An ocean of dark, curious eyes stared at Abbie, a
few of the children lightly touching her ankles to see the
contrast of her skin against their little, dark hands. Women
laughed and jabbered and pointed, and men stood stalwart and
silent.

Abbie clung to the pommel of her saddle, her knuckles white
from her firm grip. She wasn't certain she'd be able to stand

once she got off the horse, for she knew her legs would feel weak because of her nervous state. She thought for a moment about Tennessee, and her mother and father, her sister and younger brother, all of them dead now. She remembered being a little girl playing in the tall grass behind her parents' log cabin and daydreaming about a handsome prince coming for her on his white horse and taking her away to a grand castle. She did not know then that her prince would truly come—that he would be as dark and handsome as she had pictured, but that he would wear buckskins and ride an Appaloosa, and that the castle he would take her to would be a tipi, surrounded by a people totally different to her.

But it did not matter. For the man who brought her to this place was as much a prince as any she had dreamed of, as brave and handsome and honored. And now he reached up for her, lifting her down from her horse with strong hands and keeping a reassuring arm around her waist as he led her toward a handsome Cheyenne woman with graying hair.

The commotion around Abbie all seemed a blur, for she was lost in a myriad of thoughts, trying to remember Tennessee one moment, and Cheyenne words and etiquette the next, while voices and laughter and movement surrounded her. But Abbie's thoughts became centered and focused the moment the handsome woman reached out and took her hands.

"Welcome to our village, wife of Zeke," the woman told Abbie. Her hands closed warmly around Abbie's, and a great strength seemed to emanate from them and from the woman's beautiful eyes and warm smile. Abbie knew she had to be Zeke's mother.

"I'm proud to meet you, ma'am," she told her.

The woman nodded and looked up at Zeke, letting go of Abbie's hands for the moment and reaching up to her half-breed son, who enveloped her in his arms for a brief moment, ignoring the Cheyenne custom of showing little emotion in public.

"I was afraid you would not come back this time," Abbie

heard the woman tell him. "Always when you leave me I see the little boy who was taken from me."

"You know I always come back, Gentle Woman," he replied. He released her, and put an arm back around Abbie. "And this time I bring a wife, Gentle Woman. This is Abigail. Already she carries my child."

The woman looked Abbie over now, reaching out and touching her hair. Then she looked back up at Zeke. "She has no Indian blood at all?"

"None," Zeke answered. "But her heart is Indian, Gentle Woman. She thinks with an Indian's courage and honesty, works with an Indian's strength, and speaks with a straight tongue. She is alone, Gentle Woman. I'm all she has. And both of us want the Cheyenne to be our family. You shall be her mother. Her parents and family are dead."

Gentle Woman took both Abbie's hands. "In my heart, I want it to be as Zeke wishes. But it is for the council to decide, my child. If they should say you cannot stay, my heart will be heavy." She looked back at Zeke. "Come!" she told him, pulling at Abbie's hand and leading them inside a tipi. Others congregrated around the entrance, eager for Abbie to reappear so they could study her.

Inside the tipi a man stood, a tall man with nearly white hair. His arms were folded in front of his chest, and he wore only a breechcloth, like most of the men Abbie had seen so far. Zeke immediately went to the man and grasped his wrist in a handshake.

"Welcome, son," the man told him. "What is this Swift Arrow tells us about a white girl you have taken as a wife?"

Zeke smiled proudly and turned to Abbie. "This is she, my father. This is Abigail, and the only thing white about her is her skin." He nodded to Abbie. "Abbie girl, this is my Cheyenne father, Deer Slayer."

Abbie bowed slightly, not sure what else to do. "I'm glad to meet you, sir," she told the man. Deer Slayer eyed her closely, and there was a momentary silence before he turned to Zeke.

"Why a white one, Zeke? It is good that you have finally taken another woman, but you vowed not to marry another white one."

"I know that, Father. But Abbie is different. I have asked Swift Arrow to call a council so that I can tell the chiefs about her and ask that she be allowed to live here among the Cheyenne whenever I am here."

The man nodded. "A council is being arranged. You have caused much commotion throughout the village this day, my son. Come. We will go out and help make preparations. The smoke must first be offered to the gods."

Zeke nodded, stopping near Abbie before leaving. "You wait here until I come for you. My mother will remain with you." He quickly kissed her forehead and touched her cheek with the back of his hand. "Don't be afraid, Abbie."

"I . . . I think I might faint!" she whispered.

He smiled and led her to a stack of skins, telling her to sit down. He looked at his mother. "Get her some water and calm her down. She's pretty nervous. I don't want her losing the baby. She's been sick with it."

"I shall watch over her. You go with your father. She will be ready when you return."

Zeke bent down and kissed the top of Abbie's head. "I love you," he whispered. He left hurriedly, and Gentle Woman brought a gourd of water over to Abbie.

"Drink this," she told the girl, kneeling in front of her.

Abbie took the gourd with shaking hands and drank, then handed it back to Gentle Woman. "You're very beautiful," she told the woman sincerely. "I knew you would be, because Zeke is so handsome."

Gentle Woman smiled. "*Ai.* I am very proud of all of my sons, so handsome and brave, all of them. But my Zeke, he is special, for he was taken from me when he was just a small boy, and my heart cried for him for many years. Then the spirits smiled upon me and brought him back. In spite of the three Cheyenne sons I had by then, I was never happy until my

97

Zeke returned."

Gentle Woman rose and replaced the gourd, then walked to the tipi entrance to look out. "They are almost ready," she told Abbie. "They have assembled quickly, for they are excited about your presence!" She turned to Abbie and smiled kindly. "You are lovely."

Abbie blushed and looked down. "Thank you."

"It is good to have you here," Gentle Woman added. "I will have a daughter now, and soon a grandchild! When Swift Arrow's wife and son died of the spotted disease, my heart was very sad. Now there will be happiness again in our family, and my lonely half-blood son will smile again. I only hope that some day Swift Arrow will also find another woman to warm his hardened heart."

Their eyes held, and Abigail knew already that she liked this woman whose name seemed so fitting. Gentle Woman. Her eyes virtually glowed when she spoke of her sons, and Abbie could imagine the horror this woman must have suffered the day Zeke was dragged from her arms, while she was taken away by a Crow buck who had bought her from her white husband. Hers had not been an easy life. She had been stolen by a Ute at the tender age of twelve, raped, and made a slave until the Ute sold her to Zeke's father. He kept her with him until he tired of her, then sold her to the Crow buck and took her little son back with him to Tennessee.

"I thought . . . I thought you would be disappointed with Zeke's choice," Abbie told the woman. "Swift Arrow doesn't like me, and I don't think your Cheyenne husband likes me."

Gentle Woman grasped Abbie's hands. "Listen to me quickly, my child, before they come to take you before the council. My Zeke is a man of great courage and suffering. He has lived among the whites and has been to many places. He is wise for his years and knows what is good and true. If he has chosen you for his woman, it says much about your worth. The others know this. I know this. Because you are special to Zeke, you shall be special to them. Swift Arrow and Deer Slayer and

98

any others who might voice objections, they are also wise men, men who are cautious, men who have seen what the whites can do. They are perhaps more afraid only because they have not been into your world as Zeke has, and so they find it more difficult to judge you because they do not understand the whites so well and have nothing to compare you with. But in time I know you will prove yourself. You must go to the council with your chin held high and bravery in your eyes. You must speak only when they ask you to speak, and then it must be only the truth."

"But how can you . . . I mean . . . I've just arrived. How can you be so sure about me, ma'am?"

Gentle Woman smiled. "Because my Zeke loves you. His eyes shine with pride for you. He is pleased. For many moons he has been alone, and now he has a woman beside him in the night, and she carries his life. It is good! If Zeke has chosen you, it is not for me to judge, only to accept. I have great trust in my son's judgment."

Drums began beating and Abbie's heart seemed to pound harder along with them. Zeke's mother squeezed her hands and rose to walk to the tipi entrance. She looked out. Abbie could hear bells jingling and voices chanting and singing; these were mingled with clipped war whoops and coyotelike howls.

Gentle Woman suddenly moved back as Swift Arrow entered, wearing layers of beads around his neck and a brightly feathered headdress. His face was painted with stripes of blue, and his bronze, muscular arms were adorned with copper bands.

"Where . . . where is Zeke?" Abbie asked.

"Do not ask questions!" he snapped. "Come with me! Your husband is with the council. We shall decide whether or not we can keep a white woman among us! Walk behind me, and do not speak! See if you can keep that loose tongue of yours from moving!" He left so quickly that Abbie had time for only a brief backward glance at Gentle Woman, who gave her an encouraging smile.

Abbie hurriedly followed Swift Arrow, not noticing an Arapaho woman watching sullenly from a distance when she exited the tipi. The woman's dark eyes burned with hatred and jealousy of the white woman Cheyenne Zeke had brought back with him.

"Cheyenne Zeke belongs to Dancing Moon!" the woman hissed to herself. She spit in Abbie's direction, but Abbie was unaware of the gesture, for she was now surrounded by Cheyenne villagers, who pushed her along behind Swift Arrow toward the council gathering.

Six

The Cheyenne priest sat cross-legged at the head of the
council. His face was striped in yellow and his head was
adorned with a magnificent headdress of eagle feathers. A
brightly painted bonepipe breastplate decorated his chest. He
was old, his dark skin showing the wrinkles of time and sun.
And in his eyes shone the wisdom of a man who had lived many
years and had known all of life's trials and tribulations; this
wisdom gave him the requirements needed to be a counselor
for the People.

Abbie sat motionless at the center of the circle of
councilmen, Zeke among them, his face painted in white, his
prayer color, and coup feathers tied at the base of his hair,
which was pulled back into one plait that hung down his back.
Abbie's apprehension was quelled by his presence, for she
could feel his strength and reassurance without having to
touch him or look at him.

The priest raised a polished, wooden pipe to the sky. "To the
Wise One Above," he said in the Cheyenne tongue,
"*Heammawihio.*" He puffed the pipe and then pointed it at the
earth. "To the God Who Lives under the Ground, *Ahktunowihio.*" He puffed the pipe again, and Abbie watched, aware of
what the man was doing, for Zeke had taught her some things
about the Cheyenne religion, and she had seen him practice it
himself, offering a pipe to the gods of the sky and the earth, as
well as to the powerful spirits that lived at the four parts of the

compass. The priest waved the pipe in these four directions in honor of those spirits, enacting the ceremony called the *Nivstanivoo*.

The pipe was passed on to the other men, who performed the same ritual one by one and puffed the sacred pipe. Abbie sat silently, as Swift Arrow had instructed her to do. She was glad she had the beautiful doeskin tunic that Tall Grass Woman had given her to wear. At least that, with her long, dark hair, made her resemble a Cheyenne woman, but there was no way to ever have skin quite so dark. Perhaps a few years of living with the elements would help. But at this moment she felt as white as the clouds she watched in the distance.

The Cheyenne women of the village watched from the background, staring in awe at Abbie, curious to know about her, their faces friendly and eager. Dogs dashed about, and a small, fat puppy trotted up close to her. She wanted to reach out and pet it, but was afraid that anything she did or said might be a mistake, so she sat still and watched the puppy out of the corner of her eye, while the men began conversing. Her heart quickened when she noticed a couple of them arguing vehemently, certain they were arguing against her being there. She wished more than ever that she could understand the Cheyenne tongue.

Then Zeke rose, walked close to her, and stood behind her. He began speaking, turning slowly and facing them one by one as he spoke, and although he used their own tongue, Abbie knew he was telling them about her and doing his best to convince them she should be allowed to stay.

"This young woman, hardly more than a child, has shown me a strength and courage as powerful as any of our own women," he told them. "I have told you that after what happened to the white woman I married in the place called Tennessee, I would never again marry a white woman. But, my friends, my brothers, with this girl it is only her skin that is white. Her spirit and her heart are as strong and true as any Cheyenne. And even though I feared she would suffer from her own people for choosing a half-blood for a husband, I could not turn her away, for she had no one, and I knew she must belong to me. Her heart lies here, next to my own." He put a fist to his chest. "And because she knows that my heart lies here, with my mother's people, she has given up the white man's ways to come here with me. This in itself is a great sacrifice."

"And what are these things she has done to show you her strength and trustworthiness?" Swift Arrow spoke up.

Zeke eyed his brother defiantly; then he swept his eyes around the circle of men again.

"When first I met this woman-child," he told them, "I was a scout for her people who were going to the far place called Oregon. Her mother had already died, and her father brought her and her sister and small brother west to start a new life. But her small brother fell from their wagon and was crushed beneath it."

There were some gasps and whispers among them, for the Cheyenne were a people of gentle hearts. Abbie was amazed at the almost total silence in the crowd, except for an occasional whisper. Their eyes were riveted on her and on Zeke, for the Cheyenne delighted in hearing someone tell a story, whether it be fact or fantasy, a story of a warrior's conquest or a story about spirits of the night. Now Cheyenne Zeke was telling them a story, and they all listened with enthusiasm, their faces lit up like little children's, even Swift Arrow's.

"This was when I first learned about Abigail's courage," Zeke went on in the Cheyenne tongue with Abbie able only to guess at what he must be saying. "Her small brother developed a terrible infection that was slowly killing him. The pain was unbearable, a very bad thing to see, with maggots on the places where the bones showed through the skin. He was badly broken on the inside, in ways that would not mend. It was so terrible that Abigail came to me one night when he suffered worst of all, and she asked"—his voice dropped in his own grief—"she asked if I would . . . use my knife . . . in such a way that I would quickly end her brother's horrible suffering."

103

Silence hung over them, and by the inflection of Zeke's voice, Abbie knew he was telling them something that was difficult for him to talk about. She looked up at him and he glanced down at her. "I'm telling them about Jeremy," he told her quietly. She looked away, wanting very much to hold him. Never would she forget what he had done for her that night. Never before and never again would he perform a more difficult task out of love, and the memory of it brought an aching grief to both their hearts. But Abbie loved her little brother. And no one could convince her that the decision she had made to end his suffering was wrong.

Zeke pulled out his knife. "I ended the boy's life quickly with this, in a way that was easy on him. I used the knife so that Abigail's father would not know. It was quick and soundless." He swallowed. "Until this very moment, no one has ever known, other than Abigail and myself. Now you know. This honor of sharing such a sacred moment I choose to share with you, to show you this girl's courage and compassion."

His voice choked and he shoved the knife back into its sheath, pacing a moment before he continued; the People watched spellbound.

"Abigail's brother died as bravely as any dog soldier," Zeke finally continued quietly. "He had the same strength and gentle spirit his sister has. She knew her decision would burden her heart forever, but she also knew she could not let his suffering continue, with no end in sight but death. There was no sense in letting it happen slowly." He touched Abbie's hair for a moment. "But Abbie's father could not stand the loss, and in a night of drunken grief he took his own life." There were some whispers among the People. "And so Abbie had lost two loved ones within a few days of each other and was left in a strange land with no one but her sister remaining. Her sister was not strong like Abbie, nor as wise and proud. She was vain and wanted fancy things and the comforts money brings. She had taken up with a fancy man on the wagon train—a gambler. After her father died, she ran off with her fancy man and Abbie was completely alone. Only days later we discovered her sister, Lee Ann, had been captured by vicious outlaws, and her lover killed."

Abbie closed her eyes against the pain when she heard the name Lee Ann. She wondered if she would ever be able to erase the memory of finding Lee Ann dead, a hole in her forehead from a bullet, her body naked and abused.

"I will not tell you every detail, except that when I went after the men who captured Lee Ann, this brave girl insisted on going with me, thinking that if we found her sister alive, Lee Ann would need her. I tried to discourage her, but I knew if I left her behind she would follow me, and so I took her with me only because she would be safer that way. And by then I knew I loved her, and she loved me." He stopped and knelt behind Abbie, putting his hands on her shoulders. "By that time we were already husband and wife, according to Cheyenne custom."

Some of the Cheyenne women smiled and whispered, aware of the meaning of the words, but most of the men sat with unemotional faces, except that Black Elk grinned. Amid the crowd of women, the jealous-eyed Dancing Moon watched, her heart burning with hatred for Abbie and a terrible desire for Cheyenne Zeke.

"I had sent the wagon train on with a reliable man, to wait for us at the South Pass, while I and my good friend, Olin Wales took Abbie and went to search for her sister. But we were too late when we found her. When we knew she was dead I sent Abigail back to the wagon train, with Olin as her protection, while I went on to find the outlaws and avenge her sister's murder. But the outlaws tricked us. They attacked Abigail and Olin, leaving Olin for dead and capturing Abbie. When I found the outlaws, they already had Abigail with them." He stroked Abbie's hair. "Thanks to the gods, I got there before they violated her, but they had beaten her and hurt her, and I don't think I need to tell you what happened to those men."

Red Eagle grinned. "They felt your blade!" he put in.

Zeke nodded, studying the luster of Abbie's hair in the firelight. "There were many of them." His eyes lit up with burning hatred, and his lips curled at his next remark. "But I had vengeance in my heart!" he snarled. "I surprised them, and I shot many of them with arrows before they even knew what was happening. I used my knife on the rest. But during the fight I took a bullet in my side; and Abigail, in spite of what she had been through, ran to one of the horses, grabbed a rifle, and shot one of the outlaws herself—a Crow renegade!" He rose. "This shows you her courage!" he bragged. "That was the first man she had ever killed. I was glad it happened to be a Crow!"

They all laughed lightly, and Abbie breathed a little easier.

"I was badly wounded," Zeke continued. "We found a cave to hole up in, and Abigail, after all she'd been through, dug the bullet out of me. It was not easy for her to do, but she saved my life by doing it. And when she continued to show her courage and her strength after all the things she had been through, I began to be more sure I wanted her for my woman, for always. After I recovered enough to travel, we returned to the wagon train, and we discovered Olin Wales had also survived. My heart was glad, for Olin is one of the few white men who is a very good friend to me."

"What of the Crow arrow?" Swift Arrow asked. "You tell us she had taken a Crow arrow."

Zeke began pacing around the circle of councilmen. "Our wagon train was attacked by Crows. That was when Abbie shot her second Crow Indian. But she took an arrow in her back that exited her body at her chest, just above her left breast. It was a very bad wound."

There were more gasps and whispers, and stares of curiosity mingled with admiration for the white squaw who had killed two Crows and had even survived an arrow wound!

"I removed the arrow myself. Later she got a bad infection from it. I had to cut her to drain it, and then I had to burn the infection out, deep inside, with a white-hot rod. It was a terrible thing for her to suffer through, and she almost died." He turned his eyes to Abbie, and his voice gentled. "It was then I knew I must have her at my side forever," he went on. "When we reached Fort Bridger, I asked her to marry me the white man's way to make it official with her own people. But she was so weak that I had to leave her at Fort Bridger to mend. I came back for her this spring." He turned to face the priest. "And then we came here to find the Cheyenne," he finished.

The old priest grunted something to Zeke, and Zeke bent down and grasped Abbie's arm. "Stand up, Abbie girl," he told her quietly. "I think we may have won the battle."

She looked up at him and he winked, as the old man walked close to her, then circled her, eying her up and down.

"So . . . she has killed two Crow!" he exclaimed in the Cheyenne tongue.

"She has killed three Crow!" Zeke answered. "Did my brother, Swift Arrow, not tell you about the one she killed when the Crow attacked my brother's camp?"

The old priest glanced at Swift Arrow.

"I . . . I did not have the chance," Swift Arrow told him.

The old man's eyebrows lifted in doubt, and a faint smile passed over his lips. "When you are older, you will learn that telling about another's heroics does not diminish your own, Swift Arrow. Could it be that you are jealous of this small girl?"

Swift Arrow's eyes blazed with anger, but the old priest had him on the spot. Swift Arrow looked around at the others, and some of them chuckled; but their laughter ceased when the old priest cast them chastising looks.

"Swift Arrow's heart is bitter with the loss of his loved ones to the white man's disease. All of us feel some bitterness. In time, we will forget." He looked at Swift Arrow. "And forgive," he added. "For it is more noble to do so. Disease is an unseen enemy that cannot be controlled. Only the Great Spirit can say who shall and shall not get the disease. And this small bit of woman cannot control such power." He turned to Zeke. "This killing of three Crow, it is strong medicine!" he declared. "You will swear by her? You will give your oath that if this woman should become a traitor to our people, you will suffer the punishment for her and be banished from our people forever?"

"I give my oath," Zeke declared staunchly. "Because I know Abigail would never be a traitor to my people. She is one with me, as I am one with the Cheyenne, and she carries my life in her belly. She is my woman and will go where I go and love what I love and sleep where I sleep."

The old man nodded. "Your word is good, Lone Eagle. We know you to be a great warrior, and I myself watched you bear the suffering of the Sun Dance ritual. I know that you speak the truth. But as one final proof, I would like to see the scar left by this Crow arrow."

Zeke put a hand on Abbie's shoulder. "I will show only you—in the privacy of the priest's dwelling."

The old man nodded. "Very well." He turned and walked through the circle of men, and Zeke put a hand to Abbie's waist, urging her to follow.

"Zeke? Where are we going?" she asked.

"He wants to see the scar from the arrow," he told her.

"What!" She stopped but he urged her forward again.

"It's all right, Abbie. Trust me, please. Let's get this over."

She blinked back tears and followed the priest. The three of them entered the old man's tipi, where many headdresses and religious objects hung amid the priest's personal belongings. Some of these were gifts from those who were grateful for his prayers and his faithful leadership in ceremonies. The priest himself stood dark and wrinkled and rigid, his arms folded in front of him, while Zeke unlaced the front of Abbie's tunic and pulled it down over her left shoulder just far enough to reveal the scar left from the arrow but not enough to expose the whole breast.

The old priest did not seem to look upon her with evil

thoughts, only with admiration.

"*Ai.* I know wounds," he told Zeke. "This was a bad one. Your woman is strong."

"And brave," Zeke told him, pulling the tunic back up.

The priest turned and took down a leather belt with two gray feathers in it. Stepping closer to Abbie, he reached around her as she stood rigid and curious while he tied the belt about her waist. Then he stepped back.

"Tell your woman this belt is my gift to her. The feathers are from the gray eagle, our most powerful medicine. They will protect her from arrows and bullets, and she will not again suffer such a wound."

Zeke explained, "This is a great honor, Abbie. A great honor indeed."

She nodded to the old priest. "*Ha ho,*" she told him, remembering the Cheyenne word for thank you. A faint smile passed over the old man's lips.

"It is not just because she has killed three Crow that I do this," the old man added. "I admire her courage in ending her small brother's terrible pain by asking you to end his life. This took great strength and wisdom, and it will forever be a burden to her heart." He watched the agony that drifted through Zeke's own eyes. "And a painful burden on your heart also," he added.

Their eyes held. "I . . . had become very fond of the boy," Zeke replied sadly. "What I did was done out of love. It still grieves me in the night."

"I am sure that it does. It is strange, is it not that you can use that blade of yours in such savage hatred and then sometimes in love, as when you took the boy's life and when you had to cut this small woman to save her from the infection?"

Zeke nodded. "Love and hatred often lie close beside one another, my father." He used the endearing term most young Cheyenne men used toward the older, wiser men who were not actually their fathers, but who were honored and respected as leaders. "I will give you two of my best horses in return for the gift you have just given Abbie," he added.

The old priest nodded. "I go now to tell the others of what I have seen and to tell them it is my decision that she should stay. She has no family. The Cheyenne do not turn away the homeless and lost. We will take a vote."

He turned and left the tipi. Then Zeke pulled Abbie into his arms, smothering her with a kiss before she could say a word. He pressed her tightly against himself, so tightly that she could feel his heart pounding and could feel his manly hardness pushing against her belly, for his pride in her made him want her as he never had before. His lips moved to her neck and his hands grasped her hips.

"I love you, Abbie girl. There will be some celebrating tonight."

"Then . . . it's all right?"

"Yes, Abbie." He lifted her off the ground, whirling her. "You're Lone Eagle's woman, and from now on you're Cheyenne!" he told her.

She smiled and threw her arms around his neck, and they kissed hungrily. She remembered the first time Cheyenne Zeke ever kissed her, the hot, terrible need she had had to have this man be her first. The fire of his kisses had never dwindled, and his touch made her want him as she had always wanted him, for he was a man who knew about women and had taught her everything about how to please him and receive pleasure in return. To be accepted by the Cheyenne was their last barrier. They had overcome so many barriers to be together. Now he was with his people, where he was happiest. And she was carrying his baby. The old priest would recommend she be allowed to stay. Nothing could spoil their happiness now. Nothing.

After several minutes the priest reentered.

"She stays," he told Zeke. "Come."

He led them outside, where men and women began congregating around them, their faces now happy and smiling and welcoming. Zeke was shaking hands with the men and was suddenly whisked away for men's games, as the entire village had decided to spend the rest of the day celebrating before beginning the hunt the next day. Abbie wanted to stay with Zeke, but the women already had her surrounded and were babbling to her in Cheyenne, touching her, ogling her, laughing, and visiting.

Abbie was relieved when Zeke's mother came to her rescue to interpret their questions, and if Abbie had been lonely for friends before, she could not be lonely now, for all of them seemed to want to be her best friend. Already, offers were being made to show her how to construct a tipi, how to sew skins, how to make pemmican. Some offered to paint her tipi, once she had made one that would be all her own. They dragged her about, showing her their fat babies and painted dwellings, while Zeke was off somewhere participating in war games and sharing stories of conquest with the men.

The little puppy that had remained beside Abbie when she sat in the council circle now followed her again. The other women kept shooing it away until Abbie finally bent down and picked it up, cuddling it close.

"It's a darling puppy!" she told Zeke's mother. "May I keep it?"

The jabbering lessened, and some of the women giggled and looked at each other.

"You mean, until it's fattened up more?" Zeke's mother asked.

Abbie frowned. "I mean . . . as a pet . . . unless it belongs to someone else."

The Arapaho woman who had been watching sullenly and following the crowd of women laughed wickedly and stepped forward, pushing herself through the other women and confronting Abbie. She sneered at Abbie and the puppy and put her hands on her hips. She was beautiful to look at, but had a wild, animalistic air about her and a vicious look in her dark eyes. Her black hair hung long and tangled. Her tunic was open in a fetching manner, exposing more of her breasts than the other Cheyenne women did.

"I speak your tongue!" she sneered. "I know what you say!" She laughed again and pulled the puppy's ear. "Cheyenne do not keep dogs as pets!"

"Be still, Dancing Moon!" Zeke's mother said sternly. "Leave us!"

"I will leave when I wish to leave!" the Arapaho woman spat back. She turned evil eyes on Abbie. "The Cheyenne eat their dogs, especially the fat puppies!" she said to Abbie in English. Abbie's eyes widened in horror, and Dancing Moon smiled with pleasure at her obvious shock. "Do you still wish to live with the Cheyenne?" she sneered.

"That is enough, Dancing Moon!" Gentle Woman barked. She put an arm around Abbie's shoulders. "You may have the puppy, Abbie. It is yours. No one will harm it. We have many ways that you must learn to understand. There are things the white man eats that the Cheyenne will not touch. It is no different. You must understand this. Custom is custom and cannot be called wrong because someone else says that it is. We shall respect your feelings, and you shall keep the puppy." She turned her eyes to Dancing Moon. "And you will stay away from Zeke's wife!"

"Wife!" She spit at Abbie. "I should be his wife!"

"No honorable man wants one such as you for a wife!" Gentle Woman replied. "Only to make him feel good in the night. You are a disgrace!"

Dancing Moon seemed unperturbed by the remark. She only leered at Abbie, who stood staring at her, feeling small and beaten. Dancing Moon smiled. "Perhaps," she answered Gentle Woman, her eyes on Abbie. "But I am good at making a man feel good in the night. Zeke knows this, and he will remember when he tires of this little white nothing! I will have him back in my bed. Zeke is good with a woman, is he not?"

Abbie's fear and shock were replaced by burning jealousy and anger. She straightened, clinging to the puppy and looking Dancing Moon in the eyes, even though she had to look up.

112

The Arapaho woman was much taller.

"He's the best," Abbie replied calmly and quietly. "And he's mine! He won't be needing you anymore, Dancing Moon."

The woman's eyes narrowed, and she whirled and left. Abbie watched her a moment, noticing her long, willowy legs and the way she had of swaying her hips when she walked. So, Zeke had slept with this one. It stirred a terrible jealousy Abbie had never felt before, and she vowed that this night when she made love to Zeke, he would find a wild and grateful woman in his bed and would have no desire for any other. For Dancing Moon would most certainly do her best to entice him away.

"I am sorry," Gentle Woman was telling her. "She is a bad one! Zeke only slept with her sometimes to relieve his manly needs. She means nothing to him, Abbie. Nothing. She means nothing to any man! That is the kind she is. She likes all the men. Some day she will cause great trouble and be banished. Zeke knows how she is. And he loves you. You are not to worry about filth like that."

Abbie looked at the woman. "Is it true . . . about . . . about eating dogs?"

Their eyes held, Gentle Woman's full of love and patience. "It is true, my child. But that is our way, just as the white man eats the egg of a chicken. What one thinks is bad, another thinks is good. It is all the same, Abigail. You will never be asked to eat the meat of a dog if this is distasteful to you. Zeke would not ask such a thing of you. And it is as I said. The puppy is yours to keep. We will tell all the village so that no one harms it." She laughed lightly. "It will be a good joke! The Cheyenne like a good joke. The white woman keeps a puppy for a pet!" She patted Abbie's cheek. "Yes, they will laugh at that one. But they do not laugh at you, Abbie. They laugh with you. When you learn the kind of happy people the Cheyenne are—the way they like to play jokes and tease—you will laugh, too, and will not be so serious. My Zeke, he always says the white man is too serious. He does not know how to—how do you say it?—relax? He cannot be himself. You be yourself, Abigail. Laugh with us

113

and at us."

She turned and said something in Cheyenne to the women, and they all screeched with delight, laughing and poking at Abbie and pointing to the puppy. At first Abbie was offended, but she saw the friendship in their eyes, and she began to smile. There was a time when she thought she had lost everything. Then she found Zeke. Now she had an entire family again, and she was carrying Zeke's baby. Yes, she could smile. There was only one fly in the ointment now. Her name was Dancing Moon.

Abbie awoke to the smell of cooking meat, and turned over to see Zeke adding wood to a fire inside Swift Arrow's tipi, which they continued to use until they would have one of their own. Two strips of smoked antelope lay in a flat, iron pan over the fire. Zeke glanced over at her and grinned, and she quickly took in the beautiful sight of him. He wore only the loincloth which briefly covered that part of him that had planted life in her womb.

"Why didn't you wake me?" she chided him. "I should be doing that."

"I know. But you've been sick and I felt sorry for you. Besides, I'm happy about how well you've been accepted by the People." He came over to her and removed his moccasins, crawling under the robe with her. "And don't you dare tell anyone I started the fire and the breakfast," he warned her, "especially not Swift Arrow."

She giggled and kissed his chest, and he pulled her close. "By the way, woman," he teased, "you were pretty wild last night." He moved down and made a growling sound in her neck. "You must have more savage blood in you than you think."

He felt her stiffen slightly in his arms, and he pulled back to see tears in her eyes.

"What's wrong, Abbie?"

"Is that what it takes to please you?"

114

He grinned in confusion. "What are you talking about?"

She blushed slightly and looked away. "I'm talking about . . . Dancing Moon."

His grip tightened on her wrist and he raised up on one elbow. "Has that bitch been talking to you?" His instant anger surprised her.

"I . . . didn't have a chance to tell you last night. You were so happy and all, I didn't want to bring it up. Why didn't you tell me about her, Zeke?"

Her tears of wounded love tore at his heart, and he felt a sudden desperateness at the knowledge that he had somehow disappointed her.

"Abbie, there was nothing to tell," he replied. He moved on top of her, taking her face between his hands. "She was just someone to sleep with when I needed to get something out of my system. And now that I have you I have no need for such a woman. Don't you let anything she says upset you, Abbie. If she does upset you, you tell me, understand? I'll set her straight." She bit her lip and nodded. "Forgive me, Abbie. But how could I tell you? I tried once or twice, but there never seemed to be a right way, and she meant so little to me anyway."

A tear slipped down the side of Abbie's face. "She's . . . beautiful," she said quietly.

"Not like you," he answered lovingly, his own eyes watery. "There isn't a buck here who'd want her for keeps, Abbie, and if she isn't careful, she'll be banished from us. The only reason she hasn't been already is because she's Arapaho, and her people deal with their loose women more lightly than the Cheyenne do."

"She told me I couldn't keep the puppy because the Cheyenne would eat it," Abbie sniffed. "I want the puppy, Zeke."

His eyes hardened again. "I ought to beat her for saying that to you!" He wiped a tear on her cheek with his fingers. "Of course you can have the puppy, Abbie. No one will harm it."

115

He kissed her cheek. "You just have to understand that the Cheyenne have had dogs around for work and for food for centuries. It's commonplace, like the white man killing and eating chickens or pigs. Since the People migrated west, dogs have become a minor part of their diet. They eat mostly buffalo meat and elk and all the other wild game. The dog is only eaten when the hunt has not been good, when there are little children's bellies to be fed. You've never hungered that way, Abbie. If you knew what it was like to be that hungry, you would understand how a man can eat a dog." His hands gripped her hair. "Don't dwell on such things, Abbie girl. And don't let Dancing Moon upset you."

She met his eyes. "Am I better than she is in bed?"

He kissed her lips lightly. "You know the anguish I went through deciding to marry you, Abbie; I loved you so much and was afraid being married to me would bring you harm. But I gave in. Now why in hell do you think a strong man like myself couldn't fight his feelings for you and had to marry you? Abbie, you know how much I love you. You know how hard it was for me to stay away from you. How can you ask such a foolish question?"

She shrugged and sniffed. "I just . . . I don't know anything more than what you've taught me. I just want you to be pleased with me."

He grinned a little, reaching over and moving the iron skillet off the fire. "You're carrying my baby," he told her. "And surely you know when I'm inside of you whether or not I'm pleased." He moved between her legs. "You are my peace and my refuge, Abbie girl. You are the most pleasing thing that has ever happened to me."

She searched his dark eyes and knew that he spoke the truth. "Ne-mehotatse," she whispered. Her chest swelled with a sob, and it tore at his soul to know she'd been hurt by his own kind. He stroked her hair back from her face and began kissing her salty tears.

"Abbie, my sweet Abbie!" he groaned, his kisses becoming

116

quick and urgent, moving to her lips, where he lightly ran his tongue along the insides of her lips, bringing fire to her body again. She knew instinctively that he needed to make love to her now, to show her she was his only love. She knew that she must claim him in return.

She closed her eyes as he quickly removed the loincloth, and she eagerly welcomed him into her body, wanting him never again to desire Dancing Moon. Her fingers dug into the hard muscles of his back and her breath caught in her throat as he took her with determined possessiveness and unspoken apology, his lovemaking more forceful than normal. Soon he would go on the buffalo hunt with the other warriors, but first he would comfort his woman and reassure her that he belonged only to his Abbie.

The hunt was like nothing Abigail had ever seen. Specified warriors had herded the buffalo into the valley below the village campsite. The women watched, while mounted warriors yipped and howled and rode in circles around the herd, concentrating the great, black mass of bushy manes into a close group. Zeke was among those who rode around the animals, and Abbie watched with trepidation, for herding was a dangerous job and called for sure-footed horses and skilled riders. To fall under the hooves of the giant buffalo was to greet death, and Zeke's mother had told her of how many warriors had died in other hunts.

Soon the buffalo were surrounded, and other warriors rose up from hiding places and let go of their arrows, aiming for the kidneys of their intended prey. Some of the warriors who rode began singling out animals to spear with lances, and Abbie thought to herself that if she didn't already know that Zeke was a half-breed, she would never have been able to tell there was one drop of white blood in him this day. He wore only a breechcloth, like most of the others, as the morning was already hot. His bronze skin glistened in the sun, and his hair was braided. He wore his coup feathers and carried lance and bow, and, of course, the knife.

Zeke worked hard, for it took up to fifteen buffalo hides to make a tipi. He knew he would never be able to get that many, for this was a small herd, and they were getting smaller every year. But he would get as many as he could and then buy or trade for more with the other men. He was more worried that the small kill would mean a lean winter for the Cheyenne unless they found bigger herds in the fall, which was unlikely.

Already, the business of trading beaver skins for other needed supplies was falling off at an alarming rate. The Cheyenne were losing buying power with the skins, as well as losing buffalo, their source of nearly all needs: food, clothing, utensils, medicine, shelter, nearly everything. When the demand for beaver skins was reduced to nothing, the buffalo would become even more important, for there would be nothing left with which to purchase whatever items were needed because of a poor hunt. If the Indian had to resort to trading buffalo robes for more food, then there would be that much less for shelter and clothing. It seemed like a vicious circle, with nothing to look forward to but starvation.

At least Zeke had his horses. He would continue to breed them and urge his red brothers to do the same, for these animals were one more source of trade, which his people would need as they became more and more dependent on trade for survival rather than on hunting buffalo. But trade would present another problem for the Indians, who were easily cheated by white men. The future did not look good. For now, Zeke would take his herd of horses to Independence, sell most of them, and use the money carefully to buy supplies as needed, at least for his immediate family. He also had some savings in a bank there, with the one and only banker he had found who would do business with a half-breed. He decided this might be a good time to take the money out, especially if war was brewing with Mexico. To wait could mean having difficulty getting his hands on the money.

He speared a mammoth bull, and the animal staggered and fell. He grinned with pride. It had been a long time since he'd been on a hunt. He climbed down from his horse and, having waited a moment to be sure the buffalo was dead, took out his vicious-looking knife, not even thinking about what he was doing as he deftly gutted out the animal on the spot. He was only thinking about taking Abbie to Independence with him. It would be a nice break for her. He tied a leather cord decorated with white beads around the buffalo's hoof, designating the kill as his own, then mounted his horse and rode after another bull.

He hoped that perhaps some day the Cheyenne would have more rifles, which would make this job easier. But that would take away the challenge of getting close to the big animal and killing it with a man's own strength and wit and skill. He liked it better this way. Even though he had two rifles and a hand gun, he preferred the thrill of sinking his lance into the tough hide of the buffalo. He would pretend the next one was Dancing Moon. That would help him thrust the lance with more force!

Once the hunt was over, the really hard part began, and it was woman's work. The men sat in circles, smoking and telling tales about their kill, while the women began the arduous task of preserving every part of the animal for a special purpose.

Amazed, Abbie watched Zeke's mother and the other women as they rapidly cleaned out the animals, removing all flesh and gristle from the skins with a sharp-edged tool which they used skillfully. Gentle Woman let Abbie help, teaching her patiently everything that must be done, and Abbie's head reeled at the Cheyenne's ability to put to use every part of the animal, wasting nothing.

"The hair will be scraped from the hide for decorating clothing and to use for stuffing saddles and such," Zeke's mother explained. "If this were a winter kill, we would leave

119

the hair and mane on many of the hides for winter clothing and blankets. The hide of the mane, turned inward, makes very warm moccasins. The intestines of the animal are cleaned and stuffed with chopped meat and are roasted and boiled—like your white man's sausages . . . the lungs are dried and roasted . . . the bone marrow is boiled and eaten and used in pemmican. Pemmican can be made many ways and is a very good food for a warrior to take when he will be gone for many days away from his woman and has no one to cook for him. . . . The hides, of course, will be used for tipis and clothing, as well as leather straps, parfleches—many things. . . . The meat will be roasted or boiled. Some will be sliced and dried into what the white man calls jerky, and some will be used in pemmican. . . . The bladder is used for water bags, the horns for spoons and ladles. . . . The hides of the older bulls are used for moccasin soles, parfleches, and shields, because they are tougher."

All of this was said at intervals as the woman worked, wasting no time, while Abbie watched and sometimes helped.

"We will need many hides to make you a fine tipi," Gentle Woman told Abbie. "Zeke will bargain for whatever others we need. Then the women will gather and help you sew Zeke a fine dwelling."

"I . . . I don't know how to thank all of you," Abbie told her.

"It is not necessary. The Cheyenne help one another because it is necessary to survive and because they are a gentle-hearted people who care about their own. You and I will show our thanks by cooking the women a fine meal." She stopped scraping for a moment and sat back to look at Abbie. "Tonight there will be much celebrating," she told the girl. "Always there is singing and dancing after the hunt. We will roast much meat and stuff our bellies, but after tonight we will be very careful to eat sparingly, for we never know how much meat we will get from the next hunt, and the herds are getting smaller." She put a hand on Abbie's. "Do not be afraid of all the wild dancing and singing tonight. It is all done in merriment and

120

celebration. No one will scalp you."

Abbie laughed and petted the puppy that had stayed by her side throughout the day. Now it licked at some drying buffalo blood on the grass beside the animal Gentle Woman was cleaning.

"You're wonderful," she told Gentle Woman.

The woman laughed lightly. "I would not say that. I would say you are the wonderful one." She sobered. "You have given up much to be with Zeke," she told Abbie. "This will not always be so easy for you, especially when times become more difficult for the Indian as I know they will. A day will come, Abigail, when it might be wiser for you and my Zeke to be with the whites. To be with the Cheyenne will bring you great sorrow . . . and danger."

She returned to her work, and Abbie stood up for a moment, looking out over hundreds of miles of nothingness at a great, broad plain that seemed to go on forever. How big this country was! Surely the day would not come when there was no room for the Indian to roam freely this way! Surely not that many whites would come to this untamed land! She looked down at Gentle Woman and around at the others. She was beginning to realize how marvelous they were, what a beautiful people they were. Yes, a beautiful people. That was how she was coming to think of them.

The Cheyenne did not have the same lusts and desires and greed in their hearts that whites had. They cared nothing for wealth and power. Freedom was their wealth. And honesty and simple wisdom was their power. They had no desire to own land, but simply to be able to roam free on the land and use it to survive. She watched Gentle Woman expertly flesh the hide of the buffalo she was working on, and again Abbie was overwhelmed at this people's ability to survive on the simplest things provided by nature. She wanted to always remember them this way, as they were at that moment, free and happy and beautiful. She hoped it could always be this way for them.

121

For to live any other way would be to die.

Abbie picked up the puppy and petted it; then she set it down and began helping Gentle Woman again. The puppy scampered off after a bird, and from a distance Dancing Moon watched, thinking how delicious the fat puppy would taste, and what a fine trick it would be to play on Abigail Trent Monroe to make a meal out of the white woman's pet!

Seven

Campfires lit up the night; and beating drums, chanting voices, and jingling bells filled the air with the sounds of Indian celebration. To an outsider, it would be frightening to watch, for it seemed as though these Cheyenne and Arapaho were about to make war and were eagerly preparing to move out and raid and take scalps. But their hearts were full of merriment, and for some of them, their blood was full of firewater.

At dusk there had been the games, and Zeke participated with the others, coming in second at wrestling and third in the game of shooting arrows to see how many an archer could put into the air before the first one fell to the ground. His speed was very good, but Swift Arrow, whose name bespoke his reputation, was fastest.

However, in the contest of throwing knives, Zeke found no match, either in speed or accuracy, as one by one he beat every opponent. Then two pieces of rawhide were strapped in layers around a tree trunk, and only Zeke was able to slit open the outer piece without cutting or marring the leather beneath it. Abbie had to grin. She had seen him use his knife that same way once before—on a man—slitting open the man's vest without touching his skin.

Many stories were told among the Cheyenne about Zeke and his blade, and this night they were shared again as Zeke's brother, Red Eagle, reveled in describing a bloody knife fight he'd witnessed between Cheyenne Zeke and four Pawnees. All four Pawnees died. Abbie remembered stories that white mountain men had told her about Zeke while she was recuperating at Fort Bridger, and it amazed her that a man who could be so vicious with a blade could be so gentle with his woman.

The evening had begun early, with feasting on roast buffalo and wild strawberries. As the evening had progressed into games and dancing and singing, Abbie had never seen Zeke quite so happy, nor so wild. The day's kill had brought out a savageness in him that he did not often show. His eyes were full of fire; his smile was that of a man who found pleasure in wielding his knife and participating in the men's games, which at times were very rough; and his body seemed harder, more tense. He was alive with happiness and freedom, and Abbie knew that here, and only here with his mother's people, could Zeke be himself and find complete peace.

The rhythm of the drums changed when darkness fell, and most of the celebrants gathered around a huge campfire in the center of the village. There were still many buffalo to finish dissecting, but tonight the women would rest and dance. Zeke found Abbie just as many of the women began dancing in a circle around the fire, smiling at the men and carrying blankets about their shoulders, moving provocatively as the men watched.

"What are they doing?" Abbie asked Zeke.

He ran a hand over her hips. "Can't you tell? Tonight wives will entice their husbands, and young girls will tease their favorite bucks. They will single out husbands and lovers and throw a blanket around them to show their affection." He pulled her closer. "Many of the husbands and wives will go to their tipis. Lovers can only sit under the blanket and talk."

Abbie looked up at him. "Talk?"

He chuckled. "Mostly. A Cheyenne girl is very chaste, Abbie, and if a man takes liberties against her will, he suffers the consequences."

Gentle Woman hurried over to Abbie, handing her a

124

blanket. "Come! Join us!" she told the girl, moving out into the circle. Women of all ages danced, and Zeke gave Abbie a shove.

"Zeke, I can't!"

"Why not?" he winked. "Get out there and let loose a little, Abbie. Forget that you're white. Don't be so stiff. Dance for me."

She looked around at the women, holding the blanket around her shoulders bashfully. Then she glanced back at Zeke, and he flashed his handsome smile that always gave her a sweet, warm feeling. Again she looked at the women, and now some of them pulled her into the circle and began pushing her, laughing and urging her to join in the dance. At first she only walked along with them, but soon the rhythmic drums seemed to strike at her very soul, the strange chanting and the eerie firelight making her feel wild and free, making her want her man. She began moving more rhythmically, her hips swaying slightly like those of the other women. She stretched out her arms and turned, letting the blanket float with her like a cape. Then she tried to mimic the skipping steps of the other women, beginning to enjoy the freedom of the movements and joining in the laughter and excitement of the dance. In the outer circle men grinned and watched, occasionally giving short cries of delight and desire.

Some women began leaving the circle now, walking up to husbands and sweethearts and throwing their blankets over the men's shoulders. Husbands left the celebration with their wives, and some couples put blankets over their heads. Abbie continued to dance, knowing Zeke was watching and wanting her; she decided that the next time she circled near him she would stop and cast her blanket around him.

But before Abbie reached Zeke, Dancing Moon had already entered the dance and had stopped in front of him, swaying her body seductively. She took off her blanket and threw it over Zeke's shoulder. Then she smiled and brazenly unlaced the front of her tunic, pulling it open to show him her full breasts. Abbie felt the blood drain from her face and she stood still, hating Dancing Moon as she had never hated anyone before, jealousy absorbing her with such intensity that she thought she might choke.

But Zeke did not look upon Dancing Moon with eyes of desire. Instead, his eyes blazed with anger that she would do such a thing in front of Abbie. As he took the blanket from his shoulder the crowd quieted. He threw the blanket back into Dancing Moon's face.

"The dogs in this camp are worth more than you!" he sneered at her. "How dare you do this in front of my wife, bitch!"

Her eyes flashed with the fire of desire. "Some Cheyenne men have more than one wife!" she shot back at him. "I cannot bear children. But I can give you pleasure when that skinny white one is fat with child."

Zeke backhanded the woman, and Dancing Moon fell to the ground. Abbie gasped in shock, never dreaming Zeke would lay a hand on a woman. But, to Abbie, Dancing Moon was not like a normal woman.

"I regret the times I've slept with you!" Zeke growled. He yanked her up by the hair of the head, and Dancing Moon winced, putting a hand to her face where he had hit her. "Go away from me, and leave my wife alone, or by God I'll put a scar on you that will keep all the men away!" He shook her. "Do you understand me, Dancing Moon?" he asked through gritted teeth.

"I understand!" she hissed.

He gave her a shove and she nearly fell again. She pulled her tunic back over her breasts and, casting dark, hateful eyes at Abbie, picked up her blanket and ran off into the darkness. Zeke's eyes met Abbie's. As his gaze became pleading rather than angry, she saw the little boy in him who feared losing someone he loved. She slowly approached him, her heart warming at the love in his eyes. She walked closer and reached up, folding him into her blanket, and the drums began beating again and the people laughed and shouted their approval as

126

Zeke lifted Abbie off her feet and carried her away.

While Zeke carried her to their tipi, Abbie rested her head on his shoulder. Neither of them spoke, and the drums' rhythmic beating seemed to penetrate their very hearts as Zeke ducked inside the dwelling with his wife. He set her on her feet, closed the entrance flap, and then turned and pulled the blanket off her. He quietly unlaced her tunic and pulled it down over her shoulders, letting it fall to the ground.

Abbie stood with her head hanging, feeling like a new virgin wife—the virgin she had been when first he took her on that wild and lonely night the summer before when they were on that wagon train west. His hands moved down over her breasts, tantalizing the nipples and sending shivers through her body.

"Look up here, Abbie," he told her. She raised her dark eyes, blushing as she always did when this man looked upon her nakedness. "Don't ever let something like that slut get between us," he told her. "We've already been over this. I want no woman but you, and only you know how much I need your love."

He bent down and kissed her lightly, then moved his lips down over her neck and began kneeling, caressing each breast with his lips and then moving his mouth gently over her belly until he lightly kissed the soft hairs between her thighs while his hands massaged her bare hips. She could not stop a whimper of pleasure, and she grasped the back of his head in her hands and pressed against him, the drums and her jealousy of Dancing Moon bringing out her wildest desires and removing her normal inhibitions. This was her man. This was Cheyenne Zeke, a man both brutal and gentle, cruel and kind, vengeful and loving, a man greatly feared by his enemies and deeply loved by his people . . . and by Abigail Trent Monroe.

He made love to her with such passion that she felt ravished, delightfully tired, and totally in love. She gloried in the bronze-skinned man who moved over her with expertise. His body was hard and handsome, in spite of its many scars. The hunt and the provocative dance had brought out his virility and that of

127

many other warriors who would take their women this night, their manhood stirred by the activities of the day.

When Zeke finished with her, he held her close under the buffalo robe, and the drums continued to beat outside.

"It's been a good day," he told her quietly. "A successful hunt, the games, the food, and the celebrating . . ." He kissed her hair. "And this."

He kissed her hungrily, but they were disturbed by a rustling sound outside the tipi and a sultry laugh. Then it sounded as though someone was running away. They both sat up, and Zeke gave her a look, telling her to stay where she was. He picked up his knife and walked naked to the entrance flap, opening it quickly and looking out into the shadows. No one was there. But Abbie gasped, and when he looked down, he understood why. Her puppy lay at the entrance—what was left of it. There was only the head and skin, and a pile of bloody bones.

"Zeke!" Abbie whimpered. "Oh, dear God!" She turned away and wept.

"Slut!" Zeke hissed. "I'll use my knife on her for this!"

Abbie went through the movements of learning how to stitch hides together for a tipi, but actually she was struggling to forget the sight of the slaughtered puppy. Three days had passed since she had found its remains, and Dancing Moon had not been seen since that night. Zeke had gone out of his way to try to make up for the loss of her pet. He brought Abbie the best skins for their new dwelling and promised he would buy many beads for her when they went to Independence so that she could decorate the clothes she made to be more beautiful than anyone else's. He helped her with work that no other man would help his woman do, and in the night he quietly held her, not trying to make love to her; for he knew the loss of the puppy had sent her into a depression that made her want only to be held.

He wanted very much to get his hands on Dancing Moon,

but she had vanished, although he feared the woman had not given up on her hatred for Abigail. Zeke vowed to himself that somehow Dancing Moon would pay for bringing such mental anguish to Abbie, who had already had her share of suffering and who had barely begun to adjust to the new life-style of living among his people.

Abbie's spirits brightened when the tipi began to take shape, and the women of the village coaxed her to smile, joking with her and keeping her busy, all aware that her heart was broken over the puppy. They had no strong feelings for any of the dogs, but they understood that Abbie did, and they respected her feelings. So they kept her busy, and while a few of them helped sew skins for a tipi, another demonstrated to Abbie how to make a war shield by stretching rawhide over a willow hoop and hanging brass bells and beaded leather strips around the edge of the shield. Another woman painted the shield with an eagle, Zeke's sign, and the finished product was presented to Zeke the same day that the tipi was erected.

This became another occasion for celebration. But Zeke's brother, Red Eagle, drank so much whiskey while celebrating that he passed out while he was sitting with Yellow Moon, his bride-to-be. He had to be carried to Swift Arrow's tipi, and although it was humorous at the time, Zeke knew it was a grave foreboding of the future. Red Eagle's drunkenness was only one small sign, and when he and Abbie retired to their new dwelling for the night, his heart was heavy with concern, for whatever happened to the Cheyenne would affect both their lives.

"Isn't it wonderful!" Abbie was saying excitedly, whirling around inside. "It's much larger than any of the others! And it's our own, Zeke, our very own!" This was the most happiness she had felt since the puppy had been killed. She turned to face Zeke and his eyes were full of love and sadness. "What's wrong?" she asked him. "You've been very quiet tonight."

His eyes scanned the small woman-child before him. "Most white women look forward to a fancy new house with wood floors and a hard roof and glass windows, with a fireplace and a clock on the mantel," he told her. He turned away. "I'm sorry, Abbie. It shouldn't be this way . . . for you. You shouldn't have married me. There's trouble ahead for the Cheyenne—and probably for us."

"Zeke Monroe!" she chided, putting her hands on her hips. "And I suppose I should have settled for some mealy white boy who doesn't know his head from his feet and is scared of his own shadow—or perhaps some older man I can't stand to have beside me in the night—just so I can have a roof over my head and a fireplace and cook on a wood stove!"

"Stop it, Abbie!" he snapped. "You know there are plenty of brave, industrious, good men out there among the whites."

"But I married you, Zeke! I married the man that you are, not the color of your skin! You could just as well have been white, but it just so happens that you're half Indian. What's the difference? A woman's place is with her man, and as long as my man's happiness lies here with the Cheyenne, then this is where my happiness lies!"

He turned back to face her, and their eyes held challengingly. Then Abbie's softened and she smiled. "We've already made our commitment, Zeke." She stepped closer to him and took his hands. "And I've never doubted my decision."

He searched her eyes, his own tearing, to her surprise. "Are you sure, Abbie girl?" he asked in a near whisper.

She smiled more broadly. "Zeke, I'm here. And I'm carrying your child. Isn't it a little late to ask me if I'm sure?" She sighed and squeezed his hands. "I know I was upset over the puppy, but Dancing Moon is gone now, and I feel better, Zeke, having our own dwelling. Everything will be fine. And do you know what I wish right now? I wish you'd get your mandolin and sing for me, like you used to do last summer on the wagon train. Sing me a Tennessee mountain song. It's been so long since you sang and played for me, and I'm so happy tonight, so proud of our new lodge and the war shield I made for you."

He sighed in resignation and bent down to kiss her forehead.

"I'll get the mandolin," he said quietly, a sadness still in his eyes. He put a big hand to her cheek for a moment, then went to get the instrument he'd left in Swift Arrow's tipi. Abbie sat down to wait. She dearly loved to hear him sing, and remembered that night the year before, when he had sung especially for her as she lay close to dying from the arrow wound. His singing had comforted her and soothed her lonely heart. Zeke played the mandolin's magical strings with a mystic beauty, and his voice was clear and mellow. When he sang his Tennessee music for her, she was back home again, and that was all the home she needed. Tennessee would be only a memory now.

She looked around the tipi. Utah and Kansas Territories had become home to her, and this dwelling was as homey and warm as any fancy house, for a home was only a home when there was love in it, whether it was made of buffalo skins or bricks. And there was already much love inside this dwelling.

Susan Garvey sat on satin sheets, moaning about her "poor" condition. She was seven months pregnant and certain she would die when she gave birth, if she did not die before that from the strain of carrying around a fat stomach. It seemed to take all her strength just to walk from the bed to the toilet, and she kept her maids running at all hours, bringing her books, food, water, whatever she asked for. They helped her bathe and brushed her hair and, in general, made certain Mrs. Garvey did not have to lift one weak little finger.

Her heart quickened with dread at the realization that the senator would be home soon. In the two short years they had been married, she had grown to hate him, especially when he grasped at her in the night with his fat fingers. She was glad for the pregnancy, for it gave her an excuse to put a stop to their sex life, which mattered little to her since meeting the handsome young physician who attended her. She didn't care that the maids might gossip about the doctor's house calls and about the prolonged time she spent with him behind closed doors, because never had she known sex could be so deliciously exciting as it was at the hands of her physician. Perhaps it was because their secret affair was so scandalous and forbidden that she gloried in the doctor's touch. For all she knew, the baby she carried was her doctor's and not the senator's; but she was Mrs. Winston Garvey, a senator's wife, and for the sake of appearances, all must believe this was the senator's son or daughter.

Susan Garvey had been born and raised wealthy, and she intended to stay that way. Marrying the senator had assured her of that. And as his wife she also enjoyed a place of prominence. But now that she had an exciting lover on the side, life was even more wonderful. After the baby was born, her doctor lover would "fix" things so that she never got pregnant again. She wanted no more babies and was having this one only for the sake of appearances, to show her "love and devotion" for the senator. But pregnancy spoiled a woman's figure, and she did not intend to go through it again.

She smiled at the thought of how clever she and the doctor had been. The senator would be told that it would be dangerous for Susan to ever have another child, and that sex must be prohibited for the sake of Susan's health. It was a wonderful idea, for then she would never again have to sweat beneath the senator's fat body; yet she could continue her affair with the doctor without worrying about getting pregnant. The operation to keep her from having any more children would be a secret between herself and her physician.

It was a perfect plan. Let the senator smother some prostitute with his fat body and grope at some other woman with his clumsy fingers. She couldn't care less, except that it would be fun pretending she was jealous and angry whenever she suspected he'd been with someone else. After all, she was a devoted wife, who should be upset by her husband's infidelity.

She chuckled to herself. Of course, the doctor would have to continue his house calls and "examinations," for her health was "delicate," or so it would seem. It was a game that brought her great delight and entertainment. To live any other way would be boring.

She heard the door below open and close, and then her husband bellowed a greeting to the servants. She closed her eyes and made a face. She knew the routine. He would hand his papers to a servant to take to his office; then he would light a smelly cigar and heave his body up the stairs of their plush townhouse to greet his pregnant wife, who was too ill to get out of bed. Pregnant young women had to be treated delicately, and he had to be patient with her condition.

She heard the dreaded footsteps on the stairs and scooted down under the covers, hoping her face was not still flushed from the doctor's recent visit and "examination." She put on the face of a weak and ill young woman so that he would not dream of crawling into bed with her. The door opened, and he barged into the room, puffing his obnoxious cigar.

"Good evening, pet," he said to her, plopping himself on the bed beside her. "And how is the little mother?"

"I feel terrible!" she mumbled. "I'm so sick all the time, Winston. I'll be so glad when this is over and I have my figure back."

He grinned and ran a hand over her swollen belly and across her privates. "So will I, my love. So will I."

She drew up her knees and pulled the covers up to her neck. "You don't fool me, Winston! You get what you need from those filthy wenches who advertise themselves on the back steps of Washington! I'm not that stupid!"

He only smiled and rose, walking to the dresser to a tray full of various alcoholic beverages. He opened a bottle of bourbon and poured a small amount into a glass.

"What's wrong, my pet?" he asked, talking down to her as he always did. "You were reluctant in bed long before you got pregnant." He took a swallow and turned to her. "Are you tired of your fat old man already?"

She puckered her lips. "Sex is such a chore!" she grumbled.

"Only the man gets any fun out of it. All the woman gets is pregnant and sick!"

He chuckled and nodded. "Well, my dear, it's wives like you who keep women like those on the back steps of Washington busy. But you are still my wife, and you'll forget all this once you have the baby." His eyes roved her body. "And whether you're willing or not, I intend to exercise my husbandly rights when I feel like it. If I want to have at you, I'll have at you."

She turned up her nose. "Don't be such an animal!" she sneered.

"You liked it when we first married."

"I never liked it! I just pretended." She sat up straighter and fluffed her pillows. "Mother told me it would be like this, and she was right. She and my father haven't slept together for years."

He raised his glass to her. "The world would certainly be a lot better off if mothers quit telling their daughters what a burden sex is." He took another swallow, thinking how lovely it would feel to plant his hands around her throat and squeeze. She had been so enchanting and deliciously innocent when he first married her. "You really are quite a spoiled bitch, you know," he said flatly, walking over to pour another drink. "And if you don't quit lying around in that bed, you'll be fat."

She laughed lightly. "I already am fat, thanks to you. And you should talk. Do you think I enjoy having a fat husband?"

He started on his second drink. "You enjoy having a husband with a fat wallet well enough. You enjoy the fat life you lead and the clothes and fine things my fat money brings you. A few rounds in bed with me isn't much to ask in return." He studied the drink in his hand. "Come to think of it, you aren't any different from the whores I sleep with. The only difference is that you have a piece of paper saying you're my wife. But I pay for your services, just the same."

She rubbed at her belly and made a face. "And you think I'm not paying? I'm the one who's losing out on all the parties because of this horrible stomach, lying here sick all the time;

134

and now I have to look forward to the awful pain of childbirth." She burst into tears, but he just grinned and shook his head.

"What you need is to know what it's like to really work, my dear, to know some of the discomforts of life, like the pioneer women. Perhaps you'll learn soon enough at that."

"What are you talking about?" she sniffled, taking a hanky from under her pillow and dabbing at her eyes.

"I've sent Jonathan Mack west to do some investing for me. If I work things right, I'll own half of Santa Fe when the States take it over after this war with Mexico."

"So what?" she grumbled. She blew her nose. "Who cares about Santa Fe?"

He raised his eyebrows and grinned. "You should, my dear. You'll be living there, and you'll be the wealthiest, prettiest, most talked about woman there. Wouldn't that please you?"

Her eyes widened. "I'll not live in that . . . that . . . snake-infested dusty hole! I'll not leave Washington!"

He swallowed the rest of his drink. "You'll live where I tell you to live. It would be good for that sallow skin of yours to get some Western sunshine, and roughing it a little would be good for your spoiled, rotten soul!"

"I'll not live there! Do you understand? How can you think of such a thing. I'd have to leave mother and . . . and the high society parties, and the grand coaches . . . and . . . and civilization itself! Why, I could even be attacked and raped by Indians! Tortured and murdered! And what of our baby? How can you begin to consider such a horrible idea!"

He lit another cigar. "Think of it this way, my dear. I'm going to have a grand mansion built for you, and when you go out there, you'll stand out like a lily among thorns. You'll be the center of society and you'll own half the town. How can that be so bad?"

She folded her arms in front of her. "And where will you be while I'm out there sweltering and choking on dust."

"I'll be joining you. I have five years left in the senate. I've

135

won this seat often enough and I'm getting bored with Washington. Believe me, my pet, Jonathan Mack will make good use of my money. We'll be quite rich, or should I say, richer than we already are. You can move out there and get settled—get used to the place—in, oh, three or four years, after things have settled with Mexico and all my land holdings are safe; and soon after, I'll retire from political life and join you. Could be I'll get right back into politics out there, you know. In the West a man can own a whole town, my pet."

She turned her eyes to the pink satin bedspread and thought about his suggestion. To be the center of attention would not be so bad. In fact, she could be the pillar of society in a place like Santa Fe. And it could be a whole year after she arrived before her fat husband joined her. She could have quite a good time in that year. But still . . . Santa Fe . . . the West . . . Indians! It was all very frightening.

"Could we . . . could we pay Dr. Whitney to go?" she whined. "He's such a good doctor, and surely there are no doctors out there, Thomas. He says my health is not good, and I may always have need of a physician."

He waved his arm. "So, let him go, if it makes you happy. Hell, the man could get rich out there. There must be a tremendous need for good doctors."

Susan smiled inwardly. A whole year alone with Dr. Whitney!

"And don't worry about the Indians," he went on, puffing his cigar. "There are ways of handling those ignorant savages. They'll learn to either stay where we tell them to stay, or die. It's that simple. The world would be better off without them anyway, kind of like getting rid of flies and mosquitoes and rodents, wouldn't you say?"

She sniffled. "I suppose so." She dabbed her eyes and looked up at him. "Can I have a grand house? The grandest house ever built out West? With all the comforts I have here?" Her mind was racing at the possibility of a whole year with the doctor and the idea of being the belle of the West.

136

"You can have whatever you wish, my pet," he replied. He sat back down on the edge of the bed, and she suddenly realized she didn't want to spoil her chances of being with the good doctor, or of losing her position as the wife of Senator Winston Garvey, who might some day be the wealthiest landowner in the West. As old and fat as he was, she could be left a young and very rich widow. She puckered her lips again.

"I'm terribly bitchy, am I not?" she told him, feigning regret. "I guess it's my pregnancy, Winston."

"You're young, my sweet. You'll mature."

"Try not to be too angry with me, Winston." She batted her eyes at him and he reached over and pulled her soft, silk gown down over her shoulder, exposing one breast. He toyed with it a moment, grinning like a hungry wolf.

"How can I stay angry with a beautiful young thing like you?" he replied. She closed her eyes and let him touch her, hoping he would not die before he became wealthier, but that he also would not live to enjoy his wealth. The senator leaned down to plant his mouth over her breast and she felt ill.

"Please, Winston, I'm just not in the mood when I'm fat and sick," she protested. He sat up, his eyes alive with desire for her.

"Whatever, my pet." He rose and walked out of the room, and she snuggled down to dream about a whole year alone with her doctor.

The great band of Cheyenne and Arapaho moved northeast toward the junction of the Smoky Hill and Republican Rivers, where they hoped to find more game. More Indians joined them, some northern Cheyenne coming down from Nebraska and unorganized territories, telling tales of more and more white-topped wagons traversing the Great Medicine Road to the West.

These stories spread quickly among the southern Cheyenne

and the Arapahos, and they were discussed at the councils and tipi gatherings. More were coming! Hundreds more! More than the Indian could count! And soldiers were also coming. Fort Laramie was full of them now, and the Sioux were beginning to feel threatened by the presence of so many soldiers and whites. Already, they had lost thousands of their people to the white man's diseases. Mothers had lost children, and children had lost parents. Men had lost wives and sons, and warriors who were bold and skilled in battle had succumbed to the dreaded spotted disease of the white man.

But they also had a great hope, an almost childish outlook on their future and on their attitude toward the land. It was so vast! Soon the white man would stop coming. Soon the diseases would stop, and the buffalo herds would grow larger again. They were as one spirit, moving in unison, all with the same blind faith in *Maheo* and the good earth and the spirits. After all, the white man did bring some good things, like sweet sugar and iron kettles and bright cloth and beads. His whiskey caused a terrible headache, but it tasted good; and before the headache came, there was a wonderful feeling of being close to the spirits. It made a man feel stronger and happier. The white man also brought rifles. More and more Cheyenne were trading for rifles when they could, for although they preferred not to use the long guns in combat, rifles made the killing of buffalo much easier and safer, since it could be done quickly and from a distance where a man could not be trampled.

It was also a time of great hope for Abbie, for she had been accepted by this strong and proud people, and she was learning that they were nothing like the evil, ignorant savages the whites had made them out to be. Her heart was full of happiness, for she had many friends among the women, the closest of all being Tall Grass Woman, whose round, happy face was always a welcome sight.

Many of the women had taken part in painting Abbie's tipi, and now in three places it was decorated with an eagle flying alone. These represented Zeke's Cheyenne name, Lone Eagle.

Tall Grass Woman had painted a white woman beside a red man to signify the mixed marriage, and Zeke's mother had painted a row of blue stones of various sizes to represent the "crying stones" Zeke had given Abbie the year before when she had lost her family.

"When you feel all is lost, hold the stones in your hands and keep the faith, Abbie girl," Zeke had told her when he'd placed them in her hands. "Let the stones cry for you."

She had seen him use the stones once, when a little girl on the wagon train had been bitten by a snake and Zeke had buried the girl up to her neck in mud to save her life. His own faith and strong spirit had helped keep the little girl calm, and he had shown her the blue crying stones and told her a story about them that helped her not to be afraid. The stones had begun to sweat, little blue beads of water that tasted salty appearing on them. Zeke had told the little girl that the water was her own tears, and that the stones were crying for her.

Abbie treasured the stones, for they had been Cheyenne Zeke's first gift to her. Now she would give him a gift, a baby. Hopefully it would be a son. Already she felt flutters of life, and soon her belly would grow large with the tiny life it held. And although life with the Plains Indians was rugged—full of hard labor and constant wandering—she was happy, simply because Zeke was happy. She had lost all of her initial fear of the Cheyenne and was learning to accept their ways. She was also learning some of the Cheyenne language and struggling to understand their religion and social conscience. There were many rules because they lived by strict discipline and a code of ethics, and her only fear now was that she would somehow break a rule inadvertently. But she had Zeke, and as long as she had him, she would find her way among the People.

It was after another hunt and a long day of laborious skinning and stretching of hides and dissecting meat that Abbie's happiness ended. The destruction began with a weary walk to the river to wash buffalo blood from her hands and arms. Perhaps the destruction was mostly because Abbie was so young and inexperienced that she had decided too quickly she could abide by her new way of life; for what happened to her at the river brought her face to face with the reality of life in a savage land with a people very different from herself.

She had walked to the river, ignoring Zeke's constant warnings that she never leave the tribe and wander off alone. That was a strict rule for all women, but at the moment Abbie didn't care about rules. She was tired and dirty, and she was thinking only about being clean again and about letting the cool waters soothe her aching arms, after which she would get a good night's sleep.

She stepped into the river, rinsing her hands and arms and then scrubbing them with the lye soap she had brought with her. Then she knelt to her knees to wash her hair, not caring that her tunic was getting wet; she would remove it when she got back to the tipi. She soaped her hair and bent over to rinse it, the rushing waters of the river drowning out the sound of footsteps behind her.

Perhaps if she had been Indian, she would have felt the presence. But she was white, and it would take many years for her to develop the keen senses the red man seemed to be born with. Something suddenly pounced on her from behind, and she fell face down into the water.

A strong hand held her beneath the surface, and Abbie realized that whoever this was, he or she meant to drown her. A sheer desire to live and have Zeke's baby brought her the strength she needed to reach up and grasp the arms that forced her down. They felt slim like a woman's. Abbie dug her nails into them and twisted. She felt gravel biting into her cheek when she did so; but she managed to push her attacker off, and the two of them began rolling in the water.

At first Abbie was too absorbed in fighting for her life to scream as she poked and scratched and struggled and rolled. But her attacker was bigger and stronger so finally she found herself on her back, her arms pinned down and her attacker sitting upon her. Water splashed over Abbie's face, blurring her eyes, but she could make out a woman's form.

"Tonight we fight for our man!" the woman hissed.

Abbie recognized the voice. It was Dancing Moon!

"I have been waiting for this moment to find you alone, white woman!" the Arapaho snarled. She let go with one hand and backhanded Abbie. It had happened too quickly for Abbie to react and now she knew that without help she would not win a fight with this strong and vicious woman. Dancing Moon meant to kill her. When the Arapaho woman hit her again, Abbie reached up, dug her nails into Dancing Moon's face, and screamed for Zeke despite the mixture of blood and water in her mouth.

Dancing Moon jerked Abbie's hand away and pushed her arms back down. "White bitch!" she snarled. "Now you have shown your weakness! They will laugh at you for calling for help! A true Cheyenne fights her own battles! She does not call for help!"

Abbie arched upward, trying to get the woman off her, but Dancing Moon only laughed and raised up slightly to jerk Abbie around so that her face was in the water again. "Now you cannot scream!" she told Abbie. But already Dancing Moon could hear voices and footsteps; there was not enough time to wait for Abbie to drown.

Again Abbie struggled, and Dancing Moon let go with one hand to take out a small knife from a belt she wore around her tunic. She raised the knife just as Abbie managed to turn over again. Abbie screamed and struggled to get away, wiggling up just enough that the knife came down in her abdomen rather than her chest.

Pain and blackness enveloped Abbie. She could feel Dancing Moon leaving her, and for a moment there was only the feel of the cold river water splashing over her face. Then there were more voices, and strong arms were lifting her.

"Abbie!" someone groaned. "My God, Abbie, what's happened to you?"

Who was talking to her? Terrible pain pierced her belly. Was

141

it the baby? No! It was too soon for the baby! The baby! Something stung terribly at her face, and she could taste blood. Her nostrils, ears, and throat were full of water and she was coughing and choking; yet she was unable to speak or focus her thoughts. Everything hurt, and someone screamed Zeke's name. Was it coming from her own lips? No. She couldn't speak! And yet . . .

"Someone has attacked her!" a man's voice spoke up.

"Whoever it was, he'll die!" a voice close to her responded. "And he'll die slowly!" There was a tenseness in the arms that held her.

"Be calm, Zeke," a woman's voice spoke up. "She will need you to be calm. And there is the knife wound. You are the best at fixing knife wounds. You must be calm and help her, my son."

"Who would do this!" came the desperate reply.

"It is too dark to find the attacker tonight," someone at a distance said. "It is dangerous to go out among the spirits of the dead when the sun is down."

There was a sudden warmth around her, and, sensing a dim light, Abbie could smell the sweet smoke of herbs. She recognized the smell as that created by the *Shaman*, the medicine man, when he burned special herbs and leaves as part of the ritual of doctoring the wounded. But who was wounded? Was she the one who would be the object of the *Shaman*'s rituals? She felt her tunic being removed.

"My God!" someone groaned again. "Abbie!"

Eight

For the next few hours Abbie knew nothing but fits of pain punctuated by long moments of unconsciousness. The pain tore at her abdomen, as though witches' claws were gripping her insides and tearing at her. When conscious, she could hear women's voices, feel a man's gentle hands stroking her hair and occasionally sense a cool cloth on her forehead. She was aware of a soft chanting in the background and the continued sweet smell of burnt offerings. But she did not remember that she had screamed her way through the stitches Zeke had taken with a crude bone needle and thread made from the thinnest intestinal membrane of the buffalo, boiled for cleanliness and slit into paper-thin strips. Nor was she aware that the tiny life she had carried in her belly had been expelled because of the shock of her attack and stabbing, and that she no longer carried Zeke's baby. Now she sensed only awful pain and then blessed blackness.

Not until morning sunrise did she open her eyes in full consciousness, to realize she lay in the *Shaman*'s tipi. The old man, face painted, was quietly chanting and waving gray feathers that caused the smoke rising from a sweetly scented fire to waft over her body. At first she lay quietly, her eyes focusing on her surroundings, her mind finally beginning to remember and to understand.

"Zeke!" she whimpered. She did not realize he had been sitting near her head, where she could not see him at first. He was immediately at her side, bending over her and putting a hand gently to her badly scraped face, careful not to touch the deep cuts where someone's nails had dug into her. His face was drawn and pitifully tired-looking, his eyes desperate and wild with grief.

"Abbie girl!" he said in a near whisper. "I . . . thought I'd lost you!"

She started to rise but cried out with pain.

"No, don't move!" Zeke warned her. "I had to stitch up the wound on your stomach. You're in a bad way, Abbie, and you've got to lie still."

"The . . . wound?" she asked, closing her eyes and trying to remember.

He bent closer and kissed her eyes. "Abbie, who did this to you?" he asked gently. "Tell me who did this, and he'll pay."

She struggled to remember. The hands! The awful, strong hands! And the water! Choking! Struggling! "She . . . tried to drown me!" Abbie whimpered, tossing her head and breathing rapidly. "She said . . . we had to fight . . . for our man! She wanted me . . . to die! Zeke!"

"Hush, Abbie!" he told her grasping her face between his big, gentle hands. Someone else entered the tipi and sat down near her.

"Zeke," a woman's voice spoke. "She is better?"

"Damn!" Zeke groaned. "It was her! It was Dancing Moon!" His voice sounded bitter and broken. "I should have killed her the night of the dancing!"

"Be calm, Zeke," came the woman's voice. Abbie felt a gentle hand on her forehead. "Tell us, Abigail. Was it Dancing Moon who did this to you?"

Abbie's body jerked in a sob, and pain tore through her again. It hurt to cry and yet she could not stop. She was suddenly enveloped in the realization that she must have miscarried.

"Yes," she whimpered. Then the awfulness of it all hit her, the terrible knowledge that she had lost the precious life that

144

she had so wanted to carry in her womb to full term. "Yes!" she said louder. "Yes! Yes! Yes!"

"Don't, Abbie!" Zeke pleaded, grasping her hands tightly. "My God, Abbie, you've got to lie still!"

"I don't care!" she screamed. "My baby's gone, isn't it? Tell me, Zeke! My baby's gone!"

He kept a firm hold of her hands and bent down to kiss her damp hair. "Yes, Abbie girl."

She groaned and gritted her teeth, and horrible, wrenching, painful sobs swelled up from her soul.

"Abbie, at least you're alive!" Zeke moaned, trying to console her. "You can have other babies."

"I wanted this one!" she sobbed. "Oh, God, I wish . . . I was home! I want my . . . mother! I want Pa! I . . . hate it here! I hate it! Everybody dies! Everybody dies! I want to go back . . . to Tennessee! I want to sit . . . on the swing . . . in our back yard! I want my mother, Zeke! They don't . . . want me! Your people . . . don't want me!"

"God, Abbie, stop it! That's not true!"

"It is! It is! They tried to kill me!"

"Abbie, don't do this! That was Dancing Moon. The others love you, Abbie. I love you. You've been happy with the Cheyenne."

She struggled to get away from him, filled with horror at her memories of death—her mother, her sister, her brother, her father. Now her baby was gone! Everything was gone! And here she lay in a foreign land amid a foreign people. Perhaps she had been lying to herself all along. Perhaps she could not live her life with this man who understood savageness in a way she never would. Perhaps doing it for a man's love was not enough to carry her through. She felt sick and weak and small and white . . . so white and foreign!

"Make him go away!" she screamed, pushing at the *Shaman*'s hand as he held eagle feathers over her forehead. "Make him go away! I don't need his chanting and his . . . pagan rituals. I've already lost my baby! I've

145

lost . . . everything. Everything! I can't go on, Zeke. I don't want the Cheyenne. I don't want anything! It won't work! I just . . . want to die!"

She did not see his ashen face or the horror in his eyes. She felt him move away from her. He barked something to the *Shaman*, and the chanting stopped. Abbie lay there unable to control her crying while a woman's gentle hand stroked her hair. Someone covered her with another robe, and suddenly she knew the tipi was empty, and that was how she felt. Empty. Totally and agonizingly empty.

A gentle breeze ruffled the coup feathers in Zeke's hair, and birds sang nearby. He sat on a flat rock, lightly picking at his mandolin while staring absently at the dancing waters of the river nearby. He sat alone, in a place where he knew no one would come and see his tears. But when he heard footsteps in the distance, picking up the sound early with his keen ears, he quickly turned to see his mother approaching. He set the mandolin down and turned away again, wiping tears from his cheeks with his fingers as she came closer.

"Leave me!" he groaned. "You should not . . . see me now."

"Why?" she asked quietly. "Because you weep?"

He sighed deeply. "She . . . loved my music," he replied brokenly. "And she loved me. It won't be that way for us again." He rubbed at his eyes and his shoulders shook slightly, and Gentle Woman's heart ached for her lonely half-breed son. "Please . . . leave me, Mother," he again requested.

"There are many kinds of weeping, my son," she went on. "To weep over the bad fortune of someone we love brings no shame. It is natural." She put a hand on his shoulder. "Zeke, it is difficult for a man to understand what happens to a woman when she loses a child. Many things take place . . . inside of her . . . things that she cannot help. It is like . . . like it is with some women at their flowing times . . . when they may not be as patient. It is something she cannot stop from happening,

Zeke. It makes her say things she does not mean, and hurt those she loves when she does not want to hurt them. Do you understand what I am telling you?"

He rose and moved away from her. "She's right, you know," he choked out. "It won't work. I was foolish to think it would!"

"She's young, Zeke. And all of this is so new to her. Do not lose faith. She is a child, Zeke. A little girl! And she has lost too much too fast. When she is healed, and the awful loneliness of losing her baby has left her, she will be your Abbie again. You have so much love for one another, Zeke. But you are a man, and she is a child. You must be patient. Surely you knew when you married her that it would take time and patience for her to grow into a woman."

He wiped at his eyes again. "I knew that. But making her live this way . . . it's too much." He picked up a rock and threw it hard into the water. "I was a fool to marry her. A fool!" He whirled. "Not because of her, Mother. Because of me. Me! Because I'm a half-breed and life with me will destroy her! I . . . I tried so hard to keep myself from her . . . to convince myself that I must leave her—send her on to Oregon and never see her again. I'd learned my lesson with Ellen. This is what I get for breaking my vow to never marry another white woman! This is what I get for being weak with love for her. I'll ruin the very thing I love the most, just like I ruined Ellen!"

"You did not ruin Ellen! You loved her! You were good to her. You had a right to marry her, Zeke! You are a man. It does not matter that half of you is Indian and half of you is white. You are just a man. And you can love any woman you choose to love. If she happens to be white, then she is white."

Their eyes held for a moment, and her heart ached for this firstborn son who had suffered so greatly in his short life because of his mixed blood. At the moment he was four years old again, and he was being dragged away from her, for the same desperate, lonely look was in his eyes. She stepped closer and grasped his arms.

"Zeke, give her a few days. It is her pain that is talking, that

147

is all. Her physical pain, and her mental pain. Her heart is full of sorrow."

He gently pushed his mother away and turned around. "I've lost her," he said. "I intend to go and find Dancing Moon. After that, when Abbie is well enough, I'll take her back to Tennessee . . . back home." He pulled out his knife. "But first I will use this on Dancing Moon!" He threw the knife, and it stuck into the side of a tree, vibrating from the violent thrust.

"No!" his mother protested. "You are Abbie's husband, and she will need you. You will stay here and be at her side, even if she says she does not want you there. I speak as a woman, Zeke. Listen to one who is older and wiser. She needs you, whether she knows it herself or not. It is your duty to be here. The priest has already given orders that runners should go out. They are to spread the word of this evil deed Dancing Moon has done. She is to receive no help and no home in any camp, not Cheyenne, not Arapaho, not Navajo, not Sioux; no tribe that is friend to the Cheyenne will give her a home. If she tries to take shelter with any of them, she is to be whipped and scarred. She will suffer, Zeke. She will be homeless and despised. There is no need for you to go after her, for the punishment from her own people will be great, and she will have brought it upon herself. Your place is here, with Abigail."

"She doesn't want me now." He groaned. "She doesn't need me."

"Oh, my son, do not be such a fool! It is this great love you have for her that makes you speak like a child. I know you better than this. You love her so much that you cannot bear the least little bit of hurt that comes her way, and you are ready to blame all of it on yourself. But we all get hurt, Zeke. Life brings everyone pain and disappointment. If she were a Cheyenne woman, it would have been the same, Zeke. Do you not see this? Dancing Moon would still have attacked her and brought her harm, because of her jealousy. But because she is white, and because of what happened to Ellen, you are ready to say that everything bad that happens to her is your fault, just because she happened to choose a half-breed to love! Look at me, Zeke. Look at me and tell me that you could truly take her back to Tennessee, leave her there, and return to us without Abigail."

He threw his head back and breathed deeply. "I . . . saw her . . . in a vision, Mother," he said brokenly. "Before we were married. I saw her in a vision . . . and she was . . . beside me. She was beside me!"

"Then you know this is how it must be, my son. And you know this is just a little root along the pathway that has tripped you. But when we trip and fall, my son, we rise again. We brush off the dirt and we go on. It will be this way for Abigail. You will see, if you are but patient."

He walked over to the tree and jerked out his knife, wanting very much to use it slowly on Dancing Moon. It was the first time he had ever wanted to bring harm to a woman. He shoved the knife back into its sheath.

"Has she . . . asked for me?"

"Not yet, my son. She only weeps."

He sighed deeply, his back still turned. "I . . . have to go away for the night, Gentle Woman. I have to be alone. I have to think."

"I understand."

"Is her . . . her bleeding . . . is it bad? Dangerous?"

"No. At first it did look bad, but the bleeding is normal now. In a few days it will stop."

He rubbed at his neck and sighed. "I must go to Independence soon. I have money there that I should get out of the bank. And I have to take my horses to trade before all of the wagon trains have left. That is the best market for the horses. I'll take Abigail with me on a travois and leave her there with a white doctor who can care for her. When she's well enough, I will take her home—back to Tennessee—even though it is dangerous for me to go there."

Gentle Woman smiled sadly. "She will not want to go, my son. This I know in my heart."

He turned to look at her with red, tired eyes. "I pray to *Maheo* that you are right."

Abbie stirred slightly, opening her eyes to the morning sun that filtered through a slit in the door of the tipi. She realized she had been taken to her own tipi, and she saw Gentle Woman bending over a small fire. No one else was about. It was the second morning after her attack and miscarriage, and her pain had lessened. The relief from pain seemed to bring a slight relief from sorrow, and she was suddenly disappointed that Zeke was not there, although for two days she had not wanted to see anyone, not even Zeke.

Gentle Woman turned and noticed she was awake; then she smiled kindly and came to Abbie's side, taking her hand. "You look much better this morning, Abigail!" she said with genuine happiness. "You have color in your face again. How do you feel, child?"

Abbie turned her eyes up to stare at the hole in the top of the tipi, where smoke curled out. "I . . . don't know quite yet." She looked back at Gentle Woman. "Where is Zeke?"

Gentle Woman smiled. "Do you wish to see him?"

Their eyes held. "I . . . don't know. Would he . . . would he want to see me?"

Gentle Woman squeezed her hand. "He has been waiting impatiently."

Abbie blinked back tears. "You shouldn't be kind to me," she told the woman. "I haven't been very nice. Zeke shouldn't want to see me at all. I . . . I hurt him badly, didn't I?"

"You have only behaved as any woman behaves when these things happen to her. You have been in shock, and many bad things have happened to you since first you left your home in Tennessee."

Abbie looked away again. "I'm so confused, Gentle Woman. Sometimes I . . . I want so much to go home. But Zeke can't go there because he's wanted there, and even if he weren't, he

150

could never be happy in Tennessee. Here . . . on the prairies . . . in the mountains with his people . . . here is where he is happiest. I could never destroy that happiness."

Gentle Woman smiled. "And Zeke talks about you the same way, thinking that here you cannot be happy. So, what do you think can be done about that?"

Abbie sniffled. "I don't know," she whispered.

"I will tell you one thing, Abigail. For a woman to go with her man, that is what is important. It sometimes does not seem fair. But that is the way it is. Zeke's people love you. And one day, when you are older and have many children, you will forget this day and this confusion. Then you will know where you belong."

Abbie wiped at her tears, wincing with pain when her fingers touched the cuts on her face. "I'd like to try to get up today," she told Gentle Woman. "I don't want Zeke to see me like this. I want to get up and walk. Will you help me wash, and brush my hair?"

"I will help you wash. And I will brush your hair. But you must not get up yet, child. Wait another day or two. And wait one more day before you talk to Zeke. Today is the first day you have been able to think clearly. Think about Zeke, about Tennessee, and about the Cheyenne. Think about all of these things before you see your husband; for you want to be sure of what you will say, so that no harsh words will be said that you might regret."

Abbie put a hand to her forehead, her mind racing with confusion and loneliness and regret. "I said . . . such terrible things! Surely he hates me!"

"Oh, no, child, he could never hate you. It is himself he hates, for bringing you here. Now he thinks it was wrong. He thinks he should take you to a white doctor at Independence when he takes his horses there, and that when you are better he should take you home, to Tennessee. He thinks this is what you want."

Abbie closed her eyes. "I don't know now what I want. I

151

thought . . . I could be so strong . . . that I could be the perfect woman for him."

"Abigail." Gentle Woman took her hands. "Listen to me. You do not have to be anything but yourself. And you can be yourself anywhere, child. You do not have to be back in Tennessee for that. And to be yourself means you cannot deny the love in your heart. You could no more live without my son than he could live without you. You must stop worrying about proving yourself, for he loves you just as you are. And the Cheyenne love you just as you are. We do not expect you to change overnight, or to take up all the Cheyenne ways. You are Lone Eagle's woman, and you are brave and strong. That is all there is to know. And when you do feel weak, then you must let your husband be your strength. That is the way. That is what a man is for, Abigail. To be the strong one when his woman cannot be. And there will be times when the woman must be the strong one. The strength comes from both sides, Abigail, creating a power that is mighty and can bear all things."

Abbie studied the gentle, brown eyes of Zeke's mother. This truly was a woman of strength who had suffered much more than Abigail had. "You are good to me, Gentle Woman. Being with you is like . . . like having my mother with me." New tears of sadness welled in her eyes. "Sometimes I miss her so!"

Gentle Woman patted her hand. "You lost your family too quickly. You need more time to get over your loss. Zeke understands this. Let him help you, Abbie."

Abbie sniffed and looked away. "Tell him . . . to come tonight . . . when the sun sets," she told the woman. "I will think about all these things today . . . and speak with him tonight. I have so much to decide."

"I will tell him," Gentle Woman answered. She smiled and leaned down to brush Abbie's cheek with her own. "*Maheo* watches over you, woman of Lone Eagle. And always remember to follow your heart. That is most important."

*   *   *

Abbie waited with a pounding heart, hoping the cuts and scrapes on her face did not look too terrible, and wondering if he would come at all. The sun had gone down, and she knew what she must do now—what she must say. Gentle Woman had left to get Zeke, and now Abbie could hear his familiar footsteps outside the tipi. She had come to know them. Her heart beat so hard it felt as though it was in her throat when the entrance flap was raised.

He entered almost hesitantly, as though he thought she might throw him out. He wore the white doeskin shirt that was gloriously decorated with beads and paintings, the shirt he usually wore only for special occasions. She knew he had worn it for her, because she loved to look at him in it; it made him even more handsome. And her heart ached with love when she realized he wanted to look his best for her, as though perhaps he needed to woo her all over again.

Their eyes held in a moment of quickly passing emotions, from sorrow to anger to sorrow again. His jaw was set in stubborn determination to bear whatever it was she would tell him. She saw the hurt behind his defensive stance, and could hardly bear the thought that she had done the hurting.

"Zeke, I . . . I'm sorry . . . about the baby," she told him, not sure how to begin. He folded his arms in front of him.

"Why should you be? It wasn't your fault. It's Dancing Moon who should be sorry, and when I find her, she will regret the day she was born! None of this was your doing. It was hers. And mine."

Her eyes widened. "Yours! What on earth are you talking about?"

"I brought you here, didn't I?"

"I came because I wanted to come."

"But you don't want to stay."

She frowned, confused by his words. He seemed angry, and yet she felt it was a deliberate anger, staged for her benefit. Perhaps he wanted her to go back to Tennessee because he thought it was better for her. Perhaps he was trying to make

153

her want to go back.

"Zeke, the things I said, I said out of pain and depression. Surely you know that."

He lowered his arms and seemed to soften. He nodded. "I understand that, Abigail. But often the things we say in pain are like the things we say when we are drunk. We mean them but never say them when we are feeling good or when we are sober. It is only the truth that is forced out of us against our will."

"Zeke, I can't live without you!"

"But can you live with me?"

She dropped her eyes. "Zeke, I was attacked, remember? I didn't ask for any of this. I was happy here . . . with the Cheyenne. Happy with my pregnancy. I . . . I dearly wanted to give you a son." Her voice broke and it seemed that in the same moment he was at her side, putting a palm to the side of her face.

"Abbie, I know this is not your fault. But it opened my eyes, and I don't know if I can bear the guilt."

"There is no guilt to bear!" she sobbed. "What we are left with is . . . is a decision; and I've made one." She looked up at him, tears running down the sides of her face and into her ears. She wanted desperately to hold him and to feel his arms around her. But she suddenly knew she must wait, that there was something she had to do first.

"And what is this decision you have made?" he asked, his eyes showing his fear.

"Zeke, you made it too easy for me. Don't you see? When first we came here, it was too easy, because I had you and I could run to you whenever I needed to. The true test, Zeke, is to live here among the People alone. I . . . I want you to go to Independence without me." His eyes widened in surprise. "Take the horses," she went on. "Take them now while you can get a good price for them. It's already almost too late. Go on to Independence and leave me here. By the time you come back, I'll know. I'll have made my decision as to whether or not

I can truly live among the Cheyenne."

He shook his head. "I don't know, Abbie. . . ."

"Zeke, you must go soon if you want to get a good price for those horses! I'm too weak to go with you, even on a travois. And I have your mother here to care for me, and your brothers and your friends to watch out for me. I need some time alone with them, Zeke; time to face myself and them without you always in between to cushion things. I'm so sorry I've been such a child about this, Zeke."

"A child!" he interrupted. "My God, Abbie, you were attacked! Viciously attacked!"

"Just the same I said childish things that I will regret always. But perhaps . . . perhaps it was like you said . . . perhaps those were my true feelings coming out. If they were, Zeke, then I have to face those feelings, and I have to face them alone. Right now the only thing I know for certain is that . . . that I love you. And finding out if I can stay here is important to that love. Please, Zeke. Please do it this way."

He touched her hair. "Abbie, are you sure you could stay here alone?"

"No." She half smiled. "That's what I have to find out."

He frowned and ran his hand down over her side to her hip. "How is your wound?"

She closed her eyes and lay back. "Better. The pain is better."

"I did the best job I could at sewing you up. I haven't checked it out all day. I'd better have a look at it." He pulled the robe away from her, trying to ignore the rush of need and love and desire that enveloped him when he looked upon her nakedness. He looked closely at the wound, gently pressing his thumb around it, and she jumped slightly and whimpered.

"Is it bad?" he asked her.

"No," she replied. "Just sore. Nothing like the pain of infection I felt from the arrow wound."

"Well, it looks good, thank God." He sighed and covered her, resting his eyes for a moment on her breasts before hiding them again under the robe. She could see his hand trembling. "I thought . . . the night it happened . . . you looked so dead . . . lying there in the river!" His voice choked, and she grasped his hand tightly.

"Forgive me, Zeke, for hurting you!"

He only nodded, his eyes closed to prevent any tears from showing. He rose and walked toward the tipi entrance. "Perhaps because of this decision you have made . . . perhaps it is best I do not hold you, Abigail, until I return . . . and you know what you want to do."

She wanted to cry out to him that it was not so—that she wanted very much for him to hold her. But there was a strange, unwanted coldness between them, a barrier built by hurt pride and by sorrow and loss.

"I . . . I guess that would be best," she told him.

He started out. "Zeke!" she called out. He hesitated but did not turn around. "Zeke, do you think . . . is there such a thing as . . . as loving someone too much?"

He stood there stiffly for several seconds. Then he nodded. "There is such a thing," he replied in a strained voice. He swallowed. "I'm sorry, Abbie . . . about Dancing Moon." He walked out and closed the flap.

Zeke circled the small herd of Appaloosas to keep them in check; then he rode back to Swift Arrow, who stood at the edge of the village waiting for a final good-bye. He dismounted and stood before his brother, putting out his hand. They grasped wrists.

"I know that you are one of those who did not want her here," Zeke told Swift Arrow. "But you are my brother, and you are a dog soldier. She is my woman, and I can think of no man better able to watch over her while I am gone. I trust you will do this in spite of your feelings for the whites," Zeke told the man.

Swift Arrow nodded. "I will do this for you, my brother."

"Black Elk is too young and inexperienced, and Red Eagle drinks too much to be of any use," Zeke told the man.

"Red Eagle is becoming worthless because of the white man's firewater!" Swift Arrow grumbled.

"I agree," Zeke replied. "We must be careful, or the whiskey will ruin more of our people."

"This I know."

Their eyes held in a moment of silence. "Take good care of her, Swift Arrow. And try to be more understanding. She is not truly a woman yet. But this decision she has made—it's the decision of a woman, and it will not be easy for her to dwell among a people so foreign to her without me at her side. I am all she has had, Swift Arrow, for a year now. She's gone through so much . . . so many changes. For all I know her love for me was just . . . just something she needed at the time. It's possible when I come back that she'll have decided she'd be better off with her own people and that . . . perhaps what she felt for me was just a little girl's need for someone to watch over her."

Swift Arrow frowned. "You could bear such a decision?"

Their eyes held in brotherly love. "I don't think so, Swift Arrow!"

Their hands were still clasped, and Swift Arrow squeezed Zeke's wrist. "I think her decision will be to stay, my brother."

"It would help if she knew you wanted her to stay."

Swift Arrow sighed and released his hold. "I will try to understand her and accept her and forget my hatred of other whites. It is only fair, for she is trying to understand and accept the Cheyenne."

Zeke smiled a little for the first time since Abbie's attack. "Thank you, my brother." He eased back up onto his horse in one smooth motion.

"I will be gone about three weeks, Swift Arrow."

Swift Arrow nodded. "You will have to search for us. We will head north to the great flat river to join the Sioux for the Sun Dance."

157

"I'll know where to find you." Zeke looked across the village at his tipi, the one Abbie had worked so hard to help sew, the one that was painted with a white woman and a red man. He wanted to run to her, to sweep her up in his arms and run away with her, somewhere. Anywhere! But was there a place for them?

"She does not want to say good-bye," his mother had told him that morning. "Good-byes are too difficult. She said to tell you it would be too hard if she saw you again. But . . . she said she will hold the crying stones, and that her heart rides with you, and that in the night she will feel you beside her."

Zeke tore his eyes from the tipi and put his fingers to his brow as a sign of respect and honor to his brother. Swift Arrow put a hand to his brow in return. "*Maheo* ride with you and keep the wolves from your back," Swift Arrow told Zeke.

Zeke nodded to him and rode forward, whistling and swerving his mount to get the horses into motion again. He headed for Independence.

Dancing Moon crawled to a creek and plunged in, letting the cool water soothe her back. The horrible sting from the whipping the Arapaho women had given her still penetrated the muscles of her back, seemingly to the bone, and she wondered if there would be ugly scars from it.

"Damned white bitch!" she spat out. "This is her fault!"

She was amazed that word of her attack on Abbie five days earlier had traveled so fast. But then the Indians had ways of spreading talk. With runners and smoke signals, they had done a fine job of making certain that Dancing Moon's evil deed was known to all, and Dancing Moon had discovered she had no home. When she had arrived at what was once a friendly Arapaho camp where many men were normally eager to bed her, she had been met with knives and hatchets and told to leave, and before she could get away, the women had attacked her, stripping off her tunic and whipping her with quirts and

158

branches until she could barely walk. Then they carried her far from the village and dumped her, throwing her dress at her and warning her never to return, either to their village or to any other Arapaho, Cheyenne, or Sioux village.

But being in the wilderness alone was not easy, even for an Indian woman; for she had no weapon save the small knife she carried and nothing to eat except wild plants and berries. There were no friends now to help her and provide for her.

She let the water rush over her wounds for several minutes before she heard the rumbling sound of horses' hooves, the clanking of stirrups, and the squeak of saddles. She sat straight up and, grabbing up her tunic, ducked behind a large rock to watch several white men approach on horseback.

Most of them were unkempt and slovenly. Some were dressed in buckskins that had been worn too long without being changed. Their faces were sprouting ugly beards and their postures on their mounts were slouching. The man in front wore a soldier's blue coat, but it was not buttoned and was worn over a dirty cotton shirt. They all carried weapons, and Dancing Moon was afraid. But quickly her harlot's mind began to race. She had heard tales about white men—that they hungered for Indian women. She was without food and without a warm blanket for the night. These men might be able to provide for her. Ducking down she slipped her tunic over her head, ignoring the pain when it touched her back. She breathed deeply for courage. She knew nothing about white men other than rumors. But men were men, and now she would learn about the white ones.

She moved out from behind the rock just when the man in front wearing the blue coat rode by. He put up his hand. Rifles were immediately pulled from their resting places and hammers clicked as the men looked around, apparently expecting an attack.

"There is only me!" Dancing Moon spoke up, surprising them with her English. She had learned it from the few other Indians who spoke it, and from Zeke. "I am alone."

159

The leader continued to scan the horizon. "Keep a sharp eye, men!" he ordered. He rode up closer to Dancing Moon. "Who are you, squaw? What is it you want?"

"I need . . . food . . . blankets!" she replied. "And a horse!"

The man laughed. "A horse!" He looked back at his men and they all laughed. Turning to her, he eyed her up and down, thinking to himself that in spite of her disheveled appearance, she had an animal beauty that stirred a man's groin. He rode up closer and took a piece of her hair in his fingers. "Might be we could fix you up with some food and blankets, for the right payment, squaw woman. But a horse, ain't no woman good enough to get a horse in return, especially not a squaw!"

She opened her tunic and exposed her breasts. "Is this good enough for the food and blankets?"

The man's eyes grew watery with hunger and he dismounted, stepping close to her and touching a nipple with the back of his hand. "Could be." He looked around again. "If you're alone."

"I am alone. My people do not want me. See?" She turned and let her tunic fall more, exposing her back. The man grimaced.

"Why'd they do that to you?"

She laughed wickedly. "Because I am bad!" she replied, turning back to face him with hungry eyes.

The man smiled and rubbed his groin. "That so?" His eyes dropped to her breasts again, and the other men rode up for a closer look, their rifles dropping lazily as they took in the sight of her. The leader yanked her dress down farther so that it fell to her feet, and his breathing quickened. "Well, now, squaw lady. Just how do you intend to . . . uh . . . pay for that food and them blankets, with your back the way it is? Won't it hurt you to lay on it?" His hand lightly brushed her between the legs, and she felt the excitement she always felt when a man touched her. And this was a white man. There were many of them. She would find out what white men were like.

"I will get on my hands and knees," she said with a seductive

160

smile. "You have never seen how the dogs do it? And the big horses?"

The man grinned and actually blushed. The others began to dismount, shoving each other around to be next in line.

"Come behind the rock," she told the leader. "I will find out if you are like a dog . . . or like a horse!" She walked toward the rock, swaying her naked bottom provocatively. The leader turned to the others.

"Keep a lookout and remember we're volunteer soldiers and supposed to be guardin' this territory against Mexicans."

"But we never got no official orders yet, sir. We ain't even been to see Colonel Kearny yet."

"We're soldiers, Malcolm!"

"Well, sir, what I mean is, we could all take a turn at her, couldn't we? Ain't nobody gonna know."

"Of course we can all take a turn. We'd have done it even if she wasn't willin'. Everybody knows that's all a squaw is good for! This one is gonna earn her keep. We'll have us a good time before we get on with the . . . uh . . . war."

The others laughed. "Maybe we'll find us some more women on them big rancheros," one of them spoke up. "Some dark-eyed rich bitch who's been savin' herself for some lover."

"Maybe so," the leader replied. "Right now we got us a loose squaw who needs food and blankets. We'll supply her with her . . . needs."

He walked behind the rock, where Dancing Moon waited on hands and knees. She tossed her thick, black mane of hair to look back at him, and she smiled. The sergeant grinned, his blood racing with excitement at this pleasant diversion from his journey toward Fort Leavenworth to volunteer for the Mexican war.

The men sat around the campfire, exchanging stories about their experiences with the wild, hot-blooded squaw who had "purchased" her supplies. Dancing Moon was bathing. She

161

was sore but deliciously satisfied, and now she sauntered toward them to reap her reward, walking brazenly into the circle of white men and bending seductively over the fire to tear off a piece of roast rabbit.

"I have earned my food and blankets?" she asked, turning to the leader. The men all laughed.

"You've earned it," the leader answered. "By the way, my name is Baker. Claude Baker. What's yours?"

"I am called Dancing Moon. I am Arapaho." She bit into the meat.

Baker eyed her up and down. "Well, now, Dancin' Moon, got any more hot-blooded squaws where you come from?"

She looked around at them. "Maybe."

"Some say all squaw women is eager to get raped by white men," another put in. "That so, Dancing Moon?"

She laughed wickedly. "That is for you to find out!" she replied, hating all her Indian women friends now for turning her out. "But I can tell you something that is true, something your bluecoat leaders might want to know, something that could make you big men with your leaders!"

Baker threw away a bone and wiped his hands on his pants. "What's that, Dancin' Moon?"

She wiped her own lips with the back of her hand and moved closer to him, gently rubbing his inner thighs with one hand while still holding the rabbit leg in the other. "It will cost you a horse," she told him. "I must have a horse so that I can ride south to the Apache."

The man shook his head. "I don't know, Dancin' Moon. A horse is pretty valuable."

She drew back. "Then I will not tell you what I know!" She stood up and walked away.

"Wait!" Baker yelled. She whirled to face him. "Tell us and then we'll decide if it's worth a horse."

She took another bite of rabbit. "Bring me the horse first so I can see it."

162

Claude motioned and one of his men jumped up, walked into the darkness, and returned with a mount. Dancing Moon looked the animal over, checked its legs and its teeth. She looked at Baker. "And the blankets and food?"

"You'll get those no matter what."

She nodded and stepped closer to him. "There is a white woman living among the Cheyenne," she told him. "A captive slave."

Baker frowned, and the other men looked at each other in disbelief.

"I ain't heard of no white woman bein' captured by the Cheyenne," Baker told her.

"No one would have known. This one was found alone at her wagon by the Cheyenne. Her family had all died. They took her and raped her and made her a slave. One of them married her. Now she has been with them a while and she has become accustomed to them and is ashamed to come back to the white world for fear the whites would look down on her. Someone should go there and take her away. She does not belong there." She looked around at their astonished faces and smiled. "This is good enough to get me a horse?"

Baker scratched his head. "What tribe is she with? Where is she now?"

"It is hard to say with the Cheyenne. It is a big country. The last I knew, she was with them where the Smoky Hill and the Republican Rivers come together. It is possible they go north now for the Sun Dance with the Sioux. It would be hard to find them, but it would be worth it. Find them and see for yourself. Then tell your leaders to take soldiers there to take her away!"

Baker looked at his men, then back to Dancing Moon. "I think you just earned yourself a horse, squaw woman. But you'll not leave us until mornin', and anybody who feels a need to have another go at you can do it, understand?"

She grinned, thinking of the trouble Abbie and the Cheyenne would have if soldiers came for her.

"I understand," she replied. "Do what you wish. I just want the horse and the blankets. I will find my own way to the Apache!"

Baker nodded. "Then get down on your hands and knees, squaw," he told her.

"I want to eat more first."

He knocked the rabbit leg from her hand. "You'll eat when I say you can eat if you want that horse! Get down like I told you!"

She glared at him, but knew she had to obey. It was her only way out. She knelt down on her hands and knees and he moved behind her, pushing her tunic up to her waist. The others watched. There would be little sleep for Dancing Moon this night, but she did not mind so much. She would have a horse.

Nine

When Zeke reached Independence, he found it hard to believe it had been only a year since he was there last. The city had swelled with emigrants, and this year there appeared to be hundreds more preparing to head west than there had been the year before. Now he knew the Indians' tales of more white-topped wagons were true, and he also knew what the consequences could be.

From the stockyards where he sold his Appaloosas to the heart of the city, emigrants and townspeople alike talked of nothing but the war with Mexico. The town swarmed with travelers, merchants, soldiers, and scouts; and the air was static with excitement. There was constant movement everywhere. The commotion was irritating to Zeke, who already missed the peace of the Great Plains and the Rocky Mountains . . . and Abbie.

Abbie! He ached to hold her, and dreaded what she might tell him when he returned. Perhaps when the child turned into a woman, she would feel she had made a mistake in marrying him. His thoughts were full of her, and his nights were miserable. If not for Dancing Moon, Abbie would be with him now. He would be taking her into the shops and buying her things. He had planned to rent a nice room for her . . . if he could find an inn that allowed Indians. He had wanted to give her a break from the difficult life he had forced upon her when he took her to his people. But she was not with him, and she

165

had come close to dying and might even change her mind about staying with him—all because of Dancing Moon! Somehow Dancing Moon must pay! He would see to it!

A battalion of bluecoat soldiers entered one end of town just as Zeke approached the bank where he intended to take out his savings. People were beginning to cheer, and Zeke stopped to watch curiously. He took his corncob pipe from the parfleche that he carried over his shoulder. Slowly, he stuffed it with tobacco as the battalion came closer and more people gathered around him to see the soldiers.

"We're with you, Kearny!" someone behind him shouted. "Go get the Mexican devils and clean them out of Santa Fe!"

"Take California while you're at it!" a woman shouted.

"Might as well get rid of a few redskins along the way!" another man yelled. Several people nearby laughed, and bristling with anger, Zeke turned to glance at the man who had made the remark. The man paled at the dark, threatening look in Zeke's eyes and quickly darted away, melting into the crowd. Zeke's eyes quickly scanned the faces of the others who had been laughing, and their smiles faded as they feigned casual talk and averted Zeke's glare.

Zeke turned his eyes back to the street as the crowd pushed and shoved around him. There were cries of "Manifest Destiny," "Kill the Mexicans," and remarks supportive of the soldiers as the huge battalion passed directly in front of them.

Dust rose up in great clouds, swords clattered, hooves rumbled, and horses snorted. There were the sounds of squeaking leather and shouted orders; and the apparent leader, who appeared to Zeke to have an honest face for a white man, sat straight and tall in his saddle, a handsome man, with true eyes and a prominent, straight nose.

Catching a whiff of cheap perfume, Zeke turned to see a painted woman standing beside him. She wore a purple satin dress, and her eyelids were just as purple. Her hair was bright red and huge earrings dangled from her lobes, reaching almost to her shoulders. She smiled fetchingly at Zeke when he looked down at her; then she ran her green eyes up and down his body for a quick inventory. The red on her lips exaggerated their width, and the powder on her face only accented the lines that framed her eyes and lips, making her look older than Zeke guessed she really was, for her eyes and body looked younger.

"That's Colonel Stephen Watts Kearny," she told Zeke, nodding to the leader of the soldiers. Zeke looked back at the bluecoats. "Him and his men are headed for Santa Fe, to win the war for the United States and take over Mexican Territory. All them men with him are mostly volunteers, men hungry for any kind of action." She laughed lightly. "I could give them some action right here!"

Zeke turned his eyes to the woman again, taking in her full and generously exposed bosom. "That so?" he asked. Their eyes held for a moment and he puffed at his pipe, turning back to watch the soldiers. "So, there's really a war going on."

She reached over and ran a hand across his hips. "Hell, yes! Where have you been, Indian?"

"Out on the plains," he said in a distant voice. "With people who don't know and don't care about what's going on in the white man's world."

She frowned. "You sure don't talk like no Indian."

He looked down at her again. "Neither did my pa," he replied.

She threw back her head and laughed, rubbing at his hips again. "I like you, mister! You . . . uh . . . you got a squaw here with you?"

His eyes darkened, and he looked back at the soldiers. "No," he answered. She stood quietly beside him, still rubbing his hips, but he hardly noticed, for his mind was full of the ominous warning the battalion of soldiers presented. Most of the mounted men did not even wear uniforms. They were general riffraff—the worst kind of men to charge with handling Indians, which is what he was certain these men would end up doing once they were through with the Mexicans. An army of greedy white men who hated Indians

167

would be a grave threat indeed.

The procession seemed endless, as eight companies of mounted volunteers passed through. One blond-headed young man who rode by looked vaguely familiar to Zeke, but the dust was too thick to tell for certain. The young man had also noticed Zeke, and their eyes had held for a brief moment. But the soldier could not get out of formation, and he rode on. Two artillery companies followed the mounted soldiers, and a group of rangers from St. Louis brought up the rear of the huge army led by Colonel Kearny.

Zeke realized that all of these men were just a drop in the bucket. When the time came to take care of the Indians, the government could send out soldiers from the East who would vastly outnumber red men on the plains, and that seemed to him all the more reason to take Abbie back to Tennessee.

It took several minutes for the soldiers to pass. Then Zeke looked after them for a moment, while dust rolled over buildings and clothing, and people coughed and choked on it. Zeke paid no heed to the dust. His Indian senses felt a strange chill, as though a part of his life had just passed by, and the blond-headed soldier turned to look back once more. But the young man could no longer see Zeke, so he just shrugged and kept riding.

Zeke turned to look down at the painted woman who remained beside him. "Want a beer?" she asked him. "I'll buy."

Zeke glanced at the door of the bank where he had been headed and decided his business could wait a few more minutes. It had been a long day, and he was worried about all the soldiers infiltrating the West. A drink sounded good. "Why not?" he told the woman.

She smiled, her body tingling. This half-breed was indeed a handsome man, and a big man. She had never bedded an Indian, for to begin with they were not welcome in the white men's saloons. But it wouldn't matter if they were, for Indian men were not commonly known to cavort with prostitutes.

Something about pride and honor, she'd heard. But most whites said it was because their own squaws kept them too busy. Still, the half-breed who now followed her into the saloon was not with his squaw, and he just might have enough white blood in him to consider bedding her, while at the same time he was enough Indian for her to say she'd been to bed with one, something she had always been curious about.

She led him to the bar and ordered two beers. The bartender eyed Zeke and hesitated. "He's an Indian, Kate!" the man objected.

"He's also half white!" She contradicted him. "Give him a beer, Dennis, or I'll fire you!"

The man glowered at her, then turned to draw the beer. The woman called Kate turned to look up at Zeke.

"You own this place?" Zeke asked her.

She shrugged. "Half. My partner owns the other half." She eyed Zeke again as he took a long swallow of beer. "So. What brings you to Independence, half-breed?"

He set the glass down. "Horses. I raise and sell them. Appaloosas."

She smiled. "I've always heard Indians were good with horses—especially the Cheyenne. Could that be what your other half is?"

He nodded and smiled. "You guessed it."

She laughed lightly. "I'm getting pretty good at guessing those things! When I came out here from Illinois, I didn't know one red man from the next." She put a hand to his side and ran it up his ribs and over his chest, fingering the lacing of his deerskin shirt. "So . . . did you sell all of your horses?"

"I did."

She met his eyes. "Well, I guess that means you have some money in that parfleche you carry."

"I guess." He swallowed the rest of the beer.

More men began entering the saloon as the soldiers disappeared down the street, and the room became a din of voices and shouting as Kate held Zeke's eyes and continued to

169

toy with the lacing of his shirt.

"Is there . . . uh . . . anything you need before you go back? I mean, a man has needs, and . . . perhaps you've never been with a white woman."

He stood up straighter and pushed her hand away, keeping a firm but gentle hold on her arm. "I've been with one or two."

Her eyebrows went up. "Oh?" She smiled. "Other prostitutes, no doubt."

His eyes took on a dark look that frightened her, and she lost her smile. "Why would they have to be prostitutes?" he asked coldly. "Because I'm half Indian? Are you saying no decent white woman would sleep with an Indian?"

Her face paled. "Well, I, no. I didn't mean that. I just—"

He let go of her arm. "I know what you meant." He reached into a leather pouch that hung from his weapons belt and pulled out a coin, slapping it on the counter. "Thank you for the beer, but I pay my own way," he told her, his eyes glittering with anger. "I came in here because I wanted a beer, and because I knew if I walked in with you maybe I'd get one, but if I walked in alone I wouldn't get served, because my skin is burned dark from the sun and I dress like a Cheyenne. That's the only reason I came, lady. I didn't come in here because I was panting after a white woman. If I want a white woman I can get one, and I won't have to pay for her."

He turned to leave, but several men blocked his way at the door. "What did you mean by that remark, mister?" one of the men spoke up. "You aimin' to force yourself on some poor white woman?"

"Half-breed savage!" someone else sneered.

Zeke straightened, his body tensing for a fight, for he'd been through these things before. He almost hoped there would be one; he was so full of worry over Abbie and over the white migration and the soldiers that he felt ready to explode. It was people like these who would make life difficult for himself and Abbie if they lived in the white world. It was people like these

170

who had forced him to keep Abbie out on the plains, living the hard life of an Indian squaw.

"What I meant is none of your business." Zeke snarled. "I came to Independence to sell my horses and now I'm leaving. That's all there is to it. Now get out of my way!"

Another of the men looked at Kate. "Was he hurting you, Kate?"

She thought for a long moment. "No," she finally replied. "Let him go. I invited him in here, Len. He didn't ask for this."

"I think we should teach him a lesson before he leaves," another man grumbled. "He should never have took hold of your arm."

"It's all right, Casey."

"I say it ain't!" the one called Len returned. He started for Zeke, but before he set his foot down in the first step, Zeke pulled a knife, the smaller one of the two he always carried. Len hesitated and backed up.

"Indians and knives are a bad duo to go up against, Len," one of the other men spoke up.

"I'd listen to him, if I were you," Zeke told the one called Len. Then he saw a movement to his right, and Zeke's keen sense of warning and long experience at self-defense told him to act first and think later. He threw the small knife, and a man cried out when it landed in his upper arm before he could even draw the gun he had intended to use on Zeke.

"Oh, my God!" the man wailed, blood streaming down his arm.

By then Zeke had drawn his other knife, the big one, and he waved it menacingly at all of them.

"You fool!" Kate chided the gunman. "The Indian had a right to throw that knife! You had no reason to draw a gun on him!"

The others just stood and stared, awed by the speed and accuracy with which Zeke had thrown the weapon. Most of them had missed Zeke's movement altogether, and had not even realized he had drawn the knife until they saw it sticking in the gunman's arm. They all backed up farther, as the gunman slumped into a chair, his face paling and his eyes bulging. In the corner, a well-manicured, neatly dressed man sat watching the event, his dark eyes studying Zeke. The man's hands were small and lily white, and his hair was slicked back, not one piece of it out of place. The room had grown quiet and tense.

"Who the hell are you, mister?" one of the other men asked Zeke. Kate walked over to yank Zeke's smaller knife from the gunman's arm. She wiped the blood on the man's shirt and smiled, wanting to hate the half-breed but impressed by his skill.

"Name's Zeke," he told the others. He still waved the big knife, and did not remove his eyes from them for a moment. "Most call me Cheyenne Zeke."

"Cheyenne Zeke!" one of the men exclaimed. "I've heard about a Cheyenne Zeke. Supposed to be a real terror with"— the man glanced at the big blade—"with a knife."

"You heard right," Zeke sneered. He reached over and took the other knife back from Kate, his eyes still on the men. "Now, are you men going to let me through? Or do I have to show you those stories you heard about me were all true!"

They all swallowed and shuffled their feet; then they began moving aside. Zeke slowly approached the swinging doors of the saloon, looking like a sleek panther prowling around its enemy and ready to do battle. He could not resist stopping at the doorway and deftly cutting the string tie the one called Len wore tightly around his neck. Len's eyes grew wide with horror at the realization that the huge, ugly blade had been no more than a hair's distance from his throat.

"Thanks for the beer," Zeke sneered. He walked out, and Kate rushed to the door to watch him. The fringe of his buckskins swayed rhythmically, and her blood ran hot for him. But he was his own man, and was not easily seduced. The well-dressed man who had been sitting in the corner of the saloon pushed his way past her and followed Zeke.

Zeke banged on the door of the bank, wondering why it wasn't open on such a busy day. He stepped back to look at the sign again, wanting to be sure he was at the right place; then he banged on the door again. Finally it opened slowly, and Zeke looked into the face of one of the few white men he trusted. "Afternoon, Mr. Blake," Zeke greeted him.

"Zeke! I . . . I'm not open anymore, but come in, Zeke. It's good to see you. Good to see you." He shook Zeke's hand and Zeke went inside. The well-dressed man who had followed him from the saloon sat down on a bench outside the door of the bank. He would wait.

"How have you been, Zeke?" Mr. Blake was asking. "Come on in the back and sit down! How about a little whiskey?"

"One shot wouldn't hurt," Zeke answered. He followed the man into the back room, wondering why the place was closed and the front office was collecting dust. Blake offered Zeke a chair, smiling kindly at him and hurrying to a desk where he pulled out a drawer and took a flask of whiskey from it. Zeke watched him. Blake was a small, balding man who wore spectacles and Zeke was certain he could probably pick him up and throw him across the room. But he had no desire to harm Rodney Blake, for he was one of the few truly good white men Zeke had known and the one and only man in Independence who would do business with Indians.

"It's been a long time, Zeke," Blake was telling him. He handed Zeke a small glass with a half inch of whiskey in the bottom. "I wondered if you'd ever come back." He smiled and sat down. "Men like you . . . well . . . trouble seems to follow them, doesn't it?"

Zeke laughed lightly. "That it does, Mr. Blake."

Blake nodded. "Yes. That's why I thought perhaps . . . well . . . I thought you'd bought your ticket to that Hanging Road to the Sky."

173

They both laughed. "There have been many times when I thought that time had come," Zeke replied. "Fact is when I was here last I took on the job of leading a wagon train west to Oregon." His smile faded, as the pain of the memory of meeting Abigail on that trip shot through his heart unexpectedly. He looked down at his glass of whiskey and swirled it in his hands. "I . . . uh . . . I ended up getting married, Mr. Blake."

"Well! Congratulations!" Blake told him putting out his hand. "And who is the lucky Cheyenne maiden?"

Zeke met the man's eyes and did not shake his hand right away. "She's not Cheyenne," Zeke answered. "She's white."

The man's smile faded for a moment. "White?"

Zeke nodded. "Met her on the wagon train and couldn't keep my eyes off her. She ended up having the same feelings for me."

The man smiled again. "Well, where is she now? I'd like to meet this woman who snagged a wild bobcat like you!"

Zeke grinned sadly. "She . . . uh . . . she's with my people right now. She . . . lost a baby and was too weak to come with me."

"I see." The man put out his hand again. "Well, like I said, congratulations, Zeke. I'm sorry about the baby. I sincerely hope she'll recover and be able to have more children."

Zeke met his eyes and saw the sincerity in them. He shook the man's hand. "Thank you, Mr. Blake." He swallowed the rest of his whiskey. "I suppose you know why I'm here. I need my money. I got a good price for my horses, Mr. Blake, but the buffalo hunt wasn't very good this year and it looks to get worse. I probably won't get back here for a long time once I leave. I'll need everything I can get in order to buy supplies for my wife and my mother at Bent's Fort. With this war with Mexico and all, I expect prices will go wild."

Blake's face saddened and he sighed and sat back. "Zeke, I'll be straight with you. You may want to use that knife on me, but there isn't a damned thing I can do about it. I've got no money to give you, Zeke."

Zeke's eyes flashed with quick indignation. "What do you mean? I left three hundred dollars with you last year, and it was supposed to earn me some interest to boot. I need my money, Mr. Blake!"

Blake swallowed. "Zeke, it's this Mexican war. There was a run on the banks. The smaller ones, like my own, were left without a cent."

Zeke rose. "But . . . that can't be!"

"I'm afraid it can be, Zeke. We operate by investing money in land, stocks, whatever—in order to earn more money. We don't generally expect every customer to come in here wanting all of his money right away. But that's what happened. We handed out everything we had. And because of the war, some of our investments turned out to be worthless so that we couldn't recover much that way. I'm . . . I'm afraid I'm bankrupt, Zeke. I simply don't have your money. I swear to God that if I did I'd give it to you. I'm sorry, Zeke. Damned sorry."

Zeke's jaw flexed in anger. "What about the other banks? I've seen other ones in town that are open. Why aren't they closed down like you?"

"Big money back East. They got backing. Some of them were bailed out, Zeke. But me . . . well . . ." He looked down and swallowed. "Zeke, I did business with Indians. Men who do business with Indians are not included when it comes to getting help from Easterners."

There was a long moment of silence, and Zeke nodded. "I see," he said in a strained voice. Blake looked up at him.

"Zeke, there's a grand plan taking place. This is just the beginning. I . . . I feel like I should warn you that no one back East is going to want any good to come to the red man. And we're filling up fast with whites, Zeke."

Zeke walked to a window, wanting desperately to tear the room apart. "I've noticed," he answered. So, here was just one more reason why he never should have married Abigail. It

175

seemed that everyplace he turned, there was an ominous message about his future and the future of the Cheyenne. How could he involve the woman he loved in these things? And yet how could he live without Abbie! He swallowed. "I . . . uh . . . I appreciate your doing business with me, Mr. Blake, treating me as an equal."

"You are an equal, Zeke. We're all God's children."

Zeke laughed bitterly. "That is not the theory of most whites, Mr. Blake."

"I'm aware of that, and it shames me. I guess it's been that way since the beginning of time, Zeke. And I guess that's why men like me don't do well in business. A man has to be ruthless in this game, Zeke. I am simply not a ruthless man."

Zeke's eyes narrowed. "Well, I can be ruthless, if that's what it takes!" he replied. "The whites will find out just how ruthless the red man can be, Mr. Blake, once the red man is pushed too far!"

He whirled, and Rodney Blake was glad that he personally was not one of those to whom Cheyenne Zeke wanted to show his ruthlessness. Zeke stepped close, towering over him. "Good luck, Mr. Blake."

"I don't need the luck, Zeke. You do." Their eyes held in understanding, and then Zeke walked to the door. "What will you do, Mr. Blake?"

"I'm going back East. What about you? What will you do?"

Zeke sighed. "Raise more horses, I guess. Find some odd jobs. I need the money bad. I've got a woman to think about now."

"God go with you, Zeke."

Zeke nodded. "May *Maheo* walk with you, Mr. Blake. Your heart is as true as the red man's."

Zeke walked out of the back room and through the main lobby of the darkened bank, his mind racing with disappointment and confusion. His trip to Independence was to have been a happy one. He had intended to bring Abbie with him and treat her royally. He'd planned to sell his horses and get his

176

money from the bank, along with the interest it had earned. But Abbie lay weak and ill somewhere out on the Plains, and his money was gone. At least he had the money from the sale of the horses, but the addition of the three hundred dollars he had left in Mr. Blake's care would have gone much farther. He walked to the front door and entered the busy street.

He hated it! He hated the noise and confusion of the white world! He hated their attitude toward him and their intrusion into Indian Territory. He started for the stables where his horse was being held when a voice called out to him.

"Cheyenne Zeke!"

Zeke turned to see the neatly dressed, dark-eyed man who had been waiting for him on the bench outside the bank.

"What do you want?" Zeke snapped.

The man grinned and walked closer, putting out his hand. "Name's Mack. Jonathan Mack."

Zeke looked down at the hand that was no bigger than a woman's. He did not put out his own hand. He did not like this Jonathan Mack. He was too smooth and too neat. Mack looked him up and down and nodded, retrieving his hand. "As you wish," he told Zeke. He glanced at the bank door and back at Zeke. "I . . . uh . . . thought perhaps you might be in need of some money."

Zeke leaned against the post of an overhang. "Is that so? Now how would you know that, Mr. Mack?"

Mack stuck his thumbs into the pockets of his satin vest. "Well, Zeke, it's well known around here that most small banks are out of business because of the war. I noticed you going inside there and I . . . well . . . I thought perhaps you had come to get some money." He laughed lightly. "That's why most people go into a bank, now isn't it?"

Zeke eyed him narrowly. "I don't suppose you knew that the man who runs this bank dealt with Indians, and that's why the bankers back East wouldn't help him out?"

Mack's eyebrows went up. "Is that so?" He frowned and shook his head. "That's too bad."

177

Zeke sneered. "I'm sure you think so." He turned to leave.

"Zeke!" the man called out. Zeke turned to eye him impatiently.

"What the hell do you want, Mr. Mack?" he asked.

"How much did you lose?"

Zeke looked him over, repelled by the man's smoothness. "Three hundred dollars plus interest. What's it to you?"

The man pulled out a thin cigar and offered it to Zeke. "I'll pay you six hundred—to do a job for me," he replied.

Zeke frowned and studied him. He knew by instinct this was not a man to be trusted, but he needed the money badly. Six hundred dollars was a lot of money, and if he could do this service for this milky sap of a white man and then be rid of him, it might be worth it. He walked closer to Mack.

"What kind of a job?" he asked.

Mack smiled and held his cigar closer. "They're very good, Zeke. Try one."

Zeke took the cigar cautiously and Mack lit it for him.

"Come and sit down," Mack told Zeke.

"I'd rather stand."

Mack shrugged. "As you wish."

Zeke puffed the cigar. Mack was right. It was very good.

"I saw you in the saloon a bit ago," Mack told Zeke. "You're quite good with that knife," he added with a grin.

"So?"

"Well, I'm looking for a good man, one who knows the area well between here and Santa Fe. You know that country?"

Zeke puffed the cigar again. "I do. But you don't need a good man for that. Just follow the Santa Fe Trail and the soldiers. They'll take you right to the place."

Mack smiled. "You don't understand. To begin with, scouts are easy to find, I'll admit. But they're all white men, you see. I need an Indian, a man who thinks like an Indian, converses with the Indians, understands Indians. I have two wagons that have to go to Santa Fe, Zeke, and I don't want the Santa Fe Trail used. I need a man who knows the back country, one who can take the wagons south of the Trail through Oklahoma Territory and northern Texas, a man who knows the Indians in that area, knows the country. I figure a man like you, well, he'd get on better with whatever Indians he might run up against, and he'd know how to handle them better than the white scouts. But more than that, I figure a man like you would know how to avoid the Indians altogether, because you'd understand them, how they think, where they go and all."

"I don't understand what you're driving at. Why can't you just use the Trail?"

"Because we're at war with Mexico. Right now nothing attracts more attention than the Santa Fe Trail, Zeke. I don't want attention. My wagons hold valuable merchandise, you see. Now, if I take them on the Santa Fe Trail, they're much more likely to attract attention from Indians and Mexicans, simply because of all the raiding that's been going on along that route. Even if I traveled with soldiers, I'd not be safe, at least not with the wagons along. Those soldiers are going to attract attention, Zeke. They're very likely to be attacked by Mexicans, and if they are, the Mexicans would confiscate my wagons. I don't want that to happen. That's why I think they'd be safer if someone took them through the back country and traveled in obscurity. He could take the best route he knew to avoid both Indians and Mexicans. Well, I just had a feeling you might be the man for the job. How about it? As you said, six hundred dollars is a lot of money."

Zeke pushed his leather hat back from his forehead. "Just what is in these wagons, Mr. Mack?"

Mack grinned. "I intend to open a chain of saloons in Santa Fe, Zeke. I know that in the long run the States will win this war, and when they do, Santa Fe will boom again. I've invested a lot of money in this enterprise, and I'm on my way there myself. When I open, I intend to open big. The wagons carry the parts to a very expensive piano, Zeke, as well as whiskey— the best whiskey, if you know what I mean. You have an honest look about you. I think I can trust you to know that. I want to be honest with you in return and not deceive you about the contents of the wagons."

Zeke frowned. "Good whiskey is like gold to the Indians, Mr. Mack. If I'm carrying whiskey I might as well be carrying precious gems. It's a hell of a risk. It would take more than six hundred dollars to make me do it."

Mack fingered his cigar. "All right then. How about eight hundred?"

Zeke smelled deceit, but the recent loss of his hard-earned savings pressed on his mind. "You sure that's all that's in those wagons?" he asked Mack.

"As God is my witness," the man replied with a nod. "Piano parts and whiskey. The piano is worth five thousand dollars, and the whiskey is worth more than that when you figure its value when sold by the glass. This is going to be a very posh saloon, Zeke, and confidentially, part of the reason I am getting my things there the back way is because I know of a rival businessman who is planning the same type of enterprise. I intend to beat him there and get set up before he does. Taking the back way will insure my supplies get there safely. My rival will think I haven't even started shipment yet."

"You going along?" Zeke asked.

Mack grinned. "Goodness, no! I'm not cut out for that kind of rough going," he answered. "I'll take a stage along the Santa Fe Trail. A stage coach is not nearly as attractive to the eyes of raiders as the merchant supply wagons, Zeke. That's why I'll take a stage to Santa Fe, and you'll take the wagons through back country and meet me there."

"What if I don't make it?"

The man shrugged. "I know the risks. If you don't make it, I'm out my investment. That will be my problem."

"I reckon it will. But what's to keep me from selling the whiskey to Mexicans for gold and never showing up? You'd never know the difference."

Mack grinned. "I know people," he replied. "Keeping his word is important to an Indian. You're a man of your word. I see it in those Indian eyes of yours. You won't betray me." He looked Zeke up and down. "So, is it a deal?"

"I'll have to think on it. I have a woman waiting for me out there on the Plains. I have to get back to her. If I'm gone too long she'll worry."

"So? Send your squaw a message. Surely you can find someone among all these scouts and trappers and riffraff who'll get a message to her. The trip would take, oh, a month, I suppose. Then of course you would have to allow for return time. Tell her six to eight weeks."

Zeke frowned and turned away, puffing the cigar again. "I don't know if I can leave her for that long."

"Good heavens, man, squaw women get along fine on their own. They're a hardy lot!"

Zeke quelled his anger at the remark. It would do no good to bother telling this man his squaw was not a Cheyenne woman. He turned to face him again. "I don't trust you, Mack. And you can bet that if there's some trick to this you'll pay. You say you know your men, so you'd best know I'm not a man to mess with. Where are your wagons?"

"I hired some men to watch them. They're stored behind the livery right now."

"All right. I'll meet you there in the morning. I want to inspect them. Then I'll give you my answer. And I'd have to be allowed to choose the other driver myself."

"As you wish."

"If I do that, he'll have to be paid good, too."

"Eight hundred for you and four hundred for him then."

Zeke thought about it for a moment. "I'll give you my decision in the morning," he told Mack.

"Good. I hope it will be yes. I think you're a good man for the job."

Zeke eyed him suspiciously for a moment, then nodded. "Thanks for the cigar," he replied. He walked down the steps and out into the street, stepping over horse dung and jumping mud puddles as he headed toward the stockyards where he had sold his horses.

His mind raced with indecision. Eight hundred dollars was a tremendous amount of money. It was a very tempting offer indeed—one that he could hardly turn down. He wished his good friend, Olin Wales, was around. He hadn't seen his fur trapping friend since they'd gone separate ways after Zeke had gone back to Fort Bridger to fetch Abbie. Wales had accompanied Zeke the year before when he'd scouted for Abbie's wagon train, and he was a good man to have along—one of the few white men Zeke felt free to call friend. They had risked their lives for one another more than once and saved one another from death. But he had not run into Olin this trip. It was hard to tell where a man like Olin might be at any time. He was the wandering sort, a man who lived off the land as well as any Indian.

But if Zeke was to take on this business deal with Jonathan Mack, he wanted a trustworthy driver with him. The only other man who came close to Olin Wales in dependability was Luther Grimes. "Grimey," he was nicknamed, mainly because he had an aversion to baths. But the man's smell was bearable on a dangerous journey; for he was good with a gun, he'd fought Indians, and he was honest. That was the most important thing to Zeke. Grimey would go to his death for a friend, and Zeke was his friend. They had hunted and trapped together, fought Crow together, and shared intimate stories.

Grimey knew Zeke's background, and his only flaw was his love of telling stories about Cheyenne Zeke's knife—often to Zeke's embarrassment. For Grimey loved to exaggerate and add color and excitement to his stories. The man would literally strut when he called Zeke his friend. Grimey would be a good partner on this trip, if Zeke could find him. He had left him at the stockyards, where Grimey had brought in a herd of horses for a nearby rancher. The two of them had made plans to meet later at a tavern south of Independence where Indians could be served with no trouble, and there they intended to swap stories.

182

To his relief, Grimey was still at the stockyards; and when Zeke called out to him, Grimey broke into a quick smile. As the short, wiry man hastily walked toward him, Zeke ignored his soiled buckskins and yellowed teeth.

"Hey, my half-breed friend! You said we would meet tonight at the tavern. What brings you back here?" Grimey walked up and shook Zeke's hand.

"How would you like to go to Santa Fe, Grimey, through Comanche and Apache back country?"

Grimey raised his eyebrows. "Sounds interesting!" He removed his hat and ran a hand through thick, curly black hair. "Tell me more."

"A man just offered me eight hundred dollars to take two wagons of expensive whiskey and piano parts to Santa Fe. I'd need another driver. He's offered four hundred dollars for the second man. I can't think of a better partner than you, Grimey. What do you say?"

Grimey shrugged. "I don't know the details, but what the hell? If Cheyenne Zeke thinks we ought to do it, I'm game. I have nothing better to do than risk my neck riding through Apache country. At least I'd be with an Indian, eh?"

Zeke grinned. "I'll give you all the details when we meet tonight. I just needed to know if you'd consider it. I'm thinking on it strongly, Grimey. I lost all my savings in the run on the banks. I need the money. I don't exactly trust the man who hired me, but for one trip and all that money, I'm willing to risk it."

"If you are willing, then so am I, my friend. Count me in."

Zeke smiled more. "Thanks, Grimey. I have to find somebody to take a message to—" He stopped. He had not told Grimey yet about Abbie. "A message to my people. Let them know I won't be back as soon as I thought. They always worry when I come to Independence where all the white folks are."

Grimey laughed. "Hey, I know a man who says he is heading for Fort Atkinson from here. You write your message and give it to him. There are always Cheyenne around that fort. They can find a runner for you to take the message from there to. your people. No doubt this time of year they will head in that direction."

Zeke nodded, feeling better all the time about the trip. With eight hundred dollars he could settle down on a piece of land—maybe near Bent's Fort. He could build Abbie a cabin there. Perhaps they could be together and he could give her the comforts of a white man's dwelling, yet they would still be among the Cheyenne most of the time. There were few white settlers down on the Arkansas, and she would be safe near Bent's Fort. It seemed as though his answers were finally coming. How he longed to see Abbie and ask her about it! But that would have to wait. It would be a long time before he saw his Abbie again. The waiting would be difficult and he worried about how she would fare alone with the Cheyenne until he returned.

Ten

Abbie sat astride her Appaloosa, riding across the broad plains of Kansas Territory toward Nebraska Territory. The bands of Cheyenne and Arapahos with whom she rode seemed to grow daily in numbers, as more joined them on their journey northward. Travois tracks, prints of unshod hooves, and moccasin tracks left a trail nearly a half-mile wide behind the migrating bands, as hundreds of men, women, and children rode or walked toward the rendezvous point with the Sioux for the Sun Dance celebration.

For most of the day, every day, some rode and some walked, uncomplaining. For such a large number of people, they were amazingly silent as they traveled, partly because this was not a time for visiting, but rather a time for moving. Energy must be saved. And more importantly, because too much noise might attract uncooperative whites or dreaded soldiers or enemy Ute, Crow, or Pawnee.

Braves rode in front, sitting straight and silent on painted ponies, carrying a barrage of weapons, war lances, and shields. Abbie smiled with admiration for these Cheyenne warriors. They did not know the meaning of fear, and although most of their women had to walk and perform most of the hard daily labor, the men were willing to fight and die for them if need be. A Cheyenne woman need not fear when she was with her man. And there was a beautiful, almost childish abandon in the men—a need to ride free, to feel action, and to show their

185

women just how courageous and skilled they could be. They played constant war games and relished a good hunt, and at night the talk around council fires was full of excitement over the upcoming Sun Dance, where young warriors would display their courage and boys would become men. Some would change their names because of the visions they would experience while in great pain.

This much Abbie knew, although she was not yet certain just exactly what would take place and was even more uncertain as to whether she wanted to know the details. But at least she would discover what this strange ritual was that Zeke and so many of the other warriors had put themselves through.

Zeke! She thought of him with a sad longing that brought a heavy ache to her chest. She had hurt him that morning after her attack, astonished and stunned him by voicing feelings he did not know were there, fears and doubts she herself had not even known were buried in her subconscious, not until Dancing Moon's horrible attack. Perhaps it was Dancing Moon's viciousness that had reminded Abbie just how thin the line between gentleness and ruthlessness was in these people. Their passions ran high, their thirst for vengeance was keen, and they considered violence and bloodletting commonplace.

But now that Abbie was healing, her fears were subsiding, and she saw a beauty and gentleness about the Cheyenne and Arapaho that far outweighed their ruthlessness. It was true that Dancing Moon's attack had been vicious; however she was only one person, outnumbered by a host of friendly, stalwart, chaste women who doted on their little brown children and tended to their husbands needs with silent and uncomplaining faithfulness—women like Gentle Woman, who had nursed and babied Abigail as though she were her own daughter. There were those who had painted her tipi and patiently taught her the proper way to clean the buffalo hides, to tan them and stitch them together to make a home, clothing, shoes, war shields, parfleches, and the countless other items made by these people who knew not the meaning of waste.

Even the men had a gentle side. She had known Cheyenne Zeke's gentleness, and could tell by the reaction of most of the squaws to their men that although the men showed no affection in front of others, there was a generous serving of it behind closed tipis. Abbie constantly felt the guarding and watchful eyes of Cheyenne men on her, especially Swift Arrow's, since he had assumed the responsibility of protecting her, despite the fact that Abigail knew he would much rather she were not with them at all.

She felt a new closeness to all of them since her attack and the loss of her baby. The Cheyenne had a great affection for children, and they did not take a miscarriage lightly. She had learned that the small bit of life she had expelled, hardly recognizable, had been wrapped and placed, facing the heavens and the sun, high on the scaffold that would guide its soul to the great Hanging Road in the sky so that animals could not get to it. It was then that Abigail took on new feelings for these people, for their dead were always honored, and the elderly and even the few among them who were mentally afflicted, were treated with gentle patience and great affection.

To the Cheyenne there was a reason for all life, and every living soul was a part of the Great Spirit's grand scheme. Humans, animals, and plants were all combined into one spirit so that there was really no distinction. Abbie struggled to really comprehend this outlook through all her waking hours. While she was recovering, she had learned much from her long walks with Gentle Woman, and in spite of her great longing to see Zeke, now she was glad she had decided to move alone among his people. It was the only way she could rid herself of whatever fears and doubts she might have, the only way she could face the Cheyenne on her own and thus face whatever trials might arise because of their different life-style.

It had been fourteen days since Abbie's attack. Other than the slight soreness around the pink scar on her abdomen and the faint tracings of nail marks on her face, she had apparently recovered. The bleeding from the miscarriage had stopped. But she felt empty and barren. She had so wanted the baby for Zeke! She prayed constantly that no damage had been done that would prohibit her from having another, and she prayed that Zeke would still want her when he returned. For most of the past two weeks Abbie had ridden on a travois, until yesterday and today. She did not like appearing weak, and although the People understood her affliction, she was anxious to get on her feet and fend for herself.

She felt the pride of a true Cheyenne squaw now as she rode her handsome Appaloosa. To the Cheyenne, Zeke was a wealthy man because of his horses, so Abigail could ride and not feel obligated to walk like many of the other squaws. But she decided that they had done much for her, and for this reason she walked at intervals and, in turn, let the other women ride her horse, to give them a break from the long journey on foot. She also shared whatever horses there were from Zeke's herd that had been broken for riding. It was the least she could do, and she knew that these people would appreciate her kindness.

The big Appaloosa she rode was gentle with her, and it made her think of Zeke. Everything made her think of Zeke. He would be in Independence now. Perhaps he had already left to come back. Her heart pounded at the thought. She had voiced her worries to Gentle Woman that perhaps Zeke would have trouble finding them, but Gentle Woman had only laughed.

"Zeke always finds us. He knows where we will be going. Do not worry about that one, Abigail."

Abbie smiled. It was silly for her to worry about Zeke. He would come back to her as he always did. He had come for her at Fort Bridger, and before that he had come for her and saved her from the outlaws. He would come back this time. He would come back. He had to come back!

A man on a painted pony broke loose from the group of warriors in the lead and galloped back toward Abbie. She recognized the animal as Swift Arrow's before the young man had ridden up beside her. He turned his mount again and walked it slowly next to hers.

"You are still able to ride?" he asked her, his eyes looking ahead. "You are not tired?"

"I'm fine."

He turned to look at her, his eyes quickly scanning her slim white legs that showed beneath the tunic. He could understand how Zeke could love this white one, and then again in many ways he could not.

"You are lucky," he told Abbie. "Your husband is wealthy and you can ride. Do you like the horse I picked for you from the herd?"

"It's a good horse, Swift Arrow. Very gentle but sturdy."

The man nodded. "The Cheyenne raise the best horses! And Cheyenne men are the best riders!"

Abbie smiled. Cheyenne men loved to brag, yet they did not do it in a truly conceited manner. Their statements were just plain fact. And although they competed in games and in battle, there was no real jealousy felt among them; theirs were just proud, friendly challenges. There was no great exaggerating when they shared their stories of conquest around council fires, for it was a strict rule that they tell only the truth, and if they were caught lying or stretching the truth, they were promptly ridiculed and chastised and shamed.

"We go north now," he told her. "For the months when the leaves are green and the grass is dry. Then we return to *Hinta-Nagi,* the Ghost Timbers, for the winter months."

Abbie did not reply, but only waited as Swift Arrow continued to look ahead. "What will you do with Zeke's things if he does not return?" he asked her.

Abbie frowned at this strange question and turned to look at him, but his eyes remained straight ahead. His bronze arms glistened in the sun, a silver band tightly decorating the hard bicep of his upper right arm, and he wore many coup feathers at the base of his braid.

"I . . . I don't think about him not returning," she answered.

189

"It is wise to think of such things. What would you do if he did not come back to us?"

Abbie's heart tightened. "I . . . I suppose I'd . . . I'd give all but a few of Zeke's belongings to you, Swift Arrow, as his oldest brother. And then I'd have you take me to Bent's Fort . . . or maybe Fort Laramie . . . and I'd find a way to get back home . . . to Tennessee." Her eyes teared at the terrible thought of Zeke not coming back. "I . . . have an aunt there."

Swift Arrow halted his horse and grasped the reins of her own mount, making her stop. The others walked on, and Swift Arrow stayed back with Abbie.

"I do not say these things to make you sad," he told her. "I say them to make you think." He waved his arm across the skyline ahead of them. "Look out there and tell Swift Arrow that you could leave this land, or that you could even leave our people. Tell Swift Arrow that you could go back to that place and forget us, forget this great land, and the buffalo and the eagle. Tell Swift Arrow that you could truly do this, whether with Zeke or without him."

Their eyes held in a moment of understanding. "I don't know, Swift Arrow. I just . . . don't know."

"I say you do know. I say already your heart belongs here. I say already you know what you will do. You know what your decision will be when Zeke comes for his woman."

She suddenly realized he was trying to help her decide.

"Thank you," she told him quietly. She thought a trace of a smile passed his lips, but Swift Arrow did not smile easily, and it was hard to tell. He let go of her horse and they started walking the animals again.

"Do you know that if Zeke does not return, you will belong to me?" he asked, suppressing a grin when she jerked her horse to a halt again. He turned to look at her surprised eyes.

"I would belong to no one but myself!" she answered defiantly.

"You are Zeke's woman. I am Zeke's brother and you have been given over to my care. I could make you my woman, if

I wished."

She raised her chin and got her horse into motion. "Not without my consent. Besides, you'd no more want me for a wife than you'd want a prickly porcupine!"

To her surprise he laughed loudly, a rare sound from the man's lips. "You are right!" he answered. He charged his horse forward for a short way, then circled and came back to her. He frowned and rode beside her again. "Do you mean Swift Arrow would not be a good husband? That you would not be proud of him?"

Her heart raced. He was somehow testing her, and she wanted to give him the right answers. "I . . . I can't think of a better man other than Zeke," she answered. "But white women can't just go to another man for the sake of being practical, Swift Arrow. There has to be . . . well . . . there has to be love . . . feelings."

He eyed her slyly. "You have no feelings for Swift Arrow?"

She rolled her eyes in exasperation. "Of course I do! You're Zeke's brother. But I don't have . . . 'wifely' feelings." She began to redden and Swift Arrow began to chuckle, and she realized he truly was teasing her, a game the Cheyenne were very good at playing. She was surprised he had come back to speak to her at all, for Cheyenne men used few words, except when bragging about a hunt or a battle, and Swift Arrow had said no more than ten words to her during the entire trip. Perhaps Swift Arrow was finally learning to like and accept Cheyenne Zeke's white woman.

They rode on silently a while longer until Abbie spoke up again. "Why don't you marry again, Swift Arrow?" she asked him. "You should find another woman to relieve your loneliness."

His face hardened. "Who said Swift Arrow is lonely?"

She swallowed. "I did!" she answered boldly. "I can see right through you."

His jaws flexed and he stared ahead. She was afraid she had made him angry, but then he spoke up quietly. "I want no

191

other woman," he told her. "I want only to be a great dog soldier—the best! The best dog soldiers had no wives."

"I see." She rode quietly, waiting for him to speak again.

"I will sleep near your tipi again tonight," he told her.

"I appreciate that, Swift Arrow. I feel very safe with you around."

"You think about what I said," he told her. "White woman's heart does not lie just with my brother. It lies with this land, with *Escceheman*, Grandmother Earth, and with these people. Each day you will see this more." He trotted ahead of her. "*Hai!*" he shouted then, letting out a war whoop and galloping ahead to the other men. Abbie watched him, a proud, free man. If Zeke's forebodings about the future of the Indians came true, it would go very hard on men like Swift Arrow.

Zeke and Grimey drove the two huge supply wagons out of Independence. Zeke had checked the contents of the wagons' high, boxed-in beds and had been satisfied. He saw nothing but piano parts and whiskey, just as Jonathan Mack had said he would. But he still felt uneasy, and would be glad when this strange delivery was made. The eight hundred dollars would feel good in his pocket.

Jonathan Mack smiled as he watched the wagons roll away, their false bottoms filled with rifles and dynamite. He brushed off the lapels of his expensive suitcoat and hurried after a man to whom he had seen Zeke hand a note before leaving.

"Mister!" he shouted, rushing up and putting a hand on the man's shoulder. The bearded, beaver-hatted trapper turned, frowning curiously.

"Yeah?" he asked impatiently.

"I . . . uh . . . I just wondered what Cheyenne Zeke handed you," Mack asked him. "You see, that shipment he just left with is mine and it's very valuable. I don't know the man very well, and . . . well, I just need to be sure he hasn't tricked me."

The man chuckled. "Just a note to his woman, that's all. I'm takin' it to Fort Atkinson to find a runner to take it to his people—so's they know he's gonna' be gettin' back a little late. Don't worry about it, mister. Zeke's a good man."

"I see. Well, did you plan on leaving right away?"

The man shrugged. "In the mornin', I guess. What's it to you?"

Mack smiled. "I'd like to buy you a drink, that's all. By taking that note for Cheyenne Zeke you're helping him, which in turn helps me. I appreciate your doing that."

The burly mountain man licked his lips at the thought of a free drink. "Why not?" he replied. "You look like a man of means. I don't mind lettin' you foot the bill." He laughed heartily and nearly made Mack choke when he slapped the much smaller man on the back.

They walked together toward a saloon of Mack's choosing, and soon Jonathan Mack was pouring free whiskey down the trapper's throat. But the trapper did not notice the white powder that was slipped into his last drink, and moments later this burly, unsuspecting mountain man slumped to the floor. As men gathered around him, Mack bent over him, feigning concern. He checked the man over and then looked up at the others.

"Go get the coroner," he told them. "This man is dead. Must have had a heart attack."

Someone ran out, and the saloon keeper and two other men carried the dead man to a back room to wait for the coroner. In that town of migrant, busy people, no one was too concerned over the death. The men in the saloon returned to their drinking and gambling, and no one noticed Jonathan Mack go into the room where the dead man lay and slip a note from the trapper's pocket. Jonathan Mack wanted no connections discovered; he wanted no one to know what had ever happened to Cheyenne Zeke. He opened the note carefully.

"Dear Abbie," it read. "Lost the money I had saved. Run on the banks. Got a job taking supply wagons to Santa Fe. Pays

193

real good, Abbie. I have no choice but to take it. So I won't be seeing you for two months or longer. I don't know if I can stand being away from you that long. Please wait for me. I will be back like always. I love you, Abbie. That is the only thing I know. I will have a lot of money to take good care of you, if you still want me when I get back."

"Abbie," Mack mumbled to himself. "That sounds like a white woman's name." He arched his eyebrows and shrugged; then he took his thin cigar and held it to the paper until the note caught fire. "I'm afraid you won't be returning to your precious Abbie, Mr. Cheyenne Zeke," he said with a smile. He threw the note into an ashtray and watched it burn before he left to catch a stagecoach to Santa Fe.

They lined up silently along the ridge to stare down with wonder at the seemingly endless line of white-topped "houses on wheels," below.

"*Katum!*" Swift Arrow swore under his breath. There seemed to be too many wagons to count.

"*E-have-se-va!*" a frowning old warrior beside him uttered.

The Indians sat unmoving, and Abbie could see riders below galloping up and down the line of wagons, shouting. They had spotted the huge Cheyenne and Arapaho tribe and were obviously worried, for they drew up their wagons and began forming two circles.

Abbie almost laughed. What a distorted view the white men had of the Indian! She remembered a time when she, too, was afraid of the "wild savages."

A burly man wearing buckskins headed up the hill toward them, carrying a piece of white cloth on a stick. Swift Arrow began grumbling something and quickly whirled his horse, riding over to Abbie, who had sneaked up to the edge to get a better look.

"Go back with the women!" he said sternly but quietly. "This man see you, he make much trouble for us! Go back and

194

hide your white legs! *Hopo! Hopo!*"

Abbie quickly obeyed, edging her horse around and moving in to mingle among the other women. She threw a blanket over her legs. Gentle Woman hurried to her side and handed her another blanket.

"Put this over your shoulders to hide your arms!" she warned. "And keep your head down!"

Abbie got herself covered just before the scout reached the tribe, and her heart pounded with excitement.

"I come in peace," the scout said to Deer Slayer, Zeke's Cheyenne stepfather. Deer Slayer nodded.

"We want the same," he told the scout. "We want only to pass through. We go north."

The scout eyed them warily. "You aren't here to beg?"

Swift Arrow jerked as though someone had hit him, and Deer Slayer put a hand on his son's arm.

"We are not beggars," Deer Slayer said calmly. "We go north to hunt in the cool mountains during the season of the dry grass."

The scout frowned. "You speak good English for a savage."

"I learn from my woman. She learn from white man."

The scout grinned and Swift Arrow was having trouble controlling himself, for he knew what the white man was thinking about his mother. The scout noticed Zeke's Appaloosas at the rear of the migrating tribe, and he looked questioningly at Deer Slayer.

"Where'd you get them horses?" he asked.

"They belong to my stepson, a half-blood called Cheyenne Zeke."

The scout straightened at the name. "I've heard of him."

"I am sure you have!" Swift Arrow said haughtily. "He is well known among your kind—good with the blade!"

"We want to go now," Deer Slayer interrupted. "You take your wagons and go, and we will cross the Great Medicine Road."

The scout shook his head. "You might wait until we're in a

195

straight line and then attack us."

"We have women and children among us!" Deer Slayer replied irritatedly. "We are not a war party!"

The scout backed his mount. "Just the same, you go first. Soon as you're out of sight, we'll head out."

"And what is to keep your people from shooting at us?" Swift Arrow asked suspiciously.

"I'll see that they don't," the scout answered.

Swift Arrow grunted in sarcastic laughter. "Remember how many of us there are!" he replied warningly. "The Cheyenne have always been friendly to the white man—at least so far!"

The scout nodded. "I'll remember. Give me a few minutes. I'll signal you."

Abbie's horse snorted and tossed its head, drawing the scout's attention. She kept her face down, but the man noticed her hair was slightly wavy and not jet black like that of the other squaws. Her dark tresses had a reddish glint in the sun.

Abbie felt weak with dread, and Swift Arrow's hand tightened on the knife at his waist. It seemed like hours rather than seconds that the scout stared at Abbie, but he finally looked back at Deer Slayer.

"Looks to me like another one of your squaw's got mixed up with a white man," he said with a wicked glint in his eyes. "That another half-breed over there?"

"Her grandfather was a white trapper," Deer Slayer lied. "She is no concern of yours, and we grow impatient!"

When the scout nodded and turned his horse, Abbie took a deep breath of relief. After several minutes the scout signaled Deer Slayer, and Deer Slayer and other band chiefs motioned to the others to proceed. As they started forward, Abbie rode carefully so her blankets would not fall. She prayed no one on the wagon train would panic and so something foolish. She remembered some of the people who had been on the train she had taken the year before and how easily they had assumed all Indians were out to attack, murder, and steal.

She glanced at the wagons as she passed by, catching a

196

glimpse here and there of white women and full dresses. She wondered if she would ever dress that way again. The sight of the wagons caused a strange, sad ache in her heart, for they brought back memories of the loss of her family the year before and these combined with the beautiful memory of meeting and falling in love with Cheyenne Zeke.

No, she would not wear hoops and slat bonnets and full dresses again. The tunic was much more comfortable. They rode on, and the wagon train faded from view. Abbie headed north, for the summer rendezvous.

Zeke lay listening to the plaintive cry of the coyote, howling its lonesome wail. It seemed to epitomize the loneliness in his own heart. He stared up at the brilliant display of stars, wondering when his own soul would walk that Milky Road to the Great Spirit. And what would Abbie do if he did not come back to her.

Abbie! He saw her in the stars, felt her in the softness of the buffalo robe he lay on. How he longed to touch her again, to taste of her breasts and caress the sweetness between her legs; to hear her whisper his name and whimper at the ecstasy of taking him into herself. Abbie! Would he share her that way again? Or would he lose his white squaw to the life she was born to live? Perhaps just as he could not survive solely in the white man's world, neither could she survive solely in the Indian world. Abbie! Sweet Abbie! Such a child, yet such a woman. He needed her now. Needed to hold something.

But there was nothing here to hold, nothing here but the cold, arid night air of northern Texas. And the only other human being close by was a smelly scout named Grimey, who sat near the fire now playing his harmonica.

Zeke felt as empty as the land he was in. This part of Texas was not plush and mountainous like Utah Territory. And it was not soft and rolling like the Kansas and Nebraska Territories. It was a hard, brutal land, full of rock and dust and

197

thorny bushes that cut the legs of the mules that pulled the wagons. Zeke hated seeing his own horse's legs so badly scratched. He cared very deeply for his mounts and treated them with great love and tenderness. He had never quite understood the attitude of his fellow red men, the Apaches, toward their horses. They often rode their mounts until the animals fell from exhaustion, and then they sometimes killed and ate them. But that was the Apache way. He was only vaguely familiar with the "ghosts of the Southwest." That was how most people thought of the elusive and wily Apaches, who could disappear in places where it would seem no man could hide. They were crafty and distant, difficult to find and even more difficult to get to know. But they were Indians, and Zeke felt a kinship with them. He wondered how long it would be before the Cheyenne and Apache would perhaps join together in one cause, to preserve their right to exist in a land fast filling with whites. A kinship among all tribes, even the enemy Crow and Pawnee, might be necessary in the future. But for now, few Cheyenne, perhaps none, had ever even seen an Apache Indian.

Grimey stopped playing his harmonica and looked over at his half-breed friend. "You got that white squaw of yours on your mind, friend?"

Zeke smiled and sighed. "Mostly. I hope she gets that note, or she'll think I deserted her."

Grimey grinned. "She will get it. Clawson is a good man. He will get it to Fort Atkinson."

Silence hung for a moment in the cold, night air.

"Hey, half-breed," Grimey spoke up again. "You think she can live with the Cheyenne like that? A woman, at least a white woman, she likes to dress up, you know? Wear them pretty petticoats and fix up her hair and dance. You know?"

Zeke put a piece of chewing tobacco in his mouth. "I know."

"I think you are wrong—about not bein' able to live among the whites."

"You don't know what I've seen, Grimey. Sure, there's

some like you—good ones. Maybe there's more than I think. But it only takes one or two who are simple-minded and dead set against a mixed marriage, just one or two who brand a white woman who does such a thing, and they can make life miserable for that woman. I know the hurt that can bring, and I don't want that to happen to Abbie. Problem is, there's a lot more than just one or two people like that out here."

"Mmm-hmm. That's for sure, friend." Grimey chuckled. "Hey, I know you, Cheyenne Zeke. I remember when you said as how you'd never get mixed up again with no white woman. And you are a very strong man—able to control yourself 'cause of that Indian blood. This girl—she must be something. She must have all but knocked you over the head and dragged you away."

Zeke stared up at the stars. "She might as well have, Grimey. I tried. I really tried; but, damn it, she lost her whole family and there she was, lost and alone, and in love with a crazy half-breed."

"Hey, when we get through with this trip, maybe I will go along back with you and meet this girl."

"You're welcome to come along. I have to tell you, though, after that attack and losing a baby and all, it might be like you said. Might be she'll be wanting to wear those pretty dresses and dance and do up her hair. Might be she'll have decided to go back to Tennessee."

Grimey scooted down under his bedroll. "I don't think so, friend. She sounds like a strong woman, a good woman. And once this land gets into your blood, man or woman, it is not so easy to go back to the old life. Besides, she is married to Cheyenne Zeke. My guess is she would not find it easy to walk away from your bed, my hot-blooded Cheyenne warrior."

He chuckled and Zeke did not reply. He only felt an ache in his heart and a gnawing at his loins to be with Abbie.

*   *   *

199

The heavy wagons lumbered through torturous canyons and grotesque rocks, veering around dangerous talus, and sometimes scaring up coatimundi, Apache fox squirrels, but seldom finding fresh water arroyos.

The days were hard and hot, and Zeke's buckskins grew dark with the stains of perspiration. He thought to himself that he was glad Grimey was downwind of him, for the heat, combined with the man's already offensive odor, made his smell discernible even from a distance. Both were most certainly earning their money, and Zeke was beginning to wonder if eight hundred dollars was enough for the job.

They had been on the trail for over three weeks, and Zeke had been away from Abbie for well over a month. He kept his spirits up by telling himself that in just ten more days or so this trip would be over, and he could get his money and head back to her. But the road to the end of the journey appeared longer when he heard the yipping and cawing of a small band of raiding Apaches that suddenly appeared from the surrounding rocks! Zeke's mind raced! The wagons were much too cumbersome and the mules too slow to try outrunning the Apaches' swift ponies. There was only one thing to do—surprise them by not running at all. He reined in his mules and Grimey rumbled up beside him, bringing his own wagon to a halt.

"Hey, half-breed, what do we do?"

"Get your rifle and get down under the wagons!" Zeke yelled. He grabbed his own firearm and ducked down between the wagons. The Apaches were close now, their enthusiastic war cries enough to curdle any man's blood with fear, for the Apache had a great love of torturing their captives to find out how brave they were. Zeke held no animosity toward them for it, for this was the Apache way, and an offering of a brave captive to their God was great medicine. But he did not care to be the one making the sacrifice. No doubt, the Apaches would consider him a good catch, for if he was to die at their hands, he most certainly intended to die with honor and without uttering one cry of pain or one plea for release.

The small band of nomadic red men surrounded the two wagons, screeching and shooting arrows aimlessly, trying to defeat their prey psychologically rather than with weapons.

"Aim good, Grimey!" Zeke shouted, raising his own rifle. "They want us alive so they won't shoot right at us at first!"

"They won't get me alive!" Grimey yelled. He let off a shot and one warrior cried out and fell from his horse, while his kinsmen rode their horses over his body. "I don't aim to be no Apache captive, brother!"

Zeke had fired twice by then, one miss and one hitting its red-skinned, black-haired target. He thought to himself that he would go and take the man's weapons and a piece of his scalp when this was over. They would be great war medicine.

He preferred hand-to-hand combat, but there were simply too many Apaches, and to go out among them would mean certain death. He fired again, hitting yet another. But when he saw his fine Appaloosa lying dead with an Apache arrow in its neck, he lost all reason. He stood up amid swirling Texas dust and fired wildly, killing three more in quick succession, while arrows whizzed past him so closely he could feel the rush of air.

Suddenly his Indian fever for revenge and combat took hold, and while Grimey kept firing, Zeke ducked down and crawled to the wagon seat, reaching beneath it and grasping his bow. He removed an arrow from the quiver on his back and put it against the bow string. Then he stood up and let out a Cheyenne war cry, releasing an arrow which went straight through the neck of an Apache warrior in revenge for his horse's death.

The circling of the Apaches slowed, and Grimey cut down two more, while Zeke called out war cries and let go two more arrows. To hell with the rifle! A true warrior used arrows and knives! At the moment he didn't care about the wagons or his pay in Santa Fe. He was not protecting his merchandise. He was avenging the death of a sturdy, valuable, and loyal mount.

One of the Apaches, who had hung back from the attack, cried out in the Apache tongue, and the remaining warriors drew back, returning to the one who had shouted to them. Zeke and Grimey remained down between the wagons. They looked at each other questioningly but did not speak as dust settled on them. The remaining warriors spoke in their clipped tongue, apparently discussing their next move.

"Do you know what they're sayin'?" Grimey finally spoke up quietly.

Zeke frowned. "I don't understand Apache too good, Grimey. But I heard them mention Cheyenne, and I think one of them has one of my arrows in his hand."

"Hey, half-blood, you surprised them with those arrows, huh? They did not expect an Indian!"

"Maybe." They waited until finally the apparent leader rode forward, holding up his bow. He gestured, using sign language.

"Stay put," Zeke told Grimey. Zeke rose and stepped away from the wagons, answering in sign language that he was Cheyenne. They spoke with their hands, the Apache man asking Zeke if he was considered a great warrior among his people.

"I am," Zeke replied. "With this." He pulled out the huge blade that had won him a reputation, hoping that if he was to prove himself, he would be allowed to do so with a knife, for then he was sure he would win the battle.

The Apache leader eyed the big blade warily. It was held in a way that told the Apache that its owner knew how to use it.

"What is in your wagons?" he asked Zeke suspiciously.

"Just parts to a white man's music maker," Zeke replied. "It is nothing of value to an Apache."

The Apache sneered. "You lie!"

Zeke held his knife defensively. "Come closer and call me a liar!" he motioned. "And after I kill you, my friend and I will take care of the rest of your warriors! But first it will be just you and me! Unless you are afraid!"

The Apache man jerked back in anger, yanking his horse's head when he did so. He jumped down from his mount and pulled a knife of his own. His men moved closer, but waited as

Zeke and their leader circled.

Zeke's opponent's black, stringy hair hung long, dancing with its owner as the Apache moved sideways and back and forth, very quickly, feeling out his Cheyenne opponent. But Zeke remained calm. His movements were smooth and planned, and he was ready when the Apache lunged at him. Zeke dodged out of the way as he made a quick pass with his blade, slicing open the Apache's left forearm.

The Apache's eyes widened, and he lunged again, just touching Zeke's ribs enough to slit the skin but doing no real damage, as Zeke arched away just enough to keep the blade from cutting deeper. The Apache came at him again, this time raising his knife hand and coming down from above. Zeke grabbed the man's wrist with his left hand and jabbed with his knife, sinking it only about an inch into the Apache's ribcage before the Apache grasped Zeke's wrist with his profusely bleeding left arm and held him for a moment.

The two of them struggled in place, muscle against muscle, each trying to keep the other's blade from entering his own body. Suddenly Zeke hooked his right foot behind the Apache's right leg and kicked, landing the Apache on his backside while both still held each other's wrists. Zeke quickly laid a knee into the Apache's stomach and pushed hard; the Apache's eyes bulged with fury and pain. Then the Apache kicked up with a knee, ramming it as hard as he could into Zeke's side, bringing fierce pain to his old bullet wound.

The sudden pain caused Zeke to lose control momentarily, and he fell slightly forward, losing his good grip on the Apache's knife hand. He rolled away quickly but not quickly enough, and the Apache's knife caught him across the top of his shoulder, but Zeke knew it was not time to hesitate. As the Apache started to his feet, Zeke lunged fast, burying his blade deep in the Apache's groin.

The Apache cried out in surprise and agony as Zeke twisted his blade before jerking it out and moving back. He got to his feet quickly and waited as the Apache struggled to get to his own feet, but blood poured from the grave wound and part of his insides began to protrude from the incision. He stared at Zeke for a moment, then crumpled back to his knees and fell face forward.

He lay grimacing as one of his men rode forward. Zeke faced the second man challengingly.

"Let him die like a man!" the second Apache motioned to Zeke. "He was a great warrior. Let him die quickly! It is an honor for him to die by the hand of the great Cheyenne knife fighter!"

Zeke nodded. He walked up to his opponent and turned him with his foot onto his back. The Apache lay panting and gritting his teeth against a groan, and his eyes were pleading for instant death. Zeke raised his knife and plunged it deep into the center of the Apache's heart. He yanked it out and turned to the others. They all stared for a moment, then turned their horses and rode away, melting quickly into the surrounding rocks.

Grimey crawled from between the wagons and walked up beside the dusty, bleeding Zeke, whose breath still came in the quick pants of battle. "I think you have just saved us with that blade, my half-breed friend. I thank you!"

As Zeke turned to look at him, his dark eyes were still wild with a thirst for battle. "I have some trophies to collect, Grimey. Then let's get the hell out of here and get to Santa Fe. I want to get home to my woman!"

Eleven

The sweet smell of roast buffalo meat permeated Abbie's tipi. She sat near the fire stitching together a new deerskin shirt for Zeke, while Swift Arrow gnawed at a piece of the meat.

"Is good," he told her, licking his fingers.

"Thank you," she answered quietly.

"You serve me well, woman of Lone Eagle. Make good fire . . . good food . . . take good care. You are pretty good woman."

Abbie suppressed a smile. "I take good care of you because you are Zeke's brother and you take good care of me," she told him. But her smile faded quickly. "What do you think has happened to him, Swift Arrow? It's been over five weeks!"

He grunted and picked up one of Zeke's pipes that he had been smoking. He handed it over to Abbie, and she knew that he wanted her to fill it. She doubted she could ever become accustomed to waiting on a man with Swift Arrow's attitude and was glad Zeke had enough white in him not to be so demanding; but she suspected Swift Arrow was enjoying being particularly demanding, for he seemed to bask in testing her patience. She took the pipe without protest, determined that he would not make her complain.

"Lone Eagle is good at taking care of self," he replied as she stuffed the pipe. "But I worry, too. If he had no woman, I would not worry. He has gone away before for long, long time. But now he has new wife. He would not want to stay away so long."

Abbie blushed at the remark and handed back the pipe. Swift Arrow lit it with a small piece of burning kindling and puffed it for a moment.

"If Lone Eagle not back soon after Sun Dance, I and my brothers will go to fort . . . ask about him. He have friends among white trappers. They will search for him. You not worry. Lone Eagle live off land . . . strong man. He come. He leave many times before. Always he returns. This my own mother saw in a vision. Eagle come to her . . . tell her that as long as she lives, her half-blood son will always come back to her."

Abbie looked up from her stitching, her eyes red with tears. "Is that the truth, Swift Arrow?"

"Swift Arrow does not lie."

Their eyes held. "Have you had a vision, too, Swift Arrow?"

He nodded. "When I suffer the Sun Dance. I do not choose to share it with white woman. But it is when I took the name Swift Arrow. Red Eagle and Black Elk have also had visions. Theirs were from long days of fasting and staying alone in the mountains with no food and no weapons. There they learn to survive with only the spirits to guide them. Now Red Eagle has chosen to suffer the Sun Dance ritual. I pray to spirits that it will cure him of the evils of the white man's whiskey."

Abbie stirred the fire. "What will happen to Red Eagle at the Sun Dance, Swift Arrow?"

He puffed the pipe again and shook his head. "I not tell you yet. Not good for one such as you to dwell upon. It is something hard for one such as you to understand. You must be Indian to understand."

"But I need to understand. Don't you see? I must understand!"

He studied her for a long, silent moment, his eyes scanning her small body. She sat rigid and startled as he suddenly reached over and put his fingers between her leather belt and her body, pulling the belt around so that the gray eagle feathers

206

were at the front of her tunic.

"Look at these feathers given you by the old priest," he told her. She looked down at them, her heart pounding with uncertainty as to what he had intended to do when he reached for the belt. There were still times when his fiery eyes and hot temper frightened her. "Do you not know what great gift this is our priest has given you? Do you not know what an honor this is?"

"Of course I know it's an honor!"

He jerked his hand away. "You know nothing!" He moved back and picked up the pipe again. "Your people are far from the spirits. They do not breathe the earth into their nostrils and speak to the bears and fly with the eagles. When you feel as one with the land and the animals, then you will begin to think like Cheyenne—like all Indians." He nodded toward the feathers at her waist. "Do you know why we prize eagle feathers as most powerful?"

She sighed. "No," she replied quietly.

"It is because eagle flies closer to the great heavenly Gods. Because eagle touches clouds . . . has more freedom . . . more power than man. When an enemy is close, he can soar to the heavens and nothing can harm him. He lives close to the clouds . . . master of the skies." He puffed the pipe. "I would love to be eagle if the Gods made me animal."

"Tell me more, Swift Arrow. I want to be ready to understand the Sun Dance."

He set the pipe down and came close to her again, digging a fistful of dirt from the hardened floor and holding it up in front of her face. He squeezed the dirt between his fingers, letting it filter through them and trickle into her lap.

"To think like the Indian, woman of Lone Eagle, you must first move as one with the land, the plants, and all living things. This much I tell you, to think of things not as separate. Do not say, 'this is plant, with no soul'; or 'this is buffalo, with no soul'; or 'this is just dirt, with no soul.'" He took her hand with his free one and gently put the dirt into her palm. "We are one with all things," he told her, "and all things have soul, a life source. We are all one step going onward, all moving as one. Think only of this for now—one step going on. Put behind you all thought of things white man think he needs to survive. Man needs nothing but this"—he squeezed her hand—"the earth. Nothing but that which the Gods provide for man's nourishment, clothing, and shelter. This is why we ask an animal's forgiveness before we kill it, for it is one with us. It knows its purpose on earth, that it was put here by the Gods to give food to man. All things are one, woman of Lone Eagle. Think only of this."

Their eyes held, and for a brief moment she saw a hint of respect and admiration in his own eyes. She felt as though she had just won one small battle.

"It will take much more than two moons of living with our people to understand them, white woman," he told her. "We have been going on for hundreds of moons, thousands of moons, since first the Great Spirit formed us from the earth. Birth, living and dying—all are the same to us. There is no fear of death. When we know we are about to die, we sing our prayer of death. The words of the prayer say, 'nothing lives long, nothing stays here, except the earth and the mountains.' The spirits take the man's life and put it into a woman and more life springs forth. It lives and walks and breathes, and the most important thing it must do is to honor the spirits who created it—to be strong and brave and full of truth. Then, when it dies, that life can walk *Ekutsihimmiyo*, the Hanging Road between earth and heaven. Think on these things, and you will understand that if something has happened to Lone Eagle, his spirit still lives in the great bird of the sky."

He moved away again. "I go now. Tomorrow begins the ceremony of the renewal of the Sacred Arrows. This we must do before the Sun Dance. I and other dog soldiers must decide tonight who will be chosen to make the new arrows." He rose to leave.

"But what will happen, Swift Arrow?" Abbie stopped him. "What is the renewal of arrows all about?"

He walked to the tipi entrance. "You ask many questions."

"How else can I learn?"

"I have already given you much to think about." He turned and left without another word.

Abbie looked down at the dirt in her hand, rubbing it between her fingers. "We are all one," she told herself. "All one." She tried to let the thought penetrate her brain, and some of it began to make sense to her. For she realized she could be with Zeke no matter how many miles might be between them. All she needed to do was smell the sweet earth or touch the feathers or dance under the sky, and she was with him, for he was all of those things. She walked over to her parfleche and removed the blue crying stones; then she lay down and curled up under her robe. She held the stones to her breast.

"Come back, Zeke," she whispered. "Come back soon!" She fought against her own tears, remembering Zeke's instructions to let the stones cry for her. She kept her hand tight around them and was soon asleep, unaware that moisture was appearing on the stones.

The next day was filled with busy women and much visiting and laughter. It was time to celebrate the renewal of the Medicine Arrows. Abbie could get no more answers out of Swift Arrow, and so she turned to Gentle Woman who was busily refurbishing her husband's war shield. Abbie sat in the woman's tipi pounding some berries and meat into pemmican, trying to keep her mind off of Zeke.

"Tell me about the arrow renewal," she asked Gentle Woman. "What will happen?"

Gentle Woman smiled patiently. "It is a time for celebrating," she replied. "The Sacred Arrows protect us from bad things, and when we feel new protection is needed, the arrows are renewed for greater power. We have seen many white-topped wagons and know the diseases these new people bring us. We feel bad things coming, Abigail. And so we shall renew the arrows. All must attend—our tribe and all the Arapahoes who are with us, and any tribes to whom we send runners. If anyone refuses to attend, his lodge can be destroyed and his horses killed. If he still refuses, it is very bad luck for him, for he is not protected by the arrows. The warriors will purify themselves in the sweat lodges, and the *Shamans* will perform special ceremonies to cure the sick and afflicted. This renewal is being sponsored by Two Feathers, who was trampled by a buffalo on last winter's hunt and seemed certain to die. But he survived. For this miracle, he has agreed to sponsor the renewal."

She looked over at Abbie and smiled at the way the girl was listening to her, like a little child listening to a bedtime story.

"You have learned many things while you have been alone with us," she told Abbie. "I feel in my bones that Zeke will come back. But perhaps it is good that he has been away longer than he thought. You are learning many things, and you are learning not to be afraid."

"I'm trying so hard to understand, Gentle Woman." She tasted the pemmican and grinned. "It's good!" she exclaimed, surprised that she could make this Indian food by herself. Gentle Woman chuckled and returned to sewing new beads onto the fringes of Deer Slayer's war shield.

"For two days we will celebrate and feast, Abigail. The men will be purified in the sweat lodges, and the *Shamans* will conduct the healings. Then"—she put down the war shield and dropped her voice—"then all of the dog soldiers and band soldiers will tell all of the others when it is time to go to their tipis and remain there. We cannot leave. We must be very quiet, while the sponsor, Two Feathers, goes to the lodges of four of the oldest and wisest men, who have been chosen by the

210

council to make the new Medicine Arrows. Two Feathers will bring the four men to the lodge of the Arrow Keeper, who is Runs Slowly, a very wise and respected warrior. His job as Arrow Keeper will one day pass on to his son, Strong Arm. The Keeper will have a bundle of arrow shafts made of strong willow wood, and the four arrow makers will spend four days making the Medicine Arrows and will be watched by Two Feathers and Runs Slowly, members of Two Feathers' soldier society, the old chiefs, and men who have taken part in other Medicine Arrow ceremonies. On the morning of the fifth day, the arrows will be displayed in front of the Arrow Keeper's lodge, but only the men may look upon them."

"Why?" Abbie asked in surprise. "We have to wait in our lodges all that time, and can't even see the arrows?"

Gentle Woman smiled patiently. "That is the way." She reached over and tasted the pemmican. "You are right. It is good!" she told Abbie.

Abbie smiled with pride in her accomplishment. She dumped the pemmican from the stone bowl onto a piece of clean deerskin and began flattening it out to let it dry.

"I will tell you something else about the Medicine Arrows so that you understand our hatred for the Pawnee!" Zeke's mother told her, bitterness coming into her voice. "Many summers ago, maybe fifteen—sixteen, the Pawnee captured the Cheyenne Sacred Arrows. It was a great, great loss for the Cheyenne, and we believe it is why we have had bad luck with the white man's disease and with poor hunts. We have fought the Pawnee to get the arrows back, but they have never been found."

"But weren't new arrows made?"

"*Ai*. But we have never believed them to be as powerful as those that were taken. Perhaps this renewal will bring the power we need to protect us from the sickness and help us find more food. But never will we find love in our hearts for the filthy Pawnee!" She spit into the fire, and it was the first time

211

Abbie had seen any hatred in Gentle Woman's countenance. She swallowed and did not reply, but only returned to pounding down the pemmican.

The celebrating ended, and four days of quiet retreat inside the tipis began. They were long days for Abbie. Filled with restless worry over Zeke, her mind raced with a myriad of pictures of what could have happened to him. Yes, he had been hurt by her, but he was a man and she was a child and he loved her. He would not desert his wife. It was not like Zeke to do such a thing.

With so much time on her hands while the arrows were being made, Abbie found herself dwelling on the past year, starting with the moment Cheyenne Zeke had stepped into the light of her father's campfire and offered to scout for their wagon train. The memory of the first time she had laid eyes on Cheyenne Zeke still brought excited shivers to her body. He had simply stepped from the shadows, tall and lean and dark, fierce looking, yet with a gentleness in his eyes when first they rested on Abigail Trent.

He was her first and only man. She had lain with him out of a mixture of terrible loneliness and terrible need, and it had been good and sweet and beautiful, as though the life he had poured into her that night had also poured strength into her. Even the pain of their first intercourse had been beautiful. And though at the time she knew he could not commit himself, he had branded her just the same. Now she wished the Arrow Renewal would end quickly, for she had too much time to sit alone and think about Zeke. It hurt to think of him. For he was not there, and she had no idea what could have happened to him. She refused to believe he could be dead. Not Zeke! Men like Cheyenne Zeke did not die. They survived! And they always returned to their women.

On the fifth day of the Arrow Renewal the women waited in their tipis while each man took his turn at viewing the renewed arrows, and throughout the village there was almost complete silence. Abbie felt a strange new power hanging in the very air, as though God himself had come to dwell among them. She tried to tell herself it was only her imagination, but then again, perhaps this was the "oneness" Swift Arrow had told her about. Perhaps she, too, was finally caught up in this spiritual sameness, and was at last beginning to think like the Cheyenne. That thought caused her to suddenly become overwhelmingly curious to see the arrows with her own eyes, to look upon the strange, sacred objects from which the warriors seemed to feel they could gain protection from all evil. What was it about the arrows that made them feel this way? She wanted to understand. What harm could there be in seeing them for herself, if it might help her to understand the Cheyenne religion? It pushed at her as day turned to night, becoming an obsession. The child that still strongly influenced the sixteen-year-old "woman" teased her imagination and made her feel daring. Somehow she must see the arrows!

By nightfall her curiosity knew no bounds. The men had returned to their tipis, and preparations were under way to continue the march northward in the morning; there in three more weeks they would form one great village with the Sioux and northern Cheyenne for the Sun Dance.

The camp quieted with the onslaught of darkness, and owls hooted in the distance, while Abbie lay awake in her tipi thinking about Zeke and the Sacred Arrows. She seemed to be unable to separate the two of them—Zeke and the Arrows. The wonder of the magic fetish enveloped her. She longed to see the arrows, to feel their power; for she felt that if she could see the arrows, she would somehow know whether Zeke was alive or dead. She lay staring into the darkness well into the night, then rose, her restlessness and curiosity keeping her eyes from closing.

She walked barefoot to the tipi entrance. All the women had remained in their lodges that night, going out only to go to the bathroom. But none walked near the Sacred Arrows, which by

213

morning would be put back in the Keeper's medicine bag and not displayed until the Medicine Arrow ceremony was again called for. If Abbie was to see them, it had to be this night!

She quietly opened the entrance flap of her tipi and peeked out to see Swift Arrow curled up asleep beside the dwelling. She watched his rhythmic breathing for a moment; then she darted through the doorway and around the other side of the tipi. Her heart pounded with apprehension and fear, yet something urged her onward as she inched her way on quiet, bare feet toward the great central lodge where she knew the Keeper dwelled . . . and where the sacred arrows would be displayed.

She stayed in the shadows along the outer rim of the village, priding herself on her ability to remain quiet enough to go undetected by the wary eyes and ears of the men who sat up guarding the village against enemies who might choose to approach by night. She had learned that much from Zeke— how to move like a shadow.

But Abbie was not as clever as she thought, and she had underestimated the Cheyenne's ability to detect the tiniest presence. Swift Arrow had not been fooled by the white woman. He followed her silently as she circled around until the Arrow Keeper's lodge stood directly in front of her, past two rows of tipis. Her heart pounded so hard she thought she might die, yet she felt rushed along by something stronger than her own will. She waited in the shadows, listening to men's voices coming from the Keeper's lodge. Then she watched as Two Feathers exited the tipi, along with two other warriors. To her surprise, Runs Slowly himself also exited the dwelling and walked off into the shadows. Perhaps he had gone into the darkness to relieve himself. Whatever the reason, Abbie knew it was her one and only chance to see the arrows!

She darted to the first row of tipis and ducked down, waiting. Then she dashed to the second row. So close! She was so close! She took a deep breath and looked all around. No one seemed to be looking, and Runs Slowly had not returned. She dashed to the Arrow Keeper's tipi and ducked inside.

The pungent smell of burned herbs filled her nostrils, and a powerful, unknown "presence" seemed to close in around her. Her breath came in quick gasps as her eyes fell on arrows that lay at the center of the tipi. She approached them and knelt in front of them.

There were four arrows, two with shafts painted red, and two with their shafts painted black. Gentle Woman had told her the red arrows represented the procurement of food and were called Buffalo Arrows. The black ones represented war and were called Man Arrows. "They are our most sacred religious objects," Gentle Woman had told her.

Abbie stared in awe at the arrows, a wonderful peace filling her and making her forget that she should leave quickly. She did not want to leave. She felt hypnotized by the arrows, for she knew that they epitomized the root of the Cheyenne religion.

"The arrows were first given us by *Mutsiluiv*," Gentle Woman had told her, "Sweet Medicine, our prophet, who received them from the Great Spirit." The buffalo arrows pointed up, and the man arrows pointed down. And Abbie knew that to look upon them was to look upon the beginnings of the Cheyenne—the People—Zeke's people. From this blood, Zeke got his power and his strength. She felt a new understanding, and wondered if seeing her own Jesus would be like this. She wanted to touch the arrows, but an inner sense told her she should not, for it would be like trying to touch God. Only the Arrow Keeper and one who was a full-blooded Cheyenne had the right to touch the fetish. She felt humbled, unworthy to touch them, for her skin was white.

A sudden, quick movement behind her, startled her from the near trance the arrows had imposed upon her. She whirled and gasped as she looked up into the furious eyes of Runs Slowly.

"*Heyoka!*" the man roared at her. "*E-have-se-va!*" He grabbed her by the hair and she screamed as he shoved her roughly toward the tipi entrance. "*Nonotovestoz!*" he shouted,

215

pointing to the entrance. *"Nonotovestoz! E-have-se-va!"* He kicked her in the rear and sent her flying through the entrance; then another hand grabbed her by the hair, jerking it. It was Swift Arrow, who looked as though he wished to sink a knife into her belly.

"I did not think you would truly do it!" he hissed through gritted teeth. "I watched to see if you would be such a fool!" He threw her down. *"Katum!* You have done a bad thing, white woman! A bad thing! You give me much trouble now! Go to your tipi!"

Abbie choked in a sob and ran off, her mind screaming for Zeke. Swift Arrow was angry with her now! They would all be angry with her! Who was there to protect her? Perhaps a woman's punishment for looking upon the arrows was death, and perhaps they would not wait for Zeke's return before they burned her at the stake or boiled her in a pot or cut out her heart while she was yet alive! Her mind raced with visions of all the horrible things they might choose to do to her, and she dashed into her tipi, flinging herself down on her robe and sobbing for Zeke.

She heard running outside and scooted into the corner, grabbing up her carbine and making ready to fire it. In the next moment Swift Arrow darted inside, and she could hear a great commotion outside. She pointed the rifle at Swift Arrow, her breathing coming in quick, frightened gasps, tears staining her face.

"I . . . didn't do it . . . to dishonor the People!" she screamed at him. "I . . . had to see them! I had to . . . see them!" Her words came out in choked sobs.

Swift Arrow's eyes burned into her, and his hand gripped a quirt tightly. "I should whip you for this!"

"I belong to your brother! It's up to him to decide what to do with me!"

"You are my property and my responsibility while he is gone! You make me look bad!"

"You saw me going there! Why didn't you stop me?"

216

"Because I wished to see how much of a fool you still are, white woman!"

"My intentions were good! Something made me go. A power stronger than I. Something made me go there! Don't you understand?" Her body jerked in a sob. How she wanted Zeke! How she needed his reassuring arms around her now! Never had she felt so utterly desolate and set apart, not even when she had lost her family on the wagon train. "Something . . . wanted me to understand the secret . . . the power . . . the root of the Cheyenne!" she yelled at Swift Arrow. "I couldn't stop myself!"

Swift Arrow studied her silently; then he turned and barked something to the frenzied, angry warriors outside the tipi. They exchanged words of argument, but Abbie sensed that most of them were leaving. Swift Arrow turned again and walked straight over to her, paying no heed to the rifle, which he sensed she would not use on him. She kept hold of it until he grabbed it from her hands. He threw it aside and Abbie ducked down, putting her arms over her head, waiting for the sting of the quirt. But she felt nothing.

A moment later she slowly raised her head to look up at him, and he knelt down in front of her, grasping the back of her neck. She stiffened and stared at him.

"Tell me, white woman. Tell me what you think of Cheyenne men. You think perhaps I would truly beat you . . . perhaps rape you and throw you to the dogs!" He shoved her away. "I tell you now, if you think this of Swift Arrow, then you still have the heart of a white woman and not a Cheyenne! If you are so afraid of me, then you still have not learned! When a Cheyenne woman has done something wrong, she looks her man in the eye and asks for her punishment so that the Gods will be pleased with her again. She is not afraid to admit the truth—that she has done something wrong."

"You are not my man. And I've done nothing wrong," she answered through tears.

"I am your keeper. And you did do something wrong! You

217

looked upon the sacred arrows! No woman looks at the arrows, and to have it be a white woman . . ." His hands went into fists.

"I tell you I've done nothing wrong! Something made me go there, Swift Arrow. For all these days I've done nothing but think about the things you have told me . . . about the earth and the sky and the animals . . . about all things moving in one step together. And tonight . . . I had to see the arrows! I don't know why. I wasn't trying to dishonor your beliefs. I just had to see them. And when I did, I felt something . . . like if I . . . if I looked upon my own Jesus. Have you heard about the white man's Jesus?"

Some of the anger left his eyes. "I have heard he was a great prophet, like Sweet Medicine."

"Yes," she sniffed. "And he is very powerful also. Please believe me, Swift Arrow, I just had to see the arrows. I had to see them to understand the Cheyenne . . . to understand Zeke and his people. Please ask them to forgive me!"

"They will not! The only thing they will understand is punishment for atonement. And they would expect me to do the punishing! But I do not wish to bring harm to my brother's woman. Why do you make such problems for me!"

Her mind raced with remorse and fright and near pity for Swift Arrow, for she had put him in a spot. And then it came to her. "You don't have to punish me, Swift Arrow. Tell them . . . tell them I wish to atone for what I've done . . . by making a sacrifice at the Sun Dance."

His eyes widened. "No! That would be worse!"

"It would be my choosing."

"You do not know what takes place. You do not want to be a part of it. I will not allow it. They will not allow it. You must be punished here and now! If you want to walk out of here tomorrow and hope to live, then turn around now and drop your tunic to your waist!"

Her eyes widened and she backed up.

"I tell you they must know you have been punished!"

Her eyes filled with tears again. She had no choice if she

wanted to survive. She turned and unlaced her tunic with shaking fingers, letting it fall to her waist, and Swift Arrow looked with pity on her small, white back.

"It is as hard for me to do this as it would be if you were my own sister," he told her. She felt the sting of the quirt. Her body jerked, but she did not cry out. Again it slashed across her back, and again she kept silent. Three more times he lashed her, but she sensed he was deliberately not using his full strength. Then he took hold of her arm. "Do not move," he told her. He called out, and Runs Slowly and Two Feathers entered to look upon her wounds. Swift Arrow said something to them in their own tongue and the two men grunted something in reply, then left. "Where is your bear grease?" Swift Arrow asked her when they were gone.

She held her tunic up over her breasts and nodded toward the other side of the tipi where a stone bowl sat with brown bear grease in it. Swift Arrow retrieved the bowl and came back over to Abbie, who stayed on her knees but was not weeping. She had expected him to go and get Gentle Woman, but in the next moment his own hands began applying the bear grease, and she could not believe that the very hands that had whipped her were now gently applying the soothing grease.

"In a day or two it will not hurt," he was telling her. "You have made me do this. I did not want to hurt you. My brother will cut me open and stretch my hide for this. But I had no choice. What you have done will mean certain death for me at Zeke's hands."

"Then . . . we won't tell him," she replied quietly. He stopped in surprise.

"What do you mean?"

"Exactly what I said. In a day or two the welts will be gone. Tell the others and Gentle Woman, that I do not want him to know about the arrows. If I am to be a true Cheyenne, I must accept my punishment. I'll not go running to my husband to tell on you like a little child. I did something wrong. I deserved it. Tell the others it was just . . . just my ignorant white blood and poor understanding of your ways that made me do it. Tell them I beg their forgiveness."

He began applying the bear grease again. "I thank you for this," he told her, rubbing her back gently. Then he set the bowl down and stood up. "Perhaps there was a reason for what has happened. Perhaps the Great Spirit wanted you to see the arrows."

"Perhaps."

Gentle Woman came in then, and immediately she began to scold Swift Arrow in her own tongue when she saw Abbie's back. Words were exchanged, but Swift Arrow did not raise his voice to his mother. He stalked out of the tipi, and Gentle Woman rushed over to Abbie, who was grimacing as she pulled the tunic back up around her shoulders.

"Abigail! Why did you do this?" the woman exclaimed. "Why did you look upon the arrows?"

"I . . . I'm not sure," she replied in a near whisper. "Please leave me alone, Gentle Woman. I just want to be alone." She lay down on her side, and Gentle Woman watched her for a moment with a frown. Then she simply sighed, and quietly left.

Dancing Moon did not like the dry, hot country to which she had been forced to flee. But she no longer cared that she had no home among her people. It was boring to live the life of the chaste Cheyenne and Arapaho maidens, and she wondered how any woman could bear to be the slave of only one man. She liked her new freedom, and she had soon learned wherein lay her powers. She had the ability to weaken men with her hungry eyes and provocative body. She could manipulate them by making them want her and then holding back, keeping them panting at bay. And with this power, she would survive!

Already she had managed to use those powers on Mexican gun runners, who had made her their captive and had raped her. But it was not long before they felt they were the ones being raped, and the beautiful Dancing Moon soon had them under her own scheming control, playing one man against the other and offering them her services for food and supplies and a place to sleep. It seemed a very nice exchange to the Mexicans, and it was not long before Dancing Moon used her wit and bodily skills to become the property of the leader of the men, one Manuel Artigo, who was soon promising her a place at his right hand, money, and pretty clothes, if she slept only with him and not with the other men.

Dancing Moon promised to do so, although she had no intention of keeping such a promise. And all the while she watched and listened and learned about the business of gun running, quickly surmising that doing things that were against the law could bring great riches. She rode with them to a place called the Devil's Pits, where they were to set up camp and wait for two wagons bearing smuggled rifles and dynamite to aid in their war against the United States.

It was all arranged. When the wagons reached Devil's Pits, the drivers would be killed, and Manuel, Dancing Moon, and the others in Manuel's outlaw gang would be well paid to take the guns on south into Mexico, while one of their men would ride north to Santa Fe with a payment of pure gold for Mr. Jonathan Mack in return for arranging for the shipment of more rifles.

With the rifles they thought Mexico had a chance of winning the war and keeping Santa Fe. They did not know that Jonathan Mack had every confidence that the United States would win, and that to him, the smuggled guns were merely another means of getting richer. Both Dancing Moon and Jonathan Mack were hoping to profit from the Mexican War by what they considered a well-planned scheme. However, Mack had underestimated the driver he had hired; and Dancing Moon had no idea that driver was none other than Cheyenne Zeke.

Abbie rode quietly at the back of the tribe, shunned by all

except Gentle Woman. Even Tall Grass Woman was forbidden to speak to the white woman who had looked upon the Sacred Arrows. But Abbie could tell whenever Tall Grass Woman looked at her that she regretted the order not to talk to her, for the young girl's brown eyes showed regret and sorrow whenever she looked at Abbie.

Abbie missed talking to her good friend Tall Grass Woman, as she missed the sewing circles and helping in the care of the other women's little brown babies. She missed the companionship of those with whom she had made friends. She was an outcast, one whom they would tolerate simply because a promise had been made to care for her until Zeke returned. Abbie felt like something abnormal, as though she had an affliction that made her horribly ugly and deformed. For that was how some of them looked upon her. She was forced to erect her tipi away from the others, to bathe downstream from the others, to draw her water alone. No one helped her with firewood or with her horse or tipi. Gentle Woman could talk to her and advise her, but she could not help Abbie. And Abbie's loneliness was only made more painful by Zeke's continued absence. Her thoughts were full of him and her heart cried out for him.

Where could he be? Why did he not come and save her from this awful loneliness and rejection? What was to become of her?

On the fifth day after the encounter over the arrows, Abbie washed her utensils alone. They were camped at the base of the White River in Nebraska Territory, not many days from the meeting with the Sioux. Abbie dreaded the meeting now, and she tried not to think about it as she scrubbed at a tin pot with sand.

Beside her lay her personal parfleche full of memories from her former life: her father's fiddle, her little brother's marbles, a locket that had belonged to her sister, and her mother's cross. These things were all she had left of her family and of the white life she'd once led in that distant place called Tennessee.

She set the pot down on a rock and reached into the parfleche, removing a dress she had saved, a pretty yellow ruffled one. She held it to her bosom and stood up, remembering that night with the wagon train the year before, when Zeke had played his beautiful mandolin and had sung Tennessee songs for her. She had worn the dress then, wanting to look pretty for him. She twirled around, holding out the skirt of the dress; it was now badly wrinkled from being packed for so long. She pretended she was dancing for Zeke, and he was watching her with his dark eyes, wanting her in his mysterious, provocative way.

She hummed a waltz, whirling and whirling, while tears streamed down her cheeks. She pretended little Jeremy was there, laughing and watching her. Little Jeremy! Poor little Jeremy, whose horrible suffering had been ended by Zeke's blade at Abbie's request. The thought stopped her dancing, and she burst into loud sobbing, throwing down the dress and holding her stomach. She felt sick with grief and fright and loneliness. Zeke! Where was Zeke?

She wept bitterly, her sobbing drowning out the screams of Tall Grass Woman, who had been bathing her small daughter in the river upstream from where Abbie sat. But after a moment Abbie realized someone was shouting in panic, and she looked up, wiping at her eyes.

Tall Grass Woman was running along the bank, screaming and jumping up and down and pointing, while others came running, including Swift Arrow and some of the men, ready to do battle against whatever enemy had come to do harm to the women. But no enemy was there. The only thing to be seen was little Magpie being carried swiftly down river, her little brown arms flailing in the deep waters.

Abbie hesitated for a moment, wondering why on earth Tall Grass Woman did not go into the water after her child. Instead she screamed something in Cheyenne, and then held her head in her hands.

"*Ai-ee!*" she shouted, joined by the other mourning women,

who were certain little Magpie would drown. *"Ai-ee! Ai-ee!"*

Abbie looked quickly from them to the little girl, who was apparently losing her battle with the deep waters. She looked back at Swift Arrow.

"Why doesn't she save her child!" she screamed.

Swift Arrow looked at her with desperation in his eyes, and for the first time Abbie understood how deeply the religion and superstitions of this ancient people ran.

"The deep waters—they hold monsters and evil spirits!" he told her with regret. "There is nothing we can do for Magpie!"

Abbie's eyes widened in horror. "No! You're wrong! I'll show you you're wrong!" She turned and dived into the river.

"Stop!" Swift Arrow shouted. "Do not go, Abigail!"

They all stood on the bank and watched in horror as Abbie swam out toward little Magpie, struggling to reach her before the girl floated past.

"Help me, Jesus!" Abbie found herself praying as she struggled through the swift, cold waters. She coughed and choked, having trouble herself keeping afloat as she swam toward the little girl. Her ears and nose filled with water, and she grunted as her body jolted against a large rock just as Magpie floated past. Hanging on to the rock with one hand, she reached out and grabbed one of Magpie's braids with the other. The child screamed and struggled with fright, but Abbie grasped the rock, while she pulled until little Magpie's head was very close to her; then she quickly reached out and grasped the tiny girl.

"Ho-shuh!" Abbie told the crying, choking girl, remembering the Cheyenne words for be still, be confident. *"Ho-shuh, Magpie!"*

Magpie grasped Abbie tightly around the neck, and Abbie urged the little girl to move around to her back and hang on, giving her a gentle push in that direction. As Abbie let go of the rock, she and Magpie were carried from it by the powerful current. Magpie screamed and hung on so tightly that Abbie

224

was afraid she would choke to death before she reached the bank. The water carried them farther downstream, and Abbie could see the People running along beside them so they could help them out of the water. When she got close to the bank, Swift Arrow ran into the stream and grasped her arms. Pulling her up and keeping an arm about her waist, he helped her to shore, where she collapsed with Magpie.

Tall Grass Woman grabbed her little girl and screeched out a Cheyenne cry of happiness, holding up the little girl and weeping, and the others cheered while Swift Arrow helped a drenched and panting Abigail to stand.

"Get a blanket!" he ordered. To Abbie's amazement, Runs Slowly was quickly at her side, throwing around her shoulders a colorful blanket that he had been bringing to the river for his woman to wash. He pushed her ahead of him and shouted something to the others, patting her on the head, and Tall Grass Woman's husband, Falling Rock, came forward and handed Abbie his bow and two arrows. Two Feathers also came forward and, taking a coup feather from his hair, stuck it into one of Abbie's wet braids. He smiled at her and stepped back; then Swift Arrow walked up beside her and put an arm around her shoulders.

Abbie looked up at him in astonishment. "What . . . what are they doing?" she asked him. Swift Arrow grinned.

"They are thanking you and giving you their good-luck pieces. You have done a great thing this day, woman of Lone Eagle. You braved the evil spirits of the deep waters and conquered them to save one of our own. You are greatly honored!"

Abbie could hardly believe her ears. Runs Slowly was giving some kind of speech to the others, waving his arms and pointing to Abbie. Then he came up to her again, and handing her his knife, said something to her in his own tongue. He looked at Swift Arrow and stepped back.

"Runs Slowly says this is a great thing you have done,"

Swift Arrow told Abbie. "He says now the People know why the spirits led you to the Arrows and made you look upon them. It was to give you the strength you would need to brave the deep waters. You are forgiven by all for looking upon the arrows. He says"—the next words seemed difficult for him to say—"he says it is you who should forgive us for punishing you for doing something the spirits intended you to do. If the arrows gave you courage and gave you an understanding of the People, then it is good after all. Today we have seen the purpose of what you did." He moved around to face her. "Swift Arrow also asks your forgiveness," he said with near-shame on his face.

Their eyes held, and she suddenly felt warm and alive and loved again by this people who could change so quickly.

"There is nothing to forgive," she replied. "You did what you had to do. And my strength came from my own Jesus, Swift Arrow. When I looked at the arrows . . . I thought of my God then, too. Perhaps . . . perhaps your Great Spirit and God are the same."

He grinned, a rare sight for Abigail; she had not seen him smile since she'd looked at the arrows. "Perhaps this is so." He turned to the others and shouted something in Cheyenne; then he gave out a war cry and surprised Abbie by grabbing her about the waist and lifting her. He cried out again, and the others raised arms and weapons and gave out one war cry in unison in honor of the white woman who had saved Magpie.

Swift Arrow set her on her feet again and laughed. "My heart sings!" he told her. "For now we know Zeke's wife has a purpose among us! We are your friends forever, woman of Lone Eagle! Never fear us again! Whatever happens, we will be with you. We will protect you. You may speak to the other women again. The spirits have made this happen to open our eyes. Now you are beginning to understand! This I know. Come! There will be feasting tonight, and the council will gather and offer special prayers for Zeke. You will pray for us, for your prayers are powerful!" He pushed her along and the others walked with them. "You are my sister now," Swift Arrow told her. "Mine and Red Eagle's and Black Elk's. You are our mother's daughter and our father's daughter. You are a daughter of the People."

Abbie did not reply. Her throat hurt with the tears she was choking back—tears of joy. Zeke! If only Zeke were here now!

Twelve

Zeke's wagon clattered over the hard clay earth, with Grimey's close behind. Zeke squinted up into the torturous sun. The sky seemed to be all sun, and its glare hurt his tired eyes. Yet he felt compelled to stare at it for a moment, for he suddenly was overwhelmed by the sensation that this trip had been a mistake and that the spirits were trying to tell him so. He could almost hear a voice telling him to beware. He tried to shake the idea from his head as his eyes turned to the red rock canyon ahead, but the sensation would not leave him. He kept thinking of Jonathan Mack's perfumed smell and small hands, and his own uneasiness over the suspicion that Mack was not being completely honest irritated him.

But perhaps only the tedious, hot journey and his longing for Abbie had brought on this depression and this uneasy suspicion. Once he'd reached Santa Fe and was on his way back to Abbie, he would feel he'd been foolish to worry.

At least they had reached Devil's Pits, the point at which they were to veer north into Santa Fe. But Devil's Pits was a dangerous place, a rocky crevice between two great cliffs of sheer redrock—a spot avoided by Indians and traders alike because of the numerous deep holes that potted the area, holes that led to caverns below that were known to be abundant with rattle snakes. Its name was fitting, for it was a demon-infested place where only a devil would want to live.

Zeke motioned Grimey to keep moving. They would get

themselves out of the canyon and away from the danger of snakes before making camp. There was only one narrow exit, and Zeke knew that the mouth of the canyon would be an excellent place for an enemy to lie in wait for unsuspecting prey; however, in this Godforsaken place probably the only enemy to be feared were the snakes. Indians and Mexicans stayed away from the canyon because of the rattlers. Zeke used it now only for safety, at Mack's request. Traveling through the canyon was insurance that no one would be near to attack the wagons. In that respect, Zeke had to admit Jonathan Mack had thought well. There remained only one more day's fast run to Santa Fe. Then, finally, he could get his money and get back to Abbie!

He urged the stubborn mules up the rocky canyon floor. The animals were fidgety, for although snakes could not be seen, the mules sensed their presence. The canyon walls became less steep, and a wide opening gaped ahead. Zeke headed for it, anxious to get out of the canyon. Grimey was quickly bringing up the rear. But just as the wagons peaked the canyon exit, ten horsemen emerged quickly from the surrounding boulders, too quickly for Zeke to react, for he had not expected anyone to be in such a desolate place, let alone ten Mexican outlaws with rifles, all pointed at him.

Zeke's blood raced, but he told himself to stay calm. Something was amiss, and he knew instinctively that whatever was going on, it was Jonathan Mack's doing. How else could these men have been at this hellish place, ready to greet him with rifles? Now it all made sense, his strange uneasiness when he had looked at the sun.

The gunmen motioned Zeke to move forward. By then Grimey had also seen the Mexicans, and like Zeke, he knew it would be wise to do as these men said. He scowled at the Mexicans, who all looked eager to use him and Zeke for target practice.

Zeke knew that he and Grimey could get four or five of the Mexicans before going down, all of them if they had the element of surprise. But the Mexicans had surprised them, and Zeke was not willing to die for Jonathan Mack. Not even for the eight hundred dollars for it would do him no good if he was dead. He made a silent vow that if he lived through this encounter, Jonathan Mack would pay up whether Zeke delivered the piano and whiskey or not.

He urged his wagon far enough ahead so that Grimey could get all the way out of the canyon, then he halted the mules. His eyes quickly scanned the ten men, quickly evaluating each one and deciding which could be the most dangerous and should die first if he had a chance at them. But for the moment he had no chance. The leader pranced his horse forward, bringing it closer to Zeke's wagon. He sported a large sombrero and a colorful cape, and he smoked a fat cigar.

"Welcome to the Devil's Pits, *señor,*" he said to Zeke with a wide grin.

"I didn't know I'd have a welcoming committee," Zeke replied coldly. "But I believe I know the man I should thank for this."

The Mexican laughed. "Hey! You talk good English for an Indian, *señor!* Me—I did not expect an Indian. I expected two white men, like that one behind you." With that the man pointed at Grimey with his rifle and pulled the trigger.

Zeke whirled in his seat and watched with horror as his friend fell dead from his wagon. Zeke's head immediately ached with rage, for he had talked Grimey into coming with him. And in an instant, his friend had been shot down without warning or provocation. Now as Zeke stared in disbelief at his dead friend, an eleventh figure moved in the distant rocks, an added presence of which not even Zeke was aware. Slowly he turned back to the Mexican leader who had shot Grimey, and even though the man held a gun, the Mexican felt fear at the look in Zeke's dark eyes.

"You stinking scum!" Zeke sneered. "If you want the wagons, why not just take them! You didn't need to shoot him!"

"Ah, but we do, *señor*. Just like we need to shoot you. Then . . . we throw you in the snake pits. And since no one ever comes to this place, no one will ever know that this is where you died, you see?" He chuckled. "It is a good idea, no? That way, Mr. Mack, he will not be involved and there will be no one to tell where we got the guns."

Zeke frowned with surprise. "Guns? What guns?"

The Mexican leaned forward. "The ones you carry in the bottom of the wagons, *señor*," he replied with a grin.

The surprise on Zeke's face made the man laugh openly. "Did you really think Mr. Mack would go to so much trouble just for whiskey?" he asked Zeke. "He has fooled you, Indian. In the bottom of your wagons there are rifles—and dynamite—to help us poor Mexicans in our struggle."

Zeke felt he might explode at any moment; his body raged with the need for vengeance—for Grimey's murder and for the trick that had been played on him. He decided that if he was to die, he would not just sit there and take a bullet—die without honor. These men were not going to take Cheyenne Zeke's life without a fight! So before the leader could reload his out-dated firearm, Zeke's knife was out and tossed, landing squarely in the man's heart.

At almost the same instant, his second knife pierced another man's throat. A third man fired at Zeke just as Zeke dove from the wagon, and the bullet grazed Zeke's forehead. When its force spun him around, he thought he heard a woman's voice as he hit the ground, temporarily stunned.

"Wait!" the voice shouted. "I know him!" The words came from the eleventh figure who had now come closer. The outlaw Zeke still had not seen dismounted and came to stand where Zeke lay waiting for a bullet to shatter his brain or open his back. But the only thing he felt was a boot kicking him hard in the ribs, and again pain tore through the old bullet wound. Another foot pushed him over onto his back. For a moment he was blinded by the glare of the hot, unrelenting Mexican sun, but when his eyes focused, he saw the shadows of the outlaws

232

standing over him. He also could make out a woman's form. The woman slowly dropped the barrel of her rifle to Zeke's head, and the steel felt hot against his skin. He could not distinguish her face, for the sun behind her made it only a dark shadow. He could see that she wore a short tunic and her legs were long and willowy and that her hair hung straight to her waist.

"So, my Cheyenne half-blood lover," the woman sneered. "We meet again!"

He recognized the voice. "Dancing Moon!" he uttered.

Abbie was picking wild blackberries with Tall Grass Woman and some of the other squaws when Black Elk came galloping out to them.

"*Veheo! Veheo!*" he shouted, using his own tongue to tell them white men were close by. "*Hai! Hai!*" He motioned for the women to get back to camp, and Abbie ran with the rest of them, trying not to spill too many berries from her bowl. Her heart pounded with excitement. Perhaps it was Zeke returning! She ran with a glad heart toward camp while Black Elk trotted along beside her, shouting, "*Hopo! Hopo!*"

Berries bounced out of the bowl, but Abbie didn't care. Surely it was Zeke coming! But as soon as she reached the edge of the village, Black Elk slid off his horse and grabbed her, pulling the bowl of berries from her hands and handing them to Tall Grass Woman.

"Go tipi!" he ordered. "*Hai!* Do not let them see you!"

She looked at him with disappointed eyes. "It's . . . it's not Zeke?"

He shook his head. "No like how they look! Bad *Veheos*, we think maybe. Have guns. Go! Go!" The young man gave her a shove, and she darted for her tipi, but the men who were approaching down the distant slope had already caught sight of all the commotion. Their leader turned to look back to the men.

"Somebody with light skin just ducked inside one of them tipis," he called out to the others. "Somebody shoved her in. We just might of found ourselves that white squaw prisoner, boys!"

"Hope you're right, Claude," one of the men replied with a grin.

"Keep your rifles ready," Claude Baker replied. "These redskins don't have much in the way of firearms yet, but you can't trust 'em. We ain't never had a lot of trouble with Cheyenne, though. I expect they'd just as soon hand her over as get themselves in trouble with the white folks and the soldiers."

They proceeded down the gentle, green slope toward the peaceful village that had been partially asleep until the rumor had quickly spread that white men with guns were approaching. Now many Indians stood outside their tipis, and warriors, gripping tomahawks and bows and lances, remained beside their own tipis to protect their women and children.

Baker eyed the village warily as he entered. He rode straight toward the tipi where he'd seen the most commotion, determined he'd frighten off the Cheyenne men simply by showing his power and courage. He rode straight up to the tipi, and his men scattered out slightly, each watching in a different direction. Swift Arrow stood directly in front of the tipi, his arms folded in front of him and a sneer on his face.

"Why do you come to our camp?" he demanded.

Baker grinned. "Well, I'll be damned! You speak English. That ought to make things easier, Indian." His eyes scanned some of the other Indians as his rifle rested on his knee, pointed directly at Swift Arrow. Baker took a quick survey of some of the squaws, remembering what a good time he'd had with Dancing Moon; then he looked back at Swift Arrow. "Name's Baker," he told the Indian. "Me and my men are part of the new volunteers for the bluecoats that are fightin' the Mexicans. You know about bluecoats, Indian?"

Swift Arrow stepped closer. "I am called Swift Arrow!" he

answered. "And I know about bluecoats. You do not wear the blue coat. You do not look like soldier!"

Baker grinned. "Well, we are, just the same. And you redskins ought to understand that when this war with Mexico is over the bluecoats is gonna make Indians their next campaign, 'specially if you keep up your raidin' and rapin' and such. You're gonna be in big trouble, Swift Arrow."

"We have done no raiding or raping! Only white men rape!" Swift Arrow spit back in reply. "Tell us why you are here . . . or leave us!"

Abbie watched from a tiny opening in the seam of the tipi just enough for her to be able to see outside with one eye, and her heart quickened when she saw the man called Baker shove the end of his rifle against Swift Arrow's neck.

"We got word you Cheyenne bucks is holdin' a white woman here captive," he growled. "We hear tell you've treated her so bad you've got her all brainwashed into thinkin' she has to stay here now 'cause she's been molested by lowdown redskins and can't never face her white kinfolk again!" He shoved the rifle harder, pushing Swift Arrow slightly backward. "That true, red devil? You holdin' a white woman captive?"

"There is no white woman here!" Swift Arrow replied through gritted teeth.

Baker just grinned and backed his horse. "Go ahead boys!" he shouted to the others. Six of the eighteen soldiers galloped up to preplanned targets; each grasped a child, jerked it up onto his horse and held a handgun to its head. Mothers screamed in terror and warriors watched in confusion, aware of the power of the rifles and unsure what the white men intended to do with the children. To preserve the children was most important. One warrior, thinking only of saving his own small son, charged the soldier who held him. The soldier quickly shot with his handgun, knocking the warrior down with the bullet but only wounding him in the shoulder. More women screamed, and for a moment there was general commotion, with rifles pointed threateningly in every direction, while the wounded Indian struggled to his knees, groaning with pain. Swift Arrow spread his feet in a fighting stance, his hand resting on his tomahawk, and Abbie's eyes widened with horror at the realization that more of them could get hurt because of her.

"Tell us the truth, red bastard, or we'll start shootin' the lice in these little heads one by one!" Baker told Swift Arrow. Swift Arrow looked at the soldiers and the little children, amazed that these white men would be so cowardly as to use infants to get what they wanted.

"You stink like a skunk!" Swift Arrow sneered in reply. "You are lower than the belly of a snake to hide behind babies! Get down from your horse and settle this like a man, white scum!"

Baker kicked out and caught Swift Arrow in the jaw, knocking him backward. Swift Arrow grasped his tomahawk and got to his feet, making ready to attack, but Abbie screamed out his name and ran out of the tipi.

"Don't do it, Swift Arrow!" she cried out, darting in front of him and grabbing at the tomahawk. "He wants you to do it!" Swift Arrow shoved her away and made her fall; then he raised his hatchet again. "No, Swift Arrow! Listen to me! I know how they think!"

Swift Arrow's arm stopped in midair, as Baker backed his horse a little and held his rifle straight and sure. The camp fell silent, for the white woman had shown herself.

"Go ahead, redskin!" Baker challenged Swift Arrow. "Move that arm one more inch and I'll have reason to blow your balls off!"

"Swift Arrow, don't give him reason to shoot!" Abbie shouted, getting back to her feet. "I don't want anyone else hurt because of me!"

Swift Arrow backed up unwillingly, his eyes blazing. Somehow he would find a way to kill this man called Claude Baker!

"Why did you not stay inside!" Swift Arrow barked at

Abbie, his eyes still on Claude Baker.

"I couldn't!" she answered. "Not with them holding the children!" Swift Arrow still gripped the tomahawk, and Abbie's heart pounded with terrible fear.

"Hey, she's a young one," one of the soldiers yelled out. "Bet them bucks found her nice and sweet!"

Baker chuckled and pulled back the hammer of his rifle. "Put down the weapon, redskin!" he sneered. "Or I'll shoot the girl first and then you. We'll take the white woman's body with us to show the soldiers and tell them it was Cheyenne who killed her—after raping her!"

Abbie glared at Baker. "You filth! How dare you come riding in here hiding behind little children! These people have done nothing wrong!"

"They've got you, ain't they? You sayin' holdin' a white woman captive ain't wrong?"

"I'm not a captive! Would I have cared about this man and the others if I were their prisoner? I live with them of my own choosing!"

Baker's eyebrows arched and he chuckled. "Well, well. Yer mighty loose for such a little girl now, ain't you? Looks like they've done a good job on breakin' you in to their way of livin'."

"No one has done anything!" Abbie replied angrily. "None of these men has ever touched me! I belong to Cheyenne Zeke, a half-blood who lives among these people. This man here, Swift Arrow, is Zeke's half brother. My husband . . . had to go to Independence on business. I have no other family, so I am staying with Zeke's family until he returns! That's all there is to it!"

Baker sighed, running his eyes over her small body. "Ain't no white woman lives with redskins of her own free will."

"This one does!" she answered, her anger overcoming her fear. "And if you make trouble, you'll be having Cheyenne Zeke to worry about, because he'll find you!"

"Hey, Claude!" one of the others spoke up. "I've heard of

237

this Cheyenne Zeke. He ain't one to mess with. I hear tell he uses a blade as fast as a man can draw a rifle, and he takes pleasure in exposin' a man's insides."

Claude eyed Abbie, then Swift Arrow. "How many times has this one had you while your husband's been gone?" he sneered. Swift Arrow tensed.

"Swift Arrow, don't let him make you do something foolish!" Abbie pleaded.

Claude just grinned. "Well, now, we all know how some Cheyenne men have more than one wife. Maybe the women can have more than one husband. I hear tell brothers share their wives and all kinds of rituals is performed with women—regular orgies, I hear." He looked at Abigail. "That true, honey? Tell us white men what the red bucks do that's so different, hmm?"

The white men all laughed jeeringly, and Abbie blinked back tears of rage, her face coloring deeply. "You're a horrible man!" she sneered. "You're the worst coward I've ever seen!"

Claude leaned forward, unaffected by her insults. "Well, missy, just the same, you're comin' with us."

"Over my dead body!" she retorted.

Claude just grinned. "Well, if that's how you want it. But I'd just as soon have you alive. 'Course I could take you over the dead bodies of these little children here and of some of the women and warriors, if that's the way you want it, honey. Us white soldiers can't just ride out of here and leave a poor little white girl prisoner with these here savages now, can we? You've just been brainwashed, honey. Soon as you're back to civilization, you'll start rememberin' where you belong fast enough. Ain't nothin' to be ashamed about, missy. The white folks will understand. You can go to church and get cleansed, and maybe some white man will even marry you—long as you don't ever tell him you've slept with red lice!"

"You will take her nowhere!" Swift Arrow seethed. "You will not touch her, even if it means the lives of some of our people! She will not leave here with the likes of you! I made my

238

brother a promise to protect her!"

Baker spit out a wad of tobacco at Swift Arrow's feet. "Well, now, I'd say she'd be a mite safer with her own kind than with a bunch of savages. We all know how curious you Indian men are about white women."

Swift Arrow moved quickly, realizing his only hope was to leave the coward before him no time to think. In a flash he grabbed the barrel end of Baker's rifle and shoved upward. The gun went off, and Swift Arrow yanked Baker from his mount, shoving him to the ground and jerking the rifle from his hands while he was stunned and smashing Baker across the side of the head with the butt end of the gun. In the same moment, Abbie had ducked back inside the tipi and come out with her Spencer carbine to find Swift Arrow holding Baker's own rifle on the man. It all happened in not more than two seconds, and Baker's men, inwardly afraid because there were so many more Cheyenne and Arapaho present than soldiers, hesitated and did not fire their guns; for all knew their first shots would take down some of the warriors and children, but there would be no time to reload before the rest of the Cheyenne men attacked with lances, clubs, knives, and tomahawks, and none of them wanted to die that kind of death.

Baker groaned and held the side of his face, frightened now that he realized his plan to frighten the Cheyenne into giving up the white woman had backfired. Dancing Moon had convinced him that Abigail was an unwilling captive, and he had fully expected her cooperation. But this was a different matter, for the white woman herself held a rifle on him.

"Take your men and leave, white scum, or you will be the first to die!" Swift Arrow growled. "Do you think my warriors are afraid of such a few men or even of the other soldiers you might send?" He laughed wickedly. "Send them! We enjoy fighting! But I tell you this! We will die to the last man before we will give this woman over to one such as you! Do you think we are such fools that we do not know what you would do with her? She is my brother's wife! Now get out of our village before

239

I am no longer able to keep myself from pulling this trigger! If I do, I will only wound you, for I would enjoy saving you for a slow death!"

Baker swallowed and got up slowly, all his courage gone now that his rifle was in his enemy's hands.

"Tell the others to let the children go!" Swift Arrow told him. "If they do not, then tell them to pull the triggers and kill the children! But be sure they know what will happen to them when the children are dead!"

Swift Arrow's face told Baker that he meant every word of it. The warriors would sacrifice the children if need be. They would not be threatened and toyed with.

Baker picked up his hat and scowled. "Let the little savages go!" he ordered his men.

The children were dropped carelessly to the ground, and their mothers rushed to pick them up and scurry off with them.

"You and your people will pay for this!" Baker told Swift Arrow.

"No! You'll pay!" Abbie shouted back. "When the soldiers find out how you rode in here and tried to make trouble with the Cheyenne, they'll be very angry. The last thing they want is to rile up the Indians! They've done nothing wrong! Nothing! I am the wife of Cheyenne Zeke, Zeke Monroe. I have a paper to prove that I am legally married to him—the white man's way. We were married at Fort Bridger. Zeke will be back any day now, and when he finds out you made trouble for his wife and his brothers, you'll be having to look over your shoulder, Mr. Claude Baker, because you don't know just when you might find a half-breed standing behind you with a knife!" She stepped closer with her own rifle. "None of these good people has harmed me in any way! They are my family and I live with them by choice! You get your men out of here, because I don't know how much longer these warriors can hold off from chopping you into little pieces!"

"Come on, Claude, let's git out of here!" one of the other

240

men yelled. "She ain't no captive, not if she's been legally married to the half-breed."

"Like I say, Claude," another spoke up. "I done heard of this here Cheyenne Zeke. I don't want nothin' to do with him."

"But Dancing Moon said she was a captive!" Baker retorted, backing away from Abbie and Swift Arrow.

"Dancing Moon!" Abbie's face paled. "You know the Arapaho woman, Dancing Moon? She is the one who sent you here?"

Baker moved around to mount his horse. "We had a run-in with the bitch. She's like all the other squaws. She spread her legs for all of us—in return for food and supplies. And she told us about you. We come here to help you, to save you from these savages!"

"You're a stupid fool to believe the likes of Dancing Moon!" Abbie told him. "And it's you I'd need saving from, not the Cheyenne! Now get out of here!"

Swift Arrow opened the chamber of Baker's rifle and spilled out a bullet; then he tossed the gun back to the man and picked up his tomahawk.

"Leave quickly! I would love to see your blood flow!" He sneered.

Baker backed his horse, eying the hundreds of Cheyenne who surrounded himself and his men. He did not think they would dare to give him trouble, but now they had the upper hand and all looked eager to do battle. "Ride out, men!" he shouted to the others. They quickly and eagerly obeyed. Baker eyed Abbie for a moment. "You won't shoot me!" he growled. "It would bring your precious bucks too much trouble from the soldiers and you know it!" He jerked his horse back farther. "I'll leave! But folks is gonna know there's a white woman livin' with Cheyenne men out here, and you won't never be able to show your face in civilized parts again, you whore!"

He whirled his horse and rode out, all of his men disappearing over the hill down which they had come and

241

heading southwest for Fort Laramie.

Abbie lowered her rifle slowly, the blood draining from her face. Her body shook with rage and humiliation. This was the first time she had been exposed to the very thing Zeke had warned her could happen if they tried to live in the white world, for she knew that for every Claude Baker there were a hundred more like him. She had thought that perhaps it could be different in the West than it had been for Zeke in Tennessee. But it was just as Zeke said. The only whites out West were originally from the East, and they had brought with them all of their attitudes. Like the child that she was, she had not believed him, having faith in the goodness of people. But Zeke had been down that road. He knew.

"Now you are ashamed of us?" Swift Arrow asked her quietly. He stood behind her, his own heart raging at Claude Baker's last words. Abbie shook her head.

"No," she answered. "I'm ashamed of my own people . . . the ones who think like . . . him!" She looked off in the direction Claude Baker and his men had ridden and tears streamed down her face. "I'm sorry for their insults."

"Do not be sorry for that kind. It was not your fault."

She turned to face him. "Thank you," she told him, wiping at her eyes. "Thank you for not letting them take me. You could have saved yourselves a lot of trouble by letting them have me, you know. It might have been worse than it was."

He, too, looked after Baker's men. "I, Swift Arrow, should let men such as those take you? What kind of man would I be to do that? I made my brother a promise!" He took the rifle from her hands. "Come, *Kseé*, you are safe now. They will not come back."

Abbie closed her eyes and nodded, but she could not stop the tears of shame and embarrassment that slid quietly down her cheeks. "I hate them!" she sniffed. "I hate all people who think those awful things!"

"So . . . now you understand this hatred we feel . . . you understand what my brother has always understood."

242

She did not reply. The tears that choked her would not let her speak.

When Zeke regained consciousness, it was to find himself lashed by the wrists to a wagon wheel, his arms stretched out to either side, his nude body sitting on the hard, rocky ground. He struggled to focus his eyes, shaking his head and looking down to relieve his eyes from the glare of the hot sun. His mouth screamed with terrible thirst, and his head ached from the scalp wound. Sweat trickled into his eyes, burning them. He tugged at his bindings; then he was suddenly brought to full consciousness when someone tossed water into his face. It felt wonderful, and he licked his lips, trying to get some into his mouth.

Then a shadow knelt in front of him, and he looked into the beautiful but hated face of Dancing Moon. His eyes lit up with fire and he tugged at his bindings again.

"Just how did I get lucky enough to run into you!" he growled at her. He spit into her face, and the smile she had been wearing turned into a sneer.

"I would not call it lucky, my Cheyenne lover," she hissed in reply. "This day you shall die for casting me out for your white bitch!" She grabbed his scrotum and pinched, and he gritted his teeth against the horrible pain. "How is your white woman?" she asked. "Did she live after Dancing Moon attacked her?"

Zeke's stomach felt nauseous from the pain in his privates. "She . . . lived!" he snarled. "She lost a baby . . . but she lived! And I'll have my revenge, Dancing Moon! Never have I wanted to bring harm to a woman . . . until now!" He struggled again at his bindings, but she only laughed.

"Hey, Dancing Moon, we have to go!" one of the Mexicans called out to her from a distant campfire. "How long you going to mess with that half-blood? We got to take these guns south and send Miguel to pay Mr. Mack. Then maybe we get even

243

more guns, eh?"

"We go in the morning!" she replied, her eyes still on Zeke. She lowered her voice then, talking directly to Zeke. "You killed my man with that blade of yours, my Cheyenne stud! For this and for casting me out, you shall die!"

She stood up and straddled his legs. "You were the best," she purred. "But you were bad to Dancing Moon. I am sorry to have to kill you!"

He looked away. "Who are these men? Why are you with them?"

She laughed and moved back from him. "They are my friends. When my people cast me out, I came south. These men found me. And I"—she smiled more—"managed to talk them into keeping me with them. I became the woman of their leader, Manuel Artigo. Now Manuel is dead, and for the privilege of competing for my favors, the rest of these men will look to me as their leader. I have learned quickly, my half-breed lover! I have power with men . . . and there is wealth in stolen guns! I find this life exciting!" She strutted in front of him, and he could almost smell her as a male dog smells a bitch in heat. He was revolted by her. She had changed. There was a time, years ago, when he'd enjoyed her company, even though he knew she had a strange appetite for men and was not true to him. But she had never been vicious. It seemed that as she matured, her appetite for men and excitement had grown also. "After this deal, I think perhaps my men and I will raid some of the wealthy villas and see what riches we can find. For now we will get more of the smuggled rifles, and the Mexicans will pay me much gold for helping them. I think perhaps we shall ride against the Americans and take what we need to lead a good life, no? I will let my men rape the white women. I would enjoy watching that!" She laughed. "Yes, I would enjoy that! I hate the white women!"

She whirled and faced him straight on. "You! You will be sorry you ever planted yourself in a white woman, Cheyenne Zeke! Today you shall sit there and rot in the sun! Then tonight you shall freeze in the cold desert air. In the morning, you shall enjoy the company of rattle snakes when we throw you into one of the pits!" She flung her head back and went to join the remaining men. There was much laughter and drinking, after which she decided to put on a show for Zeke to demonstrate her power over her men. She sat them in a circle around a blanket and, strutting before them, picked one or more at random to perform sex acts with her in front of Zeke. She was an animal, worse than an animal.

Zeke looked away, concentrating on thoughts of cool mountains and thinking of himself as an eagle flying high in the heavens where all was peace and beauty. But his thoughts were constantly interrupted by Dancing Moon's grunts and groans and the laughter of the men; never had he hated a woman as he hated this one. Then he thought about the smooth, lily-handed Jonathan Mack, and his hatred was almost unbearable.

He closed his eyes and pressed his head back, again concentrating on the mountains, using all his discipline to take his spirit to another place and so avoid the pain and heat and his terrible thirst. He opened his eyes for just a moment when he heard the distant screeching of buzzards. He saw them picking at something several yards away, then realized it was Grimey. His body tensed with a burning desire for vengeance, and he tugged at his bindings again, but to no avail.

"*Maheo*, help me!" he whispered. "*Heammawihio*, help me! *Ahktunowihio*, help me! Keep me from death. Bless me with the glory of revenge! Allow me to go back to my woman! *Maheo! Maheo!* I walk as one with Thee. I walk as one with *Esceheman* and *Hesek*."

"*Ho-shuh*," a voice seemed to tell him somewhere in his mind. "*Ho-shuh*, my son." He closed his eyes and slipped back into the blessed relief of unconsciousness.

When Zeke awoke, darkness was falling, and he shivered

from the cold. Again he concentrated on being strong, for he had learned to discipline himself against pain when suffering the Sun Dance ritual. He struggled to ignore the terrible thirst and the pain in his head. Then he saw Dancing Moon sauntering toward him, carrying a canteen and a cloth. To his surprise she knelt down beside him and wet the cloth, applying it to the wound on his forehead. She washed his face and then held the canteen to his lips, and he drank eagerly. He said nothing, wondering why she had offered this small bit of kindness, suspicious of her every move.

"Dancing Moon is sorry to treat you this way," she told him quietly. "There was a time when it was good between us, Cheyenne Zeke. Both of us wild and free and eager in our lovemaking." She traced a finger over his finely chiseled lips. "But Dancing Moon does not like being cast out for another woman . . . especially not for a white woman, you see?"

He turned his head. "Get out of here!" he muttered, thinking only of poor Abbie and the loss of the baby. Dancing Moon only grinned.

"I came to offer you a chance to live," she told him. He turned back to face her with bitter eyes.

"And just what is this chance I have?" he asked suspiciously.

She ran a finger down over his chest. "There is still a warm place in Dancing Moon's heart for her man," she replied. "If you would show me that you are still my man, Cheyenne Zeke . . . show Dancing Moon that you still have . . . feelings for her . . ." She leaned down and kissed his nipples and he grimaced with hatred and revulsion at the memory of seeing her cavort with the Mexicans.

"Get away!" he hissed.

"But you are such a beautiful man!" she purred, moving her lips downward. She began caressing him with expert fingers, and then she began using her lips and tongue to work him against his will, for Dancing Moon knew men and how little control they had over such things. Zeke knew her intention and fury pulsed through his blood. If he had to die, he would rather have it be quickly at the fangs of snakes, than to first be humiliated and debased at the hands of this she-devil. He waited until she was more excited, letting her grope at him and devour him, and then when she raised her head slightly he came up hard with his knee, catching her on the jaw. She cried out and fell against him, and he brought up his left leg, twisting slightly and shoving her away from him with it; then he kicked her hard in the stomach.

She lay there stunned for a moment before she groaned and crawled to her hands and knees, shouting for her men.

"What has he done to you, Dancing Moon?" one of them asked. "He must be a man who does not appreciate a beautiful woman, huh?" The man laughed and helped Dancing Moon to her feet.

"Spread his legs!" she hissed.

Zeke struggled as four men took hold of him, two men on each side. They pulled his legs apart, and Dancing Moon stepped close to him, sneering down with evil pleasure.

"You are a fool!" she told him. "That was your last chance!" She drew back her booted foot and kicked as hard as she could. This time it was impossible for Zeke not to cry out. "That will keep you from having anyone else for a while!" she hissed. "But that does not matter anyway. I am tired of these games!" She looked at her men. "Throw him in the pit! We will leave as soon as the sun rises!"

Someone unlashed his wrists, and Zeke struggled; but he had no strength because of the black pain Dancing Moon had inflicted on him. He was dragged and pushed for some distance; then he felt himself falling into blackness. His body hit something hard and cold and damp.

"Throw in his knife!" he heard Dancing Moon shouting somewhere in the distance. "Let the great warrior be buried with his best weapon! It is fitting!" Zeke heard her laughter as something fell beside him and clinked against a rock. He heard a hissing sound, and although the pain in his groin was

247

almost unbearable, his instincts told him he must not move until the pain lessened and he could get his bearings. He was in a snake pit, of that he was certain. Perhaps if he could lie still until morning, the sun would shine into the hole enough to show him where the snakes were.

"We will not see Cheyenne Zeke again!" Dancing Moon told the others. He heard their laughter, and then the voices grew dim.

"I tell you, we saw her!" Claude Baker tried to explain to an officer at Fort Laramie. "She's white, and she's livin' with the Cheyenne! Take some men and go see for yourself! When we tried to take her out of there, the Cheyenne threatened us!"

"I know the Cheyenne! They don't go around capturin' white women!" a Laramie scout interrupted. "I'm tellin' you, sir, they can't be holdin' no captive. We ain't even had any reports of any missin' or stolen white women."

The officer leaned back in his chair. "I suggest you tell us the whole story, Baker. If you intend to volunteer for this war and join our ranks, you'd best be honest with us now."

Baker sighed. "All right. I'll tell you again. This Arapaho woman we met on the way here, she told us about a white woman that was bein' held captive by the Cheyenne. She said that the woman was so brainwashed by the bucks and so ashamed to face her own people again that it might be hard to get her away from them to help her. Well, we figured it was our duty to help the poor woman if we could. So, on our way here we checked out all the Cheyenne we could, hid out and scouted them, you know? Then, this here one band, we watched them awhile and we was sure we saw a real light-skinned woman with them. So we rode in, thinkin' the Cheyenne would hand her over quick enough if they knew they'd be in a heap of trouble and had been found out. But it was true, like the Arapaho woman told us. She'd been so brainwashed that she done stuck up for the Cheyenne—pointed a rifle at us and everything!

Said she was there of her own free will and wanted to stay! They threatened us, sir. I think them bucks would have scalped us all if we'd of tried to take her out of there."

The officer pressed his fingers together and stared up at a clock. "Mmm-hmm." He shifted his eyes to Baker. "Well, Baker, I'd say if she's apparently satisfied where she is, then we'd best leave it alone for now. We have a war with Mexico to worry about, not one with Indians. That will most likely come later. The woman is probably some kind of half-breed anyway. Since we've had no reports of missing white women and are presently having no major problems with the Cheyenne, we will stay out of it."

"But, sir—"

"I said to forget it, Mr. Baker!" the man barked. "Your job as a volunteer is to muster out of here in two days and head south with a garrison that will be going to Santa Fe to reinforce Kearny once his men take the city. You came here to join up with the Mexican war, not to go chasing over the plains after some white squaw, even if she does appeal to you."

Baker looked down sheepishly. "Yes, sir."

"You should be glad. You joined up to see some action. You'll see a lot more when you head to Santa Fe than you would running around chasing after a white woman who probably isn't even white! You're dismissed, Baker!"

Baker scowled at them, but decided to push the matter was useless. He rose and trudged through the door. The officer leaned forward in his chair and lit a pipe. "What do you think of that story, Windy?" he asked the scout.

"Hard to say, sir. Like I said, we ain't had a lot of trouble . . . and no reports of stolen women. And it just ain't like the Cheyenne to do that anyway."

The officer puffed at his pipe. "Well, spread the word just the same. I don't want anyone to go riding into any Indian camps and threatening anyone. Just have people keep their eyes and ears open at the trading posts. And it wouldn't hurt to ask a few questions when you're out there and run into small bands of Cheyenne."

"I'll do that, sir. But it will be awhile before I run into any real small parties. They're all headed up to meet with the Sioux for the summer ceremonies. There'll be a hell of a lot of them together, and I don't aim to go ridin' into anything like that. They get pretty worked up over the Sun Dance and all. They get mighty touchy—start feelin' their oats, if you know what I mean, celebratin' their manhood and all."

The officer grinned. "I understand, Windy. Just lay low and see what you can find out." He leaned back again. "I see bad times ahead, Windy. Bad times for the Indians and for us soldiers, and the settlers, too . . . Seems like a big enough country, Windy. But I see it growing smaller every day."

Thirteen

Abbie started awake from a deep sleep, shivering and sweating. She looked around the tipi, dimly lit by the coals of a fire. Her nightmare brought tears to her eyes, and she heard Swift Arrow call to her.

"What is wrong?" he asked her. "You called out in your sleep."

Her breath came in short gasps so at first she could not reply; for she was still filled with the terror of the dream, and a whimper rose from her throat. Swift Arrow waited no longer, but went inside, without her invitation, to find her sitting wide-eyed on her bed of robes, looking around at the floor as though something were after her. Swift Arrow went to her side, grasping her arms. She choked out another cry.

"Get them away!" she murmured. Swift Arrow looked around the tipi.

"Get what away?" He shook her lightly. "Wake up, Abigail. You only dream."

She looked at him with frightened eyes that began to focus on their true target, and she finally realized she had indeed been dreaming. But there was something about it that remained ominous to her.

"Snakes!" she whispered. "There were . . . snakes . . . all around me! Hissing at me! Crawling over me!"

He frowned. "This is a bad dream. What do you think it means?"

"I . . . don't know," she answered, searching his eyes. "But I . . . I feel it has something to do with Zeke!" she whimpered, her eyes filling with tears. "He's in trouble, Swift Arrow. I just know it! Something terrible has happened to him!"

He squeezed her arms. "If you feel this is so, my sister, then I will call the elders together and we will hold a prayer council. I will gather the most honored ones and the priests, and we will smoke the pipe and offer prayers to all of the spirits to watch over our brother and bring him back to us. Together we have much power. We will send it to him, and he will be strong!"

She nodded, and he left to summon the elders and the priests and the most honored dog soldiers. Abigail had had a dream. Zeke was in danger. They must help him.

Zeke drew on all his reserve strength and discipline to keep from moving. He even kept his breathing as light as possible. For hours he lay in the dark pit, listening to the hissing all around him. Once he even felt something crawl over his legs, but he knew if he did not move, the snakes would have no reason to attack him. He thought of himself as one of the rocks and prayed to the spirits to help him melt into the boulders and become a part of the earth, for wasn't he one with the land after all?

"Give me courage, *Maheo!*" he prayed silently. "Fill me with your great strength, and remember that in my vision I was protected by the great eagle! Help me now, my Father, in my moment of great need!"

"*Ho-shuh,*" came the voice again out of the darkness. "Be still. Be confident!"

He felt a warmth flooding over him, and he could see Abbie as vividly as if she were standing beside him. "*Ho-shuh,*" came her voice. "You can overcome this, Zeke. You must, for I wait for you."

"Abbie!" he whispered, tears filling his eyes. He heard a hissing near his ear, and he did not whisper again. But he cried

252

out to her from within. He could see her standing in a field of green prairie grass, smiling, looking lovely in her doeskin tunic. He felt warm again and strangely calm. He closed his eyes and let his body relax, releasing tension in his mucles from head to toe. If he was to defeat this pit of snakes, he must be calm and not panic. He had to remember that he was a man, and that the snake was the lowest form of life. Snakes could never conquer man, especially not a warrior who had suffered the Sun Dance.

For hours he lay there, praying and feeling warmth and power flooding through him, while the night lingered and morning seemed forever far, far away. But a shaft of light finally filtered through the hole above him, and Zeke began moving his eyes to look around, keeping his head still.

He saw that he lay on a large, flat rock that jutted up from an even deeper pit. *Maheo* had seen fit to keep him from falling even deeper. Zeke could tell that if he had gone all the way down, there would have been no hope of ever climbing back out. This was good. He could tell by the light and by a brush of warm air that the exit hole above was not so far that he could not climb to it. The problem would be avoiding snakes on the way, but at least, he was not at the bottom of the pit, where most of the snakes congregated.

The sun's rays moved slightly, and he saw something glinting on a small ledge across from where he lay. He studied the object for a moment, then realized it was his knife! His heart filled with joy, for the knife was his best weapon and gave him great power! But first he had to get it, and it lay beside a large rattler that was staring at him this very moment.

All around him he could see nothing but the deeper pit. He could not be certain just how big the rock he lay on was, but he sensed that should he move too quickly, he would go over the edge. Without changing his position and thereby risking snake bite, he could not know what was behind him. But he would not lie there and die and rot in that stinking hole with rattlers as his graveside partners! He had to get out! Even if he was bitten as he climbed, he would have time to reach the top before the venom took hold. At least that way he would die above ground, and not in this devil's pit, where evil spirits lurked, waiting to rob his soul and take him to places where his soul and body would be forever tormented. He would not die such a death!

He summoned all of his courage and raised himself ever so slowly to a sitting position, feeling the power of the spirits with him. He winced with pain, for his bones ached from the fall and from spending a whole night in the cold, damp pit with no clothing. He took another look around him, now able to see what had been behind him. A ledge jutted out, nearly touching the rock on which he sat, and on it was another rattler. Its head was straight up and its tail began shaking.

"So you are the one who hissed in my ear, are you?" he said to the snake. "I honor the spirit that controls you, oh master of the underworld. But your world is not for me, I am afraid. I ask you to let me leave."

The snake's tail continued to rattle, and its tongue flicked in and out with lightning speed. Zeke stared at the creature for several minutes, concentrating on the power of *Maheo*, and suddenly the rattler slithered farther back under another ledge where Zeke could not see it.

Zeke swallowed and breathed deeply, trying to stay in control. He turned slowly to look at the snake that was curled beside his knife. "Good morning to you, black spirit," he said to the diamond-backed monster. "I don't suppose you will let me have my knife?"

The snake hissed, and Zeke scowled.

"That is what I was afraid of," he said. He sighed. "Then I must tell you that I intend to take my weapon from you, whether you like it or not. We shall see, master of demons, who is the fastest!"

He breathed deeply again. "Guide me, *Maheo*," he whispered. He set his eyes on the knife, staring at it, gauging in his mind just how far away it was, concentrating on that one spot. He had to move like lightning and he had to get a sure grip, or the weapon would fall into the pit below. He waited another moment until the rattler beside it let its head sink down slightly. Then he moved!

In an instant Zeke's arm was out and his hand gripped the buffalo hide that was wrapped around the jawbone handle of the knife. Something brushed his wrist, and he thought he'd been bitten. But in that fraction of a second, the knife had been retrieved! He gripped it tightly in his hand and then dared to look down, his body trembling with dread. He saw no fang marks, and when he looked across at the ledge, the snake was gone. It had apparently tried to strike him and had fallen from the ledge when it did so.

Zeke breathed a sigh of relief and slowly sat up straighter, looking around at the ledges above and taking more deep breaths to help clear his mind. It would be easy to climb out of the pit using the ledges, but it was impossible to tell which ones might hold a snake; and if he slipped or a ledge broke under his weight, he would be cast into the deeper pit below, where he was sure to die almost instantly from a hundred snake bites. That would be a gruesome death indeed. He tried to remain calm, remembering again the spirits that guided him and the strength and cunning only they could give him.

"I sing to you, *Maheo!*" he said softly. He got to his knees and began to chant the Cheyenne death song. If he was to fall into the pit, he would go down singing the great Cheyenne song of courage.

"Nothing lives long," he chanted in the Cheyenne tongue. "Nothing stays here, except the earth and the mountains."

He got to his feet and continued to chant softly. "Nothing lives long, nothing stays here, except the earth and the mountains."

He took a deep breath and reached out for a ledge on the wall of the pit. He got a firm hold with his left hand. "Nothing lives long, nothing stays here," he chanted again. "Except the earth and the mountains."

He put his knife in his mouth, clamping his teeth down on

255

the blade so that his other hand would be free for climbing. Since he wore no clothes, every part of his body would be exposed to the snakes, which only made the danger worse. Every inching step upward would be filled with terrible danger, still he had no choice but to try. He hummed the chant for courage as he placed one bare foot on a ledge and pulled himself up.

Hisses seemed to come from every crack and hole, and Zeke's body broke out in a drenching sweat. He continued to hum, putting a foot on the next ledge up, then boosting himself and grasping a higher ledge with his left hand.

He summoned all of his prayer power to ask the spirits to keep the ledges from breaking off. As he boosted himself one step higher, a rattler stared him in the face. It reared back to strike, but quickly Zeke grabbed the knife from his mouth and plunged it into the back of the snake's head. Venom squirted onto his chest, and wincing with nausea, Zeke thought that he preferred killing a man enemy to killing these smelly demons of the pits. The piece of rock, to which only his left hand clung, started to crumble. Quickly he yanked the knife from the snake and put it back in his mouth, tasting snake's blood and groaning at the horror of it as he quickly grabbed hold of another ledge with his right hand.

Already he was close to the top of the hole, and he speculated that Dancing Moon and the others must have thought he had fallen all the way to the bottom. They never would have left him so close to the top if they had known, but would have found a way to push his body farther down. This thought gave him courage, for again *Maheo* had smiled upon him by keeping Dancing Moon and the others from double-checking to be sure he had fallen all the way down. Now he knew he was meant to live! He was meant to reap his revenge!

He climbed faster, shunning all fear of the snakes, scrambling toward the blessed sunlight and fresh air and freedom! Higher and faster he climbed, while rocks broke off and crumbled to the awful pit below, and finally he broke forth into the wonderful, warm sunshine!

How he wanted to cry out with his joy! But he knew it was possible Dancing Moon and the others were still about. He grasped the knife from his mouth and began slithering like the snakes he had just left, moving silently across the hardened earth, not caring that the stones dug at his body. It felt wonderful to have the earth cutting at his body, for it meant he was above the ground! He was free and alive, and cries of joy and laughter pushed at his throat for release. But he stifled them until he reached a large boulder behind which he could take a moment to compose himself and determine whether anyone was still around before deciding what his next move would be. He was alive, and Dancing Moon would pay!

Morning broke across the Black Hills—*Paha-Sapa* the Sioux called them. It was beautiful country, this place where Abigail was camped with the Cheyenne and Arapaho, waiting for the arrival of more Sioux. But this morning Abigail was not concerned with the Sioux or the Sun Dance. She was concerned only with the breakthrough of the sun, for just as it broke, an eagle flew above them, circling and calling.

"Look!" Deer Slayer called out. "It is a sign! It is a good sign. Lone Eagle lives!"

Abbie looked up, and the eagle cried out again, circling so low that it cast its shadow over the circle of praying elders and priests.

"It is good," Swift Arrow told her. "Our prayers have helped Zeke."

Abbie covered her face and bent over to smell the sweet earth, for its smell made her think of Zeke's earthy, manly scent. "Thank you, God!" she whispered, her heart feeling lighter. She prayed that the eagle truly was a good sign. Someone touched her hair.

"You should not weep," she heard Deer Slayer telling her. "This is a good sign."

257

"I only weep with joy," she replied.

He patted her head. "This we understand. There is no shame in such weeping, my daughter."

Zeke crawled to the Mexicans' campsite to see that they had broken camp and left. His buckskins still lay near the spot where he had been tied to the wagon wheel. He looked around cautiously, his all-seeing eyes scanning the cliffs and canyons around him. No living thing was about, except for the hidden snakes.

He stood up and spit. Then he vomited at the thought of the snake's blood in his mouth. He picked up some sand and, rubbing it on his chest to get rid of the venom, walked to get his clothing. He winced with pain as he walked, for he still ached badly from Dancing Moon's kick. He hoped she had not put an end to his ability to plant more life in Abigail's belly.

He tied on his loincloth, again wincing with pain. He pulled on his buckskins and his deerskin shirt. His head pained him, he felt dizzy from the superficial bullet wound on his forehead, and every bone in his body ached; but he knew he must start walking right away if he was to catch up with Dancing Moon and the others. And he most certainly intended to do so. Now that he had survived the pit of snakes, he could survive anything!

He noticed that someone had carelessly left behind a tin cup. He hurried over to it and discovered to his joy, that it was three-quarters full of cold coffee. He took a mouthful to rinse his mouth and spit it out, then drank the rest. He threw down the cup and looked around for Grimey's body, which he intended to cover with rocks before he left. But the body was nowhere to be seen, and he realized the Mexicans must have thrown it into a pit to hide it. It was agonizing to know that he was responsible for the death of his good and faithful friend.

He turned and began walking, following the very obvious imprint of the heavy wagons. Then he stopped and looked back for a moment at the hated canyon. He intended never to enter it again. He raised his arms and let out a Cheyenne war cry. He was alive. *Maheo* was good! He unbraided his hair and shook it out, letting it hang long and straight. To wear it so made him feel stronger—wilder and more vicious. He would need all these feelings when he met up with the Mexicans!

The night was a bright one, and Dancing Moon laughed as, holding up Zeke's bow and arrows, she danced around the circle of men. One of the men held Zeke's rifle in the air.

"Death has come to the great Cheyenne warrior!" Dancing Moon sang. "Death to the great Cheyenne lover! No more will he take the white woman to himself."

The men laughed loudly and guzzled down some of the whiskey from the wagons. Dancing Moon drank also, while Zeke watched from the shadows. They were making it easy for him. All he had to do was wait until the celebrating was over and they were drunk. Then they would be weak and clumsy.

His blood pulsed with the heat of joyous vengeance! These men would not live to fight the Mexican War, and the guns would never reach their destination. Cheyenne Zeke would see to it that Jonathan Mack's plan failed. Before Mack's treachery he would not have cared who got the rifles. Now he wanted no one to get them, and he wanted Dancing Moon to suffer! It was likely that someone had already headed north to Santa Fe to pay Mack for the guns, dynamite, and whiskey. But when Jonathan Mack saw Cheyenne Zeke alive, he would not be so happy about his profits. Zeke smiled as the thought of how the little, white-handed man would become whiter when he saw that the driver he had hired and tricked was still alive!

The Mexicans continued drinking well into the night, while Zeke sat in the shadows praying to *Maheo* for the skill to do his job properly. Dancing Moon also drank and danced, stripping off her clothing and gyrating suggestively in front of the men before she finally fell down and let them all have turns at her.

After heated intercourse with the woman, each man fell into a deep sleep from the liquor and the exhaustion of trying to please Dancing Moon. At last, in the wee morning hours they all slept peacefully, unaware that a tall, dark shadow, gripping a wicked knife, crept close to them.

One by one Zeke plunged the ugly blade into their hearts, feeling not one ounce of regret. For with every thrust of the blade, he thought about the horror of the snake pit, and what it would have been like if he had fallen to the bottom of it. The sight of Grimey's body being picked over by buzzards still tore at his guts, giving him all the incentive he needed to seek vengeance.

One man sensed impending danger even in his drunken sleep, and he sat up to see Zeke plunge his blade into the man beside him and rip downward. The other Mexican's eyes bulged with horror. But as he started to cry out, the blade slashed through his own throat, and his cry was cut off. However, he had aroused Dancing Moon. She stirred and rubbed her eyes.

"Hulio?" she called out. Then she gasped as someone suddenly grasped her long, black, tangled hair in a tight fist and jerked back her head. The big blade, damp with blood, was pressed against her throat, and Dancing Moon's horrified eyes looked into the face of Cheyenne Zeke. To her, his gritted teeth were like the white fangs of a devil spirit as she felt his hot breath near her face.

"Yes, it is really I, my filthy, whoring bitch!" he hissed. "Aren't you glad to see your Cheyenne lover?"

"Zeke!" she squeaked.

"You should have made certain I was dead before you threw me in that pit!" he growled at her. "You underestimated my power!" He moved and slashed downward, cutting along the side of one of her breasts, and she screamed. "You will find no help, my brown-skinned whore! They are all dead!" He jerked her up and pulled her by the hair of the head to a nearby cottonwood tree. She struggled in vain as he lashed her wrists together with rope he had stolen from one of the Mexican's horses. He pulled the rope painfully tight and then tied it around the tree so that she lay flat on her back with her arms over her head tied to the tree trunk. "You can lie here and think about the pleasant things I will do to you." Zeke sneered at her. "First I want you to watch what I will do with the precious smuggled guns and that valuable dynamite."

He left her side, and for the next few moments she could hear him ripping boards off the wagons. Then she heard shuffling noises, and a few minutes later he walked back to her, carrying his own rifle and his bow and arrows.

"Say farewell to your precious cargo," he told her. He took aim with the rifle and fired, and in the next instant one of the wagons exploded, sending whiskey bottles and rifles and piano parts high into the sky. Zeke shouted a blood curdling war cry at the wonderful sight of the destroyed and burning wagon. Then he took aim again, firing at the second wagon; a bright ball of orange temporarily lit up the desert.

Dancing Moon watched in horror and began struggling at her ropes. Zeke laughed like a crazy man; then he straddled her and knelt down, planting a knee in her stomach. He grabbed her behind the neck and flashed his big blade in the moonlight.

"I might have been able to forgive you for all of it, Dancing Moon," he snarled at her. "All of the things you have just done to me. But I cannot forgive you for attacking my woman and trying to kill her! Because of you my woman lost a baby and nearly lost her life! That I cannot forgive!"

"Please don't kill me, Zeke!" she squeaked.

He only grinned. "You are not so strong and sure now, huh?" He pressed the blade against her face. "I am going to give you a chance, whoring bitch! I have a plan! Maybe you will live. Maybe you will die. But either way, you will bear the mark of the man who did this to you!"

With that he held her jaw in the painfully tight grip of the strong fingers of his left hand while he deftly cut into the skin of her left cheek. He carved a Z deeply enough so that it would leave a scar. She screamed in horror through her clamped jaw, but Zeke's eyes gleamed only with vengeance and bore no sign of remorse. He jerked her head sideways, and carved another *Z* into her other cheek.

When he let go of her jaw, she cried out in horror, great sobs bubbling up from her throat. "No! No! No!" she groaned. "You have scarred me!"

"You have scarred yourself, bitch!" he replied. He wiped the knife on her hair, then got up from her and shoved the big blade into its sheath. "Never before have I wanted to harm a woman! My white blood kept me from killing and capturing other squaws when we raided the Crow and the Pawnee. Now, for the first time, my Indian blood tells me there is no dishonor in harming a woman, for this woman is a walking demon, whose mind is sick with evil spirits and wickedness! You are not human, Dancing Moon. Somehow the spirits of the world below have entered your soul and claimed you! Now you shall suffer the same horror you caused me to suffer!"

He walked away for a moment and then returned with a leather bag. "I have been waiting at this place for hours," he told her. "You were all so drunk you did not see me steal a canteen to quench my thirst. And you did not see me steal this leather bag which I needed to capture something I had seen. When I saw this thing, I knew how I would punish you for what you did to me!"

"No, Zeke!" she cried out, unsure of what he meant but certain it was something horrible. She could feel blood from her cheeks running into her ears, and she wondered how ugly she would be if she ever survived this night.

"Oh, yes, Arapaho lover!" he replied. "You are the first Arapaho I have ever called enemy! Now I advise you that if you want to live, you must lie very still, Dancing Moon. You must not squirm. You must not scream. Only lie still and think about all the evil you have committed!"

He opened the end of the leather pouch and laid the sack on her stomach; then he moved back out of the way. Dancing Moon's eyes widened with horror as a rattle snake slowly slithered out of the bag. Its head moved up near her throat, and she could feel its tongue flicking against her chin. Never before had Cheyenne Zeke seen such horror in anyone's eyes. It pleased him. He turned and walked away, feeling no remorse. He saddled one of the Mexican's horses and rode north, to Santa Fe, where he would pay a visit to Jonathan Mack. He left behind him the still-burning wagons and their destroyed cargo . . . and an Arapaho woman whose cheeks bore the letter Z and who lay tied to a tree with a rattle snake on her naked belly. He did not look back, but only smiled harshly.

Although nervous and excited, Abbie sat still as Gentle Woman patiently painted a small horse on one of her cheeks. On Abbie's other cheek she had painted an eagle. Both were representative of Zeke, and they were Abbie's choice of paintings for the Sun Dance ceremony. The ceremony would be sponsored by Falling Rock, father of little Magpie, who had been saved by Abbie from the deep waters. In honor of the little girl's life, Falling Rock had agreed to be responsible for the sacred Medicine Bundle, the fetish of the Sun Dance, and his wife, Tall Grass Woman, would help the ceremonial grandfather, Running Horse, complete the many preparations for the final, climactic ceremony. Abbie would be allowed to witness the ritual because she was now the honored daughter of Deer Slayer, and a sister to Swift Arrow. And she had proven her bravery.

"Now I will tell you, daughter," Gentle Woman said quietly to Abbie inside her tipi. Abbie closed her eyes and held very still. "For now I think you are ready to understand. Already you have seen them cut the Sun Dance pole and attach the Medicine Bundle to the forks of the pole. For many days you have watched us prepare for this ritual, seen the constant dancing, the building of the ceremonial lodge. You have heard the many celebration songs and seen the beautiful clothing our people will wear, and the way they are painted, as I am painting you now. This is a great honor, Abigail, that the priests, even the Sioux priests, have allowed you to be painted."

"I feel like I've graduated or something," Abbie replied, trying not to move her lips too much. "Like back home, when we get a good grade in school."

Gentle Woman smiled. "Yes. It is a good feeling. But so far you have seen only the dancing and singing and celebrating and eating. It has all been beautiful to watch. But in three days, Abigail, you will watch something that is not so beautiful—something that only one who thinks with the heart of an Indian can understand. Our young men, those who are the bravest, will submit themselves to terrible pain, to prove to the spirits their strength and courage, and to ask the spirits for a vision that will tell them their purpose in life. Some will discover they are to be *Shamans*. Some will receive a sign that will show them the animal from which they will forever get their power. Some will change their names because of their visions. But whatever the vision, whatever the pain, it is for a purpose, Abigail. For the Great Spirit cherishes those who are the bravest, and protects those who show great courage and strength. The spirits of the earth and sky give us all that we need to survive, Abigail, and in return we make sacrifices to them. The sacrifice the young men make at the Sun Dance is the greatest sacrifice, and because of it the whole tribe is renewed. Our faith and our blessings are restored."

"Swift Arrow said that Red Eagle will begin fasting today," Abbie told her. "Does that mean he can't eat at all today?"

Gentle Woman painted white dots on the rear of the little horse on Abbie's cheek because it represented Zeke's Appaloosas. "Not just one day, Abigail. Red Eagle and the other participants will not eat or drink for the next three days. They will dance around the Sun Dance pole inside the sacred lodge—dance and fast—until they reach a kind of trance, wherein they do not know what day it is or who is around them. We pray that Red Eagle's heart is sincere and he is not just showing off for his bride to be, Yellow Moon. For if his heart is sincere, the spirits will help him stop drinking the evil firewater that he now seems to depend on just to get up in the morning. That is very bad."

She put down the small willow stick she had been using to paint Abbie's face and washed it in water.

"You must understand that most of the young men are sincere in this and know what to expect; this is a very religious and serious occasion," the woman continued. "A few will go through with the ceremony just to show off to their women, or for other reasons that are not sincere. Swift Arrow was sincere, and is a religious, disciplined man. Zeke was sincere. It was harder for Zeke, because he had white blood in him and had lived with the whites, and it took great concentration for him to put aside all white feelings and beliefs and to assure the spirits that his heart was all Cheyenne. But he did it, and I was so very proud of him! Next year, Black Elk wishes to participate. He is my youngest, my baby." Her eyes teared. "When he takes part in the ceremony, all my sons will be men."

She dipped the willow brush into red paint made from the stain of berries and took Abbie's wrist. "Hold out your arm and I will paint flowers on it. The colors are so beautiful on you, Abigail, because of your white skin. You will be the prettiest girl at the ceremony . . . and you will have the honor of being one of the very few whites who have ever witnessed this ritual."

Abbie blushed and watched the woman's expert hands begin to form roses on her forearm. "You don't think Red Eagle is sincere, Gentle Woman?" she asked.

The woman sighed. "I am not certain. If he turns back to the drinking after the ceremony, we will know he was not sincere. What frightens me most is that some of the other warriors have taken to the whiskey. They think it makes them more powerful, but Swift Arrow and others feel it is an evil spirit that robs a man of his wits and strength. I believe this also."

"So does Zeke." Abbie smiled. "Not that he doesn't like to

drink whiskey!" she added. They both laughed. "Zeke seems to know when to stop," Abbie finished.

"This is good. I have seen some of our braves, including my own son, drink until they fall down; the next morning they are sick and suffer the terrible pain in the head. Then, only a few hours later, they drink again. This is bad, Abigail."

Abbie sighed. "Perhaps the ritual will help Red Eagle."

"I pray it will. But we are not talking just of Red Eagle, and I do not want to stray from the beauty and purpose of this solemn occasion. I want you to be prepared, Abigail, to go into the ceremonial lodge with an understanding heart and to realize this is a sacrifice to the spirits, for all they have done for us. To honor them is to know we shall all one day walk the *Ekutsihimmiyo* across the sky to heaven."

Abbie took hold of the woman's hand and pulled her arm away for a moment. "What will happen, Gentle Woman? I must know."

The woman put the brush down and became very solemn. "The young men will fast, as I said," she replied. "And they will dance. On the third day, the flesh of their breasts and back will be pierced with skewers, onto which are tied rawhide strips that are attached to the supports of the Sun Dance lodge. Then the men are lifted until their toes barely touch the ground, so that the skewers pull at their flesh. Weights, like buffalo skulls and gourds, are tied to their ankles to cause even more strain. Their bodies already will have been painted throughout the three days of fasting with yellow, pink, white, and black in the design of the sun, moon, flowers, and plants, in honor of nature's blessings. When their bodies are lifted, the men blow on bone whistles and strain against the skewers until finally the skewers are torn from their flesh and they fall to the ground. Through all of this, they must not cry out in pain or show any cowardliness. They must bear the pain silently, except when they blow the whistles. Neither can the women and brothers and fathers who watch cry out, for that would bring dishonor to the participant."

266

Abbie put a hand to her stomach. She was not so confident after all that she could bear to watch such a thing. And yet she knew she must, for to participate in the Sun Dance was to have the knowledge of the People's religion that she so sorely needed.

"On the day the ritual begins, the Sun Dance altar will be erected," Gentle Woman went on. "A buffalo skull will be at the center. Strips of earth will be placed around it, symbolizing the four Medicine Spirits, and the earth will be surrounded by leaves and branches from the cottonwood tree and from plum bushes, in honor of the useful plants the earthly spirits bestow upon the Cheyenne. You must look upon the altar with great respect, for it represents the whole of the earth, and the lodge itself represents the heavens. To be present is to be sitting with *Maheo*, and the participants are the sacrifice."

Abbie swallowed. "My goodness!" was all she said. Gentle Woman grinned.

"Once the rite is finished, a final pipe will be smoked, and there will be a dance in honor of the spirits of the four directions. The chief priest, his wife, and the sponsors will be purified in the sweat bath; the dance paint will be removed and the fast broken. Then it will be over. If you can survive all of that, there will be more celebrating, for Black Elk is to be inducted into Swift Arrow's warrior society, and as soon as he is recovered, Red Eagle will be marrying Yellow Moon. So . . . there will be a happy ending after the suffering."

Abbie looked at the flowers Gentle Woman was again painting on her arm, but she could only visualize the gruesome ritual she would soon witness.

It all took place as Gentle Woman had told her. Abbie discovered she was so caught up in the trancelike spirit inside the huge Sun Dance lodge that the sacrifice was not as unbearable to watch as she had expected.

For three days she had listened to the constant singing and

267

pounding of drums and the endless chanting. She had heard the Sun Dance songs so often, that she began singing along at times with the others, gradually learning more of the Cheyenne tongue as she did so. Her favorite was the song about lovers, for it made her think of Zeke.

"Look at that young man. He is feeling good, because his sweetheart is watching him . . ." the words went.

She watched Yellow Moon when they sang that one. The young girl kept her eyes on Red Eagle, her future husband, but Abbie could see love and excitement in them—and pride in her lover's sacrifice. When the skewers were pushed into Red Eagle's flesh, Yellow Moon would not cry out in horror, but would watch with love and pride. For this was the day of the People.

The Sioux danced and sang with the Cheyenne. They and the northern Cheyenne had accepted Abbie's presence with surprising ease, for the Cheyenne band with whom she traveled told a good story about the white woman and her heroics. Swift Arrow had taken great care to build Abbie up to insure none of the others turned on her. Since most of them knew and respected Cheyenne Zeke as a great warrior in his own right and Abbie was his woman, she would be accepted.

The Sioux dressed in brilliant colors and were active participants in the ritual, which was practiced by them long before the Cheyenne began using it. The Cheyenne had learned it from the Sioux, and now they all danced together to frenzied rhythmic drums and chanting, a mixture of men's singing and wild cries of excited manhood combined with women's voices trilling and calling back to the men.

When the participants' flesh was pierced, Abbie flinched but did not look away or cry out. Her stomach felt weak, and she prayed she would not be sick in front of everyone, for they would laugh at her "white man's" weakness for such things. She clenched her fists and thought of Zeke, realizing he had suffered this excruciating ritual. Seeing it now she only loved him and understood him even more.

None of the participants cried out in pain; and Abbie could see pride for Red Eagle in Gentle Woman's eyes. The men danced and deliberately pulled at the rawhide strips, dragging their weights. It was both horrible and beautiful; and the blowing of whistles, the beating of drums, and the constant chanting seemed to put all the spectators in enough of a trance to help them bear the sight.

The lodge became a mystic swirl of sweet smoke and singing and blowing of whistles, the participants' bloody bodies moving more slowly as the hours dragged and the skewers finally began to tear away from their flesh. The singing and drums built to a fever pitch as one by one the participants began to collapse to the floor, some crawling, some not moving at all, for they had not only suffered the agony of the ritual itself, but they had also had nothing to eat or drink for three days.

The final peace pipe was smoked, and the wounded men were carried to their lodges to be treated, while the priests and sponsors retired to the sweat bath. The ritual was over.

As Abbie walked out of the lodge in a near stupor, blinking at the sunlight, tears almost came. Her emotion was caused by a combination of things: Zeke's mysterious absence and the horror of the ritual, combined with an opposite feeling—pure joy at being so accepted by the People. She wore a bleached white tunic, a brand new one, beautifully beaded and painted by Tall Grass Woman, her thanks to Abbie for saving Magpie. Her lovely young face was decorated with the horse and the eagle, and her arms were painted with red flowers. She did not feel like a white woman this day, not after participating in the Sun Dance.

Someone came up behind her and put a hand on her shoulder. "You are all right?" she heard Swift Arrow ask.

"I . . . think so."

He grinned. "You did well. I expected you to faint."

She looked up at him. "I . . . don't think you were . . . far off in your thinking, Swift Arrow." She put a hand to her head. "I . . . don't feel so well."

He put a hand to her waist and whisked her to her own tipi, making her sit down inside. "Do not move," he told her. He left for a moment and returned with a tin cup full of a hot liquid. "Drink this," he told her, squatting down in front of her. "It is an herb tea. Is good. Many of the People need this sustenance after witnessing the ritual."

She took the cup gratefully and sipped the tea, eying the scars on Swift Arrow's own breasts and upper arms. Some of the participants had the skewers attached in more places than just the chest and back. Swift Arrow had been one of them; he also had scars on his arms and thighs. She closed her eyes and took another sip; then she lowered the cup.

"Zeke . . . he didn't cry out, did he?" she asked.

Swift Arrow grinned. "Lone Eagle?" He laughed. "He would have plunged his own knife into his own heart if he had cried out! Not that one!"

"And you?"

He laughed again. "Would Swift Arrow be a dog soldier if he had cried out? He would have been so ashamed, he would have run off into the hills and never shown his face again!"

She sighed. "I feel like . . . like I understand things so much better, Swift Arrow. But I guess it's my white blood that keeps telling me it's so . . . so savage."

He sat down beside her, crossing his legs and studying her for a moment. "White man has strange view of what is savage," he answered. "To sacrifice one's flesh to the spirits is not savage, woman of Lone Eagle. It is beautiful and right. It is what is in their hearts, and no one is harmed but themselves . . . and willingly. I will tell you what is savage. Savage is what those white men wanted to do with you when they came to take you away." She blushed and looked at the ground, nervously fingering the tin cup. "Savage is what Zeke's white father did to our mother, tearing her small son from her arms," he went on. "Savage, Abigail, is the Trail of Tears, and what the white men did to the Cherokee and others when they chased them to Indian Territory. Savage is taking those Indians from their homes, robbing them of all their possessions, dividing their families, putting them into prison camps where they were not fed, and where they received just enough water to keep them alive!" She could feel his rising contempt. "Savage is when your little baby throws up from hunger or runs at the bowels from disease, and there is no water to even wash the child because the white man will not give it to you. Savage is when you use your own urine to clean up your child."

"Stop it!" she groaned, closing her eyes.

He put a hand on her arm. "I only try to explain to you, Abigail, why white man's view of savage is wrong. It is when you torture and murder another man without reason—that is savage! Even in our wars with other tribes, with our hated enemies the Pawnee and the Crow, even then, when we maim and kill and raid and steal, that is not savage. Vengeance, perhaps. Survival, yes. But what the white man does to the Indian is not for vengeance, not even for survival, Abigail. It is only to rid the land they want of something that is in their way, like removing a nest of bees so that one can get to the honey. The bees are there because they belong there. They harm no one. And if the man who wants the honey moves carefully and respects the bees and thanks the bees, he can get the honey without harming them and without getting stung. But white man, he does not want to be careful and respect the bees. He wants the honey now and he does not want to wait, nor does he want the bees to come back. So he tries to drown them or burn them so that he can take all of the honey. But he must remember that the bees will come and sting him, just as the Indian will sting the white men who try to take our hunting grounds! This the white man should know and remember. We are willing to share the land, but we are not willing to give it all over to the white men and never again ride free upon it.

Neither will we allow the white man to make us prisoners like the Cherokee and the other tribes of the East. We are not insects to be stepped upon. We are men . . . and women . . . children and old people . . . all walking as one . . . all here because the Gods put us here. Think about what is savage, Abigail, and you will understand there is nothing savage in our rituals, nor in anything we do. It is simply our religion, and it gives us great power."

She took another drink of the tea and looked at him. "You always know what to say to me," she told him.

He shrugged. "Then I am wise man." He grinned again, and she smiled at his matter-of-fact boasting. He rose and went to the tipi entrance. "You rest now," he told her. "I will not tell the others that you felt ill."

She smiled and blushed. "I appreciate that, Swift Arrow."

He hesitated at the doorway. "I did not tell you . . . you are very beautiful in the paintings and the white tunic. Zeke would be proud of you this day. If he was here, he would celebrate the ending of the ritual by spending the rest of the day and night in his tipi with his woman. This is what many of the bucks will be doing."

He chuckled when she blushed even more, fascinated by the way white people turned red.

He left, and Abbie finished drinking the tea, wishing Zeke were with her to do what Swift Arrow said he would want to do. How she needed his arms around her! His lips caressing her mouth, her breasts, her whole body! How she needed to breathe his sweet scent and open herself to take him inside and know that he was alive!

The Sun Dance was over. Black Elk was initiated into Swift Arrow's warrior society, and Red Eagle married Yellow Moon.

Then the tribe broke up, the Sioux going north and east throughout the Black Hills, and most of the Cheyenne going west to the Powder River north of Fort Laramie for more hunting.

It was not long before Red Eagle returned to the bottle, and on the third night of his marriage to Yellow Moon, the young girl ran crying from their tipi and fled to her mother's lodge. Red Eagle had all but raped her because of his whiskey, and he had hit her. Gentle Woman was disgraced, and Red Eagle was whipped by his soldier society for disgracing its honor by disgracing himself and not being able to control his wife. He was given one more chance to mend his ways, and he apologized to Yellow Moon and convinced her to return to their lodge. They were soon happy lovebirds again, and as the band migrated back West, Red Eagle did his best to stay away from the firewater. But always it was a struggle for him.

Abbie herself headed west with a heavy heart. Zeke still had not returned. Swift Arrow sent out runners to all the tribes and forts. They would try to find out what had happened to Cheyenne Zeke.

Fourteen

Danny Monroe rode with head hanging, his horse plodding listlessly. Since they'd left Bent's Fort and ridden south through the desert toward Santa Fe, several men and one horse had collapsed from the relentless heat and lack of water. The one-hundred-twenty-degree weather and unending sun had sapped their strength and spunk, and even the liveliest and most rugged of the volunteers were suffering. Colonel Kearny pushed them hard, up to thirty-two miles a day, a great distance for such a large group of men loaded down with a dozen six pounders and four twelve-pound howitzers, as well as a host of supply wagons and the job of watching over 459 horses, 3,658 draft mules and nearly 15,000 cattle and oxen. But they continued on, and Danny was one of the lucky ones. He was still feeling well enough to be thinking about their upcoming entry into Santa Fe.

He wondered if there would be a big battle or if the size of Kearny's enforcement would spook the Mexicans. In just a few more days, he would find out. Already scouts were bringing in Mexican prisoners: soldiers, shepherds, priests, anyone who might have information about the enemy force in Santa Fe. Dragoons under Capt. Philip St. George Cooke, and James Magoffin, a trader with strong connections in Santa Fe, had been sent ahead of Colonel Kearny with a message for New Mexico's notorious governor, Manuel Armijo. It urged Armijo to vacate the city and thus avoid fighting and bloodshed.

Armijo immediately began appealing for New Mexican volunteers to help defend Santa Fe, and word came back to Kearny that although many New Mexicans preferred American occupation because they liked American trade, Armijo had rounded up enough volunteers to try to keep the soldiers out. Kearny had warned Danny and the others that if there was to be a fight, it would most likely take place at the exit of Apache Canyon, a chasm between high walls of stone. At some points the canyon was only forty feet wide.

But that lay ahead of them. For now there was the weary job of climbing Raton Pass, another difficult feat. But at least then they would be in the Sangre de Cristo Mountains, and once they'd gotten through Apache Pass, providing they won the battle there, they would reach Santa Fe and enjoy the fruits of their campaign—some free time in that New Mexican city, time to eat and relax and perhaps even enjoy the company of the local dark-eyed prostitutes before continuing on to claim other territory.

Jonathan Mack was already in Santa Fe. Without the burden of horses and cattle and supply wagons, the stage line traveled much faster than the oncoming American Army. Already Mack had smooth-talked his way into the confidence of some of the Mexican dignitaries of the city, those who sided with the Americans because they wanted the American trade. Mack had made many promises to send trade their way once the war was over, especially if they helped him establish his own business there.

He intended to open a bank and lend money to any Mexican merchants who needed backing to build their businesses, for trade was certain to flourish once the city was claimed by the Americans. But immediately he began to buy property from those Mexicans who feared the war and wanted to flee Santa Fe. And already he was guaranteeing loans to businessmen who would, he knew, for one reason or another be unable to repay him. He would later foreclose on their businesses and claim even more property. Some land would simply be hastily vacated by its owners without any legal transfer. This property, Mack would immediately claim, and he would have the proper papers prepared for approval by the United States government once the property became U.S. soil. Kearny would arrive in several more days, and then it would all be settled.

During his short time in Santa Fe, Mack had already established a strong hand in the city. He had set up shop in a small vacated building in the center of town, advertising it as a land office and a place for information on how Mexicans should handle their property once it was in the hands of the Americans. He kept hired men inside its walls and outside the door as lookouts, for Santa Fe was a torn city, part of its citizens wanting it to become American soil, and the rest staunchly insisting that it should forever remain Mexican. Picking sides in either direction was dangerous, but the smooth-talking Mack had done a good job of convincing both sides that whatever happened, he was there to help them. Generous contributions to businesses and free whiskey, purchased from a wagonful brought in by an American trader, helped Mack glide through business dealings and win friends in both factions.

Now he only had to sit and wait. Soon a Mexican runner would arrive with the gold from the smuggled guns, and he would send a coded message back east to send out more. He was certain he could find plenty of aimless drifters in Santa Fe to do his bidding, men who would be glad to help get his guns to Mexico for gold and whiskey. And if the war ended quickly and the Mexicans no longer needed rifles, then he would simply sell them to the Indians. Indians would much rather have the long rifles than the gold that was in their mountains. Mack would gladly take the gold and valuable stones in trade.

Not many white men realized yet how much wealth lay in the hills of the West, and even Mack only suspected. There were tales of Indians using pure gold to buy whiskey and to make

277

jewelry, but not many white men had yet dared to penetrate Indian Territory to dig for the ore. Mack knew, however, that it was only a matter of time. And when gold fever began to rise, the senator would already own, through legal government paperwork, much of the land on which the gold would likely be found. Jonathan Mack would see to that.

Zeke kept a low profile once he entered Santa Fe. In a city torn by war, a man had to be careful, and Zeke had to be especially careful because Mexicans had little use for Indians. So he entered the city wearing Mexican clothes that had belonged to one of the outlaws he'd murdered. He wore a brightly colored cape and a large *sombrero*, and with his dark skin, he easily passed for a Mexican since a casual glance was all that most people cared to bestow on this dark and dangerous-looking man who wore so many weapons.

Zeke was determined to learn quickly whether or not Jonathan Mack was staying in the city, and, if he was, where. For he wanted to get his money and his vengeance. Then he intended to go directly back to Abbie. He had been gone a long time, perhaps too long. He had enough money, taken from the gun runners, to bribe anyone who might have information he needed to know. Once he knew Mack's location, it would only be a matter of waiting for the right moment. Mack would never suspect anything had gone wrong, for by now the Mexican payoff man would have reached him with the gold. For all Mack knew, the guns had been delivered to the proper party, and the driver called Grimey and the man called Cheyenne Zeke would be dead. But soon he would find out differently!

Maria, the prostitute, lay naked and spread-eagled on Jonathan Mack's bed while he gently rubbed her voluptuous dark skin with sweet oil, lingering on her breasts and then running down to her inner thighs. Maria kept her eyes closed.

278

Mack's small, white body repulsed her. His face was handsome, but his hands were like a woman's, and his privates were not like other men's. When she felt of them, she could tell he had only one lump there instead of two, and he was much smaller than other men, more like a young boy. But he paid her well, and she was permitted to come to his plush, expensive hotel room to serve him, so she put up with him.

"I love your dark skin," he told her as he toyed with her until she began to groan. "You make me want to devour you, Maria!"

He bent down to take his pleasure in her, making growling sounds, his small, naked body curled between her legs. For a moment the pair were both lost in separate sexual fantasies; then the door suddenly burst open.

Maria gasped and moved away from Mack, and at the same time Mack turned, shocked at the sudden, unexpected intrusion. His eyes widened and his pale face became even whiter when he saw Cheyenne Zeke standing in the doorway!

Mack's ashen face quickly began to turn crimson as Zeke stood there staring in revulsion at his girlish body. Maria scooted wide-eyed to the head of the bed while Mack grabbed a blanket and wiped his mouth with it before he covered himself.

"Surprised to see me, Mack?" Zeke sneered.

"I—" The man swallowed, then put on a smile. "You . . . only startled me, Zeke, that's all. I mean . . . a man isn't often interrupted like this when he's in bed with his whore." He wiped his mouth again, his face so red Zeke thought the man's blood vessels might burst.

"You know why I'm here, Mack," Zeke said threateningly, "and you're not just embarrassed because I saw your stinking little white body. You're scared because you know I shouldn't be here. But I am, Mack! You tricked me, and you owe me!"

"I . . . I don't know what you mean."

Zeke pulled his knife and Mack's eyes widened. Maria whimpered, and Zeke glanced at her for a moment, taking in her voluptuous dark body and feeling a vague need of his own.

But that would have to wait.

"Tell the woman to get out of here!" he told Mack. "And if she sends anyone up, I'll kill her."

Maria nodded and jumped off the bed, grabbing her clothes and running out the door. Zeke kicked it shut.

"You know, Mack, I'm not sure I'll kill you after all. There is honor only in killing brave men . . . real men. You aren't brave, and you're a sick excuse for a man. You might as well be wearing a dress. But since you choose to wear pants, I suggest you put them on and walk with me to your office. I want my money!"

Mack swallowed and slowly got off the bed, reddening again when he had to drop the blanket in order to dress. Zeke literally grimaced with revulsion as he watched the man, and he wondered how the whore could have let him touch her. Mack buttoned his pants and put on his shirt, breathing deeply to regain his self-control as he dressed. "Do you really think I'll let you get out of town alive?" he grumbled to Zeke as he turned to face him.

"Who's going to kill me? You?" Zeke asked with a sneer, towering over the man and bringing his big blade up against the side of Mack's face.

Mack paled even more. "A lot of men in this town work for me, half-breed!" he threatened. "You use that blade, and you'll be in big trouble!"

Zeke instantly grasped Mack around the throat with his left hand and shoved him hard against the wall, pinning him there easily. He put the flat of his blade over Mack's lips and let the edge of it touch the underside of the man's nose just enough to make it sting.

"Don't you threaten me, you bastard!" Zeke growled, keeping his voice low so no one could hear. His hand was so tight on Mack's throat that the man could not call out and had to struggle just to breathe. "I went through back country worse than hell to deliver those wagons! I risked my life against Apaches for them! And I didn't mind that, Mr. Jonathan Mack, because I agreed to do a job and I needed the money. I was honest about my end of it, but not you. Because of you a very good friend of mine was murdered in cold blood! Because of you I took a bullet that would have killed me if it hadn't been one inch off, and I took a beating." He pricked Mack's nose just slightly, enough to make the man's eyes bulge with fright. "But that wasn't the worst, Mack," Zeke went on. "Because of you I spent a night in a dark pit filled with snakes! Do you know what that's like, Mack? It's just about the worst thing a man can go through, and goddamn you, you're going to give me my eight hundred dollars and Grimey's four hundred to boot, or I'll carve you up like a fresh-killed hog!" He moved back and threw the man to the floor, where Mack lay stunned for a moment. "Like I say, I'd kill you, but you're not worth it, Mack. There would be nothing honorable in ending your life." He jerked the man back up. "Besides, I need you. I need my money. I may not kill you, but by God if you don't pay up I'll sure as hell make you bleed good!" He gave the man a shove. "Let's go— and use the back stairway. You make one wrong move and I'll sink this blade right into your spine! You got that, Mr. Lily-hands? Move wrong, and you'll be paralyzed for life!"

Mack swallowed and rubbed at his throat, a cold sweat covering his face. He blinked back tears and took a handkerchief from his pants pocket, holding it to the small cut between his lip and his nose. "You . . . you cut me!" he said in a shaking voice. His hands trembled as he took the hanky away and looked at the blood.

Zeke only grinned. "That's just a taste," Zeke answered. "You'll be crawling to the doctor for plenty of stitches if you don't get over to your office and get me my money. And I want it in gold or in American dollars."

Mack sniffed and struggled to keep from bursting into tears of fright and embarrassment. He dabbed at his nose again; then he picked up his suitcoat and put it on, straightening the lapels and smoothing back his hair with his hand. Struggling to regain his composure, he managed to move his shaking legs and walked out the door ahead of Zeke.

As they went down the back stairs and out into an alley, Zeke watched every corner and every shadow. But no one disturbed them. Jonathan Mack had not counted on this untimely intrusion, so he had no personal body guards to help him. But when they approached his office, Zeke saw an armed man in front of the doorway.

"Who's that?" Zeke asked.

"I keep a night guard," Mack replied. "Right now there isn't much law in Santa Fe. A man has to protect his interests."

"Well right now your interest is your own life," Zeke told him. "See that we don't have any trouble." He poked Mack's back lightly with the tip of his blade, and Mack remembered how well Zeke had used a knife in the tavern at Independence. The guard pushed his hat back and nodded when he recognized Mack heading toward him, but he looked suspiciously at Zeke.

"Everything all right, boss?" he asked.

"Yes, Swanson. I . . . uh . . . I owe this gentleman some money, and he is anxious to leave town . . . so I told him I'd pay him off right away."

The guard stepped aside. "If you say so, sir. You want me to come inside with you?"

Zeke pricked Mack with the knife again.

"Uh . . . no, Swanson. It won't be necessary. I assure you."

Swanson shrugged. In the darkness, and with Mack standing between him and Zeke, the guard did not see the knife in Zeke's hand. Zeke folded his arms momentarily, hiding the blade under his left arm as Mack unlocked the door and went inside, then he quickly followed and closed the door. To his relief, he noticed the window shades were drawn. That was good. When the lantern was lit, no one would be able to see inside. Mack struck a match he'd retrieved from his suitcoat jacket where he kept them handy for the thin cigars he favored. The light of the match revealed the lantern, and he lit it. Then he led Zeke to a back room where he kept a safe.

"You can't kill me now," he told Zeke as he knelt and began turning the dial of the combination safe. "Swanson has seen you. You can't even cut me up, half-breed. Either way you'd still be in trouble."

"I've been in trouble before, and I take great pleasure in using this blade on my enemies."

Mack took out a small gunny sack. He stood up, turned, and put it on the table. "Perhaps you do, Zeke," he answered, feeling more confident and taking on his old, smooth air. "But you wouldn't want to get in trouble now, would you? I mean, if you get in trouble, you might not get back to your precious Abbie!"

This time it was Mack who grinned, as he noted the uncertainty that appeared in Zeke's eyes. "How do you know about Abbie?"

Mack's grin widened as he opened the money sack. "I believe you . . . uh . . . wrote her a note before you left Independence. I asked the man you gave it to to show it to me . . . just to make sure you weren't in some way double-crossing me."

Zeke's heart pounded. "Did she get the note?" he asked.

Mack shrugged. "How would I know? Maybe so . . . maybe not."

Zeke grabbed the man by the lapels, the tip of his knife touching Mack's earlobe. "Did she get the note!" he growled.

"I honestly don't know," Mack replied calmly, breaking into a sweat again. "Why don't you just take your money and get the hell back to her and find out, half-breed!"

Zeke let go of him reluctantly, giving the man a shove. He watched carefully as Mack took bills out of the sack and began counting them.

"There. Twelve hundred dollars," he told Zeke. "Or do you plan to use that knife to threaten me into giving you more?"

"I'm not a thief, Mack. I only want what belongs to me."

"Well, now you have it, so you can leave."

Zeke shoved his knife into its sheath and then dumped out

283

the rest of the money in the gunny sack, putting his own money into the sack to carry it. "Many thanks, Mack. And now I can tell you that your guns never reached the Mexicans, so you have nothing to brag to them about. You may have trouble convincing them to pay you any more money for smuggled guns."

Mack's eyes widened. "What are you talking about? They've already been here and paid me."

"Sure they have. But the man with the gold left before they knew I'd survived that snake pit. I caught up with them, Mack." He grinned. "Not one man is alive . . . and your precious wagons full of guns and whiskey are blown all to hell! I expect you might find parts of them clear over in Texas!" Zeke's grin widened as he looked at Mack's enraged face, and he reached across Mack's desk to pick up one of the thin cigars from the supply of the smokes Mack seemed to keep everywhere. Then he took a match from Mack's coat pocket, while the man stood there rigid with anger. Zeke struck the match and lit the cigar. Having taken a deep drag, he blew the smoke into Mack's face. "You're right, Mack," he told the man. "These are damned good cigars." He walked to the back door. "I appreciate the job, Mack. But don't ask me again. The pay just isn't good enough."

He walked out the door, and Mack stood staring after him, his body trembling with rage. He considered sending his guard after Zeke, but Cheyenne Zeke was good with a knife, and he apparently had an uncanny way of surviving the worst attacks. If he sent men after the half-breed, and Zeke survived, Mack knew that would mean certain death for him.

He sank into a chair and put his head in his hands. Picking Cheyenne Zeke for a driver had been a great blunder. He felt weak and faint from the aftershock of Zeke's threats, and he put his head down on his arms and wept, for he had truly thought Zeke would kill him.

* * *

Zeke kept his sack of money inside his parfleche and carried the parfleche with him as he approached a supply store. He was more anxious than ever to get back to poor Abbie, who probably had not even gotten his note. His mind was full of her, his body ached for her, and his heart feared she might not even be there when he arrived. After all these weeks, it was possible she had given him up for dead, and perhaps she had asked Swift Arrow to see her to Bent's Fort or to some other place from which she could find escort back to Tennessee. Yet, surely she knew enough to give him some time. She must be aware that he might be in trouble, but that he would come back to her. He always came back to her. He would leave today and ride hard all the way, leaving little time for sleeping or eating. He would just ride and ride until he had her in his arms!

But first he must purchase a good horse with some of his money . . . and more important than that, he wanted to take her something. They would have much to talk about when he saw her again, for when he'd left, the question of whether or not she could live among the Cheyenne had been left hanging. That problem was yet to be resolved, but Zeke thought he knew of a way to resolve it. For now, he could not go back to her without a present . . . something pretty for his woman . . . a peace offering . . . a love gift.

He entered the supply store. He would need a good stock of nonperishable food for the hard ride back, but most of all he needed the gift. His eyes scanned the stock as an American merchant came out from the back of the store, one of the few Americans left who were allowed to conduct business in Santa Fe. The man eyed Zeke suspiciously. Tiring of the Mexican clothing, Zeke had decided to wear his own buckskins. Since he was about to leave the city, he had decided to take the risk of being recognized as an Indian. He wanted only to be wearing his own clothes and to get out of town.

"Something I can do for you, mister?" the storekeeper asked.

Zeke looked over at the man. "Maybe. I'm looking for a

285

present . . . for a woman . . . something pretty, not practical."

"I see. Well, I don't have a lot to choose from, I'm afraid. What with this impending war and all, not many shipments are getting through. Fact is, if Mexico wins, that will be the end of my business. I'll have to fold up and go back East."

"Too bad," Zeke replied absently, walking over and fingering some material.

"Oh, now, material is something all squaws like, sir! Especially the brightly colored pieces. Perhaps you could choose some beads to go with it?"

Zeke eyed the man darkly, catching the note of derision when he used the word *squaw*. But he brushed off the insult and searched around the store. His eyes rested on a tiny gold box, its seams implanted with brightly colored stones with a deep red stone in the center of the lid. He walked over to the box and picked it up, then opened it, and to his surprise it began tinkling out a tune, a lovely melody in the rhythm of a waltz. He watched it for a moment in fascination. A music box! It was the perfect gift. Abbie would love a music box! It would be a little something from her white world—something small and easy to carry . . . something of beauty and grace.

"I'll take this," he told the clerk.

"But . . . sir . . ." The man came closer. "Excuse me, sir, but that isn't too practical—for a squaw, that is. That's more of a gift for a white woman. No offense intended."

Zeke closed the lid and set the box on the counter. "I said I wanted something frivolous, not practical. And I'm perfectly aware that it's a white woman's gift," he told the man. Then he grinned. "That's why I'm buying it."

The man looked at him curiously for a moment, then arched his eyebrows at the realization of what Zeke was saying. "Oh!" he exclaimed. He looked Zeke up and down, then frowned. "Oh," he said again, more softly.

"Wrap it good so's it doesn't break," Zeke told him. "And I'll be needing some flour and jerky, a few cans of beans, and a little sugar."

The man stared at him for a moment, then decided this tall, dark man who carried a huge blade on his weapons belt was perhaps not a man to argue with. His mind raced with curiosity, but he asked no questions as he carefully wrapped the music box. He had already learned that in a lawless city like Santa Fe, you did not ask a drifter too many questions. He collected Zeke's things and put them all on the counter.

Zeke paid him and left. He walked to the stables, to the sturdy roan mare he had purchased, and began packing his gear, glad that he had been able to save most of his belongings when he had caught up with the Mexicans.

He grinned again at the memory of the wagons exploding, and at the picture of Dancing Moon lying tied to the tree with bleeding *Z*'s on her cheeks and a rattler on her belly. Now they were all dead and he had his money and a pretty gift for Abbie. Now he could go home to his woman! There was only one thing left to do to top off his day, and that was to get his final vengeance for the snake pit!

Jonathan Mack entered the reporter's office with his usual air of importance. He had fully regained his composure since Cheyenne Zeke's attack of the night before. Now Zeke was gone, and good riddance!

Mack knew Billy Walton well, for he had made a point of knowing everyone of influence in Santa Fe; and who could be more influential than a reporter who was responsible for getting articles back to Washington for the Eastern newspapers. Billy Walton was here to cover the news of Col. Stephen Watts Kearny's entry into Santa Fe, which everyone knew was now imminent.

Mack offered Billy one of his expensive cigars and sat down across the desk from the man.

"To what do I owe this pleasure, Mr. Mack?" Billy asked, lighting the cigar. "Do you have more news for Senator Garvey?"

"I do," Mack replied, checking out his well-manicured nails. "And I want you to send a story back East, Billy. I want you to do your usual good job of . . . uh . . . presenting the truth, if you know what I mean."

Billy smiled through thin lips. He liked the feeling of importance he got out here in the West. "I think I know what you mean," he replied with a wink. "Put the words in my mouth, Mr. Mack."

Mack grinned. "Billy, I want you to tell our Eastern readers that two wagons full of whiskey I was having shipped west to start my saloon business were attacked and destroyed by Cheyenne Indians. One of the men who had been along on the trip and who had managed to hide from the Indians just came to me with the message. The other driver was viciously tortured to death."

Billy nodded. "I'll get word to the senator and to my newspaper."

Mack pulled out a wad of bills. "Do a good job, Billy. I want everyone to know it was Cheyennes—that they're raiding and stealing and killing. I want everyone to know that they stole all my whiskey—killed my driver for it! I want to make damned sure the people back East know what's going on out here . . . and that something has to be done about the savages! You could even throw in that there are rumors the Cheyenne and other redskins have been attacking ranches and raping white women. Understand? I want to make as much trouble for those bastards as I can! It's time to start ridding the West of those scavengers!"

"I get the message, Mr. Mack," Billy replied, thumbing through the bills. "I'll do a good job."

Mack stood up and put out his hand. "Thanks, Billy. I knew you'd come through." They shook hands and Mack left. Billy chuckled and thumbed through the bills again. This untamed land provided a lot of material for a struggling reporter. Perhaps it would lead him to fame. And while he was at it, he would make a lot of money from people who were willing to pay well to have a reporter influence the right people in the East to aid their various causes.

Mack walked across the street to his own office, where people had begun arriving to discuss loans and land deals. He nodded politely to them, walking through the outer room where they waited and into his office, telling them he would be with them shortly.

Once in his own working office, he remembered the night before, and the horror of Cheyenne Zeke's knife against his face, the strength of the man's handhold on him, the awful hatred in the man's eyes.

He shook off his terror, grateful that the experience was over and he was still alive. Cheyenne Zeke had left, and there was nothing more to worry about. He breathed deeply with relief and smiled. His planned news stories would cause the Cheyenne some trouble when the news broke back East. That was fine!

He looked curiously at a gunny sack on his desk. Apparently someone had already been there and had delivered some gold, perhaps one of the investors who waited outside. He grinned, went to his desk, and opened the sack, reaching inside.

Then he heard the awful hiss and felt the sickening pain of fangs sinking deeply into his wrist. He screamed in horror, his knees immediately weakening and his throat constricting. People came running in, but by then Mack's eyes were bulging and his throat was so tight that he could not utter the words *Cheyenne Zeke*. He tried desperately to tell them who had done this thing to him, but he could not talk.

He fell to the floor, and people screamed and ran out when they saw a rattler crawl over him and slither under the back door.

"What a pity!" someone safe outside said. "I wonder how a snake got into his office!"

"You know them devils!" another replied. "You can find the

damned things anyplace out here!''

Farther down the street a tall, dark man sat astride a roan mare and watched the crowd gather around Jonathan Mack's office. He saw the reporter across the street running toward the crowd, and he smiled.

"I said I wouldn't kill you, Mack," Zeke spoke up quietly. "But I never said I wouldn't let something else end your life. I'd say that was a fitting way for a snake-bellied coward like you to die!"

He turned his horse and rode north. Now he could go home. To the People. To Abbie! His vengeance had been fulfilled!

Fifteen

Abbie sat near a crystal stream watching a bluejay flit among the aspen trees. Already, the leaves were showing a hint of yellow, for it was now September, the month the Cheyenne called the Drying Grass Moon. Her heart was heavy, for some of the Indian runners had returned with no news of Zeke.

She turned to watch the other women bathe in the shallow waters of the stream that ran through a hollow not far from where the village was camped. The stream was fed by a roaring cataract several yards away. Cascading waters danced over rocks and splashed merrily downstream, bubbling music in a land full of the melody of nature. They were now in the foothills of the Rockies, and it was a beautiful, green place, where waterfalls and streams and rivers in abundance mingled with strange, bubbling mud holes that had an odd smell. In some places there were pools where the water was so warm it was as though it had been heated on a stove.

The Cheyenne said this was a place where the gods lived. Indeed, it seemed like such a place—a world of beauty and color and mystery, where most of the rock was yellow, and some of the mudholes were a brilliant turquoise or purple. But Abbie could not bring herself to appreciate the beauty today. Her heart did not dance with the waters or sing with the birds. Perhaps it would never sing again. Perhaps Cheyenne Zeke would not come back this time after all.

She wandered down toward the raging waterfall. Its

thunderous movement eased her pain. She removed her tunic and touched her toes in the cool water. It felt good, for this September day was very hot. All around the waterfall and the stream, Cheyenne and Arapaho warriors were on guard while the women bathed themselves and their children. The men frequently called out teasing remarks, saying that they were going to come to the stream and cast their eyes upon the beautiful Cheyenne maidens; and the women laughed and screamed and shouted teasing remarks back to them.

"Come, then!" They bantered with the men. "We are ready!"

But Abbie knew the men would not come. They would not even look. For they were men of honor, and each knew another's wife or lover was bathing, and he had no right to look upon the other man's woman.

Abbie stepped farther into the stream, approaching the waterfall and carrying the bar of lye soap she had had with her since arriving at that first Cheyenne camp with Zeke. The soap was worn down now to a flat piece only a fraction of an inch thick. If Zeke did not return soon, she would ask Swift Arrow to take her to a supply fort where she could purchase more soap with the money Zeke had left her, for although she had learned to live with the elements, she still liked to use real soap rather than sand or the cedar leaves used in sweat baths.

But what would she do when Zeke's money ran out? What would she do if he did not come back? Soon she would have to make a decision. She loved the Cheyenne . . . loved this land. Still, she was white. To stay among the Cheyenne without Zeke would only bring them more trouble. She would have to support herself, and she could not do that without a husband— an official provider and protector. She could not forever be a burden to Zeke's family, nor could she be practical like the Cheyenne women and become some Cheyenne man's second wife.

It was not uncommon for a Cheyenne man to take in a widowed squaw, especially if she was his wife's sister. This was a practical move, not for a buck's sexual pleasure, as most whites thought. This was an angry, vicious land, and survival was the key word. Death lurked everywhere, and preservation of the People was the all-important goal. If a woman lost her man, and another man was willing to take on the burden of an extra wife and children, for whom he would have to provide food and protection, then the woman went to him—for survival. But never was a woman forced into such an arrangement. It was a free decision, and seldom was the first wife jealous; for then there were two women to do the chores and to help one another with the care of the children.

At times Abbie had witnessed a Cheyenne man casually touching his wife's sister, on some of these occasions in the presence of the sister's husband. But Abbie had learned that this was the Cheyenne way of preparing for the very real possibility that one day the sister might be a part of the household—their way for a man to demonstrate his capacity to love and to show his willingness to take on another family. The teasing and joking shared in the confines of the tipis was a means of preventing jealousy, and a way to create a situation in which a dual marriage, if called for, could work. But seldom did a man take a second wife only for the sake of having two wives, for an additional wife was a tremendous burden.

Sex among the Cheyenne was viewed with beauty as well as practicality. The unmarried women were chaste. Even after marriage, a young wife had the right to refuse her husband's desires until she felt she was ready to become a woman. A man almost never violated that right, for to do so was to bring dishonor to himself and his family. Incest was strictly forbidden and was cause for a beating and possible banishment from the family, perhaps even from the band. Relatives never married, no matter how distant; this was forbidden.

And there was a lot of love. Abbie sensed it strongly. In most of the Cheyenne families she had come to know, there was a strong bond between the man and the woman, and a very intense love for the children. In times of danger, women and

293

children were the first to be protected, and after them, the old people. The warriors were prepared to die willingly in order to provide such protection. It was their honorable duty.

These were the beautiful People that Abbie would probably have to leave. She did not want to go. She loved them.

She walked behind the waterfall, enjoying a private retreat in the little cave that left enough space behind the falls for her body to stand without being directly under the cascading water which splashed up from the rocks and wet her down. She lathered up with her soap. Behind the roaring waterfall she could hear no sound, but she knew someone would come for her if there was danger, so she did not worry.

"Jesus, help me know what to do," she prayed. She put her head back and let the water soak it. She did not love any other Cheyenne man, and she was certain she could never love any man in the way she had loved Cheyenne Zeke. She and Zeke had something very special. They had suffered together. He had been there when she'd lost her family, they had fought outlaws together, and she had dug a bullet out of his side. He had removed the Crow arrow from her back and had cut and stitched her and burned out the infection.

They had been through so many hardships and heartaches in the short time they had been together, but most important of all, Cheyenne Zeke had been her first man. How could there ever be another? She could not marry for practical purposes as some Cheyenne women had to do. She had too much white blood in her veins for that. Nor could she be some man's second wife. No. Never could she share her man. She had too much white blood in her for that, also.

But soon she must decide. She knew the only sensible decision was to go to one of the forts and find a guide to take her back home to Tennessee. She had an aunt there who would take her in. But that sounded so dull now. How could she ever go back to such a life after what she had been through! It seemed impossible. And how could she leave this savage land she had learned to love? She was white, and yet she was not white. She didn't know anymore what she was, except that she was Cheyenne Zeke's woman, and that was all she wanted to be.

She bent to her knees and wept, while the cascading waters splashed back upon her and rinsed her body. What was left now to live for? She felt like a half-breed herself, belonging to two different worlds yet not truly fitting in either, for her heart and soul had learned a different way, and her body had been claimed by the man who had put her in this predicament. She did not blame him for it. She only loved him; but he was not there, and she was alone with her decision.

She had no idea how long she was behind the waterfall crying and praying, no idea that outside secret bird calls had been exchanged, sending coded messages to the warriors who had then signaled the women to leave the stream. By the time Abbie emerged from behind the waterfall, everyone was gone. She did not notice right away. She wrung her hair and walked to her blanket, picking it up and putting it around her, thinking about the fact that the waterfall had torn her little piece of soap from her hands.

For some reason, the lost soap made her even more sad, as though a remnant from the life she'd once known was gone forever and she had lost the old Abbie in the process. She forced back tears as she sat down on the grass. She must decide. Tomorrow the Cheyenne would head due south, hunting buffalo along the way. Most of the northern Cheyenne and all of the Sioux already had left. Zeke's family and their band, accompanied by some of the other Cheyenne bands, would return to the Arkansas River in southern Colorado Territory— to *Hinta Nagi*, the Big Timbers. There they would spend the winter. Abbie could not be a burden to them during those harsh months, so the wise thing to do was to go to Bent's Fort after the People arrived at the Arkansas. There she could find a scout to take her back home.

The thought of doing this wrung at her heart, but what else was there to do? She wanted to cry again, but she had no more tears to shed. She felt small and alone and drained of all energy and life. Cheyenne Zeke was her life. Without him she felt empty.

She rose wearily and dropped the blanket, preparing to put on her tunic, but she suddenly realized she heard no screaming and laughter from the others. She looked around and found no one in the stream or on the banks! They had vanished!

Her heart began pounding with fear, and she grabbed up the blanket again, covering her nakedness. Where had everyone gone? Why did no one warn her or come for her? Had an enemy arrived at camp? Surely it was so, for the women and children had vanished!

She swallowed her fear, telling herself to think clearly. She would not be afraid. She would simply pick up her things and hurry back to the village. Perhaps they just did not realize she was missing. After all, she had been hidden behind the waterfall. And yet, Swift Arrow would surely be aware of her absence. Perhaps he was dead! Perhaps the village had been attacked and enemy Crow or Pawnee had snuck up on the women and children and had stolen them!

Her breathing quickened when there was a rustling in the bushes behind her. She whirled and stared in that direction, her eyes wide with fright.

"It's all right, Abbie girl," came the voice. "I sent them all away."

Her stomach tightened. It sounded like Zeke's voice, but did she dare believe it was he? Was someone fooling her?

"Zeke?" Abbie's own voice sounded strange to her.

There was another rustling and suddenly he emerged, leading the roan mare, wearing the handsome smile that she loved. "Have I ever told you how pretty you are when your hair is wet?" he asked her softly.

She stared wide-eyed at him for a moment, chills sweeping through her at the sight of him. He wore the white buckskin shirt that she loved, and his long, black hair was clean and shining. It hung long and loose, with a colorful ornament braided into one side.

"Zeke!" she whispered. She ran to him then, opening the blanket and enfolding him in it as he embraced her, his hands gently caressing her naked body as they meshed tightly together. He embraced her so firmly she could barely breathe, and she broke into uncontrolled sobs of joy, blubbering something about thinking he was dead, while his lips gently caressed her neck and his very life pulsed through her veins. "Zeke! Zeke!" she cried, her arms tight around his neck. Was it truly Cheyenne Zeke holding her . . . whispering her name?

"Abbie girl!"

Those were blessedly sweet words. Only her Zeke called her that! His lips moved over her neck, her cheek, her eyes, her mouth. Oh, yes, there it was! That wonderful, sweet kiss that belonged to only one man! Her own lips parted in welcome, and her hands let go of the blanket so that she could grasp his hair, touch it! Feel it!

"Ne-mehotatse!" He groaned the word passionately.

The blanket fell from her body, but it didn't matter! All that mattered was that Zeke was here, alive and holding her! He had come back! He always came back! His lips left her mouth and moved again to her neck, her shoulder, his hardness pressing against her in great yearning for his woman, and both knew without speaking that whatever decision they made, they must be together, for their togetherness was life, and being apart was like death. Hard feelings and misunderstandings were gone, and there was only a man and a woman and their love!

He set her on her feet, but she clung to him so tightly he could not remove her arms from around his neck.

"Don't let go!" she pleaded. "Don't ever let go!"

"It's all right, Abbie girl," he told her quietly.

"No! If I let go you'll be gone! I know it! I'm just dreaming!"

"You're not dreaming, Abbie. And there you go again, making me out to be something I'm not, talking about dreams and such."

"Oh, Zeke, hold me just a little longer!"

He gladly kept his arms around her, and she kissed his neck, breathing in the wonderful, manly scent of him, running her hands across his broad, strong shoulders. He moved his lips back to her own in one long, lingering, hungry kiss, his gentle hands moving over her bare hips again. Then he swung her up in his arms. She rested her head on his shoulder and asked no questions as he bent down and picked up her blanket while she still clung to him. It did not matter at the moment where he had been or why. All that mattered was that he was here now; he needed his woman and his woman needed him. There would be time later for questions and answers.

He carried her to a spot near the waterfall where Yucca bushes hid them.

"You've got to let go for a minute, Abbie," he told her with a soft smile. He kissed her hair and set her on her feet, and she finally released him. He threw out the blanket; then he turned to look at her, his eyes running over her beautiful nakedness. He smiled as she began to blush, but before Abbie dropped her eyes she had seen the tears in his own eyes and the tired, drawn look about him. Wherever he'd been, it had been just as hard on him as it had on her, and it was obvious he'd ridden hard to get back to her.

"I thought . . . maybe you'd be gone," he told her, his voice strained.

She looked back up at him. "And I thought you weren't coming back!" she answered.

He grasped her face between his big hands. "Don't I always come back, Abbie girl?"

She studied the dark eyes that she loved so much. "If I shouldn't doubt that, then you shouldn't have doubted that I would be here waiting," she answered.

He kissed her forehead. "Then let's neither of us doubt the other again . . . in any way."

She smiled through her tears. "Oh, Zeke, I'm so sorry for what I said before you left!"

"Hush, Abbie." He kissed her lips to still them, and this time his kiss was more urgent, a hungry, demanding kiss that made her whimper. When he finally released her lips, he picked her up in his arms and knelt to lay her on the blanket. She watched as he straightened and removed the white buckskin shirt. She studied his broad chest, feeling a new respect for him at the sight of the scars left on his chest and arms from his own participation in the Sun Dance ritual. In the afternoon sun, his bronze skin glistened with the heat of desire, and she felt a wonderful pain in her groin at the sight of his hard muscles and flat stomach, and that which was most manly about him when he removed his buckskin leggings and his loincloth.

She closed her eyes then and blushed. In the next moment his lips were covering her mouth again, and his body was pressed tightly against her own—the wonderful sensation of skin against skin. His breathing quickened as his lips left her mouth and traveled down her throat.

"God, Abbie, I have to have you!" he groaned, moving down to taste the taut nipples of her breasts. "I've thought about you this way every night for so very long!"

"And I've thought about you," she whispered, reaching down and touching his hair as his lips moved over her belly and caressed her thighs.

The talking was finished then. There was only the glorious touching, the eager, hungry, intimate sharing of two lovers who have long been apart. It mattered little what he did to her, for this was Zeke. He was back, and he needed his woman. She would let him have whatever he wanted, realizing her own sweet dreams and intense pleasure in the giving and taking.

His lips touched every part of her, his urgent moans and her own soft whimperings drowning out the sounds of the birds; their ecstasy made the roaring waters seem far away and the pain of their months apart quickly vanished. It seemed neither of them could give enough or take enough. She arched up to him rhythmically, as he filled her with that part of him that brought her some pain, for his own terrible need made him take her more roughly than he wanted. Yet he could not stop himself. He wanted to ravish her, make up for all the lonely nights, prove to himself she was really here, waiting for him as he had hoped she would be.

He wanted to cry out, for the scar on her breast and the one Dancing Moon had left on her abdomen only pulled at his heart and made him love her more. Such sadness and pain this woman-child had suffered since giving herself to him! He watched her lovingly as she lay with her eyes closed, her long, thick hair still damp from bathing, her body small but welcoming, her firm, slim thighs parted for him. He came down closer, wrapping strong, rock-hard arms around her lithe middle and moving his hands down to grasp her hips and push. She cried out and kissed his chest over and over, her fingers digging into the dark skin of his back. His hair hung down, touching her shoulders and cheeks, and she felt lost beneath his masculinity.

This was Zeke! The half-breed scout she'd loved since first he'd stepped into the light of her father's fire back in Independence, Missouri. Zeke! Her friend, her protector, her father, her brother, her lover! He was everything . . . and he was here! Alive! Oh, so alive! She felt that life pulsing inside of her as it poured forth from him in surges he could no longer control. A guttural, almost mournful groan exited his lips as he breathed a sigh of spent relief, and they were suddenly both limp and weak.

When their first wave of lovemaking was finished, they lay together without speaking. It was too soon. They did not want to talk yet. They only wanted to touch, to know that this was real. They had to make love again, more slowly, more deliberately. And it was only moments before he moved over her again, this time more carefully, more gently. Again he pushed himself inside of her, holding himself up on his elbows to study the beautiful contours of her face. Her eyes were closed, and he knew that if she opened them she would blush, for she was still bashful about doing these things in the light. She was Abbie, his virgin wife. He had been her first man, and he suddenly felt a terrible jealousy at the thought of any other

300

man touching his woman. If any man tried, he would die a terrible death!

She cried out and he felt her pulsing again. He struggled to hold himself back so that she could enjoy him, for it was different for a woman. When a man climaxed, he was finished. But when a woman climaxed, she was just beginning. He wanted her to have this moment, for her own needs had been as great as his. He moved slowly and deliberately, relishing every whimper and whisper, every grasp of her fingers on his arms. He came down closer and teased her lips, whispering to her in Cheyenne words she did not fully understand, but which she knew were provocative and teasing.

His whispers made her feel as though her body would soon be consumed by fire, and she cried out his name and arched up to him in wild desire. It was almost painful for him to restrain his need to pour his life into her belly. Finally it was impossible for him to hold back. Once again it was over.

They lay in the afternoon sun, touching but not speaking. They were spent from their heated lovemaking, yet both knew they would stay there that night and make love again . . . and again. For their hunger and their happiness was for this day and night insatiable.

After several minutes he began stroking her damp hair away from her face, and she turned her head to meet his dark, adoring eyes.

"There is so much to tell you, Zeke," she told him softly. "So much. I feel . . . like a true Cheyenne. I've learned so much! I witnessed the Sun Dance ritual."

He raised up on one elbow. "The Sun Dance! You watched?"

She smiled with pride. "Yes. Gentle Woman painted my face and everything! Oh, Zeke, you don't know how much I've learned. I love it here now. I love the people, and Two Feathers and Runs Slowly . . . they've given me presents for saving Magpie, and—"

"Slow down, Abbie!" he said with a grin, putting fingers to

her lips. "You saved Magpie? From what?"

"From drowning! Oh, Zeke, I just don't know where to begin."

He kissed her lightly. "How about at the beginning?" he replied. "You go first, and then I'll tell you where I've been." His face darkened. "I am sure what you have to tell me is much more pleasant."

She studied his godlike build as he stood up and walked to his horse to get his parfleche. He returned with the bag and with another blanket so she could cover herself; then he sat down beside her again, lighting a thin cigar.

"That looks like an expensive smoke," she told him, watching him take a long puff. He took it from his mouth and studied it a moment.

"It is," he replied with a grin. "You might say it cost a man his life." With that he began to chuckle, then broke into all-out laughter. Abbie grinned in confusion, as he laughed for several seconds at the cigar. Then his laughter dwindled, and he suddenly scowled at it. "I have a whole handful of these," he went on. "Kind of a keepsake, you might say."

She put a hand on his arm. "Zeke, let's talk about me later. I want to talk about you. Tell me what happened," she said quietly. "It was bad. I know it was, or you'd never have stayed away so long. And when you laughed, it wasn't a happy laugh. It was a bitter laugh."

He turned his dark eyes to meet hers, and she saw the frightening need for vengeance she had seen there before when he was aching to kill someone. It was a part of the wild side of him she did not fear, but knew she'd never fully understand. It was the Indian in him.

"You're right, Abbie girl. It was a bitter laugh." He threw the cigar aside. "I'll tell you where I've been, Abbie," he went on. "But I'm not ready to talk about it yet. I'd rather talk about the decision I've made, and I have something to show you." His face brightened again; his eyes became gentle. He reached into the parfleche and pulled out the music box, wrapped in

302

thick, brown paper. "For you," he told her.

Her eyes began to dance with a child's curiosity. "For me?" She took it carefully. "You mean . . . a present?"

"A present. A love gift."

She smiled and eagerly tore away the paper. Then her eyes widened and began to fill with tears as she looked upon the glittering gold box with its seams of jewels and beads.

"Zeke!" she whispered. "It looks so . . . expensive!"

"It was. Open the lid," he urged.

She looked up at him and a tear slid down her face. "Zeke, you shouldn't have spent your money this way! There is so much we'll be needing. Swift Arrow says the hunt may not provide enough meat for the winter and—"

"Open it," he interrupted her. "And don't worry about money. I have plenty of money. That's part of the reason I was gone for so long." He kissed the tear on her cheek. "I am your man, and I command you to open the lid or I'll beat you."

She smiled and leaned forward to kiss his cheek; then she carefully raised the lid of the box which was lined in red velvet. Her eyes widened as a waltz tune tinkled forth. A revolving drum, with little teeth on it, was set within the box, and when these teeth struck slender golden rods, they made music. She watched the drum turn with a heart so full of love she thought it might burst.

"It's a music box!" she exclaimed, her eyes tearing more. "I've always wanted a music box!"

He touched her hair. "Well then, I got the perfect gift. But I didn't mean to make you cry, Abbie."

She closed the lid and laid her head against his chest. He kissed her hair.

"Abbie, I've decided what we'll do," he told her, stroking her hair gently. "I have quite a bit of money—enough to set us up on a little piece of land. I figure we can build us a cabin, down near Bent's Fort. That's where my people are most of the time. We'll winter there. I'll build up my herd, buy you some furnishings. You can have a fireplace and a wood floor and a real bed. You'll be warm and—"

She straightened and met his eyes. "But I can live with the People, Zeke. I can! I know I can! I've learned so many things. And you said we couldn't live among the whites."

He grasped her arms. "Abbie, living around Bent's Fort would be like living with Cheyenne. There are white traders there, too, I'll grant you, but most of them know me and would respect my woman. It's a way, Abbie. A way to be with the Cheyenne and away from most whites, least ways the kind I'm sure we can't live with. In the summers that you feel up to it, we can ride with the Cheyenne on the summer hunts, go north with them for the celebrations; and in the winters, you'll be safe and warm and live like a white woman was brought up to live. I can't make you turn away from what you are, Abbie girl, any more than you would ask me to forget that I am Cheyenne. And just like I give you a part of home when I sing and play the mandolin for you, I can also give you a part of home by giving you a real house."

"But Zeke—"

"No, Abbie. I've made up my mind. Since the day you agreed to marry me, you've been willing to give up all your old ways, to give up your identity and turn your back on your own people, all for me. But never once did you ask that of me. I know you could probably live with the Cheyenne and survive. Hell, you've been doing it. But it's only been one summer, Abbie girl. I've lived with them a lot longer, and I know how hard it is. And it's going to get harder, honey. A lot harder. I can't make you be a part of that. It isn't fair to ask it. And it's like . . . like a good friend of mine told me just a few weeks ago. He said that down deep in that white woman's heart of yours, there'll be times when you'll want to fix your hair, and put on a pretty dress and petticoats . . . and dance." He grasped her arms tighter. "Look me in the eyes, Abbie girl. Look me in the eyes and say you'd never want those things."

She studied his dark eyes and could not lie. Her answer lay in her own tears. "But . . . I love the People," she whispered.

He smiled softly. "Of course you love them. I knew you would. And that's why I love you. But they know you love them, Abbie, and you don't need to live with them night and day year round for them to know that. They'd understand if you wanted to live in a white woman's home part of the time."

She sniffed. "Tell them . . . you made me do it . . . that it was your idea because you thought it would be better for me. I . . . don't want them to think I asked not to live with them."

He smiled softly. "I'll tell them."

She looked down at the little gold music box. "Zeke, what happened to you? Where did you get enough money to buy something like this?"

The strange vengeful look returned to his eyes. "It was my pay, from a man called Jonathan Mack," he replied. "I met him in Independence and agreed to take two wagons to Santa Fe for him for a good sum of money. . . ."

Danny rode farther south into Mexico with the rest of the volunteers who were under Kearny's command. He was refreshed. Taking Santa Fe had been simple, because all of the men Governor Armijo had gathered to fight the oncoming American soldiers had run from the bluecoats. There had been no one in Santa Fe to give Colonel Kearny a fight, and the city now belonged to America.

There had been a brief rest for the soldiers in the city, and whiskey and prostitutes had put new life in the men. Now they marched toward a villa where it was rumored Mexican soldiers were hiding. After taking that, they would move westward into California, and more troops would come in to secure Santa Fe.

They were four days out of the city when they crested a rise and gazed down at the sprawling *ranchero* that supposedly held the Mexican soldiers. Kearny did not hesitate. He surrounded the main *hacienda* and rode slowly toward it, his cannons waiting silently on the hillside behind him, ready to be fired if necessary. But all appeared quiet.

Kearny motioned to a second lieutenant to move in with a small troop; among these men was Danny Monroe. They would carry a white truce flag, and the Spanish-speaking lieutenant would order all Mexican soldiers who might be hiding on the premises to show themselves.

The lieutenant rode forward with his nervous men, and Danny waited silently as the command was barked in Spanish. There was no reply, nothing but the wind. Kearny and the rest of the men watched carefully, their guns positioned and ready. The lieutenant gave the order again, and again silence was their reply.

It was then that Danny saw the glint of the sun on steel. A man stood up from behind a statue and pointed a rifle at the lieutenant, and in that split second, Danny yelled at the lieutenant and jumped from his own horse to knock the lieutenant to the ground. The Mexican's bullet caught Danny in the back, just beneath his right shoulder blade. The lieutenant's life had been saved.

Daylight faded from Danny's eyes, and it seemed that every gun and cannon had exploded around him. He could not move, but felt himself being dragged; that was all he remembered until he woke up in a hospital tent, his right arm wrapped tightly against his side so he could not move it. He felt excruciating pain in his right shoulder, and knew that if he dared to move, the pain would be even more unbearable. He started to speak, but the words stuck in his dry throat, and he began coughing and choking, the slight movement making him groan with the terrible pain.

"Here, drink this," someone was telling him. The whiskey burned his throat, but he swallowed it eagerly, anxious for its dulling effects.

"What . . . happened?" he asked the voice.

"You were shot," came the reply. "But you're not hurt bad. You'll live. No vital organs damaged. You'll just be in a lot of pain for a few days, and then uncomfortable for a few more. But you'll be okay, son."

Danny blinked and tried to focus his eyes. He could smell alcohol and blood, and he knew he was in the Army doctor's tent. He blinked again, and finally focused on the doctor's face leaning over him.

"My arm—"

"Your arm is fine. I've just bandaged it close to your body so you won't move it for a few days," the doctor replied. "You need to keep it stationary, Private Monroe."

"What about . . . the Mexicans? What happened?"

"We took the villa without too much trouble. The cannon blew them out of there good, I'll tell you. Those Mexicans came running out like rabbits!" He chuckled. "And there is a lieutenant waiting outside to thank you for saving his life. The position you were in when you took the bullet—it's likely the bullet would have gone right through the man's heart or lungs if not for you. You earned yourself a medal yesterday, son. Maybe even a promotion."

"Yesterday? It was . . . yesterday?"

"Yes, sir. You've been out cold ever since. Lucky for you. I didn't have an easy time getting that bullet out of you."

Danny sighed. "Now I won't be able to finish the Mexican campaign with Colonel Kearny," he moaned.

"I wouldn't let that bother me!" the doctor replied, putting the ends of a stethoscope to his ears. "You should be glad to quit this campaign. It will get a lot rougher, I guarantee. That trip to California will be one long journey. Men will be walking until they have holes in their shoes. They'll catch cold in the mountains, run at the bowels from bad food and bad water, and I don't doubt some of them will desert. It will not be the romantic campaign they were expecting. You'd best be glad you don't have to go along, son."

"But . . . I joined up. I . . . have to go."

"You don't have to do anything but get well. The colonel is sending you and some other wounded back to Santa Fe to mend. Then you'll be sent to some other place of duty."

Danny sighed. He felt tired and depressed. It seemed his

307

Army career was all but over already. The doctor listened to his heart, then rose without speaking and left the tent. Minutes later Colonel Kearny himself entered, accompanied by the lieutenant who had carried the truce flag. Both grinned and nodded at Danny, who smiled back in spite of his pain, feeling honored by their presence.

"I've come to thank you, Private," the lieutenant told him. "There's no way I can ever repay you for what you did. It seems a very unfitting gift in return, but I'd like you to have my mount, Private. It's one of the best in the garrison."

Danny's eyes widened in surprise. "Thank you, sir! But . . . it isn't necessary. I just reacted naturally, sir."

"Bravely is the better word," the colonel put in. "I am recommending you for a medal, Mr. Monroe, and also for a promotion to first sergeant."

Danny smiled more in spite of his pain. Things were not so hopeless after all. "Sir, I . . . I don't know what to say! Thank you, sir! I'll . . . make a good sergeant." He winced with pain. "But . . . can that be done, sir. I mean . . . what about corporal and all—"

"Out here we like to encourage our good men, son. We can promote any way we choose," Kearny replied. "I'm sure you'll make a good officer of a much higher rank some day. You're real Army material, Monroe, not like most of those other ruffians out there. You're sincere. I've watched you." He leaned down closer. "And I . . . uh . . . I've heard the rumor that you have a brother out here—a half-blood Cheyenne— and that you've been looking for him. Is that true?"

Danny studied the man curiously, wondering why he had asked. "Yes, sir, it is. His name is Zeke. I . . . haven't seen him for six or seven years. I was only . . . fourteen when he . . . left Tennessee to come out here to find his Cheyenne family."

The colonel frowned and stood up again, folding his arms. "Mr. Monroe, I'll be frank with you. Washington knows that once this thing with Mexico is finished, the real problem for

Americans will still be ahead of them, which is namely Indians. I was told when I left Washington to keep my eyes open for good material, men who would make good officers for the Western Army, especially men who might be good at handling Indians."

"But sir, I don't know anything about Indians!" Danny spoke up quickly. "I just have a half-breed brother, that's all. I've never even been west till now!"

The colonel held out his hand to quiet him. "I understand all that. But you're good Army material, Monroe, and since you have an interest in the Indians because of this brother, you'll have more reason to learn about them and want to understand and work with them. If you ever find this brother, he could be a good connection in helping you understand. The time is coming, Monroe, when such understanding will be very important. I just want you to think about it . . . think about a career in the Western Army, son . . . and especially a career in working with the Indians. And since I suspect it is very important to you to find this brother of yours, I am ordering you to report to Fort Laramie after you recover in Santa Fe. I'll give you orders to take along, and someone will see that a letter is sent to higher authorities recommending you for the medal and the promotion. It shouldn't take too long for you to begin calling yourself first sergeant. Once you're stationed at Fort Laramie, it shouldn't be too difficult to find this brother of yours. Scouts go in and out of Fort Laramie all the time. It's in the heart of Cheyenne country. There is bound to be someone around the area who knows about Zeke and where he might be."

Danny studied the man in near worship. He could hardly believe what the colonel was telling him, or that so many good things could be happening to him. What better way to find Zeke than to be an officer in the Western Army and to ride the very lands that Zeke was likely riding!

"I don't know what to say, sir, I'm . . . deeply grateful."

"The look on your face is thanks enough," the colonel

replied. "Just hurry up and get well and get yourself to Fort Laramie."

Danny grinned. "Yes, sir!"

The lieutenant stepped forward, his hat in his hand. "Thank you, again," he told Danny. "What else can a man say?"

"It's okay, sir," Danny told him. "If it earned me a promotion . . . and a chance to serve at Fort Laramie and maybe find my brother . . . it was worth it."

They both grinned, but the lieutenant was obviously close to tears in his gratitude. "Far as I'm concerned, the Good Lord set you next to me, Private Monroe," the lieutenant told him. "I doubt there's another man out there who would have done what you did. They'd all have ducked to save their own necks." He put a hand on Danny's uninjured shoulder. "Thanks again. And good luck in your own Army career."

"Thank you, sir."

The lieutenant and Colonel Kearny left, and Danny closed his eyes. He would rest better now, in spite of his pain.

Zeke and his three brothers sat inside Zeke and Abbie's tipi, smoking fine thin cigars. They were gathered around the fire to ward off the chilly night air of the mountains. Abbie sat behind Zeke, picking sandburs from a pair of his leggings.

"This Jonathan Mack smoked fine cigar," Swift Arrow said with a wicked grin. "I only wish I could have seen his face when he reached into the sack, huh?"

The four of them chuckled, and Abbie smiled herself at the thought of it.

"You aren't the only one, my brother," Zeke answered. "But I thought it wise not to be close by." His face darkened. "The death I truly should have stayed to watch was Dancing Moon's."

"Mmm," Swift Arrow replied, puffing his fine cigar. "It is fine ending for that one, with your letter carved into her face. You had good idea there, Zeke. Good idea."

Zeke sighed. "I just hope she is dead," he told his brother. "Evil seems to have a way of surviving to go on to commit more evil."

"*Ai,*" Red Eagle agreed. But Swift Arrow waved him off.

"She is dead!" he declared. "And good riddance to her!"

Abbie shuddered at the thought of what Zeke had done to Dancing Moon, finding it difficult to visualize Zeke harming a woman. Yet she could feel no remorse for the Arapaho who had tried to murder her and had caused her to lose Zeke's baby.

"It is good your woman dreamed of the snakes," Swift Arrow was telling Zeke. "She is full of the spirits now . . . one with them. The vision shows she has the all-seeing heart of the Cheyenne . . . and because of her dream, we all prayed for you."

Zeke nodded. "I felt a special power and greater courage that night, Swift Arrow. It must have been the same night Abbie had the dream. You all prayed to the spirits, and they helped me."

"*Ai,*" Black Elk put in. "She is good, this woman you marry."

Zeke grinned and reached back to pat Abbie's leg. "I told you she was," he replied to his youngest brother. He gave Abbie a wink and she blushed.

Talk turned to the small hunt and the predictions of a long, cold winter. Abbie knew Zeke was concerned that they would not get back to the Arkansas River in time to build her the cabin before winter set in, but she was not worried. She had talked Zeke into forgetting the idea until the next year, for she wanted to spend one winter with the People. She had argued and insisted until Zeke had given in; but she knew he would buy an extra supply of warm clothing and blankets at Bent's Fort, and he would do everything he could to make their tipi extra warm. Already, Abbie was working on sewing more skins for an extra layer around the tipi and was making moccasins from the thickest fur of the buffalo hide. The furry side would be turned inward for extra warmth. But that was for the waking

311

hours. She knew that with Zeke beside her at night, she would not have to worry about being warm then, even if the fire dwindled before dawn. Indeed, she felt warm just thinking about it, for their lovemaking had been more heated and passionate than ever since his return.

"There is still much talk among our northern brothers of a great treaty," Swift Arrow was telling Zeke. "They say Fitzpatrick is still trying to make this happen."

"There's a lot of talk, Swift Arrow," Zeke replied, puffing his cigar. "But among the white men, there are always rumors. You should never believe what they say until you see the proof. Take my word for it."

Red Eagle took a flask of whiskey from beneath his blanket and swallowed some. Zeke scowled at him.

"Where do you get that stuff?" he asked his brother.

Red Eagle grinned. "Traders. They come around," he replied. "Other warriors buy it, too."

"And you're a fool!" Zeke snapped. "It's rotgut whiskey, full of water and sugar! Those lowdown traders are robbing you!"

Red Eagle's smile faded, and his eyes flashed with anger. "I am a man and make my own decisions! And I know how to control it now. I do not hurt Yellow Moon, and I know when to stop." He rose, his temper quick to flare when he drank the firewater. The friendly nature of their talk only a moment before had vanished. Red Eagle walked to the tipi entrance, then looked back at Zeke. "If you choose to be angry at a brother, then be angry at Swift Arrow—for beating your wife!" he sneered.

Abbie froze at the words, and Swift Arrow jumped up, glaring at his brother and clenching his fists. "Traitor!" he growled at Red Eagle. Red Eagle just grinned and walked out.

"*Katum!*" Black Elk swore. "Now there will be trouble."

Zeke got up from where he sat and turned confused and angry eyes to Abbie. "What is he talking about?" he asked in a threatening voice.

312

Abbie looked at Swift Arrow, and there was a long moment of silence while their eyes held. She looked back at Zeke. "I . . . promised I wouldn't tell," she told him. "I do not break promises. It's a private matter—between myself and Swift Arrow."

"Private!" Zeke roared. Abbie jumped and paled. She had never seen him quite so angry. "There is nothing private about another man hurting my wife! Brother or not! Now someone had better tell me what's going on!"

Abbie swallowed and nervously put down the leggings, getting to her feet.

"She looked upon the Sacred Arrows!" Swift Arrow replied, straightening himself and holding his head proudly. "I had no choice!"

Zeke whirled to face him, and Abbie could see Zeke's jaw muscles flexing in anger. She walked over to plant herself between the two men, facing Zeke.

"He had no choice, Zeke. I did something that was forbidden. I deliberately disobeyed instructions and sneaked over to the Arrow Keeper's lodge and looked at the Sacred Arrows after the Arrow Renewal. The Arrow Keeper caught me."

Zeke glared down at her. "Why in God's name did you do that?"

Her eyes began to fill with tears, for she did not like him to be so angry at her. "I . . . don't know. I just knew I had to do it. Something made me do it. I . . . I knew that if I looked at them, somehow I'd understand the People better. I'd understand you better. I . . . I can't explain it, Zeke!"

Zeke's eyes turned back to Swift Arrow. He gently pushed Abbie out of the way. "And you beat her for this?" he asked. "You couldn't wait for me to get back, even though you knew she was ignorant of how serious her error was?"

Swift Arrow did not flinch. "I had no choice!" he replied flatly. "The other dog soldiers and the Arrow Keeper were outside the tipi. If I had not quickly punished her, they would

313

have done it, my brother! Do you not see? They would not have been as kind to her! It was for her own protection that I did it . . . to quiet their anger. You know how sacred the arrows are . . . what happens to a woman who looks upon them! Would you rather I had turned her over to them? I would have waited for you, but they would not have waited!"

"Zeke, it was only five lashes, and he didn't hit me as hard as he could have. He . . . he put bear grease on the cuts right away, and I don't even have any scars!"

Zeke turned to her, his eyes full of hurt for her and anger at Swift Arrow. "No scars!" he groaned. "My God, Abbie! You were alone among them. You must have been—" He stopped and turned away from both of them, letting out a strange groan of frustration. "I can hardly believe you waited for me after that. What a terrible thing for you!"

"Zeke, I wanted the punishment!" Abbie told him. "I deserved it! And he tried not to hurt me any more than he had to! Please don't be angry, Zeke. It's just as he said. He had no choice. Swift Arrow took good care of me. And don't forget that he saved me from those awful white men who wanted to take me away. He risked his life for me that day, Zeke! If he had not, I might . . . I might have been dragged off by those men, and God knows what they would have done with me!"

He closed his eyes and sighed.

"She tells truth," Black Elk put in. "Other warriors very angry when she look at the arrows. Would have hurt her more than Swift Arrow hurt her. He do right thing, my brother. And those white men, they were bad—very bad. Swift Arrow would not let them take her, even though one put his gun against Swift Arrow's throat."

"I . . . have since asked for her forgiveness," Swift Arrow put in, his voice weak. "When she saved little Magpie, all of us knew then why the spirits had made her look upon the arrows. It was for the strength and courage she would need to go into the deep waters and brave the evil spirits in order to save Magpie. Then we knew. All of us asked her forgiveness, my

314

brother, and gave her some of our prized weapons and possessions."

Zeke nodded, his back still turned. "So . . . there is more to the story of the drowning than you told me," he said to Abbie.

"*Ai,*" Swift Arrow replied for her. "But I tell you this, my brother. Abigail is my sister now. She is true Cheyenne, and I . . . care for her. To hurt her brought me pain, and I would not have done it if I had a choice. But I had no choice. It was the only way to keep her from greater harm."

"That stupid Red Eagle!" Black Elk grumbled. "I should break his whiskey bottle over his head!" He got up and stormed out. Swift Arrow looked helplessly at Abbie.

"I never would have told him, Swift Arrow," she said quietly.

He nodded. "This I know. But perhaps it is better he knows."

Abbie turned to Zeke, wanting desperately to soothe his anger. "Zeke, if I can forgive Swift Arrow, surely you can. He's your brother. He kept his promise to you to watch out for me—risked his life for me because of that promise. He has taught me many things. He's helped me understand the People. Don't make me feel responsible for bad feelings between you and your Cheyenne brother. Please, Zeke. Don't do this!"

Zeke finally turned to face Swift Arrow, some anger still in his eyes.

"If you had been here, my brother, you would have had to do the same," Swift Arrow told him. "It would have been your duty to still the anger of the other warriors. You are Cheyenne. You know the law."

Zeke nodded. "I know the law," he replied wearily. "I just don't know whether to thank you or split your gizzard!"

"Zeke!" Abbie gasped.

The two men studied one another. "Then I tell you this, my brother," Swift Arrow replied, his eyes true and steady. "If this thing I did brings hatred to your heart for Swift Arrow, then Swift Arrow will stand still while you split his gizzard. For

315

he would rather die than to bring unnecessary harm to Lone Eagle's woman. What I did was for her own protection."

The words were said with such sincerity, Zeke could not help but feel forgiveness in his heart. Swift Arrow had meant every word he'd spoken, and he would have stood there and let Zeke cut away at him without protest if Zeke so chose. Zeke reached out and put a hand on Swift Arrow's shoulder.

"Then let us smoke a peace pipe, Swift Arrow," he told his brother. "And we will never speak of this again."

Swift Arrow nodded, pride and love showing in his eyes. "*Ai*. It is good we do not speak of it again. We will smoke the pipe and erase all memory of this night."

Abbie looked down, wiping tears away. "I'll put more wood on the fire," she said quietly. "You should both have something to eat."

Zeke and Swift Arrow's eyes held steadily, as Zeke slowly removed his hand from Swift Arrow's shoulder.

"She is no longer white woman," Swift Arrow said quietly. "She is Cheyenne!"

Zeke's heart ached with pride. He nodded. "I reckon she is at that," he replied.

Sixteen

It was the Moon of Strong Cold, January, 1847. Zeke and Abbie shared Tall Grass Woman's tipi, to which they had been invited by Falling Rock for supper. Tall Grass Woman and her husband still felt indebted to Abbie for saving Magpie, and Zeke and Abbie were often their guests. Each time they were told they must bring no gifts in return, for the life of Magpie was gift enough.

Now they all sat in a circle, bundled in buffalo robes, for this night was exceptionally cold. Extra clothing was usually not necessary inside the tipis when a good fire was going, but this night the fire could not keep up with the bitter January sub-zero temperatures.

The meal was finished, and Tall Grass Woman, her husband, and children sat listening in fascination as Zeke played his mandolin and sang Tennessee mountain songs.

"'Love, oh love, oh careless love, Just look what careless love has done,'" he sang in the mellow voice Abbie cherished. He winked at her as he sang, and Abbie blushed. Little Magpie and her brother, Wolf's Paw, seemed spellbound by the songs, for white men's tunes were much different from the Indian songs. They stared with big, brown eyes from beneath the robe they shared, and their round, perfect faces were framed by jet-black hair. They sat quiet and obedient, aware they must not speak unless spoken to.

Abbie rubbed at her full stomach. According to Cheyenne

317

custom, guests must never turn away any food offered by the host, and Falling Rock had offered Abbie more than she could handle. Zeke had helped her out by sneaking some of the meat off her plate when Tall Grass Woman and Falling Rock were not watching; but the children caught him at it once and began to giggle. Zeke winked at them and then gave them a warning look not to tell, and they just giggled more. Abbie herself had trouble not laughing; and now, as Zeke sang his songs, the children cast her sidelong, knowing glances and covered their mouths to keep from making any noise. Once, when they could not subdue another giggle, Falling Rock gave them a dark scowl, and they immediately stopped, not out of fear, but simply out of respect for their father.

It occurred to Abbie then that she had never once seen a Cheyenne father or mother strike a child, nor had she ever heard Cheyenne parents raise their voices. All teaching was done gently, patiently, and with a soft voice. Much of it was done by the elders and by relatives. Everyone seemed willingly to share in the upbringing of the children, and when a child misbehaved, the looks of disappointment and digust on the faces of parents and elders were usually all it took to bring that child so much embarrassment and shame that he or she never misbehaved in that way again. Only the adults, who should know better, were chastised for wrongdoings.

"*Wagh!*" Falling Rock told Zeke when he finished another song. "*Ha, ho, Nis'is.*"

Zeke nodded.

"*Ha ho,*" the little children said in unison. They looked at their mother with pleading eyes, and Tall Grass Woman smiled and nodded.

"They want you to tell them a story," she told Zeke in the Cheyenne tongue. "Earlier, they say no one tell story like Lone Eagle."

Zeke grinned and looked over at Abbie. "They want me to tell them a story," he told her. "You listen close and see how much of it you can understand, Abbie girl. It will be a good test

318

of how much Cheyenne you've learned."

Abbie smiled and scooted closer to him, pulling her buffalo robe closer around her neck. Zeke set aside his mandolin and leaned forward, resting his elbows on the knees of his crossed legs. His shoulders seemed broader than ever in the big, shaggy buffalo coat he wore, and as he took on a somber attitude for his story, he suddenly seemed large and dark and menacing. He leaned closer to the fire and waved a hand across it, blowing smoke toward the children.

"Do you know about the Screaming Moon Monsters?" he asked them in a near whisper.

Their eyes widened. They looked at one another and then back at Zeke. Both shook their heads "no" but did not speak.

Zeke grinned wickedly. "The Screaming Moon Monsters dwell only in deep canyons, and come out only when the moon is full," he continued. "They breathe through the rocks of the canyons and make the rocks move. When they are angry, the whole canyon shakes, and when they are not angry, the canyon is still and quiet. They scream at night," he went on. "*Aieee!*" he added in a soft, but eerie wail. "*Aieee! Aieee! Send us the children!*"

Magpie and Wolf's Paw looked at one another again and huddled closer, and it was difficult for Abbie to keep from laughing. She did not understand all of what Zeke was saying, except that it must be a story of ghosts or monsters, because of his tone of voice, his inflections, and the eerie wail. Even Falling Rock and Tall Grass Woman listened attentively, as though they believed Zeke; and Abbie decided they probably did, for the Cheyenne believed in ghosts and monsters and night spirits. Storytelling about such things was a favorite pastime in the dead of winter, when the People had little to do but stay inside their tipis and entertain themselves until they could again enjoy the freedom that warmer weather brings.

"But no children go to the Screaming Moon Monster canyons," Zeke went on, "especially not on the night of a full moon. No children have ever been found to be brave enough to

319

face the monsters, except . . ."

He stopped and lit his corncob pipe, while the children and their parents waited anxiously. Zeke puffed on the pipe for a moment, then leaned toward the children again.

"Except a little boy and a little girl—a brother and sister—who one day, long ago, decided they would show their bravery by answering the call of the Screaming Moon Monsters!" he continued.

Little Magpie's mouth dropped open, and Wolf's Paw wiggled closer to the fire.

"The little boy and girl had been bad," Zeke told them. "They had disobeyed their father and had made a noise when they were supposed to be very quiet; and because of the noise they'd made, an enemy had found them, and many of their people lost their lives. And so, the little girl and boy were very ashamed, and they wanted to do something to make up for what they had done. So they decided they would go to a nearby canyon at the first full moon—a great, deep canyon near their village, where no one else dared go. It was said that the Screaming Moon Monsters lived there and carried the skulls of the dead. Often the little boy and girl had heard their people say that if anyone could ever take one of these skulls from the monsters, he or she would be a great and honored warrior. But there was not a warrior among them, even among the adult dog soldiers, who was willing to go to the canyon and try to get a skull. So the little boy and girl knew that if they could do this, they would be forgiven for their error and would be honored and loved again."

He stopped to puff the pipe again, enjoying the looks on the children's faces. Abbie thought about what a fine father he would make some day; for he loved children, and the loss of his son in Tennessee had left an emptiness in his heart that could not be filled. But Abbie would try her best to fill it. Already she was making headway; she was almost certain she was pregnant again, although she had not yet told Zeke.

"And so," Zeke continued, "on the next night when there

320

was a full moon, the little boy and girl took weapons and ventured out into the night. They sang songs to *Maheo* as they walked to the canyon, praising the gods and asking for protection. The little boy had a medicine bag, filled with good-luck items his father had given him. He clung to it, and his sister clung to him, and together they reached the edge of the canyon. They looked down, and something white, with vacant holes for eyes, looked up at them. Then it moved—very fast!"

He waved his hand and made Magpie and Wolf's Paw jump with fright.

"It came toward them, screaming '*Aieee! Aieee!* Send us the children!' It swooped past them, blowing cold air on them, but it did not touch them. Behind it, it dragged an ugly skull, and the children were very afraid! But they could no longer face their people in shame, and so their fear was overcome by their desire to win back their honor.

"And so they did not let the first monster frighten them away. They began descending into the canyon, holding hands and closing their eyes every time another Screaming Moon Monster brushed past them, screaming '*Aieee! Aieee!* Send us the children!'

"They kept walking, holding their heads high to show the monsters they were brave. Skulls of the dead bounced past them, most of them very small—the skulls of children! But the boy and girl kept walking until, finally, they were at the bottom of the canyon, where Screaming Moon Monsters congregated and danced around them, screaming and laughing and dragging skulls! It was a horrible sight! The most horrible sight the children had ever witnessed! And they were certain that their own skulls would be the next to be tied to the tails of two of these monsters!"

He stopped for a moment, leaning back and puffing his pipe, waiting as the adults and the children looked back and forth at each other and then turned to him, waiting for him to continue. He deliberately prolonged this pause until the listeners could take no more.

"What happened? What happened?" Tall Grass Woman asked.

Zeke kept a serious face as he finally continued. "Because of the brave hearts the little girl and boy displayed, the Screaming Moon Monsters were unable to cut off their heads. They tried and tried, slashing at their necks with swords and knives and hatchets, but the children's necks were as stone, for their hearts were brave and *Maheo* protected them. It was the first time the Screaming Moon Monsters had ever come across a child or even an adult who was not afraid of them in the canyon during the full moon. It made their screaming weaker, and they danced around the children more and more slowly, until suddenly they had no more strength.

"The little boy and girl pounced upon this opportunity to get a skull. The little boy took his hatchet and the little girl her knife, and each cut off a skull from a monster's tail! Then they began to feel stronger and braver. The little boy puffed up his chest and threw back his shoulders and pointed skyward.

"'Go!' he told the monsters. 'Be gone with you! This is our land—our canyon! *Tsis-tsis-tas!* We belong here! We are the People!'

"The monsters were so surprised by this bravery that they did not know what to do but obey, and with their last strength they began flying skyward, away from the little boy and little girl who frightened them by their bravery. The little boy and girl began to laugh at them, pointing to them and watching them fly away, and then the canyon was quiet. The Screaming Moon Monsters were gone!

"By then much time had passed, and the sun began to rise. The little boy and girl started to climb back to the edge of the canyon, for they heard their mother and father calling for them. When they reached the top, they called out to the People and held up the skulls they had cut off from the tails of the Screaming Moon Monsters. The People came running, then stopped and gasped when they saw the skulls. The little boy and girl told their story, and the People believed them; for they had

322

been missing all night, and now they stood at the edge of the canyon, holding the skulls.

"And so, the little boy and girl were greatly honored. And when they grew older, they became leaders—even the little girl. She rode and fought with the male warriors, and she was as good as they. She and her brother carried with them the skulls they had taken from the monsters, and they were great medicine; for arrows and lances and knives bounced off them in battle and did not harm them. The People thought them to be the bravest of all warriors. But time took hold, and finally they grew old. Their bodies died and the life went from them, as happens to all old ones one day. They were laid out on scaffolds and raised up for burial, and many came from far and wide to see their bodies and pay tribute to them. The skulls were tied to the scaffolds, and their weapons were laid beside them. And then, the night after they died, there was a full moon!"

He stopped again, and little Magpie gasped. She clung tightly to her brother's hand, as both waited for the ending of the story.

"The People continued to watch over the bodies, even that night," Zeke went on, "for they wanted to be sure no harm came to them. But just as the moon was high in the sky, the People witnessed a terrible thing! A frightening thing!" He leaned closer to the children again. "White spirits rose up out of their dead bodies and began screaming and laughing. They flew around the People, grabbing the skulls from the scaffolds and tying them to their tails! Then they flew off toward the moon! The People were so afraid, they fainted; and when they awoke, it was morning, and the bodies of the man and woman who had once been the brave boy and girl, had vanished! They were never found, and the People were certain they had gone to be with the Screaming Moon Monsters. And so the very thing they had bravely fought against had finally come to claim the children after all! Again the canyon was to be feared, for the monsters had returned and could be heard screaming there on the nights of the full moon. To this day, not one man or woman, old person or child, has ever been brave enough to go back to the canyon and rid it of the monsters. Until that very brave person steps forward, the Screaming Moon Monsters will always be with us!"

Silence hung inside the tipi when he finished. Zeke leaned back and puffed his pipe, and the little children scooted back from the fire. Falling Rock finally broke into a grin and touched his brow to Zeke in a sign of respect. "We thank you for a good story," he told Zeke. "It has been good to have you here with us this night."

"And I thank you for inviting us, Falling Rock," Zeke replied. "It has been good to be here . . . good food . . . quiet children . . . a pleasant dwelling. Abbie and I always like coming here. The winter is long and cold. It is good to share stories and friendship."

"*Ai.*" Falling Rock nodded. "And is good to share woman, too, hey? You go now to your tipi and keep woman warm, and I do same."

Tall Grass Woman giggled, and Zeke chuckled and touched his brow. Abbie watched innocently, not realizing what had been said. "I'll go along with that, Falling Rock," Zeke was saying. He motioned to Abbie to leave, and she rose and nodded to Tall Grass Woman.

"*Ha ho,*" she told her good friend.

"*Wagh,*" Tall Grass Woman replied with a wide grin. She grasped Abbie by the shoulders and touched her cheek with her own cheek. "*Momata.*"

Abbie and Zeke left, hurrying through the deep snows to their own tipi, where Abbie immediately began building up the fire that had begun to dwindle. "What does '*Momata*' mean?" she asked Zeke.

"Very blessed," he replied.

She smiled. "I am very blessed," she answered. "I have you . . . and the People. I have everything I want." The fire began to burn harder and she straightened to face him. "I even have life inside me again," she went on quietly, unable to keep the secret any longer. "Again a son or daughter grows in my belly, put there by my husband. I am very blessed."

Zeke had been shaking snow from his moccasins when she said it. He suddenly stopped and looked at her when he realized what she was telling him.

"Abbie!"

She smiled. "I'm sure of it, Zeke. I only flowed once after you came back from Santa Fe. I haven't flowed since. That would make me at least three months along."

His eyes glowed with love, and he walked over to her and opened her robe, studying the small girl beneath it. "Abbie, I— Maybe it's too soon. I wouldn't want anything bad to happen again."

"It won't," she replied confidently. "This will be a good one, Zeke! And there is no Dancing Moon here to spoil it!"

Their eyes held in shared joy, and he pulled her into his arms, determined not to show her his fear. There was no sense in making her worry, too. She was happy. But he remembered the awful, helpless feeling he'd had when she miscarried . . . and she was still so young. But perhaps this time it would be all right, for she had not even been ill, and she was healthier now. She had color in her cheeks and was not so pitifully thin.

"We'll make this a good one, Abbie girl," he told her. "I don't want you doing any hard work, understand? No more lifting wood and carrying heavy bundles of skins and such. You'll get plenty of rest and always be warm. I'll see to it." He hugged her tightly, his heart pounding at the thought of finally having another child. It would not matter if it was a girl or a boy, and yet . . . a son would be good. A son to replace the one he had lost.

He released her and they smiled and kissed lightly. Then he helped her build the fire up even more, and the tipi began to warm, although just as with Tall Grass Woman's tipi, a comfortable warmth would not be reached on this bitter night. Zeke led her to their bed, which was built high on grass and leaves that were covered with the softest buffalo robe they

325

owned. Zeke had purchased several woolen blankets for her at Bent's Fort before winter set in, and they were layered between a cover of buffalo robes, so that when they slept the wool would not scratch them. They removed their moccasins and crawled in between the robes, and Zeke pulled her close.

"Tomorrow when midday makes it a little warmer, I'll help you bathe," he told her. "And I'll put that cream on you that we bought at the fort. I want you to stay soft and pretty, Abbie girl. I won't let the prairie sun age you. And next summer we'll have that cabin. I'll make things good for you and the baby, you'll see."

"I know you will. You don't need to tell me those things."

He kissed her again, this time harder, and his hand moved down to the hem of her tunic, then beneath it. He caressed her slender thighs and her small, round bottom.

"Zeke, it's too cold to undress," she whispered.

"Then don't," he replied. "We'll just pull up your tunic."

She laughed lightly as he pushed at the tunic, and she felt a wonderful, tingling sensation in her blood when she knew he was removing his own leggings and loincloth.

"Come here, Abbie girl," he told her, moving on top of her. "I'll warm you, *Kseé.*"

Late the next day the sky darkened with an oncoming winter storm, but the howling of the wind was dimmed by sounds of great commotion in the village. Cries of death, anger, and sorrow combined with shouts of vengeance.

"Zeke, what is it?" Abbie asked, her heart pounding. He was already pulling on his moccasins.

"Stay here," he told her, throwing on his buffalo robe against the cruel cold outside. "I'll be right back." He quickly left, and Abbie hurried to the tipi entrance to look out. The warriors had gathered at the center of the village, shaking their fists and shouting angrily, and at first Abbie thought that perhaps an enemy was nearby. Already some of the men were bringing horses, as others approached carrying war lances and weapons. She recognized the word *Mexicans,* and she noticed that eight Cheyenne men who had been to Bent's Fort to trade for supplies were in the middle of the confusion, shouting and waving their arms. Zeke was there now also, trying to reason with the men, but already many of them were mounting up, including Zeke's brothers.

After several minutes, Zeke hurried back to his tipi. "Get my rifle!" he told Abbie, reaching over and slinging a quiver of arrows over his shoulder. He picked up his leather weapons belt and cinched it around the outside of his buffalo robe. Abbie retrieved his rifle and turned to face him with fear in her eyes, shivering not just from the cold but from fear. She pulled her own robe more tightly around herself.

"What's happening? Where are you going?" she asked.

"Just to Bent's Fort, that's all. It's all right, Abbie."

"But . . . why?"

"The men who just came from there tell us Charles Bent was murdered by Mexicans, at San Fernando de Taos. All the Bent brothers are good friends to the Cheyenne. My brothers and the others are angry. They intend to ride to Bent's Fort and offer their services to William Bent. They're hellbent on riding south and scalping every Mexican they can find!"

Her eyes widened. "You . . . you wouldn't go with them!" It was more of a statement than a question.

He walked over to her and bent down to kiss her cheek. "I won't go with them, not to Taos anyway. I'm trying to convince them to stay out of it. They don't need to go getting mixed up in the Mexican War. I just want to ride to the fort with them and try to keep them out of trouble." He took the rifle from her hands, and their eyes held for a moment. He kissed her once more, as a few horses thundered past the tipi. "Don't worry, Abbie. I'll be back in just a couple of days. Keep the fire burning and the robes warm." He gave her a wink and quickly left. She walked to the entrance of the tipi again. More warriors were riding out, and in moments Zeke had his

327

Appaloosa ready to ride. He mounted up with a natural ease to ride off into the darkening sky, snow flying from beneath his horse's hooves.

Abbie's heart felt tight and painful. She walked back to the fire and huddled next to it. She knew then that she would spend the rest of her life worrying every time Cheyenne Zeke rode away, for in this savage land, danger lurked around every boulder and in every shadow and behind every tree.

"Keep him safe, *Maheo*," she whispered.

Bent's Fort swarmed with angry Indians, all arguing about what should be done. William Bent was the center of attention; he was surrounded by several other trappers and traders, all arguing with one another and with the Cheyenne. Zeke watched his brothers carefully. He was not extremely fond of William Bent, because unlike George and Charles Bent, William had sold whiskey to the Indians. Zeke had seen him sell it to Red Eagle, even though the man knew Red Eagle had a drinking problem. Still, the Bent brothers were basically honest traders who had been good to the Cheyenne and counted most of them as friends, and William Bent had a Cheyenne wife and two half-breed sons. All three brothers had worked together to try to thwart illegal whiskey traders who were unlicensed and who sold worthless, watered-down whiskey to the Indians for valuable skins.

Illegal whiskey running had become rampant along the Arkansas. A four-dollar barrel of heavily diluted whiskey, sold at the rate of one to four pints of whiskey in return for one buffalo robe, could bring a cheating whiskey trader up to eight thousand dollars in St. Louis for the robes. The profits to be made from the unwitting Indians were tremendous, and Zeke had tried to explain this to his brothers. But they did not think in terms of American dollars. Money meant little to them. If they could get whiskey and supplies for the robes, if they could keep themselves and their families from starving, or keep them warm, or buy their wives and lovers pretty trinkets or needed cooking pots with a buffalo robe, then to them it was a fair trade, even though the trader would reap tremendous profits in St. Louis for the robes.

The biggest profiteers were those who traded the diluted whiskey, especially those who were unlicensed and who undercut the legal traders. And Zeke knew it could only get worse. For as long as the Indians failed to understand the white man's thinking and the value of the white man's dollar and as long as there were white men eager to get rich quick, there would be cheating and eventually trouble. But the imminent trouble was the murder of Charles Bent and the eagerness of the Cheyenne to avenge it. Charles Bent had been their friend, a good white man, one of the few who had been fair with them.

The arguing continued, and on the perimeter of those involved in heated conversation, warriors circled on horses, holding up bows and lances and belting out war cries. Zeke managed to make his way into the group of traders and trappers, many of whom he knew from his own days of mountain wandering and from the days of the great northwest rendezvous. There were solemn handshakings and greetings, like those friends used to greet one another at a man's funeral. Zeke shook William Bent's hand and managed to get his attention.

"You can't let the Cheyenne get involved in this, Bent," he told the man. "They'll end up getting blamed for the wrong things. You know how stories get twisted."

"I don't intend to let them get involved, Zeke," the man replied. His eyes were red and tired-looking. "This is a white man's war. They don't need to get into it."

"I'm sorry about your brother. We were all fond of him."

William Bent nodded. "I need your help in calming down your red brothers. I want them to go back home and stay out of this, Zeke. I have plenty of white trappers and traders here willing to go to Taos with me. And I hear a Colonel Price has already been dispatched in that direction. We have all the help we need."

"Good. I'd come along myself, except I've got a woman to look out for now."

Bent nodded. "I understand. And I don't blame you a bit. When am I going to meet this little lady you married, Zeke?"

"Soon, Bent," Zeke replied with a proud smile. "I'll be bringing her in soon."

"Good!" Bent replied. "I look forward to it. We'll give her a royal welcome!"

A shot rang out, interrupting their conversation, and both knew it was time to bring some kind of order to the meeting. Zeke, William Bent, and the trappers spread out among the Cheyenne, signaling for them to dismount and gather together for a powwow.

General commotion continued to prevail, even after the men managed to gather the Cheyenne into a circle with William Bent at the center and his trader friends around him. Bent held up his hand, signaling the Cheyenne to be still and to listen. The angry warriors, always eager for a good fight, managed to calm down enough to listen, but their blood ran hot and they were restless for a fight.

"This is the white man's war!" Bent shouted to them, using their own tongue. "It would be bad for you if you joined it."

"We kill the Mexicans!" one of the warriors shouted. "We avenge your brother's murder!"

"No. That is my job. I am white. My brother was white. My trader friends here are white. It is our duty to avenge the murder, not yours. Your duty is to avenge the deaths of your own people, and to go home and protect your wives and children and provide them with food. You have your own enemies to worry about: the Crow, the Pawnee. Listen to your half-blood brother, Zeke, who has warned you not to get involved in this war. He knows. He understands the trouble it could bring you."

"How can helping our white friend avenge his brother's death bring us harm?" another shouted angrily.

330

"Listen to me, my red friends," Bent replied. "Most white men do not know a Cheyenne from a Sioux or a Comanche or an Apache. Many Comanches, even some of the Arapahos that you call friend, have been aiding the Mexicans in this war. They do it because the Mexicans give them guns and whiskey. Some do it just because they like war. But I tell you this. The Indians who help the Mexicans will be in big trouble with the American soldiers. They will be considered enemies, just as the Mexicans are. You have enough trouble right now, my red brothers, with your own Indian enemies and with the settlers who continue to invade your land. If you get into this war now, the soldiers and the settlers will becomed confused. To them you are all the same, and they will think you are helping the Mexicans instead of your white friends. I tell you it is better to go home and remain peaceful. Show the Americans you love peace, that you are not warlike. Let the Americans take care of their own war. Go home, I tell you. Stay out of it, and then you will not bring trouble to your women and children. Besides, there are not many of your people on the Arkansas this year. Most of them remained in the north. If half of your warriors ride to Taos with me, there will not be enough left to defend your families. The Crow and the Ute will find this out quickly. Then they will come and carry off your women and children, and you will come home to empty villages, just because you went to avenge one white man's death. This is not wise, my brothers."

The wind kicked up and cut at their faces as the warriors mumbled among themselves.

"I am deeply grateful that you have come here, my Cheyenne friends," Bent spoke up again. "You have called me friend, even though other whites have brought you trouble and sickness. You men are brave, and I know that you are great fighters and would do a good job in helping me against the Mexicans. You would take many scalps, and do a fitting job of avenging Charles' death. But because you are my friends, I cannot let you go with me. For it would only bring you more

331

trouble. Please. If you are truly my friends, help me by going back home, so that I do not have the additional burden of worrying about my red brothers. It will go better on my mind if I know you are back in your villages where you belong. Fight only the wars that are necessary. Do not fight a war that does not concern you. Save your strength and your energy for wars that pose a threat to your own people. This one does not."

Again there was a mumbling, and some of them were nodding, their hot, fiery readiness to take scalps somewhat subdued. The tension was easing.

"We will listen to the advice of our white friend," one of the leaders spoke up. "He speaks true to the Cheyenne. But our thoughts go with you, William Bent. Our hearts wish to avenge your brother's death. We will pray for you at our council fires."

"I thank you for this. Go home now, brothers. Take whatever supplies you need and go home to your families."

After some hesitation, the Cheyenne finally began to disburse, Zeke along with them. But someone called out Zeke's name, and he turned to see a white trapper who was one of the few white men that Zeke would call a true friend. He had been at Fort Bridger the year before when Zeke had arrived there with Abbie's wagon train.

"Dooley!" Zeke answered as the man approached with eager, friendly eyes.

"Zeke! Hey, my half-breed friend, it's been a good many months! I got here late and didn't have a chance to speak to you." They approached one another and shook hands.

"How are things, Dooley?"

The man shrugged. "Not so good. The fur trading business is going bad, Zeke—real bad. Back East there's not so much demand anymore for the beaver furs."

"I've heard that. I'm back to raising horses myself."

"Hey, my friend, how's that little white girl you left at Fort Bridger last year? Did you come back for her?"

Zeke grinned. "I came back. She's my wife now. Having a

baby next summer."

Dooley laughed slyly, shaking Zeke's hand even more firmly then letting go of it. "So, you devil half-blood, you made a woman of that one, heh? Where do you hide her now?"

"We live with my people right now."

His eyebrows arched. "With the Cheyenne? The little white girl lives with the Cheyenne?"

Zeke nodded, grinning more. "Tipi and all. She can keep up with the best of the squaws at tanning a hide and stitching a shirt or stretching a war shield."

Dooley laughed. "I'll be damned!" He slapped Zeke on the shoulder. "She does it for you, you devil! Don't kid me! She'd probably slit her wrists to be with you, right? You got her so goggle-eyed over you, she'll do anything to stay with you. I saw it in her eyes when I met her at Fort Bridger last fall."

Zeke shook his head and laughed, but he felt a strange pain inside because he realized that the man was right. Abbie was living as she was for him, and perhaps it was harder for her than she let on. He must build her that cabin in the spring.

"Dooley, what do you hear of Olin Wales?" he asked the man, wanting to get his mind off Abbie. He had not seen his good white friend in a long time. Olin Wales was a burly, hardy trapper who had traveled with Zeke the year before on the wagon train. Their friendship went back many years, and included saving each other's lives and fighting Crow and Blackfeet together, as well as fighting outlaw trappers who murdered men to steal their furs. Few men had shared Zeke's intimate thoughts or understood Zeke's heart the way Olin did. And he had been a good friend to Abbie on that wagon train west, understanding her love for Zeke and helping both of them through the hard times the trip had brought. Dooley's face became grim at the mention of Olin's name, however, and he looked down at the ground as he answered Zeke's question.

"Hey, my friend, Olin, he bought a ticket to the Promised Land, you know? The Blackfeet did him in, up in northwest territory last fall."

333

Zeke watched him for a moment without speaking. "Are you sure?"

Dooley faced him. "I wish I wasn't, Zeke. But I am. Olin's dead."

"You . . . saw him?"

Dooley nodded. "What was left of him."

Zeke closed his eyes and turned away. Dooley put a hand on his shoulder. "Hey, friend, that was how a man like Olin would have wanted to die."

Zeke nodded. He knew Dooley shared his grief, for men of the mountains felt a certain kinship that was not shared by other kinds of men, and the few white men Zeke called friend were mountain men with whom he had trapped and traded, lived and fought enemy Indians.

"It was good seeing you again, Dooley," he said in a strained voice. "I'd . . . have a drink with you, but I don't feel like it right now. I'd better get back to Abbie. It's . . . been a couple of days. She worries."

"Sure, Zeke. We'll meet again. I'm always wandering around these here parts. Maybe I'll come on by and we'll talk some more. I'd like to see the little gal that's putting up with the likes of you."

Zeke nodded and walked away. Dooley kicked at a rock. It was a cruel land, this Western place. Even the best of them died. He wondered to himself how the little white girl he had met the year before at Fort Bridger was going to survive out here. But then she had Zeke, and if anyone survived this land, it would be Cheyenne Zeke. The man was as much a part of the land as the rocks and the wolves. He turned up his collar against the bitter winds and headed inside the fort.

Thomas Fitzpatrick sat across from Superintendent of Indian Affairs, Thomas Harvey. Outside, the streets of St. Louis rattled with carriages and busy people. Women wore the latest fashions, theaters and restaurants flourished, and businesses made tremendous profits. Traders continued to bring in buffalo robes, as well as copper and valuable stones, and talk of the war with Mexico abounded, as well as talk of the thousands of settlers who would pass through St. Louis on their way west that coming spring. St. Louis was a rapidly growing, civilized city, the center of trade between East and West.

Fitzpatrick managed to hold a pipe in his "broken" hand; it had been crippled by a bullet that had shattered his wrist years earlier in his scouting days. He lit the pipe, then took it in his good hand and puffed it.

"So . . . you still think a treaty is necessary?" Harvey asked him.

"Absolutely," Fitzpatrick replied.

Harvey studied the famous scout, whose hair had turned white at an early age. "There's no other way?"

Fitzpatrick shifted in his chair. He was not accustomed to hard chairs and enclosed rooms. He had grown accustomed to riding free on the Plains, to the wild life and the feel of the wind on his face. But his body was feeling the effects of that hard life, and he had brushed death too often to count. Right now he preferred his new assignment as Agent for the Western tribes, a title given him by Senator Thomas Hart Benton in the fall of 1846, when Fitzpatrick was in Washington.

"Sir, the Indians are getting restless. They're afraid. White men's diseases have taken their toll, and that hasn't won their hearts over to our side, for damned sure. Whites are killing off their buffalo, dividing up the land, and prohibiting their free travel. Free travel and buffalo are vital to the Indian's survival. If we want to stop trouble before it starts, we've got to begin talking to them, reasoning with them and showing them our friendship and good intentions."

"And what do you think we should offer them?"

Fitzpatrick shrugged. "Land, of course. Enough land to keep them happy—land they can call their own and where they can ride free and hunt . . . land that will be off limits to white

335

settlers. And it will be important to offer them gifts to boot. It's the Indian's way when making a pact to offer presents and to receive presents in return as a sign of good friendship. They're getting hungrier every year, Mr. Harvey. I suggest we bring them a lot of nonperishable food—sugar, for one thing. They love sugar. Flour, dried beans, and such. Utensils, pots and pans. And plenty of beads. They love beads."

Harvey ran a hand through his hair. "Washington doesn't want to give them any more than necessary, Fitzpatrick. Our first aim is to please the settlers, our own American citizens, not the Indians."

Fitzpatrick puffed his pipe. "You'd best worry about pleasing the Indians, or it won't go well for those settlers you're so concerned about. And don't think just taking out a bunch of troops and showing some force will 'scare' the Indians into doing what you tell them. Those savages don't scare, Mr. Harvey. They love a good fight and never run from one, and most of them have more courage in one finger than a white soldier has in his whole being. Death does not frighten them. A show of force and weapons only excites them. The only thing they understand is a man's word—his honesty— and the sealing of that word with gift offerings. It's their way. With your permission, I'd like to head out there come spring and start laying plans for a treaty—start feeling them out a little—see how they'd feel about it. I'll send runners to all the tribes and kind of get their thinking into gear. Do I have your permission?"

Harvey leaned forward and studied the sturdy scout who had earned the name Broken Hand and was better known to some of the Indians as White Hair. "You should know better than anyone," he told Fitzpatrick. "See what you can get started. Where do you think the best place would be to hold this treaty council, Fitzpatrick?"

"Well, sir, I'd say Fort Laramie would be the best place."

Harvey nodded. "Laramie sounds good to me. But don't be

promising those Indians any fast action. You know Washington. Could be two or three more years before this really gets into gear. We're still pretty involved in this Mexican thing."

"I understand." Fitzpatrick rose, putting out a hand to Harvey and clasping his firmly. "We'll talk more," he told the Superintendent. Harvey nodded, and Fitzpatrick left. Harvey watched him through the window as he crossed the street.

"Walking history," he muttered to himself, feeling envious of the famous man who had just left his office. Fitzpatrick had been there. He knew that wild and frightening land west of the Missouri River. But few men in Washington knew it, or the red men who were as wild as the land itself. This job of Superintendent was not going to be an easy one, but it was a government job, and he liked the prestige of a government job. As long as he could stay in the comfortable city of St. Louis, he didn't mind. Let men like Fitzpatrick do the dirty work.

Abbie came to sit beside the fire with Zeke. He put his arm around her and she rested her head on his shoulder, while outside the wind whipped around the tipi piling snow high outside the entrance.

"I feel like it's partly my fault," she told him.

He sighed and picked up a stick to poke at the coals in the fire with his free hand. "Why would you think that?" he asked her, his voice distant and strained.

"If you hadn't come back to Fort Bridger for me—if you'd gone on with Olin after you left Oregon—maybe you would have been with him. Maybe together you could have helped each other and Olin wouldn't be dead."

He squeezed her lightly. "Then again, maybe we'd *both* be dead. Ever think of it that way?"

She moved her head to kiss his cheek, knowing he was only trying to make her feel better. "Tell me you don't blame me, Zeke."

He patted her shoulder. "You know I don't. Coming for you was my own decision. I love you. Olin was an independent man. And a wanderer. If it hadn't happened when and where it did, it would have happened someplace else. He died the way a man like him would want to die."

They both stared at the fire silently for several minutes. "How do you want to die, Zeke?" she asked. "I mean . . . if you had a choice."

He grinned a little. "In one royal, goddamned hell of a fight!" he replied. "Just like Olin did."

She had to smile then, but her heart was worried. "Don't you miss it . . . that kind of life . . . wandering the mountains with Olin and others like him?"

He sighed. "In a sense. But Olin wasn't a man torn like I was, Abbie. He didn't have the kind of memories I did. I wandered because I was looking for something." He kissed her hair. "And then I found it. Now we'll just wander together, with the People. And when you want to stay put, we'll live in our cabin. Hell, we can even go to the mountains any time we want, just you and me alone. I know places where the Crow and Ute and Blackfeet would never find us."

"I'd like that. I like being completely alone with you, like when we came here from Fort Bridger."

They sat quietly for several minutes, then Zeke patted her shoulder and got to his feet.

"Abbie, I . . . I've got to go out for a while. I've got to feel the wind on my face and wrestle with a few memories."

She sighed and looked up at him. "Zeke, it's blizzarding out there. It's so cold."

"I'll be all right." He turned away, his voice strained. "I want to feel the cold, Abbie. I want the wind to sting my face. Please try to understand. I . . . have to go out for a while."

"I understand," she said softly.

She got up, too, and placed a hand on his back. She knew he was hurting over Olin Wales, and her own heart ached, for she had come to think of Olin as a good friend also. It was Olin

Wales who had helped her understand Cheyenne Zeke on the wagon train journey the summer before. He had understood her love for his good friend. "Go and greet the wind, Zeke."

He turned to face her with watery eyes; then he grabbed his buffalo robe and left without another word. He did not return until the morning.

Seventeen

The spring of 1847 brought welcome warmth, and just as the wild flowers began to blossom on the plains and prairies and in the mountains, so did the life in Abbie's womb blossom. By April, according to her own calculations, she was six months pregnant. This child would hang on and be born healthy, she was certain. She felt good, and the baby gave her lively kicks to tell her all was well.

Although it hurt her not to be able to travel north with the People for the summer, she knew Zeke was right in deciding not to go. He wanted nothing to happen to this baby or to Abbie, and he wanted to build her the cabin he had promised. So they stayed behind when the southern bands headed northward, making only the short trek to Swift Arrow's village in order to bid them a sad farewell. Abigail Monroe now had many friends among Zeke's people, but it hurt her most to say good-bye to Swift Arrow, Gentle Woman, and Tall Grass Woman. Her memories of her experiences of the summer before remained vivid and were something she would forever treasure, for that was the summer her white heart had learned the Cheyenne way.

"*Maheo* ride with you," Zeke told Swift Arrow, who lagged behind as the rest of the band moved out.

"And with you," Swift Arrow replied, looking from Zeke to Abbie and holding Abbie's eyes for a moment before looking back at Zeke. He seemed even more reluctant to leave Zeke and

341

Abbie behind than Zeke's own mother had been.

"The Pawnee are kicking up again, I hear," Zeke told his brother.

"Then perhaps we shall kick a few Pawnee!" Swift Arrow replied with a wicked gleam in his eyes. "It would not upset me to see all of them dead."

Zeke grinned. "I'm sure it wouldn't. Watch out for the devils and take care of our mother."

"This I have always done." Swift Arrow looked at Abbie again. "This time you do not go with us. But we have many memories of our last journey north, when you learned how to be Cheyenne woman."

Abbie smiled. "Maybe next year we can go with you again," she told him. "And when you return, I'll have a grandchild to present to Gentle Woman."

Swift Arrow grinned. "*Ai.* That will make her very happy." Their eyes held again, and she knew he was thinking of his own dead son.

"I hope it's a good hunt, Swift Arrow," she told him.

He nodded and looked at Zeke. "I will bring you meat and hides!" he said.

"I wish I could go with you, Swift Arrow. You know how I enjoy the hunts."

Swift Arrow nodded, and Abbie felt guilty, as though it was her fault Zeke could not go with his people and hunt buffalo and fight the Pawnee and feel the freedom of that life. She had begged him to go, but he would not budge in his decision that she should not travel.

At least this year Swift Arrow and the others would be back earlier, for they would not go all the way into the Black Hills as they had done the summer before. They had been warned by northern Cheyenne runners that traveling across the Great Medicine Road was becoming increasingly dangerous, that hundreds and hundreds of the white-topped wagons traversed the road almost daily now, and that the nervous white travelers often shot at Indians without reason. It was a bad place to be, for more soldiers also traveled the road. The forts were growing larger with soldiers, and more and more white people were seen stopping and settling in Indian Territory, rather than just passing through it to the land beyond the mountains where the sun sets.

"They have frightened away most of the buffalo and killed what remains," the runners told them. "There are few buffalo now. It is best you hunt again at the Smoky Hill River and maybe the Republican, but do not go on north from there, or you will find only trouble. Go back home to your land on the Arkansas."

Zeke had urged his brothers to listen to the warning, and he repeated it now to his brother.

"Don't go farther than the fork of the Smoky Hill and Republican," he told Swift Arrow. "And try to be back by the Moon When the Geese Shed Their Feathers," he added, signifying August.

Swift Arrow nodded reluctantly. "I do not like being told I cannot go north to the Sioux!" he complained. "Since this white man's war, everywhere we go, we find trouble. Our own Arapaho brothers fight with the Comanche against the Americans, and the blame goes to the Cheyenne also, just because we have always been friends with the Arapaho. We try to stay at peace with all sides, but they do not let us have peace. The soldiers and white-topped wagons press down on us from the north. The Mexicans and soldiers and more settlers press up against us from the south. The mountains keep us from going west and your white brothers are so many in the East we cannot go that way. I do not like this feeling of being in a cage, my brother. I wish that you could tell us how to get out."

"I wish the same, Swift Arrow. But I don't know what to tell you, except that I'm here and I'll always be here to help you. I can help with supplies, give you advice if you have a run-in with soldiers or settlers, help you in the trading."

Swift Arrow breathed deeply to quell his anger at the white intrusion. "Perhaps it will not get worse," he replied. "Here

343

we can still ride . . . hunt." There was a sadness in his eyes. "Our great council chiefs, Black Kettle, Yellow Wolf, White Antelope—they tell us to keep the peace, that the white men who come do not want war and that not many more will come now. They say when the war with Mexico is over, many will leave. Do you think this is so, my brother?"

Their eyes held and Abbie had to look away. "No, Swift Arrow," Zeke replied. "I don't think it is so. The chiefs are great men, but they don't know the white world back East. They don't know how many white men there are, all eager for more land, and for the treasures that lay beneath this land."

"But the land is big!" Swift Arrow replied, a note of hope in his voice. "It can be shared! And if they stop killing the buffalo, we can survive."

Zeke did not have the heart to reply to the contrary. "Maybe," he answered. "Go now, Swift Arrow. May you have a good hunt."

Swift Arrow nodded, and after casting his eyes once more upon Abbie and giving her a smile, he turned and mounted his painted Appaloosa, riding off to catch up with the others. Gentle Woman waved from her horse, and Zeke and Abbie waved back, watching the small band slowly disappear into the rolling plains.

"It *is* a big land, Zeke," Abbie said quietly. "So terribly big."

He stepped ahead of her and gazed out at the empty plains. "I don't think it's going to be big enough, Abbie girl. And that's the hell of it."

They erected their tipi on a beautiful piece of land along the Arkansas River, a green, gentle slope of land surrounded by granite boulders and cliffs. The sound of the river water splashing over rocks was soothing to Abbie, and she cherished this piece of land they would now call home. Far to the West the peaks of some of the higher Rocky Mountains could be seen on the horizon, and yet to the East there were only soft, rolling plains that melted into the blue horizon. The sharp contrast of this "middle land" always fascinated Abbie, for the plains seemed to lead directly to the jutting Rockies, like a floor to a wall. It was as if the great granite mountains suddenly sprung up from the earth to create God's barrier to the West. But man had surmounted that barrier, and now by the thousands settlers plunged onward and westward, more and more of them every year, while the Rockies watched silently.

Here where they would settle, though, there was little contact with the migrating settlers. Mostly they were alone, their main worry raiding Comanches who might try to steal Zeke's Appaloosas. Abbie wondered how long their peace would last in this little green hideaway from the restless world. It was good land—beautiful land—and it was theirs, all five hundred acres of it. William Bent had helped them claim it, preparing the proper papers so that they could officially call it their own. Zeke wanted to start the cabin right away, but first he had to build a fence to corral his Appaloosas and help protect them from raids. The horses were his primary income now, and must be properly cared for and guarded. He would not always have the help of his brothers, and he knew that in the future, income from his own means would be important, for it was becoming less and less possible to rely on the land for all of their needs.

To his relief, it had not been necessary to go all the way to Independence that spring to sell his horses. The war with Mexico had made the demand for good mounts high, and William Bent had bought several horses from Zeke that spring. All along the Santa Fe Trail there were travelers and soldiers who had ready money for Zeke's fine Appaloosas, and Zeke knew now that this was how he could make a living and properly provide for Abbie and their future children. It was not easy for a half-breed to find work, and with a white wife, he could not travel with the Cheyenne and roam and hunt. This was a happy medium, making his own way by raising good horses and living near his red brothers, but staying in one place for Abbie's sake.

Abbie loved him even more as she watched how hard he worked trying to get the land in shape, tending his horses and chopping at logs for fence posts. The spring was lovely and welcome, smelling of sweet wild flowers and clean air. Abbie enjoyed watching Zeke work, seeing his bronze, muscular arms and shoulders glistening with sweat from the May sun.

But in spite of her happiness over their land and the beauty of spring and the life in her belly, she hurt inside for Zeke; for she knew that his mind would forever be tortured by the middle road he was forced to walk. And just as she had given up much to be with him, he, too, had given up much when he'd married her. For he would rather be wandering the mountains or hunting with his people . . . doing all of the things that were natural to his Indian blood. And so, both had compromised, both lived in two worlds, belonging to both and yet belonging to neither. They would have a cabin and hard floors and windows like whites. They would raise horses and do a little farming and earn money like whites. But at times they would wander with their red brothers, and Zeke would hunt with them and play war games with them and let his heart be free, like the Indian that he was. Being together would mean sacrifice and hardship for them both, yet life apart was unthinkable.

It was a sweet and peaceful interlude in their lives, that May of 1847. Wild strawberries grew in thickets along the river, and Abbie picked them daily, while the sound of Zeke chopping wood assured her he was close by and all was well. The whacks of the hatchet echoed out over the river, and they were good sounds—signs of hope for the future. She would not ask him when the cabin would be done, for she sensed that perhaps it would not get built at all this first summer. There were so many things to do to get the land in better shape, and Zeke had to spend considerable time with two foals that had been born weak and sickly.

She did not mind waiting for her house. She'd grown

346

accustomed to living in a tipi now, and was not even sure she wanted to leave the dwelling she and Gentle Woman and the other Cheyenne women had worked so hard to build and decorate. Outside it appeared to be a dwelling made only for an Indian's life. But inside a mahogany mantel clock chimed from where it sat on a fat, upended log. It was another gift from Zeke. Abbie liked to touch its oiled, rich wood, and tears would come to her eyes when she remembered Zeke buying it for her at Bent's Fort. He had promised her that some day she would have a fireplace with a mantel where she could set the clock, and the gift had just been another way of trying to bring her the white world he thought she should have.

It was a beautiful clock . . . too expensive. But he was always buying her such things, as though he feared that at any moment she might run back to Tennessee. The trip to Bent's Fort had been exciting for Abbie and surprising, for the fort was much larger than she had pictured. Its adobe walls were three feet thick and fourteen feet high, and there were round, castlelike towers at their corners, where guns and cannons could be placed for defense.

It was no wonder the Mexicans had not tried to storm the fort, for it was virtually impossible. And inside was every kind of supply anyone could ever ask for—a half acre of supplies. Zeke had bought her lovely smelling soaps, a new washboard, and special creams for her skin. He had even bought her a new dress, a white woman's dress, but she wondered if and when she would ever have reason to wear it.

Zeke had treated her like a queen that day, letting her be white again, letting her look and touch and choose supplies and treating her to a royal meal of beef and potatoes—everything she delighted in eating—prepared by the Bents' famous cook, Charlotte Green. Abbie ate real apple pie for the first time in well over two years. She had been fifteen and living in Tennessee the last time she had had apple pie. Now she was seventeen and living in a tipi with a half-blood Cheyenne. It all seemed so odd, as though the Abbie who had lived in Tennessee and had once had a brother and sister and parents was a different person. It seemed impossible that it had only been two years since she had been that innocent child headed West with her father.

Another month passed, and the land Zeke and Abbie had claimed began to look like home. The corral was finished and held the grand Appaloosas; four more of the mares were heavy with foals.

"Spring seems to be a time for big bellies," Zeke teased Abbie, gently patting her own heavy stomach as they stood at the fence watching the pregnant mares lumber about.

Abbie smiled and blushed, looking down at his big, reassuring hand. She put her own over his, her smile fading. He sensed her fear and had seen it growing. With the nearby Cheyenne village vacant and no doctor at the fort, there would be no one but himself to help her when the baby came. He moved behind her, enfolding her in his arms, with one hand still over her swollen stomach and his other arm wrapped across her breasts. He held her tight against him, kissing the top of her head.

"Abbie, I've delivered plenty of foals, and I delivered Ellen's and my son. I took an arrow out of you, girl, and burned out the infection. And there's nothing on God's earth I love more than my Abbie. We'll have this baby together and we'll do okay. You just trust me same as you always have."

She nodded quietly, and he felt a tear spill onto the skin of his hand.

"Don't be afraid, Abbie girl. *Maheo* wants us to have this child, and by God we'll have it. All you have to do is trust me, just like you trusted me to watch over you on that wagon train, and like you trusted me to help Jeremy and to rescue you when them outlaws got hold of you, and when you took that Crow arrow. I haven't failed you yet, have I?"

She leaned her head back against his chest. "No," she

replied quietly. "It's just . . . I've never been through this. And I want so much to give you a healthy baby, Zeke."

"Of course you do. And you will. You're stronger and healthier than you've been since you took that arrow last year. You'll be okay, Abbie. You trust me and hang on to me and you'll always be okay."

He felt her body jerk as she tried to stifle a sob, and he held her even tighter.

"Oh, Zeke, don't go away! Don't go anywhere before it's born. I'd be terrified if it came and you were gone!"

"Don't you worry about that. I'm going nowhere, little girl. I'll be right here with you twenty-four hours a day till this baby comes. That's one promise that won't get broken."

She nodded and sniffed, reaching around herself and clinging tightly to his strong, sure arms. "I'm so happy, Zeke. It's just that I'm so scared. I'm sorry. I want to be brave about it."

He kissed her hair again and smiled. "You've always been brave, Abbie. Just look at all you've been through, and you never cowered from anything—never once."

"I was brave for you. Inside I was falling apart. If it weren't for you, I would have."

He laid his cheek against her hair. "Nonsense. When you boil it down, Abbie, strength comes only from within ourselves. You don't give yourself enough credit. This thing you feel now is only natural, because you know that baby is going to come whether you're ready for it or not, and that's pretty scary. But if you get times when you don't feel so brave, then you just let me be your courage, and I'll do the same. Sometimes you'll be the strong one. That's what husbands and wives are for, Abbie, if they really love each other."

She smiled through her tears. "You always know what to say."

He shrugged and turned her to face him. "Just saying what comes naturally," he replied with a reassuring smile.

He gently took her face in his hands and she studied his dark eyes and all the love that lay behind them. What a handsome man he was, with the kind of looks that would only grow more handsome with age. Even the thin scar added to his looks, for it told of a rugged, experienced man, one who did not shy away from a fight or from danger. And she was suddenly calm. If Zeke would be with her when the baby was born, what was there to be afraid of?

"You're a good man, Zeke Monroe," she told him sincerely. He only laughed lightly.

"There are many who would disagree with you on that!" he replied. He put an arm around her shoulders and they walked back toward the tipi, where a campfire still burned, above it two roasting ducks.

"Maybe they would," she replied. "But they don't know you like I do. I married the best man west of the Mississippi."

She put an arm around his waist as they walked, and he did not reply. For to him no man was good enough for his Abbie, and he felt lucky that she belonged to him at all.

They sat outside the tipi beside the fire. Abbie had just put another piece of duck on Zeke's plate when they heard a bird call. Abbie thought nothing of it, but Zeke stopped eating and set his plate aside. When Abbie started to speak, Zeke put up a hand to still her, and they heard the call again.

"By God, I think that's Dooley!" he told Abbie.

"Dooley? You mean from Fort Bridger? The one you saw last winter at Bent's Fort?"

He nodded; then he stood up and gave out a call of his own. The man emerged from a thick cluster of cottonwoods several yards down river.

"Come and sit with us, you old drunk!" Zeke yelled out. "Come and have some supper!"

Dooley walked a little faster at the invitation. "You got good whiskey?" the man called back. "I don't want any of that rotgut the unlicensed traders sell!"

350

"Only the best!" Zeke called back.

Dooley came closer, and his eyes rested on Abbie. He grinned at the sight of her swollen belly, and she blushed as the man came closer to Zeke and put out his hand. "Well, my friend, you told the truth! You did make her your wife, and you've been a good husband, I see!"

Abbie blushed more and the two men laughed and shook hands. Then Dooley put his hand out to Abbie. "Don't get up, fair lady. I know it's not easy for a woman in your condition to get up and down."

She reached up and shook his hand, still blushing, but smiling. "It's good to see you again, Dooley," she told him.

"The last time I saw you, you were a skinny little thing, half dead from a bad arrow wound. I see you're much better. Being Cheyenne Zeke's wife apparently agrees with you."

She laughed lightly. "Very much. Won't you sit down and have a piece of duck meat, Dooley? It's fresh. Zeke just shot them this morning."

"Sounds good to me." The man sat across the fire from them, and Abbie prepared him a plate of food.

"So, where have you been, Dooley? Fill me in on what's going on out there in the wilderness."

Dooley seemed to fake his smile. He shrugged. "Ah, you know how it goes. Mexicans killing Americans. Americans killing Mexicans. Indians killing Indians. Indians killing trappers." His smile faded. "And, uh, whites killing Indians." He stopped and let the words sink in, and Abbie handed a plate to Dooley as Zeke studied the man's eyes.

"Something tells me you didn't come here just to see Abbie again and pay us a visit," Zeke told the man.

Dooley sighed and set his plate down. "I'll tell you, Zeke. I intended to come here to see where you are living now with your woman, see the horses you often told me about, and see Miss Abigail again. But it just so happens that on my journey down from Wyoming Territory, I, uh, I went to Fort Atkinson first, and I heard some bad news there."

Zeke tensed. "My brothers?" he asked quickly. "My mother?"

"No! No! As far as I know, your family's band is safe out there somewhere hunting buffalo. But another band that was camped near the Santa Fe Trail, Old Tobacco's band, they had a run-in with some Comanches. You know most Comanches have been raiding along the trail, attacking supply trains and all, getting paid by the Mexicans to do them things."

"I know. Get on with it, Dooley."

"Well, Zeke, like I said, Old Tobacco and his people had a little skirmish with the Comanches and then they went to camp farther up the trail. While they was camped there they seen some fancy wagons coming. Turns out they was full of government people from Washington, people sent out here by the government to scout around, see what's happening with the war and the Indians and such. Old Tobacco, being the peace-loving man that he was, he thought he should warn these people that there was raiding Comanches ahead. Old Tobacco, he always thought the Cheyenne should be friends with the whites, you know, do their best to cooperate and all."

"You talk like he's dead, Dooley," Zeke remarked.

Dooley sighed. "I'm afraid he is, my friend. One of those damned, ignorant, greenhorn government men seen him coming to warn them, and he shot Old Tobacco. Them Eastern sons-of-bitches don't know one red man from another. All's they knew was that Indians had been raiding along the trail, and they figured that's what Old Tobacco was aiming to do, I guess."

Zeke snapped a twig he had been whirling in his hand and threw it at the fire. "*Katum!*" he swore. "*Heyokas!*" He got up and walked away for a moment.

"I agree," Dooley replied. "They are fools."

Abbie listened quietly, feeling her own grief. For she had met Old Tobacco. He was a good man, a wise and kind man, loved by the Cheyenne.

"The old man, he begged his family with his dying words to

352

forgive the white men for what they did. Said they just didn't know what they was doing and shouldn't be blamed. He knew that if he didn't make his family promise, they'd avenge his murder and bring trouble to the Cheyenne. Old Tobacco wouldn't have wanted that."

"Stupid sons-of-bitches!" Zeke growled. "The worst part is that this is going to happen over and over, Dooley! This is just the beginning. The Cheyenne, even other tribes, will get blamed for things they haven't even done. And they'll take the blame just so long and then they'll start fighting back, which is just what the government would love to see happen, because then they'd have an excuse to wipe them off the face of the earth!" He kicked at a stone.

Dooley sighed and bit off a piece of meat, chewing silently for a moment. Abbie just stared at the fire, wanting to cry and yet unable to do so. She suddenly thought of the mantel clock and its loud tick. Often she had pictured each tick as representing the face of someone she'd loved and lost: her father and mother, sister and brother; the people she'd befriended on the wagon train. Now Old Tobacco must be added to the list.

How she hated death! She had seen so much of it, and she feared it would one day claim her Zeke or one of her children too early in their lives. She shook off the terrifying thought and turned her attention back to the conversation.

"I'm afraid you are more than right, my friend, about the wrong Indians getting blamed for things," Dooley was telling Zeke. He swallowed another piece of meat before continuing. "Much of the Comanche and Arapaho raiding is being blamed on the Cheyenne. Somehow stories have got back to Washington that the Cheyenne are as much a part of it as the Comanche. There's something in the works, Zeke. I smell something very foul. This country is about to explode like dynamite; and when the dust settles, you will see whites scattered in every corner and Indians surrounded. And with the whites will come greed, whiskey, disease. You'd best advise your brothers and the others to be very careful where they go, and very careful when they deal with the whites. Washington will be looking for any excuse to make the red man look bad. They're already doing it." He took another bite of meat, and Zeke turned to look at Abbie. Their eyes met in the agony of understanding, and she had to look away to avoid the pain in his.

"Thanks for coming to tell me, Dooley," Zeke said in a strained voice.

"I have a couple more things for you," Dooley told him, wiping his lips with the back of his hand. He was in his early thirties, a slightly built man, but wiry and tough, never clean-shaven and yet never with a full beard. His dark, curly hair stuck out in shaggy disarray from beneath his worn, leather hat, and his buckskins looked clean but were well worn, their knees and elbows polished smooth.

"More bad news?" Zeke asked, coming back to sit down.

Dooley shrugged again. "Mmmm . . . maybe . . . maybe not. Runners have been sent out from Bent's Fort and from other forts to tell all the Plains tribes that Broken Hand Fitzpatrick is coming out to talk treaty. He'll come to Bent's Fort sometime in August, and is already up at Fort Laramie."

"Treaty? What kind of treaty?"

"I haven't figured that out yet. Can't get any straight answers. The way I gather, there's no actual treaty being offered yet. All's they're doing right now is letting the Indians know that something is in the works—kind of getting their minds used to the idea, you know? Feeling them out, seeing what the Indian would think is fair, that kind of stuff."

Zeke stared at the fire. "A treaty." He thought for a moment longer. "I don't like it. I wouldn't mind if the government and the whites could be trusted. But they can't. If any treaty is made, Dooley, the Indians will hold to their end of it. But I'll lay odds of ten to one that the whites won't. I've seen the government's idea of what is fair, when I walked the Trail of Tears with the Cherokees."

Dooley threw aside a bone. "I would not even take that bet, my friend. Because I think you're right."

Zeke sighed. "I told Abbie when she married me that the future didn't look good for my people. I just didn't think things would begin happening this soon."

Dooley looked at Abbie. "You know that whatever happens, this husband of yours will be mixed up in it, maybe even fighting against your own people?"

Abbie met his eyes. "I know. And if it comes to that, I'll be fighting right beside him, against my own people. I've come to love the Cheyenne, Dooley. They're my family now."

He grinned. "You're quite a woman, Miss Abigail. I could tell that the first time I met you at Fort Bridger."

"And I remember that wild story you told us about Zeke in a knife fight in a tavern against an unbelievable number of men," she answered, trying to change the subject and lighten up the conversation. "I believe you said something about the whole place being covered with blood and that not a drop of it was Zeke's."

Dooley chuckled. "Yes, ma'am. I like to tell that one. But it's no exaggeration, Miss Abigail. No, ma'am. That story is true."

"Including the number of men?" she asked, hoping to shake Zeke out of his deep thoughts.

Dooley grinned. "Well, maybe I add one or two sometimes. The truth is, there were five of them, all against Zeke and all with knives."

"Five!" She looked at Zeke. "Is that the truth, Zeke?"

Zeke finally smiled a little. "Yeah, it's true."

He got up and went to the tipi, returning with a flask of whiskey and his pipe. He took a long drink of the whiskey, then handed it to Dooley. "Sometimes a man just has to have a drink," he told Dooley. But Abbie knew the words were meant for her, a way of telling her he just might get drunk that night. Dooley took the whiskey and Zeke lit his pipe.

"Zeke, I wanted to ask you something," Dooley told him.

"Ask away," Zeke replied, sitting down beside Abbie.

"Well, the fur trading business has gone sour. I've been kind of lost lately, not sure what to do with myself. I was thinking, well, with all these fine horses here, you've got your job cut out for you keeping out horse thieves, especially the Comanches, let alone white rustlers. I thought maybe you could use some help in guarding the herd, you know?"

Zeke grinned. "I'd be glad for the help, Dooley, but I can't pay much, if anything."

Dooley grinned. "Hell, I don't need no pay, long as I can take my pick of a horse and can eat my meals with you. I can build my own shelter, and once you get more settled, maybe we could build a little outbuilding for me to sleep in. I could run errands for you, go to the fort for supplies in times when the Missus can't go along and you don't want to be leaving her here alone. She should never be left alone out here."

"That's one thing I'm very much aware of."

"Well, what do you think? I'd stay out of your way. You and me have been good friends, rode together, trapped together, fought Crow and Blackfeet together." His smile faded. "I, uh, I know I ain't no substitute for Olin Wales. He was the best white friend you ever had. But I admire you, Zeke, trust you. I'm glad to call you friend. And I admire this good woman you married. You ought to have some help in protecting her and the herd."

Zeke chuckled and took back the flask of whiskey. "You don't need to talk me into it, Dooley." He took another long swallow. "Fact is, I was thinking the same thing, only I wasn't sure who I could get that I could trust. Now I know."

Dooley smiled and nodded. "Thanks. And if there's times you want to take off with your people for a while, I'll just stay right here and guard the horses for you. Heck, maybe you can build this place up to a full-fledged ranch!"

Zeke shrugged. "I don't know right now what I'm going to do. I claimed the land so I could build Abbie a cabin. She's willing to live with the Cheyenne, and that's what I'd rather do.

But it's too hard for her, and it's going to become too dangerous to be with them all the time, although there are times when we'll go with them on the hunt."

Abbie started to rise, and immediately both men were on their feet to help her up. She blushed at their attention and brushed off her tunic, which she had to wear loose now without a belt.

"Zeke, I'm going inside the tipi. You two should be alone to talk and it's getting dark anyway."

"You all right?" he asked her.

"I'm fine. I just feel like lying down, and you two probably want to talk about things you can't talk about with me around."

"Hey, now, there is an understanding woman!" Dooley said with a chuckle.

As Abbie walked to the tipi, the men were already sitting back down to talk. She went inside and lay down on their bed of robes; feeling unusually tired, she fell immediately to sleep. She had no idea how much later it was when Zeke finally came inside, but he was feeling his whiskey, as well as a desperate need to know his woman. He needed proof that she was alive and that they could be happy in spite of all that lay ahead for his people. He stripped off his clothes and crawled in beside her. She was barely awake when she realized he was moving between her legs, gently pushing them apart with his knees while his lips kissed her mouth hungrily.

"Zeke," she murmured in a sleepy voice, as his lips moved over her cheek and to her throat.

"I'll be careful, Abbie girl," he whispered. She could smell the whiskey on his breath, but she knew his heart was heavy and he needed her.

"Just don't press on my stomach," she whispered.

He raised up on his knees and grasped her under the hips, supporting her while he pushed himself inside of her, feeling passionate and eager in his desire for her. He could see her by the light of the full moon that shone down through the opening

357

at the top of the tipi.

He looked down at her swollen belly. To him it was beautiful and did not take away his desire for her, for it was his life she carried. Her eyes were closed, and her young face was beautiful in the dim light.

The whiskey in his blood made him take her with less romantic foreplay and with more haste than was normal for him, and when he finished he felt a tinge of guilt and shame. But she had not protested or complained, and he loved her all the more for it. He moved in beside her and pulled her into his arms, wishing he did not have the whiskey on his breath.

"Say you'll never leave me, Abbie girl," he told her.

"You know I won't," she replied, still sleepy. She was warm and sweet, curling up to him like a child. "I'll never leave you, Zeke."

He laid a big hand to the side of her face. "Thank you, Abbie," he whispered. But she did not hear him. She was asleep again.

The labor started early on a Tuesday morning during the third week of July. Abbie had been wondering how she would be warned that birth was about to begin, and now she knew. She dropped the iron pot she had been carrying and called to Zeke as she bent over with the awful pain. It seemed he was instantly at her side, even though he had been far out in the corral with the herd. He shouted to Dooley to heat some water, then he helped Abbie into the tipi.

"Try to relax, Abbie," he was telling her. He quickly spread out a blanket and left for a moment, returning with a fat stick, which he pounded into the earth floor of the tipi. He knelt down beside her, and she whimpered with fear.

"Abbie, squat on your knees and grasp the stick," he told her. "Don't lay down, honey. Stay on your knees and push when the pains come hard, just like I explained to you before. This is how the Cheyenne women do it. It's easier than lying down like white women do. Don't be afraid, Abbie girl. This is our baby, and we'll make it good."

"I'm . . . scared!" she whimpered as another pain came. She gripped the pole tightly. "I . . . don't want it to come!" she yelled. "I don't want it to come! It hurts too much!"

"Hang on, Abbie," he said calmly, pulling her hair back from her face. "Nothing could hurt as much as burning out that infection. You can do it, girl. I'm going to stay right here beside you every minute." He pulled her tunic up and tied it above her belly; then he put a hand gently on her back and kissed her hair. "You have to go with it, Abbie girl. Let it happen naturally. Just let it happen. Don't fight it. White women fight it and that only makes the pain worse. Go with it, Abbie."

The pain subsided and she blinked back tears. "Oh, Zeke, I want to give you a good baby!" she gasped, starting to cry.

"You'll do just fine, Abbie."

The first hour grew into many hours, and her groans turned to screams as the pains grew worse and came closer together. It seemed as though giant, black claws were reaching into her and pulling out all of her insides, but through it all Zeke's gentle, calm voice comforted her.

"Remember when I took out that arrow, Abbie girl?" he reminded her. "That was a lot worse than this, and that pain didn't lead you anywhere. This is good pain, Abbie. Good pain. It's going to bring us our baby."

More horrible pain . . . more screams . . . Her body was drenched with sweat. Dooley paced outside the tipi feeling helpless, but Zeke kept talking to her.

"We've been through hell together, Abbie girl. We'll get through this together. Push, Abbie. Push with the pain. Let it happen, honey."

"You . . . shouldn't . . . be here." She tried to joke with him between pains. "The Cheyenne say . . . if a man . . . looks upon the birth of his child . . . the man will be deformed."

"That's not a religious belief, Abbie girl. Just superstition. I don't hold to superstition. I delivered my first son and my looks didn't do any changing though Lord knows I'd be in a bad state if they got any worse."

"You're . . . the handsomest man . . . I know!" she moaned.

"There you go again, woman, saying those crazy things about your husband."

"It's true," she whimpered, another pain coming. "That's why I'm in this . . . mess now! Because . . . you're so . . . handsome. I can't . . . resist you!"

He had to grin in spite of his worry. He could hardly bear her suffering, and he knew the pains had gone on for too many hours. If she did not begin to deliver soon it could mean something was wrong. Her youth didn't help matters any. The pain filled her again, raking at her, pulling at her. He watched helplessly as she gripped the post so tightly her knuckles turned white. Her whole body trembled from her effort not to scream, but it was useless, and again he had to listen to her agony, all suffered just to give him a child. At the moment, he was not so sure he could even bed her again after this, although he realized that soon after the baby was born the pain would be forgotten. She would want him again, and he would want her. It was human nature, the process of life that had gone on for thousands of years.

"It's coming!" she suddenly shouted. "It's coming!"

His heart pounded with relief and he placed his hands gently on her waist. "Push, honey. Are you sure it's coming?"

"Yes! Yes!" she panted, beginning to smile. Then she held her breath and grunted, grasping the pole tightly.

"I see the head!" he told her, kneeling down to check her. "Thank God it's finally nearly over."

Now her body began to push of its own accord. The birthing movements were no longer under her control, and nature took its own course. It seemed only moments later that Zeke was telling her the baby was out. He took out the big blade he had used so wickedly on his enemies, and now he used it to sever the umbilical cord.

"Stay right there, Abbie. We've got to get the afterbirth."

"What is it! What is it!" she whimpered.

He was silent for a moment, and her heart pounded with fear. But then she heard him gently pounding the infant's back, and there was a choking whimper followed by a slow buildup to a good hard cry. He laid the infant down in front of her beside the pole on a piece of clean deerskin.

"It's a boy," he said in a choked voice. She looked down at her son, its tiny body bloody and covered with membrane except for the mouth and nose where Zeke had cleaned the tissue away so the baby could breathe. But in spite of its bloody appearance, Abbie could see all the parts were there. It was very obviously a little male baby, and a strong, fine-looking son at that. Its wrinkled arms and legs kicked wildly as it began crying out its anger at being tossed into the cruel world outside its mother's body. Its skin was dark red, and its small head was covered with a mass of straight, black hair. It appeared to be a perfect, unblemished and very Indian child. Abbie smiled and looked at Zeke who stared at the boy with tears in his eyes.

"You have . . . a son," she said softly. "Thank God! I wanted so much to give you a son!"

He turned his face to look her in the eyes, and a tear glistened on one cheek. "Thank you, Abbie," he whispered.

"It took both of us to do it," she replied with a smile.

He shook his head. "Not just that, Abbie. It's . . . all the other . . . the things you gave up to be with me. And now . . . you've given me a son. The Gods have smiled upon me this day!" He turned and left the tipi to get some water from Dooley. He had to wash his son, and help Abbie with the afterbirth. Dooley met him outside the tipi with anxious eyes.

"I have a son, Dooley!" Zeke said brokenly. He could not continue. He walked to the fire to get the water.

Eighteen

The summer of 1847 was a restless one, and while Zeke and Abbie worked at building up their livestock and land and enjoyed the wonder of their little son, the Pawnee were again raiding in Cheyenne territory. When Swift Arrow and the others returned to the Arkansas, Swift Arrow rode to the home of his half-blood brother carrying two Pawnee scalps. It was the first time Abbie had seen Swift Arrow in his most warlike manner, and the first time she had seen fresh scalps. For although Zeke had taken scalps himself, he had not let Abbie see them, fearing he would offend her. Abbie was glad there had been no Pawnee attacks during the summer she had spent with the Cheyenne, because she would not have cared to be in the middle of warring tribes without Zeke.

But talk of the Pawnee was quickly forgotten when Swift Arrow's attention turned to Cheyenne Zeke's new son. The pride that shone in Zeke's eyes when he presented the child to his brother swelled Abbie's heart with love.

The boy was all Cheyenne, with skin even darker than his father's. His bright eyes were deep brown, and his hair was straight and black as coal. Immediately, Swift Arrow began talking about how the boy should be taught the Cheyenne ways and how proud he would be to do the teaching, for Zeke had already promised Swift Arrow he would be the chosen uncle to teach his "little warrior" if Abbie should have a son. Although the future looked bleak for the Cheyenne, Zeke believed the

People must live on through their children and the grand-children. His son would be brought up in the warrior's ways, for then he would know he was a man.

"Have you named him?" Swift Arrow asked, touching the baby's tiny hand and grinning at the strength of the child's grasp.

"No," Zeke replied. "We want to let Gentle Woman name him."

Swift Arrow nodded. "It is good you wish to name him according to custom. The old ones should choose his name." He looked at Zeke. "But one day he will choose his own name, when he is a man. He will have a vision, and he will know."

Zeke nodded. "He will know."

"You have given my brother a fine son!" Swift Arrow said to Abbie. His eyes quickly scanned her slender body. "And already you do not look like a woman who has just given birth." Abbie blushed and Swift Arrow looked at Zeke again. "It is custom that the man does not sleep with his woman when the child still nurses. In this way the woman does not have too many babies too quickly. But Swift Arrow had trouble keeping that law. Is it same for you?"

Zeke chuckled and Abbie blushed even more and took the baby from Zeke's arms. "I think I should leave now!" she told them chidingly.

"It is the same, my brother," Zeke replied, watching Abbie walk to the tipi. "I have already disobeyed that law."

Swift Arrow waited until Abbie went inside the tipi before he spoke again. "There is a beauty about a woman when a child suckles at her breast," he added. "It makes a man want her more." There was a distant pain in his eyes.

"You should marry again, Swift Arrow," Zeke told his brother. "There was a time when I, too, wanted no other woman. The pain of my loss was so great I wanted nothing but to kill everyone in sight and perhaps die myself. I did not think I would find a woman like Ellen again. But I did. And there are many young Cheyenne maidens who would give anything to be your wife. You're an honored warrior. I've seen how some of them look at you. There isn't a Cheyenne girl in the whole tribe who'd not remove her chastity belt for you the first night of your marriage."

Swift Arrow grinned. Then he shook his head. "I want no woman. I want only to be good dog soldier." He breathed deeply and put on the face of a man who did not care. "When the Pawnee raided us, we chased them back! I counted more coup than any of the others!" He began strutting. "It was a good fight. The Cheyenne took the Pawnee hunting grounds, and the Pawnee will never get this land back. When they stole our Sacred Arrows many winters ago, they forever destroyed a chance for peace!" He turned and faced Zeke haughtily, but Zeke was sober.

"Swift Arrow, I'm afraid it isn't the Pawnee who will give you the most trouble eventually. Don't you understand what's happening?"

The man sobered. "I understand more than you think, my brother. When we return, we see them building new fort on the Arkansas. It is called Fort Mann, and already many white men were there, white men fresh from the East, soldier volunteers like those who tried to take your woman from us last summer. I myself spoke with their leader, who is called Gilpin. He tell me he is here because of all the fighting on Santa Fe Trail. Many Americans have died. I tell him it is not Cheyenne who help the Mexicans; it is Comanche and Kiowa. He look at me like he not believe me. And he tell me it would be good if the Cheyenne did not befriend any Comanche or Kiowa—not even the Arapahos, who have always been our friend. And he tell me he might even come here to Big Timbers to camp for the winter, where he can keep eye on the Santa Fe Trail, and keep eye on Cheyenne. He say it is good we are friendly, but that he make it bad for us if we help the Comanche and Mexicans."

"I'm told Fitzpatrick will be down this way soon, Swift Arrow. He wants to hold a council at Bent's Fort to discuss plans for a treaty, among other things. Fitzpatrick can be trusted, but I don't know about the big men in Washington who will be making the promises. I do think you should go, though. Promise me you'll talk the People into going."

"You will go also?"

"You know I will."

Swift Arrow nodded sadly and looked out at the horses. "This is good place you have chosen for your wooden house. Do your horses do well here?"

"They do. I hired a trapper friend of mine to help me watch them. Name's Dooley. He's at the fort right now getting me some supplies. Abbie shouldn't be making any trips yet, and this way I can get what I need without leaving her alone."

"You can trust this man?" Swift Arrow asked.

"I know men," Zeke replied. "Dooley and I go back a long way. I can trust him. Fact is, he helped me run off some renegade Comanches just the other night. They came sneaking around with an eye on my horses."

"You have something valuable to them. They could sell those horses to the Mexicans for much money and for women. I send some braves here to camp for winter, help you watch horses. No Comanche will dare come and bother you when there are Cheyenne warriors here!"

"I'd appreciate that, Swift Arrow. In fact, I'd just as soon it was you and our brothers. Maybe you could talk Deer Slayer and Gentle Woman into camping here also. Do you really think that Gilpin fellow will show up with soldiers?"

Swift Arrow nodded. "I think so. I do not like him coming here."

"A lot of things are happening I don't like," Zeke replied. He smiled at his brother. "But it's good to see you back, Swift Arrow, and to know everyone is all right."

"Soon we hold dance of the warrior societies," Swift Arrow told him. "It would be good time to introduce child to the band . . . and give him name. I would like honor of piercing the ears."

Zeke nodded. He wanted his son's ears pierced by a brave

warrior, as was the custom. The piercing represented being struck by lightning, and was believed to help make the child invulnerable to arrows. Zeke realized this was more of a superstition than a reality, but he wanted his son brought up as a brave and honorable Cheyenne man. The ceremony was a part of that upbringing, and he knew it would make Swift Arrow proud to participate in it. His Cheyenne brothers had been Zeke's whole world. They had given him love and friendship, and he intended to do the same in return.

"Swift Arrow, I—" He stopped and studied his brother, who was an honored dog soldier and full of pride. He dreaded what might be coming for his people, and hoped he could do something to prepare them, perhaps help them to understand that they would not forever be allowed to roam so freely. It hurt to see the fierce pride in his brother's eyes, and he knew already that whatever was to come, the Cheyenne would not go down easily. Zeke's mind was haunted by the Trail of Tears and what he had seen happen to the once-proud Cherokee of Alabama. Few Eastern Indians were even living now.

"What is it, my brother?" Swift Arrow asked, watching the agony in Zeke's eyes.

"I just . . . I hope you understand what this treaty could mean. The leaders in Washington will probably tell you what land you can call your own, and they'll expect you to stay within its borders."

Swift Arrow shrugged. "We go where the buffalo go. That is the way."

"No. It is not the way!" Zeke said almost pleadingly. "Swift Arrow, the only way I got this piece of property was to file for it in Abbie's name. Bent advised I put it in her name because . . . because I'm half Cheyenne. He told me"—Zeke sighed—"he told me the day might come when anything the Indians supposedly own—even men who are only part Indian—will be taken from them. Indians aren't even considered American citizens, Swift Arrow!"

The man laughed in indignation. "Our people were here

long before these white bastards came. What do you mean, not citizens? They are the ones who are not citizens! We go where the buffalo go. If the white man wants to use our land, he may use it. If he wants to cross over it, then let him cross. We do not stop him. Let him build his cities and his forts. Let him use the land to fight against the Mexicans." The man waved his arm. "Land is big, big enough for us all. The Great Spirit gave us this land to use, not to own. We do not own it. They do not own it. We all share it! *Nohetto!*"

The word signified he was through with the conversation. He walked to his horse and mounted up. "I come back soon . . . two, three days. Bring Gentle Woman to see her grandchild." He turned his horse in a circle. "And let the white man come. Perhaps we will even sign this treaty. But I, Swift Arrow, have nothing left to live for, and so I am ready to die for something. I will die for my people, and for this land, if that is what the white man wants! We have been peaceful. We do not fight him. Some of our women even marry the white man. We give white man no trouble. But let him understand that he also should not give us trouble!"

He turned his horse and rode off.

Outside Bent's Fort the drums beat rhythmically, and the warriors of the various soldier societies danced around fires, dressed in their most brilliant regalia, their faces and bodies painted in many colors, fine war bonnets on their heads, and bells jingling on their ankles and wrists. Abbie sat watching, with little *Hohanino-o* on her lap. She was pleased with the name Gentle Woman had given her son. It meant Little Rock, for the boy was as strong and sturdy as a rock; and sometimes it already seemed he was as heavy as one! Zeke Monroe had sired a boy as strong and sturdy as he was, and Abbie was proud to prove to the People that she could mother such a son.

She dabbed again at Little Rock's ears with the special herb the *Shaman* had given her to clean his lobes to prevent infection. Like a good warrior, the boy had cried for only a moment when Swift Arrow had pierced his ears. Then Zeke had held his son up for them all to see, and the warriors and women had all cheered the half-breed's new son and praised him for his fine offspring. The white woman had done well.

The celebrations had gone on all day and lasted into the night, while the Cheyenne waited for the appearance of Broken Hand Fitzpatrick who was inside the walls of Bent's Fort with a group of volunteer soldiers. It felt good to Abbie to be among the Cheyenne again. She was proud to be able to show off her little brown son, even more proud when she saw the look on Zeke's face as he carried the child around to display him to the warriors. On this night Zeke was all Indian again, and in her heart, Abbie was Indian also. The Dance of the Warrior Societies was thrilling to watch, and she became entranced by the near magic of the celebration. It was not long before Zeke himself stripped to his loincloth, donned the covering of only an apron, and painted his body to join in the dancing, waving his most-feared weapon, the big blade, his hair brushed out long and loose, his whole countenance once again savage.

It was not until the wee hours of the morning that the celebrating ended, and by then Abbie lay inside the tipi nursing Little Rock. When Zeke entered, he would have frightened any unwitting white woman, but the sight of him only excited Abbie, for she had seen Cheyenne Zeke wield the knife. She knew of his courage and skill. He was her man, and when he was painted and wore only the apron, his body displayed the man that he was.

He came to her and knelt beside her to watch his son feed at her breast, the baby's tiny brown hand pinching at her milky white skin. Manliness seemed to pour forth from Zeke, for he was worked up by the dancing and celebrating and was feeling his power and strength—remembering his vows as a warrior. And he was full of pride over his strong son.

He reached out and traced the scar on her breast, where he had cut her two summers before to drain the infection from the

369

Crow arrow. She blushed and looked down at Little Rock, saying nothing.

"Tell our son to finish quickly, so that his father can feed at your breast also," he told her, his voice strained with desire.

She smiled and blushed as he sat down beside her, gently stroked the baby's soft, black hair, and then reached over and pulled her tunic all the way to her waist so that her other breast was exposed. He liked her breasts this way, full with milk for his son. He moved around to kiss the back of her neck, then her shoulder, but soon his lips glided to the other side of her and down to gently suck her other breast.

"Zeke," she whispered, her body raging with terrible, sudden desire at this sensation. He left her breast and moved his lips over her throat. "Your milk is sweet," he whispered, moving up to her mouth.

They kissed hungrily as he grasped her free breast in his palm and caressed the wet nipple with his thumb. He kissed her eyes, then moved back as she pulled her son away and laid him aside on his own little bed of robes. The child was asleep.

She turned to face her savage-looking husband; then she raised up on her knees and offered her breasts. He sucked at them lightly as he pulled her tunic to her knees. Then his lips moved down to her now-flat belly.

"Again I disobey the law," he said softly. "A Cheyenne man should not do this to his woman for many months after a baby is born."

"I don't like that law," she replied, as he slipped her tunic the rest of the way from her body.

"Nor do I," he agreed. He quickly removed his apron and loincloth, and his dark, lean, muscular body bent over hers. Caressing her with his lips, he moved them over her knees and thighs, his hands moving up either side of her body. He kissed her in secret places that only Zeke Monroe had ever touched, places that belonged only to him. She was again struck by the fact that he seemed far too much man for her, not only physically, but in his experience and in the savage side of him that she knew she would never fully understand. But for her he had only gentleness and patience, tender touches and sweet words that made her ever vulnerable to his advances so that she was completely free with her body when it was in his hands. It was as though she had no will of her own, except to enjoy the pleasures he could give her.

"Have I told you you're more beautiful than ever since the baby?" he asked her as he stretched out beside her, pushing one knee between her legs.

"You told me just today," she answered with a smile. "You flatter me too much, my husband."

"I only speak the truth," he replied, holding her gaze with his own hypnotic look. His eyes were glittery with love and with the aftereffects of the celebrating. His body was tense and alive and urgent as he moved his other leg between her own; her slim thighs parted for him, her own eyes becoming hungry and provocative.

"I want to feel your power, Lone Eagle," she told him daringly, using his Indian name in private conversation for the first time. It filled him with sweeter desire and great personal pride, and he gave her that most manly part of him, pushing hard and filling her with fierce possessiveness so that she cried out from the sweet and welcome pain of it. He knew she belonged only to him. It was a good feeling. White blood or not, he was a good Cheyenne warrior. He had danced the dance of the warrior societies and he bore the scars of the Sun Dance ritual. He was Cheyenne! This was his woman! And now he had a son. The son would also be Cheyenne! Only Cheyenne and nothing else!

He smiled at her closed eyes. She was sweet and beautiful. This was a good way to end the celebrating—with his woman. It was fitting.

They gathered the next day for the powwow with Broken Hand Fitzpatrick. The warriors sat in a circle, their women

371

behind them and the children even farther back. Soldiers lined up between the fort and the Indians, some on foot, and more behind them on horses. Fitzpatrick began his speech to the Cheyenne, and the few Arapahos who accompanied them, using an interpreter he had hired in Santa Fe by the name of John Smith.

Abbie had stayed behind in the tipi, for Zeke was not certain she should be seen sitting among the warriors. He was not sure just what Fitzpatrick would have to say, and with the presence of soldiers, there might be trouble.

Fitzpatrick warned the Cheyenne that they must at all costs stay out of the Mexican war and not join up with their brothers to the south, the Comanche and Kiowa. Zeke listened with foreboding, as Fitzpatrick warned the Cheyenne that a Lt. Col. William Gilpin would be watching the area along the Arkansas carefully, to see that the Cheyenne did not make trouble, to keep all raiding Indians off the Santa Fe Trail, and to protect American citizens. Gilpin would be wintering at Bent's Fort, he told them. So, Swift Arrow's warning about Gilpin had been true.

It was announced that all raiding Indians would be promptly and severely dealt with. Swift Arrow received the news with an expression of sneering haughtiness; indeed, he almost laughed. But the Cheyenne spokesman, Yellow Wolf, promised the Cheyenne would make no trouble and asked if the Great White Father in Washington intended to give the Cheyenne gifts for obeying the white man's request to stay out of the war. Fitzpatrick replied that he would see what he could do. The Cheyenne reiterated that if they were to stay out of the war and not move from the Arkansas, then the white man must provide them with food and supplies, for their ability to hunt the buffalo would be severely restricted. Again, the only reply from Fitzpatrick was that he would see what he could do.

"Do not give us half promises!" Swift Arrow spoke up. "If you tell us we must stay here, then we must have food. Otherwise, we go where the buffalo go! We hear talk of treaty.

When will this treaty come to be, so that once and for all the Indian will know where he can ride without offending the white settlers and soldiers?"

"I'm working on that also," Fitzpatrick replied. "These things take time."

"How much time?" Swift Arrow asked.

"I can't say as yet," Fitzpatrick replied. "Maybe another year. Maybe two. That's the most I can tell you."

Swift Arrow snickered and rose to leave the council. Red Eagle took out a flask of whiskey and began drinking, and there was general unrest among the warriors. Fitzpatrick warned them again to be careful—that Lieutenant Colonel Gilpin would be watching the Cheyenne and intended to protect the Santa Fe Trail from Mexicans and raiding Indians who helped the Mexicans.

"We do not help them," Yellow Wolf replied. "We only hunt the buffalo . . . and sometimes war against the Pawnee, who continually raid our villages and steal our horses. We do not bother the white people or the Mexicans. And we do not ride with the Comanche and raid the supply wagons. You must not mix up the Cheyenne with our red brothers to the south."

The powwow ended without much being accomplished, except that the Cheyenne were more restless. Zeke rose to leave with the rest of them when Fitzpatrick called out to him.

"I thought it was you," Fitzpatrick said in a friendly fashion when Zeke came closer. "Haven't seen you since about five years ago, when I was scouting for a wagon train and you were trapping—saw you at Fort Hall up in Oregon, I believe it was."

"It was," Zeke replied. "Good to see you again," he added, putting out his hand. Fitzpatrick took it and they shook hands firmly. Then Zeke looked toward the Cheyenne. "At least I think it's good to see you."

They released hands and Fitzpatrick followed Zeke's eyes and watched the warriors, who were grumbling and heading back to their own camp.

"You live with the Cheyenne now, Zeke?"

"Some of the time. They're my only family."

"Well, I suppose you're prejudiced, Zeke. As for myself, I've had a lot of experience with Indians, too, and for the most part I find them untrustworthy. Sure, they keep their word and all. But they're a passionate people, Zeke; don't understand the white man's way one whit. That ignorance and stubbornness is going to bring them great trouble. You know that, don't you?"

Zeke nodded. "I know that. They're quick to anger, Fitzpatrick. They get their pride hurt real easy. And they don't like someone speaking to them with a forked tongue, making vague promises. Something either is or it isn't, and I don't think they're real sure why you're even here."

Fitzpatrick grinned. "Trouble is, I'm not sure myself, Zeke. I've been trying to reason with Superintendent Harvey in St. Louis that we need to do the very thing you're talking about: give some firm answers, make promises we can keep, and outline to your red brothers just where they can ride and hunt. I'm not making much progress, and I know the Indians are getting restless with this war and more and more whites coming out here and all. I'm doing what I can to stabilize things until Washington decides just what the hell they want to do. And I need help from men like you, Zeke. You live with them. You are them."

Zeke sighed. "I do what I can."

"I'm sure you do," Fitzpatrick replied. He folded his arms and studied the half-breed. "You know, Zeke, army scouts make good money."

Zeke eyed the man warily. "I have no desire to lead soldiers against my own people, Fitzpatrick. That's a job for men like you and Jim Bridger and Joe Meek. You men pave the way for the whites. I'll go as far as helping a few settlers cross this land to reach the other side, Fitzpatrick, but I can't help them settle right here, and I sure as hell can't help the soldiers."

Fitzpatrick frowned. "Just thought I'd plant the idea, Zeke, that's all. The army could use men like you. You know this land inside and out, and you know the Indian. Some full-bloods scout for us now, you know."

Zeke's eyes narrowed. "Traitors, you mean—renegade Crow and Blackfeet and Shoshoni who'd turn in their own mother for the whiskey and rifles."

Fitzpatrick sighed. "They aren't all that way, Zeke, and you know it. Most of them are just smart. As time goes on and the Indians begin to understand there's no hope in fighting the white man, more and more of them will come over to our side and help us bring some peace to this land."

Zeke's smile was more of a sneer. "Well, then, I'm one dumb Indian, because I'll never turn my people over to soldiers. I may not fight right beside them, and I may even try to talk them out of too much resistance, but I'll be goddamned if I'll work for bluecoats and lead soldiers to my people's villages."

Fitzpatrick's eyebrows arched in surprise. "You're more Cheyenne than I thought, Zeke."

Zeke nodded. "Mostly all," he replied with a haughty grin. "And I'd say you and your soldiers and your government men have your work cut out for you. There's nothing my red brothers like better than a damned good fight!"

Fitzpatrick nodded and their eyes held. "Zeke, the glory days of the mountain man and the free Indian are just about over. You know that, don't you?"

Zeke nodded. "I'm aware of that."

Fitzpatrick grinned. "It was a good time, wasn't it? It didn't matter out there if a man was red or white or a mixture of both."

There was a moment of understanding, and both men knew that although they had once been one of a kind, they must now choose sides and go their separate ways.

"Good-bye, Fitzpatrick," Zeke told the man sadly.

"Good-bye, Zeke."

The famous scout turned and walked back to the soldiers, and Zeke walked in the direction of the departing Cheyenne.

*   *   *

Winston Garvey looked up from his desk as Anna Gale pushed her way into his office, her gaudy, red satin dress almost hurting his eyes. His secretary stared at the woman angrily, for Anna would not take no for an answer when she came in and asked to see the senator. She barged inside, carrying her head straight and proud as she pranced toward the senator's desk, the feathered plumes of her hat blowing with the briskness of her walk. The satin and bustles of her clothing rustled loudly, and the senator rose, his face puffy and red with anger.

"What in God's name are you doing here?" he asked her. He motioned for his secretary to close the door. She did so, arching her eyebrows knowingly, but the senator shot her a look that warned her to keep her mouth shut. Meanwhile, Anna stood staunchly in front of the senator's desk.

"What is this I hear about closing down my business above the saloon?" Anna sneered through painted red lips. "And where in hell have you been lately, Senator? Have you decided to play the role of doting husband and father since that bitch of a wife of yours had her baby?"

"Watch your tongue, you slut!" the man replied. "I suspected someone was watching me, that's all. Now you've really fixed things. How dare you come prancing into this office!"

She smiled a crooked smile. "Not good enough to come here, am I?" She tossed her head. "No matter. I want to know why the police raided my place last night."

"We're stamping out gambling and prostitution," the senator replied. "It's as simple as that."

Her eyes flashed. "It is, is it? I say it isn't! You tell the police to leave me alone, or I'll tell all of Washington that you were once a primary customer of mine, Senator Winston Garvey. I'll put a quick end to your prestigious career!"

"Try it, and I'll make arrangements for you to be found dead in some alley," he replied threateningly. "Don't think I can't do it!"

Her dark eyes blazed. "You're a fat, no-good, double-crossing—"

"Save it, Anna!" he interrupted, putting up his hand. He walked over to the door and turned the lock. He had to think fast before this woman destroyed his reputation. He walked back to her, studying her phenomenal beauty, the raven black hair and milky white skin, the supple young body and exquisitely beautiful face. She watched him suspiciously but stood still as he began unbuttoning the front of her dress. "Why don't you do us both a favor, Anna, and just quietly leave Washington," he told her. "I'll give you money—all you need."

Her breathing quickened as he opened the front of her dress and unlaced her undergarment, pulling it apart and exposing her full breasts. He toyed with them, his face reddening and his lips pursing.

"And just where would I go, may I ask?" she replied.

He met her eyes as he gently stroked her breasts with the back of his hand. "West, my dear. West."

She threw her head back and laughed. "West! Do you recall that our good friend Jonathan Mack died out there of snake bite? And you expect me to go to that godforsaken, barren, horrible place?"

He bent down and kissed her breasts; then he pulled her close. "Anna, my dear, don't you realize how rich you could be out there? The West is filled with drifters: mountain men, trappers, traders, men running from the law, lonely preachers, wild Indian bucks, all kinds of men from all walks of life. The variety is endless, and they all need women like you. A lot of them don't see anything prettier than their horse's rear end six months out of the year." He looked down at her breasts, now resting atop his fat belly. "And when they see something lily white and soft like you, get a good look at that nice round white bottom and these pretty fruits I'm looking at now, they'll pay a fortune to have a roll in bed with you! Why, you could be a millionaire out there. And I'll give you the money you'll need to get set up. I've sent men out there to replace Jonathan Mack, and already plenty of land out there will be mine when the war with Mexico is over. In four or five years I'll be out West myself. When I get there, you can repay your debt to me. How about it?"

She smiled a little. "Do you really think I could get rich?"

"I know you could! Just think about it—all those men, all needing a woman. Not only would you get rich in bed, but you can charge a fortune for whiskey. I'll give you enough money to set up a regular business, open a real fancy saloon. There's no law out there, Anna. You can have all the gambling and prostitution you want, and nobody will stop you. I'm handing you the chance of a lifetime, my little orphan lady. All you have to do is leave Washington quietly."

She pulled away from him and began lacing up her undergarment. "When do I get the money?" she asked.

"Soon as you're ready to leave."

"Then I'll leave in the morning. Shall I go to Santa Fe?"

"Fine. I'll give you some money right now." He walked to a safe. "And . . . uh . . . we'll call your business, Santa Fe Enterprises. Use that name to withdraw money from the bank I've set up in Santa Fe. It's called the Washington Union. I'll send word that you are legally allowed to withdraw money under that name, but I'll keep a close watch on your withdrawals, my dear, so don't go too far overboard." He turned around with a wad of money in his hands as she buttoned her dress.

"I'll be careful," she replied. She scanned his fat body. "How's your poor, darling little wife?"

He reddened. "Once a bitch, always a bitch. I can't touch her. According to the doctor, if she gets pregnant again, she'll die. If I get to have her once every two months, I'm lucky. And to get that far I have to get her drunk."

She pursed her lips. "Oh, poor Senator Garvey! Then why haven't you been to see me?"

"I couldn't. It's like I told you. They're clamping down on

378

prostitution, and if I were caught going to see you, I'd be in a fix." He walked over and handed her the money.

"I see," she replied, fanning through the bills. "Well, then, I'll just tell anyone who asks that I came here because I was angry that you were doing your duty and putting me out of business. I pleaded and begged with you, but you refused to listen and chased me right out of Washington. They'll all know what a good senator you are."

He grinned. "You think fast, sweet Anna."

Her eyes turned cold. "That's the only way for a girl like me to survive, Senator." She shoved the money into her handbag. "Will your lovely wife come out West with you?"

He sighed. "She'll have to. I'm sending her out sooner, probably in a year or two."

"I'll bet she's thrilled about that."

"Not exactly. But when she realizes she'll be the center of society out there, she'll like the idea well enough."

Anna sauntered toward the door. "I've taken in a couple of girls off the streets—young ones. One is only thirteen. Do I have your permission to take them along?"

"Certainly. You'll need them to get set up good."

She nodded and started to turn.

"Anna," he spoke up. She turned back around. "Thirteen?" he asked.

She grinned slyly. "You interested, you old bastard?"

"Perhaps I could . . . manage to sneak over there just once more . . . to say good-bye. How about if you and one of those little girls work on me together? That would be worth quite a lot of money, wouldn't it?"

She smiled a crooked smile. "We'll be waiting, Senator." She adjusted her dress. "And by the time you get out West, I'll be running the fanciest saloon and best whorehouse west of the Mississippi!"

"I'm sure you will, my dear," he replied with a grin.

She sauntered out the door, and he returned to his desk to work on his speech. Soon he must present his reasons for considering treaties for the Indians and his plan for putting them on reservations. He would have to do a good job. If men like him were going to go West and reap the rewards, they would have to get the Indians out of the way. That was a vital first step. If he had his way, he would simply line the Indians up and shoot them down with rifles and cannon. It would be no great loss.

He tried to concentrate on his speech, but the delicious thought of the young girls at Anna's place kept interrupting his thoughts, and he found himself wondering what young Indian girls were like. Were they any different? He would have to find out once he got out West.

Nineteen

The next year and a half was hard and dangerous, for Zeke and Abbie as well as for the Cheyenne. Lieutenant Colonel Gilpin did indeed come to the Big Timbers, and he launched a campaign against all who would dare to raid along the Santa Fe Trail. Gilpin and his troops clamped down on all Indian movements, cutting off their ability to hunt necessary game. Swift Arrow and the others were enraged, and Swift Arrow pleaded with Broken Hand Fitzpatrick to tell Gilpin to ease off, to convince him the Cheyenne had nothing to do with the raiding. But Fitzpatrick himself did not get on well with Gilpin, and the two men went their separate ways, Fitzpatrick heading back north to the Platte River.

Fitzpatrick left on friendly terms with the Cheyenne, again warning them to stay away from their Kiowa and Comanche friends who were doing the raiding; but as soon as he was gone, Gilpin threw a chain of soldiers around the southern Cheyenne and cramped them even more, constantly harassing and threatening them.

Through it all, Abbie had to watch Zeke's agony, in silent pain herself. He was a man more torn than ever, aware of the power of the soldiers and the government back East, and also bleeding inside for his red brothers who did not understand this power. Again in 1848 the cabin did not get built. Just protecting their land from raids was a job in itself, and they had to help the Cheyenne do some hunting; for the area in which they could hunt had been severely limited, and the People were

381

hungry. Several times Zeke was compelled to take Abbie to Bent's Fort for protection and leave Dooley with the horses, so that he could help Swift Arrow and the others find game, as well as find food for himself and Abbie.

While all of this was going on, Fitzpatrick was pleading to no avail that posts should be established along the Arkansas and manned by experienced men who knew the country and who knew how to deal with Indians without angering them. But Washington seemed to be turning a deaf ear, and mass confusion was running rampant along the Santa Fe Trail and among the Arkansas River Cheyenne.

Swift Arrow and other Cheyenne began calling for another "big talk." Agent Fitzpatrick was reluctant to speak with them again, because the government had issued him no gifts to offer the Indians as a sign of peace; but the Cheyenne were persistent and growing more restless all the time. Fitzpatrick finally came to Bent's Fort once again for more council talk. The Indians complained about the destruction and scattering of hunting game by the heavy flood of emigrants and of the cutting of timber from the river bottoms. Wooded areas were becoming bald, and the destruction of the trees was causing erosion and changes in the river courses. In some places the water was unfit to drink. Fitzpatrick again promised he would see what he could do about a treaty and about setting up land that the Indians could call their own and on which they could ride and hunt peacefully.

Again the Indians walked away with promises in their ears and nothing in their hands or stomachs. It was a bad time for all. The Mexican war was taking its toll on the Indians, as well as opening new roads for outlaws and renegade volunteers who used the war as an excuse to raid and rape and steal. And it was not long before the white travelers and settlers had as much to worry about from their own outlaws as they did from the Indians.

* * *

Abbie walked around the pile of logs that had been stacked next to where Zeke planned to build the cabin. She tried to visualize her house, but she had lived in the tipi for so long that it seemed impossible she would ever truly live in a house with wood floors and a roof, a fireplace and a mantel—a hearth to sit beside and rock her babies.

Times were bad, and Zeke still had not got around to building the cabin. Tears welled in her eyes. She hurt for her husband, who was riding a dangerous middle road. She pulled her buffalo coat closer around her shoulders and glanced over at the tipi. There was no sound. Little Rock still slept.

She looked out over the broad plains to the east, thinking about that first year she had spent with the People. It had been good after all, and she missed it. She knew that if she yearned for that wonderful journey to the Dakotas, it must be terribly painful for Swift Arrow and the others to be confined to the Arkansas as they were now—free but not free. And she was certain that they would not long abide the treatment they were receiving. They would break loose like a bull kicking and charging its way out of a stall.

She shivered. It felt as though there had just been a great rumbling beneath the earth, a rumbling that would one day explode into a great volcano. And she wondered what part she and Zeke would play in that explosion.

She felt helpless and depressed, as torn as her husband, for Zeke was suffering greatly from the skirmishes, loving his people yet understanding what would happen to them if they tried to remain free, while at the same time he was concerned over his own son and the second child she now carried in her swollen belly. He was trying to make a home for his white wife, but she knew it would have been much easier for him if he had married a Cheyenne girl, for then he would know where he belonged. Now in their life they seemed to be forever hanging between heaven and hell.

She wiped at her tears and strained to see Zeke. He and Dooley had ridden off after some straying horses. It was necessary to keep the growing herd close by because raiding Comanches continued to try to steal them. She could see neither man at the moment and turned to walk back to the tipi when she saw riders approaching from the opposite direction, their horses splashing through the river. They rode hard, as though on an attack, and her heart pounded with fear; for in these times, one did not know if a stranger was friend or foe. She started to run to her tipi to get her rifle but a shot rang out and hit the dirt at her feet, stopping her in her tracks.

She stood her ground, praying that Zeke and Dooley had heard the shot, as the men came closer. There were six of them, a sorry-looking bunch of white men who were taking advantage of the unrest in the territory to do their own raiding. They quickly surrounded her, and with great fear she recognized one of them. It was the leader of the men who had tried to take her away from Swift Arrow well over a year earlier. Claude Baker grinned when their eyes met, and he dismounted.

"Well, well," he gloated. "If it ain't the little white squaw!"

He came toward her and she backed away, but another man poked a rifle in her back, while another went inside the tipi to check it out.

"Get away from me!" Abbie spit at Baker. "My man is close by, and when he finds you here, you'll die!"

He laughed and grabbed her coat, jerking her toward him. "Seems like I've heard that story before, white squaw! And we can take care of any Indian buck that wants to come and try to save you!" He tore open her coat. "Well, looky here, boys. The little white squaw really did let one of them bucks at her! She done got herself knocked up by one of 'em!"

"More than once!" another looter shouted, emerging from the tipi with Little Rock, who squirmed and kicked and began to cry from being so rudely awakened from a good sleep. The man held the naked boy up high in the cold air and laughed.

"Put my baby down!" Abbie screamed, starting to lunge toward them. But Baker stopped her, grabbing her across the breasts and holding her tight against himself, her back to him.

He squeezed one breast painfully as she struggled to get away.

"Let's take her then steal the horses, boss," one of the other men spoke up. "Any white woman that lets a red buck in her won't mind a few white men doing the same!"

Abbie struggled violently, in spite of her pregnant condition. All she could think of was Little Rock; she could not see just what was being done with her son. She could hear him crying, but strong hands pushed her down and held her pinned in the snow. Someone pushed up her tunic and more hands pulled her legs apart.

"When we're done, cut that red baby out of her stomach!" someone growled. "We don't need any more little red varmints runnin' around. And go drown that hollering brat, Harvey!"

"No! No! My baby!" she screamed. Something hit her across the face and she was stunned, the sky and the ugly faces spinning around her. She felt something probe rudely between her legs, and it brought vomit to her throat when she realized it was someone's hands tearing at her.

"I've been wantin' to have a lick at this ever since I seen her with them Cheyenne bucks!" she heard Baker's voice speak up. She could feel his hot breath and then the sickening wetness in places that had belonged only to Zeke, and she screamed and struggled, her mind tortured with worry for Little Rock, whom she could still hear crying.

But as her world began to go black, she heard a terrible but beautiful war cry! The hands let go of her and men began screaming and running. One fell near her, an arrow in his back, and Abbie turned on her side and struggled to get to her feet, pulling at her tunic to cover herself. She blinked and looked up to see Zeke and Claude Baker. Baker was trying to get away from the enraged half-breed, but he'd been ready to rape his captive, and his pants were down around his ankles so he couldn't run or get to his rifle.

In one sudden, swift movement, Zeke grabbed the man's penis and sliced it off with the big blade. He shoved Baker to the ground, and the man lay there screaming and rolling, blood spilling forth from between his legs while Zeke went after another man who was running.

In the distance Dooley was fighting hand to hand with another of the men. Two others lay dead nearby, their bodies split open like hogs. Abbie knew who had done that. It was Zeke's specialty.

The sixth man had apparently fled, for he was nowhere in sight. Abbie crawled away from Baker's ugly, bleeding body and screamed for her son. The little boy came wandering toward her from behind a large rock, where he had apparently gone to hide. He had been sleeping naked but warm and comfortable under many robes inside the tipi, but now his bare little body shivered as he walked barefoot through the snow toward his mother. She grabbed him and immediately enclosed him in her buffalo robe coat to get him warm. As she struggled to get to her feet, black pain grabbed at her abdomen, and she knew that this ordeal had brought on an early labor. She lay back down in the snow and kept Little Rock inside the coat next to her body, waiting for help.

Zeke came back and stood over Baker, who still screamed. The white man stared wide-eyed at Zeke as though Zeke were the most horrible monster he had ever seen. Zeke reached down and grabbed Baker by the hair of his head, and Abbie looked away when she realized Zeke was going to scalp the man. She kept Little Rock inside her robe so that he also would not see. Baker's cries were sickening; then there was a strange grunt and a gushing sound. She knew Zeke had sunk his knife into the man and slit him from penis to throat. There were no more screams from Baker.

In the next moment this man who had just gladly and easily murdered his woman's attackers was at Abbie's side, pulling her into his arms.

"Zeke! Zeke!" she wept, clinging to his coat and pressing Little Rock between them.

"Tell me they didn't rape you!" he groaned, grasping her head tightly to his chest. "Tell me, Abbie girl!"

386

"No! No!" she cried. "There wasn't . . . time."

His grip was so tight it was beginning to hurt. "I saw them touching you." His whole body trembled violently. "God, Abbie, what have I done making you live here with me! It's just like . . . with Ellen!"

"It's all right, Zeke. It's all right!" she told him. She curled up in pain and groaned. "Take . . . Little Rock! Get him warm . . . or he'll be sick. Zeke . . . I'm having the baby! Help me!"

His eyes filled with fear and he laid her gently back in the snow, taking Little Rock from her and handing him up to Dooley, who was now beside them.

"Did they hurt her bad?" Dooley asked.

"I don't think so, Dooley," Zeke replied. "But she's having the baby. Take Little Rock inside the tipi and go heat some water." Dooley nodded and started to leave. "Dooley." The man turned and their eyes held. "Thanks, Dooley," Zeke told the man in a strained voice.

Dooley nodded. "Any time, friend." He walked to the tipi, and Zeke picked Abbie up in his arms and followed him. Inside, when he saw that her face was bruised and her lip was bleeding, he was so filled with rage that he shook. He wished he had saved her attacker for a slower death. But that was over now, and she was having a baby. The tipi was chilly because the fire had begun to dwindle and the January day had been extremely cold.

Little Rock was still crying and trying to crawl to his mother. Zeke called out to Dooley again, and he entered the tipi hesitantly.

"It's all right, Dooley. Build up the fire, will you? I've got to warm it up in here." He put several robes over Abbie. "Lie there and get warm, Abbie girl," he told her. "Soon as it's warm enough we can get you set up the way you ought to be." He bent down and kissed her forehead. "Just relax, Abbie. It's only two or three weeks early. It'll be okay. We'll do this together, just like last time."

"Little Rock . . . take care of Little Rock," she whimpered. Zeke picked up his son and coddled him, wrapping a robe around the boy and talking soothingly to him. The child finally ceased crying, for his father held him; he was never afraid when his father held him.

Dooley built up the fire, and Zeke sat and rocked back and forth with Little Rock until the boy fell asleep sucking his own fist and feeling safe against his father's chest. Abbie lay sweating and gritting her teeth to keep from screaming, because she knew her screams would waken and frighten her son. It was important to keep him inside the tipi, near the fire, and if he could sleep now, that was even better.

Zeke laid the child down on his own little bed of robes and covered him well, secretly thanking *Maheo* that his son was unharmed. But he was not so certain about Abbie.

"I'll go outside now," Dooley said quietly. "I'll get a pot of water from the river and bring it in and hang it over the fire for you, Zeke."

"Thanks, Dooley," Zeke replied brokenly, bending over Abbie.

Dooley sighed. "She'll be okay, Zeke. She's good and strong."

The man left, not knowing what else to say. When he returned a few minutes later, Abbie was on her knees and Zeke was helping her get her robe off. Dooley looked away and hung the water over the fire; then he left to wait.

This time Dooley heard no screams—just quiet grunts and moaning and gentle talking. It couldn't have been more than an hour later when Zeke came outside.

"I have a daughter," he told Dooley. His voice broke on the last word, and he turned away. His shoulders shook, but he made no sound, and Dooley blinked back tears of his own.

"Zeke, they didn't rape her," he told his friend. "You have a little girl, and your son sleeps without a scratch. It's all right." His heart hurt for Zeke, for Dooley was certain Zeke had never before wept in front of another man . . . but he had never been so afraid for Abbie.

"I thought . . . they'd killed her," Zeke said quietly, wiping at his eyes. It was dark by then, and he was glad Dooley could not see his face. "I'd die without her, Dooley." He sighed deeply and hung his head. "We'd . . . better report this . . . at Bent's Fort tomorrow."

"Let me do it. I hate to say it, but I'm white, Zeke, and it will all set better coming from me. There won't be no trouble over it."

Zeke nodded. "I hope not." He threw back his head and breathed deeply. "Make damned sure they know it was just you and me. Don't let them say the Cheyenne attacked a bunch of white men and hacked them up."

"I'll make sure they get it straight."

Zeke swallowed. "And I don't want Swift Arrow to know about this if we can help it. Thank God he didn't happen to be here just now. If he finds out about it, he might go attack some innocent whites just for revenge. You know how he thinks."

"I know, my friend. You go back now and be with your woman. And with your new little girl."

Zeke nodded and returned to Abbie who lay quietly nursing her daughter. She looked up at him when he entered, and she knew he had been weeping.

"Zeke!" she whispered. He stared at her with wild, angry eyes. "Come and lie beside us, Zeke," she pleaded.

He turned away. "I'm too angry right now, Abbie!"

"Zeke, I'm all right, and the baby is fine. Little Rock is unharmed. We have to be thankful for all of that, Zeke."

He let out a disgusted sigh. "I'm having trouble feeling thankful right now, Abbie," he replied bitterly. "I think I'll go back out—clean up the mess out there. I don't want you to have to see it in the morning." He sighed. "God, I'm sorry, Abbie!"

She lay quietly watching after him as their new baby daughter fell asleep in the crook of her arm. How she wished she could comfort her husband! But there would be no comfort for him this night.

Dooley came inside the tipi to add wood to the fire.

"He's coming yonder," he told Abbie, averting her eyes.

"Thank God!" she whispered, pulling her new baby daughter closer. Little Rock still slept. After helping Dooley bury the men they had killed, Zeke had been gone all night. He had insisted on burying them far away from the tipi, loading them on a travois and dragging them over the crest of a distant ridge. He buried them deep, with no mounds, so that eventually there would not even be a sign of the graves. He wanted no reminders of the night before and would not tell Abbie where the men were buried.

It was nearly sunrise when he returned. Abbie knew he had been tortured all night over her attack—feeling guilt because she had suffered and blaming himself for everything bad that happened to her just because he was a half-breed.

"Don't be too upset with him," Dooley was telling her. "He's hurting."

"I've been through this before, Dooley," she answered softly. "And I'm not one to be angry with a man for being gone all night . . . not a man like Zeke. He had to be alone."

Dooley nodded. "You're a good woman, Abigail, good for him."

She smiled. "It isn't hard to be good to him."

Dooley returned her smile. When they heard Zeke's horse come closer outside, Dooley stood up and left, exchanging a glance with Zeke before taking his horse for him.

"She's been waiting for you," he told Zeke. "Why don't you go in there and take a good look at that new baby girl. She's a damned purty little thing just like her ma."

Zeke looked back at him with red, tired eyes. "She all right?"

"If she wasn't, I'd have come looking for you. Figured you'd stay close enough to hear me holler if she needed you."

A faint smile passed over Zeke's lips. "I was close enough."

He put a hand on Dooley's shoulder. "Thanks for your help, Dooley."

Dooley just shrugged. "You've been good to me, letting me stay here and all. I'm going to my soddy to get some rest. And you'd best do the same. You look terrible." He winked at Zeke and led his horse away.

Zeke swallowed his doubts and hesitation and ducked inside the tipi. He stopped when he met her eyes. She looked beautiful, lying there with a new baby in her arms, their son asleep nearby. Everything was so peaceful it was hard to believe the terror of the night before.

"I'm sorry I got you into all this, Abbie girl, living in the middle of nowhere, having your babies with no doctor. You deserve better."

She looked at him steadily. "If you think I deserve the best, then I'm getting what I deserve. I have you, and my babies. My son and my daughter are healthy, and I'm living in this beautiful land with my beautiful husband. I'm happy, Zeke. There's nothing more I want."

He looked around the tipi with a frown; then he turned around, sighing deeply. "Oh, Abbie, Abbie," he said with a note of resignation. "I just don't know any more."

"Well, I do know! If we were living in a fancy house, those men would still have done what they did. They were after a woman and looking to steal horses. It wouldn't have mattered who I was. And women all have their babies the same way, whether it's in a fancy house or a tipi, with a doctor or by letting nature take its course. They nurse them and love them just like I do. Living where we do and the way we do—that doesn't make any difference at all!"

He shook his head, finally turning to face her. He came over and knelt beside her, touching his daughter's soft, red cheek with his big, rough hand. "Abbie, you have so many years ahead of you," he told her, his eyes watching the baby. "I hope you don't spend them regretting the day you married a half-breed who's given you nothing but a tipi and a hard life."

"Zeke Monroe!" she said chidingly. She reached up and touched his cheek, and he took her hand. "I sold my soul to you that first night you stepped into the light of my pa's campfire and offered to be our scout. Remember when I gave you that cup of coffee?"

"I remember," he answered, meeting her eyes.

She smiled and her eyes teared. "You touched me for just a moment, and I thought I'd up and die right there, I got such a tingle in my body!"

He smiled a little, almost bashfully, and she squeezed his hand. "I still get that tingle when my strong and handsome half-breed husband touches me," she continued. "My sister said once that if I married you, all I'd ever get was a tipi and ten kids, and I told her that was just fine with me, if you were the one I was getting pregnant by. I meant that, Zeke. That's why I made that vow to God to love you and be true to you for the rest of my life."

"But that's just it, Abbie. I'm afraid some day you'll sit back and wonder why in hell you did all this, wonder what life might have been like if you had gone back to Tennessee and married a nice, quiet white boy who farmed and—"

"Zeke!" she interrupted him with a frown. "What would I want with a boring life like that. And how dare you say I'd be so fickle as to think such things!" He looked at her, surprised at her anger, for her eyes began to blaze with determination and scorn for his remark. "I knew before I ever met you the kind of man I wanted. He was going to be all man, strong and sure, willing to die for me. It wouldn't matter what his station was in life, only that he was a real man who could be brave and never turn tail on a fight, but who'd be gentle with his woman. And I figured I'd set my sights too high, till I saw you that first time. It was like . . . like getting struck by lightning. I felt like God was all but pounding me over the head to tell me I'd best not ever let you out of my sight, and I didn't." Her eyes softened again. "We have to take one day at a time, Zeke. That's all we can do. We don't know what lies ahead. We only know there's you and me . . . and Little Rock and now our new daughter. We're together and safe. And I wouldn't take all the fancy houses and rich men in the world in exchange for life without my Zeke. You and I, Zeke. That's how it has to be. We can't let anything that happens destroy what we have—that special love we have."

He closed his eyes and held her hands tightly. "There's so much trouble ahead, Abbie, for this land, for the People—"

"There's nothing we can do about that, Zeke. All we can do is hang on to our love and never let anything that happens separate us. And God knows what stories we'll have to tell our grandchildren some day, Zeke Monroe, about how this land got settled and how you and I had a part in it. We've got to help the People through these bad times, and we can't do it if we have problems between us." She searched his troubled eyes pleadingly. "Don't let your anger get in the way of our love, Zeke. Don't let those awful men out there put doubts in your head about you and me."

He let go of her hand and stroked her hair back from her face. "Abbie, people will insult you because of me. They'll—"

"Let them!" she flashed. "Cheyenne Zeke is my man, and I'm damned proud of him. You're my legal husband, and I've got nothing to be ashamed about. What I'm ashamed of is you, Zeke Monroe! The way you're talking right now. Doubting my love for you when I just gave birth to your second child." Her words broke and tears of anger welled in her eyes.

He flinched, looking like a little boy who had been severely scolded, and she wanted to smile in spite of her tears; for although he still had blood on his leggings, the blood of the men he had so ferociously attacked, she had the power to reduce him to a scolded child.

She pulled her baby girl close to her breast. "You'd best get cleaned up," she told him quietly.

He sighed and rose obediently, not sure what to say to her. He went to the tipi entrance and stopped.

"Abbie, I'm sorry. I didn't mean—"

393

"I know you didn't, Zeke. It's just that I made a choice, and I don't want to have to worry about your doubting my love."

"I've never doubted that. I just . . . I love you so much. If I ever see you hurt bad because of me . . ." He left quietly without finishing.

The summer of 1849 brought two things that were much more devastating for the Cheyenne than all the bluecoats the East could have sent against them; they were worse than being attacked by every Pawnee tribe and all the Ute and Crow combined.

Gold was discovered in California. Not only did the gold bring a new surge of emigrants, who raped the land, killed the game, and shot the Indians without reason; but the emigrants themselves brought something much worse than their guns and destruction. They brought more disease.

At first the summer seemed peaceful enough. Little Rock was two years old that year, and Zeke and Abbie's daughter, named *Moheya*, meaning Blue Sky, was six months old when the news began to trickle in.

Cholera. It raged through the Pawnee and did more destruction than all the years of fighting with the Cheyenne. Before it was over, eleven hundred Pawnee had been wiped out, and it was rumored the Sioux had also suffered severely from the dreaded "big cramps."

Most were certain the disease had begun with polluted water, made that way by the thousands of westward travelers who left dead animals lying where they dropped in their tracks, and who bathed in the rivers and left behind a trail of garbage and human waste.

The disease seemed confined mostly to the Platte River area, so the northern Cheyenne began fleeing south, bringing the disease with them to the southern Cheyenne. The northerners didn't know what else to do but run to their brothers in the south, thinking that if they fled fast enough, the disease would be left behind. But it followed them, and men and women fell from their horses or fell in their tracks as they walked, screaming in agony from the horrible cramps, dying terrible and, to them, dishonorable deaths.

The numbers of the Cheyenne along the Arkansas were swelled by those fleeing from the north, and although after several weeks, the disease began to wane, it picked up again, becoming so bad that William Bent sent his own Cheyenne wife and half-breed sons east with other Cheyenne, away from the Santa Fe Trail, where the disease seemed to be most rampant. But before it was finished, the Cheyenne had lost nearly half their people.

The ravages of the disease signaled the end of many things for the Indians, for in that same year, with the fur trading business ruined by the decimation of so many Cheyenne, William Bent's business began to fold. Bent had flourished on Indian trade, but the demand for furs had dwindled, and that situation, combined with the loss of so many southern Cheyenne and the severe restrictions on the Indians' ability to hunt and trap, meant the fur trade was over.

A new era was coming, and the old fur trading posts were being turned into Army posts. No post was planned for Bent's Fort, and William Bent could not bear to see his fort sit and fall into ruin. So, once his wife had been sent away, he stripped the fort of its valuables, rolled powder kegs into the fort's main rooms, and set a torch to it. There was soon a great explosion and fire. The fort smoldered for days, and the mecca of the fur trade for the Cheyenne and the other Indians on the Arkansas River was no more. The end of Bent's Fort brought even more confusion to the Cheyenne, who saw their old way of life fading before their eyes.

By the fall of 1849, Gentle Woman had died of the horrible cholera, as well as little Magpie. Their loss cut deeply into Abbie's heart, and her soul cried out in agony as she watched Tall Grass Woman dig her nails into her cheeks and slash at her arms with a knife to express her grief over little Magpie. The little girl had died such a terrible death that Abbie wondered if perhaps she should have let the girl drown in the river the day she had dived in to save her.

Three days later brought Gentle Woman's final release from the painful sickness. Swift Arrow slashed his chest with a knife and cut off the end of a little finger in his grief over his mother. When Zeke's brothers committed similar self-mutilations, they were joined by Zeke, who again cut at his chest several times.

Abbie knelt to the ground in her grief, holding her children close to her, as Deer Slayer and his sons placed many gifts and beautiful jewelry and new moccasins on the scaffold that held Gentle Woman. Finally Abbie could bear it no longer. Her heart was as heavy as when her own mother had died, for Gentle Woman had truly been a mother to her. With patience and love, she had taught Abbie so many things. Her name had been most fitting. And Abbie's grief was made worse by the knowledge of how deeply this woman's death would affect Zeke, who had been so close to his Cheyenne mother—Zeke, who had searched for Gentle Woman years after being torn from her arms by his white father and who had promised Gentle Woman he would always come back. Now Gentle Woman was gone. She was the one who would not be coming back.

Abbie was filled with all the Cheyenne beliefs Gentle Woman had instilled in her soul, and she could not stop herself from digging into her own cheeks with her fingernails. She wanted to hurt. She wanted to feel pain. It was necessary.

By 1850, Fitzpatrick was again talking treaty, but this time it was serious talk. There was a new superintendent in St. Louis, named Mitchell, and he agreed that a treaty was needed. Most tribes still ran wild and were confused as to their rights and territories. The government was awakening to the fact that the Plains tribes could not be forced into anything with military show, that infantry was useless against these experienced and very skilled warriors, and that cavalry mounts could not match Indian mounts. And most important, a treaty seemed a much less costly answer to the Indian problem than a war.

A treaty council was planned for the summer of 1850, so the wheels began rolling in Washington, but very slowly. Because of the involvement of Congress in the Compromise of 1850, its members were slow in attending to the problems of the Indians, and money was not appropriated for enactment of the treaty until February of 1851.

During all this time, Fitzpatrick crossed the Plains, holding small meetings with tribes and trying desperately to keep them calm. Finally he convinced most of the southern Cheyenne and Arapaho to begin a journey north to Fort Laramie for a great meeting. The Indians saw a ray of hope. They would go and sit in on this council. Besides, it had been a long time since they had gone north and met with their Sioux brothers. It would be good for them all to be together again, to feast and dance. They could hold ceremonies that might bring them the strength and wisdom they would need to cope with the changes taking place in their lives.

Zeke and Abbie prepared to accompany them northward, for Zeke wanted to see for himself just what kind of promises the government intended to make. And both he and Abbie looked forward to the trip, which would be good for them all.

Abbie would again ride like a squaw woman, carrying her little girl papoose on her back. Little Rock would ride proudly in front of his father on his father's finest Appaloosa, and Zeke would take some of his herd along to sell at Fort Laramie, for Bent's Fort, at which he had done business, no longer existed. Yes, it would be good to make the trip. They packed a travois and made ready for the journey; meanwhile the pile of logs still lay where it had remained for nearly three years. The cabin still had not been built.

*   *   *

Susan Garvey and the doctor laughed and rolled on the bed together, lost in another sexual interlude. They did not share a love affair, merely naughty games for the thrills and pleasures they brought them. But this time their fun was interrupted by Senator Winston Garvey, who had paid a servant to tell him the truth about his wife and the doctor, about whom he had become suspicious. He had only to surprise them to get his final proof.

The bedroom door burst open, and the doctor jumped up from the bed, wide-eyed with fright and staring at the enraged senator. Susan screamed and curled up, pulling the covers over herself.

"Get the hell out of my house!" Garvey sneered at the doctor.

The doctor was speechless. He quickly put on his pants and grabbed his black bag, not even giving Susan a backward glance as he rushed past the senator, his face beet red. Garvey slammed the bedroom door, and Susan began whimpering and shaking her head as he came closer to her.

"Winston, I . . . I'll let you do . . . whatever you want!" she whimpered. "I'm so sorry, Winston! Please, don't hurt me! You can come to our bed whenever you wish! Don't turn me out, Winston! Don't tell anyone about this! Please, Winston!"

He backhanded her across the face and she screamed. He ripped the covers away from her and began unbuttoning his pants.

"You are going to lie here, my sweet, and you're going to let me do whatever I wish. You owe me. You owe me plenty!"

He grasped her hair and pulled it until she screamed again.

"You slut!" he growled. "You filthy tramp! All this time telling me you couldn't lie with me because pregnancy might kill you!" He hit her again. "Well, my sweet wife, I'll have you all I want and whenever I want, and in a day or two you'll get your ass to Santa Fe! Because after I'm through with you, I won't want to look at you for a while. If I do, I just might kill you!"

He hit her again, and she began crying uncontrollably. He smiled, laying his full, heavy weight over her naked body. "In two days you'll be on your way west, my dear," he told her. "I might hate your guts, but I still like your lovely little body, and you like the importance of my name, so we just might get along after all. You can pay for your keep like a whore by letting me bed you. And maybe you'll get lucky on your way to Santa Fe and get raped by some Indian buck. I'll bet you'd just love that!" he sneered.

She covered her face and wept, as his lips moved down over her body. "By the way," he told her as he groped between her legs. "Don't think you can make arrangements with your doctor lover to go out there with you. I've already made plans for the doctor's untimely death."

She cried harder, but he was not touched. He proceeded to take her forcibly, feeling a certain excitement at the sound of her weeping.

The stagecoach clattered over the Santa Fe Trail, carrying the prim, proper, and beautiful senator's wife and their little four-year-old son, Charles. Susan Garvey held her head high, for she noticed the way the men looked at her at the stage stops, as though she were a goddess. She would be a queen out here, admired by all. And no one would know about her affair with the doctor.

She turned to straighten Charles' bow tie and her son smiled up at her, excited by this new adventure. She had decided that perhaps she liked her son after all, for he was an obedient boy and he did seem to love her, in spite of the cold way she treated him. She had tried her best to keep him away, but he always came around wanting a hug, like a dog always wanting to be petted even though its master kicks it every time it comes near.

Charles was like that. A sweet boy . . . too sweet. But children were such a bother, and he had caused her pain when he was born. She tried to love him, but could find no feelings for her son. Perhaps that was because she could see traces of his father, the fat senator, in her son's eyes. Perhaps that was why she hated him.

Susan also hated the dirty, dusty, hot country through which the stage now bounced and rumbled. This land could ruin a woman's skin in no time at all. Still, she felt lucky to still be married to the senator. He had forgiven her and had promised that as soon as she reached Santa Fe she could stay in the finest hotel while she supervised the building of their mansion. He had promised she could have any kind of house she wished, and she would make sure it was nothing short of a castle. It would be exciting! Everything she needed would be shipped from the East. The West would be their kingdom and she would be its queen. For that she would put up with the senator. She would simply wait for him to die. At her age, she would still be young and beautiful enough to have her share of men once her husband was gone.

Her thoughts were interrupted by sudden gunshots and war cries, and she frowned and looked out the window of the coach to see half-naked Indians chasing them.

"Comanches!" she heard the driver shout. "What the hell are they doin' this close to Santa Fe!"

A small troop of soldiers had accompanied them most of the way, but there had been an Indian skirmish a few miles to the north, and with the stage being so close to Santa Fe, the driver had told the soldiers to go ahead and see to the problem. Now only two soldiers accompanied the stage, and before Susan's horrified eyes, both fell from their mounts in quick succession, arrows in their backs!

The driver whipped the horses into going faster, and the coach lurched forward. Susan screamed and crouched to the floor, leaving her little boy confused and afraid. She was not concerned for his welfare—only her own—and she wondered if the Indians might take the boy in exchange for her own life if it became necessary. That would be a good way to get rid of

400

Charles and save her own skin.

To her, it seemed hours rather than minutes that they were chased, bullets and arrows whizzing by the coach while it rattled and rocked and bounced over the trail. Then Susan heard the driver cry out. Little Charles huddled near his mother between the seats, crying. The shooting continued, as the rifleman hired to accompany the driver continued his duty of fighting the raiding Indians, but there were too many. An arrow pierced his skull, and his body rolled off the coach.

The unattended coach and its horses ran wild, then hit a large rock and flipped over, breaking loose at the tongue while the horses thundered on, chased by some of the Comanches. Susan was tossed against the side of the crashing coach and everything went black. The grand life she had planned to lead in Santa Fe was not to be. Susan Garvey was dead.

Moments later the Comanches reached the coach, to find a little boy standing over his mother crying. They discussed whether or not to steal the boy, but they decided his crying meant he would not make a good warrior. Besides, taking a white boy would bring them much trouble. When they stared down at the woman, they decided her pretty hair would make a fine scalp, and Little Charles watched in horror as they deftly removed his mother's hair from her head. Then they took the driver's weapons and stole all the luggage and supplies that were on the coach before setting fire to it.

"Cheyenne!" one of the Comanches said to the little boy. "Say Cheyenne!" The raider laughed. It would be a good joke on the Cheyenne when the little boy told the soldiers it was Cheyenne who had done the raiding. He mounted his horse and rode off with the others.

Little Charles stood beside the burning coach and watched the "Cheyenne" ride away. He hated them for taking his mother's hair. Tears streamed down his cheeks, and he trembled with hatred and fright. He knew by instinct that his mother would not wake up again, so he watched the Indians

401

until they were out of sight.

Charles Garvey would not forget this day, not for the rest of his life. He knew that he would hate Indians forever . . . all Indians. Some day he would be big and important like his daddy, and he would make the Indians suffer—especially the Cheyenne!

Twenty

It was one grand migration, a sight that Abigail Monroe would not forget through all the turbulent years that lay ahead of her. The walk to Laramie was like walking toward the light at the end of a tunnel. It was a walk filled with great hope, not only for the Cheyenne, but for the Oglala and Brule Sioux, the Shoshoni, the Arapaho, and the Crow Indians.

Kiowas and Comanches, who feared the Sioux would try to steal their horses, would not attend. They had not yet learned that making a treaty with the Great White Father was more important than warring among the tribes. Those who did head for Laramie were beginning to understand that they must band together and try to forget old grudges, for there was power in numbers. And even though they understood that this treaty primarily would set aside land for the Cheyenne only, they also understood it was the beginning of bargaining with the Great White Father for all tribes. They came to learn, and to try to cooperate with the Great White Father's plea for the tribes to stop warring among themselves, for they knew that as long as they remained divided, white settlers would find it easier to take their land.

They came from all directions: Shoshoni and Crow from the west, Cheyenne and Arapaho from the south and southeast, the Sioux from the north and east. In great, colorful, impressive tribal order they came, dressed for the occasion in their most honored war paint and bonnets, their ponies painted, their tipis and clothing and faces painted, beads and hairpipes wound beautifully into their glossy black hair, bows and arrows and lances decorated with brilliant feathers.

They did not all arrive at once. The Cheyenne arrived first, and Zeke sold several horses inside the fort for a good price to soldiers and scouts who were eager to acquire these fine mounts. For the first few days Abbie stayed away from the fort, remaining within their tipi, which was staked with those of Swift Arrow's clan amid the greater circle of tribal dwellings.

It was a happy time for Zeke and Abbie. Four-year-old Little Rock ran wild and free through the camps, playing with the other Indian children, shooting his toy bow and stick arrows, and sometimes riding the pinto pony his father had given him for his very own. Already, Little Rock was as natural on a horse as his father and uncles; and wearing only leggings, with his straight, black hair hanging over the deep brown skin of his shoulders nearly to his waist, Little Rock bore no resemblance to his white mother. He was Cheyenne, totally and completely. He could speak the tongue fluently, as well as his mother's English, and he was a bright, proud child. When Swift Arrow would take the boy with him to ride, he would tell Little Rock about the warrior ways, and Little Rock would hold up his chin proudly and screech out war cries in his little-boy voice.

Blue Sky, almost two now, still spent some of her time inside her cradleboard, contented as long as the board was situated near her mother. She was a shy, quiet child, insistent on being near Abbie during all of her waking hours, clinging to her mother's skirts and following her around whenever she was not snug and safe in her cradleboard. She was dark and beautiful, with the kind of beauty that seems to come only to those born of two different races. Her eyes were large and surrounded by long, dark lashes; her tiny face was perfect and fetching, her skin as smooth as satin. To Zeke, she was a vision of perfection. Both his children were the source of his greatest pride and joy, and they were the root of his deepening love for the woman who had delivered them.

Those first three weeks of waiting for the arrival of more Indians and for the government men were a time of celebration for the Cheyenne and for Zeke and Abbie, whose pleasure was marred only by the absence of Gentle Woman. Zeke's mother was sorely missed, and her death had embittered Swift Arrow's heart even more, for again the white man's disease had claimed someone he loved. Zeke and Abbie both feared the trouble that lay ahead because of Swift Arrow's haughty dislike of most whites, as well as the growing problem of alcohol among the Cheyenne. Red Eagle's own addiction now seemed permanent, and even the birth of a son by Yellow Moon that summer did nothing to thwart his drinking.

Red Eagle had been expelled from his tipi numerous times after spells of drunkenness when he beat his wife, and all knew it would not be long before poor Yellow Moon would give up and divorce herself from the relationship. Red Eagle was fast becoming an unfit husband, who would rather drink than go and hunt for the game necessary for the feeding and sheltering of his family. Whenever Zeke or Swift Arrow or Black Elk, or even the ruling members of Red Eagle's warrior society, tried to talk to him about his drinking, Red Eagle would only get angry and want to fight them.

It was a vicious circle of dependence for Red Eagle, one that had been going on for six years and was likely to bring him banishment from his family as well as his warrior society. But Red Eagle seemed concerned only over where his next bottle of whiskey would come from.

For now, Zeke had decided he would not allow Gentle Woman's death or Red Eagle's drinking to ruin the pleasant break the trip to Fort Laramie had become for himself and Abbie. In the five years since he had brought his new young bride to his people down on the Arkansas, Abbie had seen mostly hardship. Before that, she had suffered incredible emotional torment at the loss of her family. She had given him two children, still they lived in the tipi she had helped sew with her own hands. She did not have the house he had promised her, for they had both been too involved with helping the People survive and with the dangers of life near the turbulent Santa Fe Trail, where raiding had continued even after the war with Mexico was over. It had been impossible to work steadily on anything; and so, all they had done so far was notch out the ends of the logs for the corner fittings and lay the first two tiers of the foundation logs. This year Comanches had raided them, and Abbie had been taken to Swift Arrow's camp for protection while Zeke and Dooley had rounded up Zeke's scattered herd. That had taken most of the spring and summer, and then they had to leave to go to Laramie.

Zeke watched Abbie now, thinking how hard the past five years had been. Yet she remained uncomplaining. At the moment she carried little Blue Sky, who often refused to be put down. Abbie talked softly to her shy, clinging daughter, giving her a kiss and placing her in her cradleboard. Abbie was a good mother, a doting, coddling mother, much like the Cheyenne women. She never raised her voice or grew impatient, and never once had she brought up the fact that she still did not have a house, or a mantel for her clock, or a hearth where she could rock her children. She seemed content now just to be with the People again, and she had been as excited as a child over the trip to Fort Laramie.

Zeke watched her. She was Abbie—just Abbie—the woman-child he had branded and claimed. She had only been fifteen then. Now she was twenty-one, and the lovely child he had claimed was blossoming into a gentle and beautiful woman, who had nearly forgotten what it was like to live as she had been born to live.

It was a mild autumn dusk, and the air smelled fresh and sweet. Zeke felt invigorated by the trip and by his present happiness. At the fort he had seen some men he knew from the days of the rendezvous, and he decided that they and the white soldiers should meet his beloved wife and know the truth. It was time for more than just the Cheyenne and a few white men at Bent's Fort to know of Abbie's existence, and time for

Abigail Monroe to remember she had white skin.

"Abbie!" he called out to her. She turned quickly, causing the fringes of her doeskin tunic to dance fetchingly. A wave of desire coming over him, he thought that bearing two children had added a pleasing fullness to her figure in just the right places. "Put on that blue dress I bought you back at Bent's Fort."

She frowned curiously. "Zeke, it's surely wrinkled from being folded for so long!" He came closer as she spoke. "The only reason I even have it along is because we had to bring practically all our belongings with us so the Comanche wouldn't steal our things while we were gone, and—"

He put his fingers to her lips. "You've not worn that pretty dress since I bought it for you. Get it out and heat the flat of a skillet and press it." He looked lovingly at her hair. "And unbraid your hair. Brush it out and pull it back at the sides." He reached into a small pocket on his buckskin shirt and pulled out two blue ribbons he had purchased secretly for her at the fort. "Here. Tie it back with these."

She took the ribbons from his hand and, looking at them curiously, met his eyes. "Zeke, I don't understand."

"I'm taking my woman into the fort tonight to meet some friends of mine and to show her off to the soldiers. I'm taking my mandolin with me, and me and a man I know there who plays a fiddle are going to make some genuine Tennessee music, and if a scout or a soldier there wants to dance with my woman, he has my permission, long as he stays in my sight and watches how he touches her, because it's been a long time since my woman danced to white man's music and whirled her skirts and showed off just how pretty she is."

She reddened and looked down at the ribbons again. "Zeke, we don't have to—"

He reached out and gently lifted her chin. "Yes, we do. We'll take the young ones with us, and everyone will see our little brown babies and understand that you and me are man and wife and live in two worlds. And every last one of them will

407

respect you or answer to me!"

Her eyes began to show their excitement. "Oh, Zeke, I haven't dressed that way for so long! I . . . I don't even know if that dress fits me!" She put a hand to her bosom when she said it, and she suddenly blushed, realizing she had filled out in the bodice; Zeke had bought the dress before Little Rock had been born. Zeke flashed the handsome smile that made her blush even deeper.

"If it's a little snug, you'll just look prettier," he told her.

She pushed at him and put her hands to her hot cheeks. Their eyes held and hers filled with love for her gentle half-breed husband, whose knife and ruthlessness were feared by so many men. It seemed impossible sometimes that the man who wielded the knife was the same man who bedded her so gently.

"Will you wear the white doeskin shirt that makes you look so handsome?" she asked him.

He grinned almost sheepishly. "I'll wear it for you."

"And promise to play the mandolin and sing for me?"

"I promise."

Their eyes held a moment longer, and then she dashed off to dig out the blue dress.

Blue Sky started to whimper and Zeke pulled her from her cradleboard, tossing her into the air and making her giggle. The child was content with her father, whose strong arms always comforted her when she was afraid.

"Don't cry, my little Blue Sky," Zeke told her. "Tonight we are going to take you and your brother to meet some of your mother's people, and they all will see my beautiful wife and children." He swung her around to sit on his shoulders. "Let's go find Little Rock. I'll bet my little warrior is off riding his pony again!"

Lt. Daniel Monroe sat down to his desk to work. He had just ridden into Fort Laramie that morning, straight from Fort Leavenworth, where for the past six months he had been on special assignment recruiting men for the Western Army. He was finally back at Laramie, the place he now considered home. He had learned much about the Plains Indians since he had been stationed here, and he liked Wyoming Territory . . . and the Indians. He was proud of his new gold second lieutenant's bar. He had worked hard to earn his rank, and the breast of his uniform also sported the gold medal he had earned in the Mexican War. It was set off by a bright green-, gold- and red-striped ribbon. He was happy here, his feelings of accomplishment marred only by the fact that he still had not found his half-blood brother.

Danny had not gone out yet to meet the leaders of the Cheyenne and Arapaho or those of the Sioux who now surrounded Fort Laramie by the thousands. The sight was an impressive one as he rode in that morning, and it was more than a little frightening. For the Indians, angry and troubled, were a passionate people, quick to defend their honor. Danny had spent a good share of the day going over with his men what their instructions were in case there was trouble. Under no circumstances was one shot to be fired without orders. That was the first rule.

"One shot could excite them into an all-out state of confusion and lead to more trouble," he had told his men earlier. "We are here to talk peace, not to create a senseless war." His men had listened and would obey, for although their lieutenant seemed much too young to be an officer, he had a knack for winning a man's respect. Most of them knew about the brave act he had committed down in Mexico that had earned him his first promotion. In these Western lands, a man was not surprised by anything that he saw, including a youthful officer with medals on his chest.

Danny began signing some papers for government issue of Army supplies, but he couldn't stop wondering about all the unrest brewing with the Indians, let alone all of the other problems that necessitated a buildup of the Western Army. He sat back and pondered for a moment on the lawlessness of this land that was filling up with prostitutes and outlaws and gamblers, land-hungry profiteers and cheating traders, and renegade Mexican outlaws. Now there were gangs who dealt in gun smuggling and the slave-trading of women. Such outlaws were running rampant, raiding supply trains and feeding off of others, selling guns and women to Mexicans for gold. There was a rumor that the leader of one of the most notorious of these outlaw gangs was a woman, an Indian woman whose beauty had been marred when she'd had the letter Z carved into both her cheeks. This was an intriguing tale and probably true, for many had seen her, and many had suffered one of her vicious raids. It was amazing that a woman could be at the head of cruel outlaws, but in the West, nothing was truly surprising.

He sighed and returned to his papers. Right now his problem was helping to keep the peace at Fort Laramie while government representatives made promises and offers that were intended to appease the restless, angry redmen. Only six weeks earlier, a senator's wife had been killed in a stagecoach accident on the Santa Fe Trail while being chased by Indians. Her poor little son had cried that Cheyenne Indians were the culprits who lifted his mother's scalp, but the arrows found in the drivers belonged to Comanches. It was not like the Cheyenne to do such raiding. Most whites didn't know one Indian from another. That made his job more difficult and would create even more problems for the Indians.

His thoughts were again interrupted when a young private came through the doorway and saluted. Danny rose and returned the salute.

"At ease," he told the man, returning to his seat. "Come in."

The private entered and stood at Danny's desk.

"How goes it, Mead?" Danny asked. "Are the Indians quiet?"

"Yes, sir. There's a little singing and drinking going on, sir, but they don't seem to be getting out of hand or causing any problems."

"Good." Danny returned to his papers. "Thank you, Mead. Go on back out there and keep your ears open."

The young man hesitated. "Sir?"

Danny looked up at him. "Yes? I thought you were through, Private Mead."

Mead shuffled his feet. "Well, sir, I just thought you should know there's . . . there's a white woman just outside the fort, sir, dancing with one or two of the scouts . . . just innocent dancing, Tennessee high stepping, that sort of thing."

Danny frowned. "I've been listening to the fiddle music and some other instrument. Kind of like a guitar or harp or something. But so what? There have been white women around the fort before, from the wagon trains. We have three women here right now."

"I know, sir, but . . ." The man hesitated again and Danny set down his quill pen and frowned.

"But what, Mead?"

"Well, sir, the other instrument you heard was what they call a mandolin, and the man who's playing it is this woman's husband and . . . he's a half-breed, sir. I'm told they live most of the time among the Cheyenne, down on the Arkansas. Don't you think that's strange, sir? A white woman living among the Cheyenne?"

Danny leaned back, surprised. "I have to agree with you there, Mead." He thought for a moment. "You sure she's all white?"

"Yes, sir. No doubt about it. The scout I spoke with says she usually wears deerskin tunics, like the Cheyenne women, and she and her half-breed husband live in a tipi, and they have two little ones, both of them dark as any Indian. This girl, sir, they say she's from Tennessee, and so is her half-breed husband, so they say. Something about being a wanted man there."

Danny frowned, slowly rising from his chair, his heart pounding. "Wanted? In Tennessee?"

"Yes, sir."

Danny came around the desk and stood beside the private.

411

"Did they tell you the half-breed's name?" he asked excitedly.

The private looked at him curiously, surprised by the lieutenant's sudden and intense reaction. He swallowed. "Yes, sir. It's Zeke, Cheyenne Zeke, better known as Lone Eagle to the Cheyenne."

Danny's eyes glistened with tears of hope. "Zeke! Are you sure, Mead?"

"Sure of what they told me, sir."

Danny turned away, afraid to hope against hope it could be his half brother.

"Excuse me, sir, but . . . do you know this man?"

Danny took a deep breath to prevent tears from coming and he nodded to the private. "Oh, yes!" he replied in a near whisper. "If it's who I think it is, he's my half brother, Private Mead. I've not seen him since he left Tennessee, almost twelve years ago!"

Mead's eyebrows arched in surprise. "Brother, sir?"

"Yes," Danny replied, smiling through tears the private could not see. "He's the reason I originally came West, Private Mead." He sighed deeply. "I think I'll go listen to some Tennessee hoedown music, Private." He turned and smiled, and the private was touched by the tears in the man's eyes. "Dismissed, Private," Danny told him. Mead saluted and smiled.

"Congratulations, sir. I hope it's the same man."

"Thank you, Private. So do I." He returned the salute and Mead left. Danny straightened his uniform and donned his officer's hat. He felt sweaty with nervousness and took deep breaths to control his excitement, but he said a quick prayer before heading out the door. He walked in the direction of the music.

The small crowd that had gathered around the music makers included the fort's cook and a soldier's wife. She whispered to the cook as they watched.

"Do you suppose that young woman is truly married to that . . . that Indian man?"

The cook watched Zeke for a moment, listening to his mellow voice and the soft music of the mandolin, while the pretty white woman in the blue dress sat beside him on a log, holding a charming small Indian girl.

"Why not?" the stout cook replied. "That 'Indian' man is the most handsome specimen I've seen in all my fifty years."

The soldier's wife frowned. "Martha! He's an Indian!"

Martha smiled. "He may look Indian, but he certainly doesn't sound like one. He must at least be half white."

The other woman shook her head. "That's even worse!"

"'I met a girl from Tennessee,'" Zeke sang softly in his smooth, mellow voice, smiling at Abbie as he sang. The music drifted romantically through the night air. "'She was pretty as she could be. Took my heart and won't set it free . . . that girl from Tennessee.'"

Lieutenant Monroe walked up behind the crowd to listen, moving quietly toward one of his scouts as the music picked up again and soldiers and scouts laughed and clapped and stamped their feet while Zeke strummed the mandolin and the fiddler behind him moved bow and fingers rapidly as Zeke sang "Big Rock Candy Mountain."

A trapper bowed to Abbie and tilted his hat toward Zeke for permission to dance with his wife. Zeke just grinned and nodded as he sang the happy song, and Abbie blushed and set little Blue Sky on the log. The trapper took her hands and they side-stepped to the music, while Little Rock clapped his hands and jumped up and down to the music and Blue Sky moved over to cling to her father's pantleg.

Danny watched, moving up beside a scout who was looking on and waiting for his turn at a dance. The grinning scout turned, surprised to see the lieutenant there.

"Evening, sir!"

"Hello, Boston."

"Just doin' a little singin' and dancin'. The Injuns has been

413

doin' their version of the same. Just thought we'd make a little white man's music tonight. The half-breed there, he kin sing either way."

Danny grinned and watched Zeke, more sure than ever he was his half brother. He turned his gaze to Abbie and grinned more. So, his brother had married another white woman. It was good to know he had found happiness again.

"Purty, ain't she?" Boston told the lieutenant with a grin.

"Very," Danny replied, thinking to himself that the girl must be even younger than he, and perhaps eight or ten years younger than Zeke.

"The half-breed got himself one purty lady there," the scout was saying. "Would you believe she even lives with the Cheyenne a lot of the time, just because her husband there prefers to live with his Indian half?" The scout shook his head. "She must be some woman, givin' up a white woman's ways to live like a squaw most of the time. One of the other men says he heard her say this was the first time she'd worn a white woman's dress in years."

Danny watched in fascination, glancing at the two children who stood beside their father. "What else do you know about the half-breed, Boston?"

Boston shrugged. "Just that he spent part of his life in Tennessee. And he's got one hell of a reputation with that big blade he wears. I'll tell you one thing, I pity any of these men here who'd dare try to move in on that little white gal he married or treat her disrespectful. Cheyenne Zeke ain't a man to mess with. They say he can throw that blade as fast as a good gunman can draw his gun, and he always hits his mark."

Danny studied Zeke. The white buckskin shirt he wore accented his brother's handsomeness. The weapons belt he wore at his waist held a sidearm and two knives, one small one and one of menacing size, its buffalo jawbone handle protruding from a large, brightly beaded sheath that obviously held a big blade.

414

Zeke began to sing a slow tune, and Danny moved to the center of the celebrating as Zeke sang "'Love, oh love, oh careless love.'" Danny was a tall, well-built, handsome figure in his deep blue uniform, both he and Zeke having inherited their builds from their father, who was a big man. He stepped up to Abbie, and bowed low, the gold, fringed epaulets on his shoulders making him seem even broader and creating a striking, impression.

"May I?" he asked.

Abbie blushed at this surprising intrusion by an officer. She hesitated and looked at Zeke, who stopped his singing. He had not minded the rough-hewn scouts and their innocent dancing with his pretty wife, but this was different. This was a handsome young, blue-eyed lieutenant in an impressive uniform. Perhaps the uniform would turn Abbie's head. Here was a man who could offer her the kind of life she had given up, and jealousy sprang up in his heart as he looked darkly at the blond-haired lieutenant who sported a neat mustache. The lieutenant tipped his hat and grinned.

"May I dance with your wife?" he asked Zeke.

Their eyes held.

Abbie thought there was something vaguely familiar about the man: he actually resembled Zeke a little when he smiled. A strange silence hung in the air.

"I . . . I'll just sit down on this one," Abbie spoke up, worried about the look in Zeke's eyes.

"No!" Zeke answered. "Dance with the lieutenant, Abbie girl," he said rather coldly.

Abbie swallowed and looked from Zeke to the lieutenant, who grinned and removed his hat, handing it over to Boston. He put his hand to Abbie's waist and Zeke began strumming the mandolin. Abbie looked protestingly at Zeke, but he looked down and began singing again as the lieutenant took her hand and began gently whirling her in slow circles to the music. She was compelled to put her left hand on the lieutenant's shoulder

415

and follow his steps, while Zeke finished his song.

"Love, oh love, oh careless love . . .
Just look what careless love has done."

He sang more, repeating the lines as the fiddler played the tune in a whining, romantic wail and hummed in harmony with Zeke.

When the number was finished, Danny kept his hand at Abbie's waist, enjoying the game he was playing with his brother, testing Zeke's jealousy and wondering how long it would take Zeke to realize who he was. Boldly, he bent down and kissed Abbie's cheek before she realized his intentions.

Abbie's eyes widened in indignation, and Zeke was immediately on his feet, setting down the mandolin and storming up to the two of them, stepping between Abbie and the young lieutenant, his eyes blazing.

"Appears to me you take advantage of a man's generosity!" Zeke growled. "Perhaps you'd not be so sure of yourself if I cut off a few of them golden curls, Lieutenant!" He reached for his knife, but several soldiers had already surrounded him, their rifles cocked.

"Zeke, don't!" Abbie begged.

Danny just grinned. "Put your guns away, men," he told the other soldiers, his eyes on Zeke's. "I was just kissing my sister-in-law—welcoming her into the family."

Zeke's eyes turned from angry to confused.

"I wish you'd take your hand off that knife, Zeke. This is one hell of a way to greet your little brother after twelve years!"

Abbie's eyes widened, and Zeke frowned, studying the blue eyes intently.

"Don't you recognize me, Zeke?" Danny ran a hand over his mustache. "Maybe it's this thing." He studied Zeke's tall, broad frame. "Jesus, I think you're even bigger than when you left Tennessee, brother. I thought you were through growing back then."

Zeke stepped back and looked him over. "Danny?" he finally asked.

Danny bowed. "I've been looking for you, Zeke, for a good long time. Came out here five years ago to find you . . . ended up in the Army."

Zeke glanced at Abbie, who was beginning to smile. He looked back at his brother, his eyes softening and a smile beginning to show. "Danny!" he said, smiling more. "But you're . . . you're supposed to be a kid!"

"I was, when you left!" Danny laughed. "That was twelve years ago!"

Zeke finally broke into a full grin and they grasped hands, teasingly testing one another's strength as they shook hands, then hugging spontaneously.

"I'll be goddamned!" Zeke swore, slapping the lieutenant on the back. They both laughed and then stood back to look each other over. "I guess I don't need to ask how you've been," Zeke laughed. "You look great . . . healthy . . . handsome . . . and what's with the gold bar, little brother!" Zeke fingered the emblem, while others watched in curious surprise. "And what's this? A medal of bravery!" Zeke continued, tugging at the striped ribbon.

Danny smiled almost bashfully. "I made the stupid mistake of diving in front of a bullet a few years back down in Mexico, dodged in front of my commanding officer and quite by accident saved his life. Earned myself the medal, and a promotion."

Zeke firmly gripped his shoulders. "So, you're a hero, are you?"

Danny shook his head. "Of sorts, I guess." He glanced at Abbie. "You going to formally introduce me to this beautiful lady I had the pleasure of dancing with?"

Zeke smiled and pulled Abbie close to him. "Danny, this is Abigail. Met her when I was scouting for a wagon train six years ago." He sobered. "Abbie lost her whole family on the trip and, well, it's a long story. At any rate, she snared

417

me good."

Abbie blushed and put out her hand to Danny. The lieutenant eyed her up and down, admiring the way she filled out the bodice of her dress. He grasped her hand. "I'm very glad to meet you, Abbie."

"And it's wonderful meeting one of Zeke's brothers from Tennessee!" she replied. Danny squeezed her hand.

"I'm so happy to see Zeke found someone who—" He sobered and looked up at Zeke, letting go of Zeke's hand. Their eyes held, and Zeke knew Danny was wondering about Ellen and the murders back in Tennessee. "Let's go to my office. We have a lot to talk about, Zeke."

Zeke nodded. "We do, Danny." He turned and reached down to pick up Blue Sky. "Danny, this is our daughter, *Moheya*, Blue Sky. And the little boy running over there and howling like a warrior is our son, *Hohanino-o*, Little Rock. He's been half-raised by my Cheyenne half brother, Swift Arrow, and he's all Indian!"

"I can see that!" Both men laughed, but worry shone in Danny's eyes when he looked back at his brother. "Zeke, if you're living part of the time with the Cheyenne, you're going to have a lot of problems."

"We're aware of that. Let's go talk, Danny. You want to know about Ellen, and I want to know what's in store for my people."

Danny took Abbie's arm and started walking toward the fort, while the crowd looked after them in disbelief. An Indian and a fair-haired officer—brothers!

"I'd like to meet your Cheyenne brother, Zeke," Danny was saying.

"Actually I have three Cheyenne brothers, Danny. But Swift Arrow is the most rebellious of the three. I'm not sure whether he'd think it's bad luck or good that I have a brother who's a bluecoat."

Danny smiled and shook his head. "I hope that doesn't put you in a fix, Zeke." He looked at Abbie for a moment as they walked, Zeke carrying Blue Sky and Little Rock running behind them. "I must say, Abigail, you must be some woman, agreeing to desert your natural way of life to live half the time with Indians."

Abbie smiled bashfully. "After Zeke's experience in Tennessee, he felt it would be best," she replied.

Danny frowned. "Well, I can tell you must love my brother very much. Not many white women would do such a thing—live in a tipi and all. Most of the soldiers can't even get their wives to come out here to the fort to live, even though they would have fine quarters. St. Louis is about as far as they'll go."

They went inside the office, and Zeke was impressed and pleased to know his "little" brother held such an important position. Danny nervously pulled out chairs for them all, and Abbie sat down hesitantly, feeling strangely awkward and out of place in the dress and sitting on a hard chair.

"I'll get you some whiskey, Zeke. Good whiskey," Danny told his brother.

Blue Sky crawled up on Abbie's lap and put her head on her mother's shoulder, and Little Rock stood staring around the room, intrigued by the wooden floors, the strange furnishings, and the cabinet full of rifles in the corner.

Danny poured himself and Zeke a drink, bringing the glasses over to his desk. "Abbie, would you like some lemonade? I can have someone fetch some from the cook's quarters. We have ice for it."

Abbie smiled eagerly. "Oh, yes! I haven't had lemonade in a very long time."

Danny grinned and walked to the door, calling out to someone to bring a pitcher of lemonade and three glasses. "We'll let the little ones try some," he told her as he walked back to his desk. He sat down behind it, and Little Rock stood behind his father's chair, peeking around wide-eyed at the fascinating light-headed man with the blue eyes and dark uniform with gold buttons.

419

When Danny grinned and winked at the boy, Zeke turned and said something to Little Rock in the Cheyenne tongue. The boy pointed at Danny and replied in Cheyenne. Zeke nodded. The boy spoke again and Zeke laughed.

"He can't understand how you and Swift Arrow can both be his uncles and look so different," he told Danny. "I'll have a time explaining this to him!"

They both laughed and Zeke sipped his whiskey while the room quieted.

"I can't believe I've finally found you, Zeke," Danny spoke up after drinking some of his own whiskey. "I looked for a long time. Originally, I only joined the army for grub and a little pay while I looked for you. Then I got mixed up in that Mexican thing, and well . . . here I am! I asked for Western duty so I could keep looking for you."

Zeke sighed and looked at his whiskey. "I thought about you a lot, Danny. Especially you. But I couldn't go back to Tennessee."

Danny glanced at the knife again, aware of the size and the dark, wild look of his half-blood brother. He remembered the horror stories about the murders in Tennessee. He leaned forward, resting his elbows on his desk.

"Tell me, Zeke. What really happened back there? When you so gently and patiently cured that puppy of mine, I guess it was then I decided you were my favorite brother. And I couldn't believe you'd kill your own wife and son. You loved Ellen."

Abbie's heart was suddenly heavy, for she knew it was difficult for Zeke to talk about the murders. Zeke twirled his glass in his hand and did not reply right away. He shifted in his chair, and the tenseness of his emotions already seemed to vibrate from his body, filling the room and making it seem close and warm.

"They killed her," he replied quietly. "When I got there, she wasn't even dead yet. My little boy was . . . lying on the floor with his head"—his hands began to tremble, and Abbie

420

looked away from him—"his head chopped off," Zeke went on. "And Ellen was . . . alive enough to tell me there were eight of them . . . all men who knew her . . . men she'd called friend!"

He growled the words and quickly drank the rest of the whiskey; then he stood up and walked over to the gun cabinet, his back to his brother. "They all . . . took turns with her, Danny, with my woman!" He whirled, his dark eyes frightening, and Danny Monroe could see he would never want to be on Cheyenne Zeke's bad side. He pitied any man who might dare to harm Abigail. "When I got there she just stared in shock, talking real clear and calm, like she didn't even know her arms were gone . . . cut off because she'd put them around a half-breed! Her long hair was cut off, too. I had to pull it out of her mouth, where they'd stuffed it, so she could talk." His eyes teared and Danny closed his eyes and put his head in his hands.

"She died just a couple of minutes later," Zeke went on. "And her last words were to ask me never to blame myself. She told me she'd marry me all over again, even if she knew that would happen. And after she died, I used this!" He whipped out the big blade and held it out, pointed toward Danny. Danny raised his eyes to look at the weapon. "The buffalo knife Pa gave me that once belonged to a dog soldier!" Zeke went on. "For the first time I felt an Indian's vengeance and hatred in my blood! And I found those men!" he snarled. "Every last one of them. And they died, just as slowly as Ellen died! Yes, I did kill them all, Danny. And if I had the chance I'd do it twice over! And I've killed men who tried to hurt Abbie. I don't call that murder, brother! What they did to Ellen and my son was murder. What I did was rightful vengeance! It's a code the Indian understands and one I stand by."

The men's eyes held steadily, and Little Rock watched his father with wide-eyed wonder, while Blue Sky began to whimper at her father's raised voice. Abbie kissed the girl's hair and soothed her, while Zeke turned away from them all, shoving the knife back into its sheath as someone knocked on

421

the door.

Danny leaned back in his chair. "Come in," he called out.

A private entered, looking curiously at Lieutenant Monroe's guests and setting a pitcher and glasses down on the desk. "Thank you, Greenley," Danny told the man.

The private saluted, glancing again at the large Indian man whose hair hung straight and wild and who wore many weapons.

"It's all right, Greenley. Leave us, please."

The private saluted again. "Yes, sir." He cast another glance at Zeke before he turned and left. Danny sighed as he poured two more drinks, feeling sorry for Abigail as she wiped at quiet tears.

"Have some lemonade, Abbie," he told her. She smiled through her tears and nodded quietly, reaching over to pour some as Danny turned his attention to Zeke.

"Zeke, I have a little pull now. Not a lot, but a little. The lieutenant I saved five years ago is now a colonel, and he has a couple of good connections in Washington. I'll see if I can't set the record straight in Tennessee and maybe get you off the wanted list there. It's been twelve years. It's over, and any man who understands the whole story ought to be ready to hang the whole thing up. Besides, Ellen's parents are dead now. And her brother—well, I don't know about him. He hated you and I expect that won't change. But he at least should understand it wasn't you who killed Ellen. It was his own friends."

Zeke nodded as Little Rock guzzled a glass of lemonade, liking the new drink very much and handing out his glass for more. Abbie poured some and then looked at Danny, smiling gratefully.

"Thank you, Danny. It would be a wonderful relief to get Zeke's name cleared in Tennessee. I never knew him there, but still, it would be nice to know he's no longer a wanted man."

Danny looked back at his brother. "Come and sit down, Zeke. Have another drink."

Zeke turned and walked to the chair, his face showing the

strain of having to talk about Ellen. He reached over and patted Blue Sky's leg. "It's all right, *Moheya*," he told the girl. He avoided Abbie's eyes as he leaned forward and picked up his glass of whiskey, slugging down the second drink quickly. He pulled a pipe from a leather pouch that hung from his belt and stuffed it with tobacco from the same pouch.

"Think you'll ever go back, Zeke?" Danny asked.

Zeke shook his head, then lit the pipe and puffed it for a moment. "I have no desire to ever go back," he replied.

"Not even to see our father?"

Zeke removed the pipe from his mouth and looked darkly at his brother. "Especially not to see our father."

"I think he'd like to see you again. He loved you, you know."

Zeke snickered bitterly. "If he loved me, he wouldn't have dragged me screaming from my mother's arms and sold her off to a Crow buck! The only reason he took me to Tennessee was for proof, so he could brag to his men friends about how he'd been living with a Cheyenne squaw. I never blamed your mother for hating me, Danny. She resented me and that was natural. Her blood wasn't in my veins. But my father—him I blame for all the things that happened to me back home! I didn't belong there! I belonged here. And I have no reason to go back."

Danny nodded. "I know how you feel. But Pa, he talked about you a lot, Zeke. Talked about how it was all his fault, what happened, his fault for bringing you back. You were his son, and he missed Tennessee—wanted to come back. He knew it would be impossible to bring a Cheyenne wife with him. I'll agree he probably never really loved her, but he did love you, and he couldn't bear to leave his son behind."

Zeke puffed the pipe again. "Well, I'm sorry, Danny, but I have no fond feelings for our father, and certainly not for my stepmother."

Danny sighed. "My mother is dead, Zeke. Died ten years ago." Their eyes held. "She was still young when she died. Pa

423

took it hard. Took him a long time to get over it."

Zeke puffed the pipe again and sighed. "I'm sorry. But at least you always had her, Danny. I had to come back and search for my mother. And I only had her a few years. She died last year of the cholera epidemic."

Danny frowned and took a cigar from his desk drawer. "Then I'm sorry, too. I guess all we can do now is start from here and try not to think too much about the past."

Zeke nodded. "If you want to write Pa and tell him and our brothers about me, you have my permission. But I'll never go back. How about Lenny and Lance? I wasn't as close to them, they were so small when I left. But they're still my brothers. How are they, Danny?"

Danny puffed the cigar. "Last I knew, Lenny got married and lived near Pa, farms like Pa, has a couple of kids. Lance still lives with Pa, far as I know. He'd be eighteen now. Lenny is twenty-two."

Zeke nodded. "And you? You must be about twenty-five."

"You got it." He glanced at Abbie. "And my guess is my brother here robbed the cradle by about ten years," he said with a wink. "How old are you, Abbie?"

Abbie smiled bashfully. "Twenty-one."

Danny nodded. "Just as I thought, only I thought maybe even younger." He smiled. "You have any relatives back home in Tennessee?"

"Just an aunt," Abbie replied. "But I don't really consider Tennessee home anymore, Danny." She reached over and took Zeke's hand. "My home is with Zeke down on the Arkansas. We have a beautiful piece of land there, with a view of the Rockies in the distance, and the river at our doorstep. Zeke raises Appaloosas, and some day we'll build a cabin. But we've been so involved with Zeke's Cheyenne family and their problems, there just hasn't been time for anything else."

Danny nodded. "I can understand." He sighed. "I wish I could tell you how this treaty thing will all turn out, Zeke," he added, turning his eyes back to his brother. "But you know

424

about as much as I do about it right now. We'll both know more when the government people from St. Louis get here. All I can tell you is I want to be fair and honest with the Indians, to the extent of my ability. But I have only so much authority, and no say in the final decisions on Indian policy. And if push comes to shove . . ." His eyes saddened. "I wear a blue uniform, Zeke, and there's no Indian blood in my veins. I understand their viewpoint, but damn it, people are coming out here to settle and nothing can stop it. A lot of those people are perfectly good, innocent men and women, coming out here to settle to find more land, start a new life, to dream dreams."

Zeke nodded. "I understand all that. But you have to understand the Indians—I mean really understand them—to know how they feel about what's happening."

"Then help me understand, Zeke."

Their eyes held and Zeke nodded. "We'll help each other, Danny. Come out tomorrow and meet my brothers. We'll hold a little peace council of our own before the 'big talk.'"

Danny grinned. "Promise me first your brothers won't scalp me?"

Zeke laughed lightly. "Promise."

"How about when the Crow and Shoshoni arrive? Will there be big trouble?"

Zeke puffed on his pipe. "Let's just say things will be a bit touchy. I don't hold any love for the Crow myself. I've lifted a couple of their scalps, and it was a Crow who put this scar on my cheek."

Danny studied the fine white line on the dark skin of his brother's left cheek. "I suppose the Crow is dead?"

Zeke just grinned, and Danny shook his head. "My brother, a Cheyenne warrior. The future will have an interesting effect on both of us, Zeke. I hope to God it doesn't ever come between us."

Zeke stood up and put out his hand. "We won't let it, little brother."

Danny rose and took his brother's hand, gripping it firmly.

"It's a pact, then."

"It's a pact. I'd no more bring harm to you than to my Cheyenne brothers."

"You're in a bad position, Zeke. I'm sorry for you. You're right in the middle." He glanced at Abbie, and she hugged her little girl closer to her breast. "But we won't worry about the future right now," he continued, looking at Zeke again. "Let's just be damned glad we've found each other. And I'll try to get you off the hook in Tennessee."

Zeke squeezed his brother's hand harder. "Thank you, Danny. That's a fine thing for you to do."

Danny shrugged. "You saved my dog when everybody else wanted to shoot it, and I always hated the way people treated you back home, Zeke. I'm sorry about that."

Their eyes locked sadly. "So am I, Danny," Zeke replied with pain in his eyes. "So am I."

Twenty-One

The numbers of incoming red men of the Plains swelled when the Shoshoni arrived, and Lt. Daniel Monroe watched guardedly as Jim Bridger rode into Fort Laramie at the head of the Rocky Mountain Indians. The Sioux and Cheyenne, who outnumbered the arriving Shoshoni by at least six to one, watched with proud dignity and bitter sneers, for although there were many more Sioux and Cheyenne than Shoshoni, only about one of every hundred Sioux and Cheyenne men owned a rifle, whereas nearly every single Shoshoni warrior was so armed.

"It is too bad two of the traitors' scouts were killed two days ago," Swift Arrow said haughtily to Zeke, who sat beside him astride his Appaloosa. They were among the Cheyenne, Sioux, and Arapaho leaders who were lined up with Danny and some of his men to greet the newcomers.

Danny and Zeke looked at Swift Arrow, who had denied having any knowledge about who might have killed the Shoshoni scouts two days earlier, but Swift Arrow himself had been strangely absent for a day and a night, and now he sat grinning as the Shoshoni arrived.

"It is hard to control the warriors when they see old enemies who have stolen their horses and women and have turned traitor to their own people!" He sneered.

Danny met Zeke's eyes, and both men had to grin, certain that Swift Arrow knew exactly who had killed the scouts. Then they turned back to the grand pageantry of the almost military way in which the armed and painted Shoshoni arrived.

"I suppose it is difficult," Danny answered Swift Arrow. "But you should remember that you must befriend your brothers, Swift Arrow, even those you call enemy. You have your freedom to think about now—your dealings with the Great White Father. And there is more strength in numbers. It is not wise to be divided." He turned to meet Swift Arrow's eyes again, and Swift Arrow nodded.

"Perhaps. But old hatreds die slowly, my bluecoat brother," Swift Arrow answered.

"And yet how swiftly they are born," Zeke put in.

Danny smiled sadly. "Well put," he replied.

The three of them directed their attention back to the Shoshoni procession. Swift Arrow liked Zeke's white-haired, bluecoat brother. He was not like most white men. He was true and brave, like his half-blood brother. Swift Arrow sensed this already. And he was certain that Lt. Daniel Monroe spoke with a straight tongue, for he was Zeke's brother; and even though he was white, he had courage and compassion. Swift Arrow was pleased that he had a friend among the bluecoats who in a sense was related to him. Although their blood did not truly run in each other's veins, they had a vital connection that could help the Cheyenne cause in the years ahead . . . and that connection was Cheyenne Zeke.

But that fact worried Abbie, who watched from a distance, for one day Zeke was bound to be torn in his loyalties, and that could destroy her man. The future appeared treacherous for Zeke Monroe, and Abbie felt that this coming together of the tribes was the beginning of a whole new chapter in their lives. She thought about that first journey to *Hinta Nagi* from Fort Bridger in the spring of 1846. It had been a sweet time for them . . . a time of total aloneness and quiet love, free of cares . . . a time for sharing only love and bodies. She wondered if there would ever be such a time for them again.

Someone shouted, interrupting her thoughts, and the

warriors at the front of the Cheyenne-Sioux line began yelling out clipped war cries, their horses prancing nervously in place, some moving out of formation.

"Don't let him through!" Danny ordered.

Abbie strained to see, quickly moving closer toward Zeke while the children stayed behind with Tall Grass Woman.

"There'll be trouble if he gets through!" she heard Zeke shouting. Swift Arrow was only grinning and raising his fist as a Sioux warrior who had broken rank galloped forward, his lance in the air, screeching out a war cry and heading straight for the Shoshoni.

"What's that fool think he's doing!" Danny growled.

"He intends to count coup on a Shoshoni, brother," Zeke replied. "And if he does, you'll have a battle on your hands!" Zeke started to ride forward to go after the Sioux man, but a French interpreter had already started after him. Zeke backed his horse, thinking it best to let the Frenchman try to subdue the Sioux warrior. No Sioux or Cheyenne dared try to stop him without starting an all-out battle, and if a soldier tried the same, it could cause hard feelings and perhaps even a fight between the Sioux and the soldiers.

In moments the Frenchman caught up with the Indian and leaped across onto the Indian's horse, knocking the Sioux man to the ground. There was a momentary scuffle before the interpreter managed to whack the Sioux man across the side of the head with his rifle butt, and the near disaster was averted.

Danny and Zeke breathed a sigh of relief, but Swift Arrow was disappointed. He would have liked to have seen what would have happened if the Sioux warrior had reached the Shoshoni. A good fight was always fun to watch!

The Shoshoni delegation, which had temporarily halted, resumed their entrance, led by their great leader, *Washaki*. Now there would be nearly ten thousand Indians camped around Fort Laramie. This was a gathering never before achieved, and one that would never again be repeated in the course of history. There were formal greetings and challenging looks between the Shoshoni and the Sioux and Cheyenne, after which all tribes returned to their campsites to await further proceedings.

Zeke rode back to Abbie and reached down to lift her to sit in front of him on his mount. Little Rock ran behind them, and Tall Grass Woman carried Blue Sky. Since the death of little Magpie, Tall Grass Woman had a special affection for Blue Sky, and was like a second mother to Abbie's daughter, as well as the only person besides Zeke and Abbie that Blue Sky would go to.

"I'll bet you never thought you'd be a part of something like this back when you first left Tennessee, did you, Abbie girl?" Zeke asked her. She smiled and kissed his cheek.

"I would have been frightened to death if someone had predicted this in my future," she replied. Their eyes held and he rubbed a big hand over her stomach, bringing the warm desire that his familiar touch always created in her soul. She put her head on his shoulder and he kissed her hair.

"I'll be needing your love and the strength it gives me over these next few years, Abbie girl," he told her softly.

"I know," she replied, moving an arm around his waist.

He continued to rub a hand over her stomach, while his horse plodded along slowly, so well trained it needed no guidance.

"I'll build you that house next spring, Abbie. I promise."

"It doesn't matter, as long as I have this strong shoulder to lean on and these arms around me. I'm never afraid of anything when I'm with you."

She expected his usual laughter and teasing when she made such remarks, but he only hugged her tightly against him as though to protect her from something. "I love you, Abbie," he said in a strained voice. "Why don't you ask Tall Grass Woman to keep the children for a while? I want to go back to the tipi and be alone with you."

She breathed in the sweet scent of him and felt the hard muscles of his arms tense from his sudden need. Yes, she would have Tall Grass Woman keep the children. For Cheyenne Zeke wanted her and she wanted him. She moved her lips close to his ear.

"*Ne-mehotatse*," she said softly. The Cheyenne word for "I love you" came easily to her now.

Night fires burned brightly, and Danny sat with Zeke, Abbie, and Swift Arrow, enjoying a royal feast put on in his honor and watching the wild chanting and dancing of the warrior societies, while drums filled the night air with a sound that would have sent chills through the blood of any white person who did not understand what was taking place.

Swift Arrow was determined to impress Cheyenne Zeke's white brother. Wrestling matches, war games, and horsemanship had been presented for the bluecoat's entertainment all that day. Swift Arrow himself performed superbly in the shooting arrows contest, getting six arrows into the air before the first fell to the ground, astounding everyone with his speed.

Danny was impressed with the precision of the Cheyenne horsemanship. The warriors pranced their mounts in near regimental order, making quick turns, galloping and halting with amazing quickness, even doing acrobatic stunts on their animals, and making mock charges, during which they knocked one another off their mounts using only their arms or blunt sticks so that no one would actually be injured.

The ability of the Cheyenne with weapons and in riding, combined with tales of what the warriors endured at the Sun Dance ritual, made Danny wonder just how well soldiers would fare against these Plainsmen, who were such expert fighters and who knew no fear of pain or death. Zeke himself bore the scars of the Sun Dance, and it was becoming more and more apparent to Danny that even though they shared the same white father, Cheyenne Zeke recognized little of his own white blood.

It was that same night that Danny was allowed to see, for the first time, his brother's skill with the big blade that he carried. But it was not in a contest that Zeke used the knife. The situation was much graver than that, for when a delegation of Shoshoni and a few Crow came to their camp to request an apology for the murder of the two Shoshoni scouts, the Cheyenne only sneered at them. After some argument, one of the Crow noticed Abbie and began to laugh, saying the Cheyenne must be soft to allow a white woman to live among them, and wanting to know who was the man who wore skirts who would marry a silly white woman.

Danny was not certain what was going on, for they all spoke in their own tongues and through sign language, understanding each other but confusing Danny, except that Danny saw how the Crow Indian warrior sneered at Abbie. The warrior's manner indicated he was insulting her, and Danny knew he was right when Swift Arrow and Zeke both got to their feet, their bodies tense and their eyes blazing, while several Cheyenne warriors began to congregate restlessly around the intruders.

"I am the white woman's husband!" Zeke told the Crow flatly, hatred for his old enemy in his eyes. He was taller and broader than the Crow, and his dark eyes were menacing as he stepped closer to him. "Do I look like I wear skirts?"

The Crow grinned haughtily, looking Zeke up and down and summing up the odds against him.

"That is my brother!" Red Eagle spoke up to the Crow. "He is a half-blood Cheyenne, and a good warrior!" He laughed then, too drunk to realize that to call Zeke a half-breed in front of the Crow was to invite trouble, for the Crow would think a half-breed was not a real man.

"*Voxpas!*" the Crow sneered, using the Cheyenne word for "white belly," an insulting term for half-breeds. "Your woman no good! Only bad white women sleep with Cheyenne dogs!"

Zeke's knife was out more quickly than the eye could discern. It almost instantaneously ripped upward through the

Crow's vest, slitting all its ties, while Zeke grabbed the Crow's hair with his free hand and jerked hard. The hair had been tied to one side and hung in front of the Crow man's shoulder, and as Zeke's knife came up through the vest, Zeke finished his amazingly rapid and unexpected slash with a swift sweep through the Crow's mane, cutting it off in one chunk.

Danny gasped at the speed of Zeke's movement. He had jumped to his feet when Zeke first whipped out the knife. Now, he took Abbie's arm and pulled her back out of the way of danger, picking up Little Rock in his free arm while Abbie hung on to Blue Sky and watched her husband steadily. Danny was surprised to notice that Abbie did not appear extremely upset over the incident; he did not realize Abigail Monroe had seen her husband use his knife before, and if the fight was to be with the blade, she was not afraid for him.

The Crow stood staring wide-eyed at Zeke, who stepped back, grinning and holding a good share of the Crow's hair in his left hand. Swift Arrow chuckled with delight and folded his arms, stepping haughtily in a circle around the visiting Crow and Shoshoni, enjoying the look of horror and shame on the face of the one who had insulted Zeke and Abbie.

"Do you see the scar on my brother's face?" he asked, stepping closer to one of the other Crow. He put a finger to his own left cheek and traced it downward, and Danny knew he must be talking about Zeke's scar and his encounter with the Crow who had put it there. "A Crow warrior gave my half-blood brother that scar!" Swift Arrow continued. "And that Crow man's heart and guts saw the sunshine that day!" He chuckled again, and Red Eagle let out a war cry at the remark, lifting his flask of whiskey and taking another drink. They were playing a good joke on the shocked and shamed Crow man.

Black Elk grinned proudly, while Zeke stuffed the Crow's hair into his belt and the man from whom he had taken it trembled with rage and shame. He reached hesitantly for his own knife, but stopped when Red Eagle called out to him.

"Hey, stupid Crow! That is Cheyenne Zeke! Lone Eagle!"

The Crow gripped the handle of his knife, but did not remove it from its sheath when he heard the name. Danny watched cautiously, noticing with some pride how hesitant the Crow became at the mention of Zeke's name.

"You should apologize to my half-blood brother!" Swift Arrow told the Crow. "Or your own heart will see the sunrise! My brother is a mighty Cheyenne warrior, and beneath his wife's white skin there lies a Cheyenne heart also. You will apologize to them both, or none of you will leave our camp alive!"

The Crow whipped out his knife then, and Swift Arrow stepped back, looking excitedly at Zeke, who crouched for battle.

"I will apologize, Cheyenne Zeke." The Crow sneered. "The Crow will not again call you white belly, or insult your woman. But you have shamed me, and I must avenge my shame!"

"Fool!" one of his Crow friends growled. He gestured toward Zeke, and Danny understood the gist of the conversation. "That is Cheyenne Zeke. No man goes against that one with a knife!"

The Crow gripped his blade nervously, sweat breaking out on his body, making his skin glisten in the firelight.

"It does not matter!" he glowered. He lunged at Zeke, and everyone stepped back farther, as Zeke arched backward, avoiding the Crow's blade. Zeke slashed back at him in a swift succession of swipes that kept the Crow man backing up until he tripped over a log and fell onto his back. Zeke immediately kicked at the Crow's knife hand, knocking the blade away and coming down on the Crow with his knee in the man's stomach and his blade at the Crow's throat.

"Zeke, don't!" Danny yelled out.

Zeke hesitated. If he killed the Crow, there would be a ruckus that could destroy the entire treaty gathering, and this treaty was all-important to the Cheyenne. Already hard feelings ran high over the two dead Shoshoni scouts and the handling of the Sioux warrior who had ridden out earlier in the

434

day to count coup on the Shoshoni.

The Crow man stared wide-eyed at Zeke, waiting for the blade to slit his throat. Instead, Zeke moved it slowly across his opponent's throat, without cutting him, and deftly nicked the Crow's ear so that it bled. Then he rose, and everyone gasped with surprise when, in a flash, he tossed the knife so that it stuck fast in the ground, so close to the Crow man's head that it pierced his headband and pinned the man to the earth.

"I accept your apology!" Zeke glowered. "You are lucky that a soldier is present, and that there is a treaty to be settled! I do not take insults lightly, especially when they are made about my woman!"

The sudden talk was a mixture of clipped Cheyenne and Crow, but Danny could guess at the content. He glanced at Abbie again; she watched calmly. Zeke bent down and jerked the knife from the ground, ramming it into its sheath and stepping back.

"The Shoshoni also deserve an apology!" one of the Shoshoni warriors present said. "Let the Cheyenne come to our camp and apologize to the families of the scouts they killed!"

Zeke looked at Swift Arrow, who nodded with a proud grin. "Let it not be said that the Crow and Shoshoni are trying harder than the Cheyenne to bring peace," he replied, obviously considering it all a joke. "The Cheyenne will come," he agreed. "Soon we will show you how good the Cheyenne can be at apologizing. But I will tell you that the scouts were killed because the Cheyenne were angry that the Shoshoni have so many rifles."

The Shoshoni man grinned. "There are ways, my Cheyenne friend, to get the rifles. Make the Great White Father give you rifles as part of the peace pact. The Shoshoni make peace with the white men . . . get rifles in return."

Their eyes held, and Swift Arrow realized to his chagrin that perhaps there were things the Shoshoni could teach the Cheyenne about ways to get rifles, and perhaps other things

435

the Shoshoni could tell them about how to deal with the Great White Father. The Shoshoni man nodded, and both knew that the time was soon coming when enemy tribes must stop their fighting and join together in saving the land and the buffalo from being stolen from them.

"Take your Crow friend and leave us," Swift Arrow told the Shoshoni warrior. "We will wait and see what the Great White Father wants of us, and then the Cheyenne and the Sioux and the Shoshoni will talk. We will bring a peace offering to your camp."

The Shoshoni man nodded. And the Crow man, who had slowly gotten to his feet, glowered at all of them; then he turned and left, secretly glad to still be alive. He had heard of this Cheyenne Zeke, and guessed he was one of the few men who had faced the half-breed with a knife and lived to tell about it.

The next day brought the arrival of Agent Fitzpatrick, Superintendent D. D. Mitchell, and a detachment of dragoons, as well as a Col. Samuel Cooper, Office of Adjustment; A. B. Chambers, Editor; and B. Gatz Brown, a reporter for the St. Louis *Missouri Republican*. The new arrivals were greeted by representative groups from the tribes, and Abbie's heart was proud when Danny told them the editor and reporter had both remarked that of all the tribes present, the Cheyenne appeared the cleanest and most proud. They had used the words *"stout, bold, and athletic"* in their conversations, he said. The governmental representatives, as well as the newly arrived soldiers, were also more impressed with the Cheyenne than with the other tribes; knowing this made the Cheyenne more sure of themselves and more certain that the government would give them special consideration.

The Council was to be held the next day, but because the swelling numbers of Indians created a need for more grazing land and for water, the treaty site was shifted thirty-five miles south of the fort to Horse Creek. Three days were spent in a grand march to the creek, thousands of horses, travois, warriors, women, and little children moving together—friends and enemies, walking into destiny.

During the march, Jim Bridger made it a point to seek out Zeke and Abbie. He was amazed that the young girl, who had stayed at his fort on the Green River six winters earlier to recover from a Crow arrow wound, was still alive and well and happy, living among the Cheyenne Indians. He had not truly believed such an arrangement could work and had had many doubts in that spring of 1846 when Cheyenne Zeke had come back to take her to his people down on the Arkansas.

Zeke and Abbie both were glad to see the famous trapper-trader again, for he brought back the memory of their first spring together as man and wife. And as they rode with Bridger, Abbie was more certain than ever that this life had been her destiny—God's plan for her. She was a part of something few whites would be able to tell their grandchildren about, and she could no longer imagine living the calm, quiet life of a Tennessee farmer's wife.

The original date for the great council—the first of September—was moved to the eighth, to allow time for the final arrival of all those who were coming to get their camps settled again. On the sixth, one thousand Sioux warriors rode to the Commissioner's tent in a column, four abreast, carrying an old American flag they claimed had been given them by William Clark on his first exploration of the West. Later that same day, hundreds of Cheyenne warriors also rode to the tent to officially present themselves as participants in the treaty and to receive gifts of tobacco and vermilion.

It was a time of grand excitement and for new friendships among the tribes. On the seventh of September the Oglala Sioux hosted the Cheyenne and Arapaho to a dog feast and a dance that lasted all night long.

Finally, on the eighth, the firing of cannon announced that formal talks were to begin. All chiefs assembled at the

437

commissioner's tent and smoked the peace pipe, and the commissioner stood and made his speech to them through an interpreter.

Swift Arrow listened haughtily, certain that since the commissioner and the soldiers had seen the skill and strength of the Cheyenne, they would keep whatever promises they made and would honor this treaty they offered. The commissioner explained that the Great White Father wanted only safety for his people—safety from raiding and looting, especially along the trade routes and the Great Medicine Road. His government wanted the right to build forts in Indian territory, places where soldiers could stay while they protected the Great White Father's people. And most of all, the Great White Father wanted to define Indian territory and to give the Plainsmen definite boundaries within which they could ride freely and hunt buffalo without fear of being shot at and harassed.

In return for the loss of buffalo due to the loss of hunting territory, the Great White Father would pay the Cheyenne and Sioux fifty thousand dollars a year for the next fifty years. This, the Cheyenne considered, was an overwhelming sum of money, but Zeke knew that even if it was paid, which he strongly doubted would ever come about, it would not be much once it was divided up among all the Cheyenne. The underlying threat of what the commissioner was saying worried his heart, for the government was now setting boundaries for the redmen—something that had not been done before—giving the Cheyenne a territory to roam that was much smaller than the borderless hunting grounds they had always been accustomed to and was likely to be reduced as more settlers filled the Western lands. But the Cheyenne, in particular, were pleased, certain that the Great White Father would keep his word and oblivious to the numbers of whites there were in the East and of how many more might still come into their lands.

Tribal representatives were appointed to be the official signers of the treaty once it was decided it would be accepted, and the Cheyenne spokesman was *Wan-ne-sah-ta*, Who-Walks-With-His-Toes-Turned-Out, now the Keeper of the Medicine Arrows.

The new boundaries for the Cheyenne were explained: from Red Buttes (Kansas Territory) north to the North Platte River, then west to the main range of the Rockies, south to the headwaters of the Arkansas, east along the Arkansas River to the Santa Fe Trail, then in a northwest curve back up toward the fork of the North and South Platte Rivers and west along the North Platte to Red Buttes, a basically square piece of land with a kind of tail at the southeast corner.

It was a big piece of land—good buffalo land, with access to both the Platte Rivers and to the Arkansas River—all prime Cheyenne territory. It sounded like a reasonable offer, and Agent Fitzpatrick urged the bands to counsel among themselves and to seriously consider the offer they had been made. The Plainsmen broke up the meeting, telling the commissioner they had much to think about and that they would discuss the offer in council. It did not occur to them that no mention was made of what would happen to them if they happened to stray outside the treaty boundaries to hunt or fish.

For the next nine days they counciled, arguing the pros and cons of the offer. There was more feasting and entertaining among the tribes, and on one occasion the Cheyenne warriors, stripped and painted for battle and armed with guns, lances, bows, and arrows, gave another impressive exhibition of horsemanship and war maneuvers, carrying out their military-like quick turns and charges and again leaving the white onlookers thoroughly impressed and entertained. They concluded the show with songs and coup counting, and never before and never again would there be such a gathering and such feasting and entertaining among the red men of the high plains.

During the nine days of counseling, more Crow arrived, led by Father Pierre Jean DeSmet, a Roman Catholic missionary who had been living among the Crow and had succeeded in converting some of them to Christianity and to white man's ways. Father DeSmet had worked with Crow and Blackfeet and Potawatomi as well as Sioux, and was often used by the government as a peacemaker on such occasions as treaty signing.

The Crow were accompanied by Assiniboin, Minnataree, and Arikaras, who had all come along for the adventure, to see the great gathering of Sioux, Cheyenne, and Arapaho and to learn what the treaty was about, as well as to answer the Great White Father's plea that all tribes of Indians gather together and make peace among themselves, for warring among the tribes was the cause of considerable problems for white settlers who got caught in the middle of the fighting.

But with the absence of the Kiowa and the Comanche, this two-fold purpose of the treaty gathering could not be fully accomplished. And so, there was still much work ahead for the United States government, for not yet was there peace among the tribes. Even the Sioux had come mainly to see their Cheyenne friends and to find out what the treaty offer would be; they were not prepared to do any treaty signing of their own. They were much less trusting of the white man than the Cheyenne; and in the years to come, the Cheyenne would come to understand that the Sioux were right in their distrust. The day would come when Sioux and Cheyenne would be brought closer together in their fight for freedom, but for now, the Cheyenne felt strongly inclined to sign the treaty, because it offered good land and the white men who made the offer seemed sincere, even though the wagons full of promised gifts from the East still had not arrived.

The nine days of counseling included a great show of apology, made by the Cheyenne to the Shoshoni. The Cheyenne staged a great feast for the Shoshoni and presented their old enemies with tobacco, blankets, and cloth, as well as the scalps of the two Shoshoni scouts the Cheyenne had killed. Several children were traded between the two tribes to symbolize the supreme demonstration of their melding together and their oneness that should not be broken. It was a practice not often used, but one that brought with it the highest form of representative friendship, to trust one's child to another tribe; and it was accepted by the families involved with pride and courage. It was the way of the People.

It was finally decided. The Cheyenne would accept the treaty. Four chiefs signed, including the great peacemaker, Yellow Wolf. The treaty was attested by the interpreter, John Smith, and the Indians were given Army uniforms for warm clothing in winter and flags to remind them that they were now a part of the United States and must be loyal to the Great White Father and keep the word of the treaty.

Three Cheyenne men—Little Chief, White Antelope, and Alights-On-The-Cloud—agreed to accompany Agent Fitzpatrick to St. Louis and Washington to see for themselves the power and might of the great United States. The chiefs were given a copy of the treaty, rolled up and tied with a scarlet ribbon; but to Zeke, the scarlet ribbon only represented the blood the Cheyenne would surely shed in the years to come. Already, part of the bargain had not been kept. The wagons full of badly needed food and supplies promised the Cheyenne still had not arrived.

It was not until three days later that the supplies finally reached the treaty site, and annuities were distributed, after which the tribes parted. For most of them, it was a touching and sad leavetaking, for they had spent weeks together, feasting and dancing and enjoying friendships—finding a peace they needed to regain their strength from the terrible cholera and the other diseases that had brought so much sorrow and confusion and havoc to the Plainsmen. They left feeling stronger and more united, and the Cheyenne had land they could call their own now. *Wagh!* It was good!

But their simple hearts did not understand the red tape that must be waded through in Congress in order to ratify the treaty, or that such ratification could take a year or more, or that even though they had already signed the treaty agreeing to certain terms, Congress had the right to alter it if they chose. This, the Cheyenne could not understand, for to them a man's word was his word, and it could not be changed.

Abbie rode her fine Appaloosa, with Blue Sky in front of her, slowly moving with her own band as the thousands of Plainsmen departed in all directions. The Treaty of 1851 was finished, at least for the Cheyenne. They would go home now, the Cheyenne and Arapaho, to the land that was to be their own; the Crow and Shoshoni would head back to the Rocky Mountains, the Sioux northeast to *Paha-Sapa*, the Sacred Hills of the Dakotas.

Zeke bid farewell to his white brother, knowing they would meet again and hoping it would still be under friendly circumstances, but both were aware of the precarious future that lay in wait for them. Lt. Daniel Monroe watched his half-breed brother leave with a heavy heart. He knew that if it came down to a fight between Indians and soldiers, Cheyenne Zeke would fight for his red brothers, and Daniel Monroe did not relish the torment that could bring to them both.

Zeke and Swift Arrow rode to catch up with their band, but Swift Arrow stopped his brother at the top of a ridge. For a moment they both quietly looked down on the procession of horses, dogs, warriors, women, children, and travois below. Then Swift Arrow turned to Zeke and put out his hand.

"I leave you, my brother. Go in peace to the Arkansas. I stay here with our northern brothers."

Zeke frowned. "What are you talking about, Swift Arrow?"

Swift Arrow looked out at the band again and nodded. "Down there rides a white woman—your woman." He looked back at Zeke. "I will say it simply, my brother, so that you will understand. It is easier for me this way—to not go back with you. For although it would have been foolish and her answer

442

would have been no, I must confess to you that if you had not returned those winters back when you took the wagons to Santa Fe, Swift Arrow would have asked your white woman to be his squaw."

Their eyes held for several long seconds, and Zeke felt a terrible ache in his heart, a mixture of sorrow for his lonely brother and anger that he would have such feelings. Yet knowing Abbie, he could not blame Swift Arrow, and he knew his brother meant this as the highest form of compliment for her. Zeke nodded and took his brother's hand. They gripped wrists firmly and for several seconds.

"May *Maheo* ride with you, Swift Arrow."

"And with you and your loved ones, my brother," the man replied, his eyes watery. "Our mother is gone now. I have no reason to stay on. But our paths will surely cross in the years to come."

"They surely will," Zeke answered.

"I shall miss *Hinta Nagi*."

"Come and see us, Swift Arrow. You know you are welcome always."

Swift Arrow studied his brother. "Perhaps . . . in time." They released hands. "You are good man, my half-blood brother. You have enough white in you that she can love you. Her eyes shine for you, and her heart beats for you. Her blood runs hot for you and always will, even in old age. This anyone can see, for she has given up much for you and that is what I admire in her. Always it will be Zeke and Abbie, Abbie and Zeke, always. A woman does not free her heart of a man like you. You were the first to brand her, and the burn runs deep." He backed his horse. "I will miss the children, my brother. Black Elk is young, but he is also a fine warrior and your brother. He will be glad to take over the teachings of Little Rock to become a Cheyenne warrior. Give him to Black Elk."

Zeke nodded.

"Red Eagle!" Swift Arrow spit. "He has become worthless! Do not let him spread his evil influence on my nephew, for the

443

whiskey has warped his brain. I am sorry for our brother, Red Eagle—and ashamed."

"So am I, Swift Arrow," Zeke answered. "It is a sad thing. I am glad our mother did not live to see Red Eagle as he is now."

Swift Arrow nodded. "Go now. Go to her . . . to the white woman with the Cheyenne heart." Their eyes held a moment longer, and then Swift Arrow left him, riding north.

Zeke watched Swift Arrow go, his chest aching at the parting. It seemed life was always a tangle of loving and hating, living and dying, greeting and saying good-bye. He wanted to weep, but he could not. He looked toward the departing Southern Cheyenne.

"You're some woman, Abbie girl," he said softly. He goaded his Appaloosa into motion, building to a fast gallop, and sod flew as he rode across the rolling plain toward his woman. He knew that tonight he would claim her with more passion than he had ever felt before. It was as Swift Arrow had said. Always it would be Zeke and Abbie, Abbie and Zeke, forever.

Epilogue

The autumn of 1851 was the end of an era, and the dawn of change for the Great West, a time when young privates like Danny Monroe could become officers overnight, army forts had begun springing up like mushrooms, and the Great Medicine Road and other westward trails were congested with long white lines of moving "houses on wheels." It was a place where women like Anna Gale and men like Winston Garvey could become instant millionaires, and children like little Charles Garvey learned hard lessons they would carry with them forever.

In the Great West, the peace and freedom the Indians had once known were fast disappearing, and the wild tribes of the Plains soon would no longer drink the wind. In the Great West, long-lost brothers could find one another again, only to fight on different sides and a woman with the letter Z carved deeply into her cheeks could become a legendary leader of notorious outlaws and could flaunt her evil ways with no law to stop her.

In the Great West, a white woman could love a half-breed and live with Indians and be proud.

In the Great West, life was due for dramatic changes, and yet some things would never change, just as the Cheyenne death song foretold. . . .

Nothing lives long.
Nothing stay here
Except the earth and the mountains.

TODAY'S HOTTEST READS
ARE TOMORROW'S SUPERSTARS

VICTORY'S WOMAN (4484, $4.50)
by Gretchen Genet

Andrew—the carefree soldier who sought glory on the battlefield, and returned a shattered man . . . Niall—the legandary frontiersman and a former Shawnee captive, tormented by his past . . . Roger—the troubled youth, who would rise up to claim a shocking legacy . . . and Clarice—the passionate beauty bound by one man, and hopelessly in love with another. Set against the backdrop of the American revolution, three men fight for their heritage—and one woman is destined to change all their lives forever!

FORBIDDEN (4488, $4.99)
by Jo Beverley

While fleeing from her brothers, who are attempting to sell her into a loveless marriage, Serena Riverton accepts a carriage ride from a stranger—who is the handsomest man she has ever seen. Lord Middlethorpe, himself, is actually contemplating marriage to a dull daughter of the aristocracy, when he encounters the breathtaking Serena. She arouses him as no woman ever has. And after a night of thrilling intimacy—a forbidden liaison—Serena must choose between a lady's place and a woman's passion!

WINDS OF DESTINY (4489, $4.99)
by Victoria Thompson

Becky Tate is a half-breed outcast—branded by her Comanche heritage. Then she meets a rugged stranger who awakens her heart to the magic and mystery of passion. Hiding a desperate past, Texas Ranger Clint Masterson has ridden into cattle country to bring peace to a divided land. But a greater battle rages inside him when he dares to desire the beautiful Becky!

WILDEST HEART (4456, $4.99)
by Virginia Brown

Maggie Malone had come to cattle country to forge her future as a healer. Now she was faced by Devon Conrad, an outlaw wounded body and soul by his shadowy past . . . whose eyes blazed with fury even as his burning caress sent her spiraling with desire. They came together in a Texas town about to explode in sin and scandal. Danger was their destiny—and there was nothing they wouldn't dare for love!

Available wherever paperbacks are sold, or order direct from the Publisher. Send cover price plus 50¢ per copy for mailing and handling to Penguin USA, P.O. Box 999, c/o Dept. 17109, Bergenfield, NJ 07621. Residents of New York and Tennessee must include sales tax. DO NOT SEND CASH.

FROM AWARD-WINNING AUTHOR
JO BEVERLEY

DANGEROUS JOY   (0-8217-5129-8, $5.99)

Felicity is a beautiful, rebellious heiress with a terrible secret. Miles is her reluctant guardian—a man of seductive power and dangerous sensuality. What begins as a charade borne of desperation soon becomes an illicit liaison of passionate abandon and forbidden love. One man stands between them: a cruel landowner sworn to possess the wealth he craves and the woman he desires. His dark treachery will drive the lovers to dare the unknowable and risk the unthinkable, determined to hold on to their joy.

FORBIDDEN   (0-8217-4488-7, $4.99)

While fleeing from her brothers, who are attempting to sell her into a loveless marriage, Serena Riverton accepts a carriage ride from a stranger—who is the handsomest man she has ever seen. Lord Middlethorpe, himself, is actually contemplating marriage to a dull daughter of the aristocracy, when he encounters the breathtaking Serena. She arouses him as no woman ever has. And after a night of thrilling intimacy—a forbidden liaison—Serena must choose between a lady's place and a woman's passion!

TEMPTING FORTUNE   (0-8217-4858-0, $4.99)

In a night shimmering with destiny, Portia St. Claire discovers that her brother's debts have made him a prisoner of dangerous men. The price of his life is her virtue—about to be auctioned off in London's most notorious brothel. However, handsome Bryght Malloreen has other ideas for Portia, opening her heart to a sensuality that tempts her to madness.